FIC
PYWELL

Pywell, Sharon L.

Everything after.

$24.95   05/02/2006

Everything After

Everything After

Sharon Pywell

G. P. PUTNAM'S SONS • NEW YORK

G. P. Putnam's Sons
Publishers Since 1838
Published by the Penguin Group
Penguin Group (USA) Inc., 375 Hudson Street, New York, New York 10014, USA ° Penguin Group
(Canada), 90 Eglinton Avenue East, Suite 700, Toronto, Ontario M4P 2Y3, Canada (a division of Pearson
Penguin Canada Inc.) ° Penguin Books Ltd, 80 Strand, London WC2R 0RL, England ° Penguin Ireland,
25 St Stephen's Green, Dublin 2, Ireland (a division of Penguin Books Ltd) ° Penguin Group
(Australia), 250 Camberwell Road, Camberwell, Victoria 3124, Australia (a division of Pearson
Australia Group Pty Ltd) ° Penguin Books India Pvt Ltd, 11 Community Centre, Panchsheel Park,
New Delhi–110 017, India ° Penguin Group (NZ), Cnr Airborne and Rosedale Roads, Albany,
Auckland 1310, New Zealand (a division of Pearson New Zealand Ltd) ° Penguin Books
(South Africa) (Pty) Ltd, 24 Sturdee Avenue, Rosebank, Johannesburg 2196, South Africa

Penguin Books Ltd, Registered Offices:
80 Strand, London WC2R 0RL, England

Excerpts from *The Antigone of Sophocles, an English Version* by Dudley Fitts and Robert Fitzgerald,
copyright 1939 by Harcourt, Inc., and renewed 1967 by Dudley Fitts and Robert Fitzgerald,
reprinted by permission of the publisher. CAUTION: All rights, including professional, amateur, motion picture,
recitation, lecturing, performance, public reading, radio broadcasting, and television are strictly reserved.
Inquiries on all rights should be addressed to Harcourt, Inc., Permissions Department, Orlando, FL 32887-6777.

Library of Congress Cataloging-in-Publication Data

Pywell, Sharon L.
Everything after / Sharon Pywell.
p.   cm.
ISBN 0-399-15350-0
1. Brothers—Fiction.   2. Fratricide—Fiction.   3. Vietnamese conflict, 1961–1975—Fiction.
4. Domestic fiction.   I. Title.
PS3616.Y94E94   2006   2005054952
813'.54—dc22
Printed in the United States of America
1   3   5   7   9   10   8   6   4   2

Book design by Stephanie Huntwork

This is a work of fiction. Names, characters, places, and incidents either are the product of the author's
imagination or are used fictitiously, and any resemblance to actual persons, living or dead,
businesses, companies, events, or locales is entirely coincidental.

To Claire and Mark

Everything After

Another Way of Forgetting

AMONG THE MANY THINGS MY ADOPTIVE FAMILY GAVE ME WAS a romantic reverence for the Fourth of July. Every year on that day they offered up a reliably cheerful tangle of Popsicles, softball, sparklers and patriotically inspired cake designs. I recall every Fourth of July as perfect: no unexpected rain squalls, no weeping skinned-knee children or dropped hot dogs in the dirt. But then, memory is just another way of forgetting: you place a picture in your mind and the longer you entertain it, the further it pushes all other possible truths away.

On the last Fourth of July before my two older brothers went to Vietnam I sat on our porch and regarded my paradise. There in the denim bikini that Uncle Charlie disapproved of so much was my sister Angie surfacing after a quick dive into the lake. She pulled herself up out of the water and onto the dock and her hair reflected light like black glass. She smiled at me and I got the same happy lift in my chest I always did when she smiled.

Our brother Eddie had the same electric grin but it didn't always make me happy to see it. Angie's happiness, on the other hand, always seemed symbiotically linked to my own. I am the youngest of my siblings, and that summer I was nineteen. Angie was the oldest among us at twenty-two, with Perry and Eddie sandwiched between us at twenty and twenty-one. We saw ourselves as organized in pairs: Eddie and Perry had each other; Angie and I had each other.

And all of us shared Hank, Uncle Charlie and Aunt Eleanor's son. None of us remembered a time without him because even before we were adopted into his family, our parents were inseparable friends. There were times when I swear we were more comfortable in Uncle Charlie and Aunt Eleanor's house than Hank was, but that could simply be because we outnumbered him.

I heard my brothers in the living room, charging through a duet on the pianos they bought in May so they could play together all summer. Perry and Eddie played competitively, aggressively, badly, wholeheartedly. It was Eddie's idea to get a second piano. They played *Scaramouche* with a galumphing bravado, Eddie adding trills and then dark minor chords for comic effect. In previous years they'd sold the second piano back to the dealer when school began, but on this particular summer Angie and I had promised to do that for them so they could play right up until the very last moment without any distractions.

Uncle Charlie and Hank were assembling some kind of grill, and from my seat on the porch I saw Hank bending over the tools, as graceful and beautiful as my sister. He was twenty-two that year—the same age as Angie. He raised his head from his work to watch her shake the lake water from her arms and start raking our two-ton delivery of sand by the lake's edge. He watched her intently.

Every Fourth of July we constructed this artificial beach, and by every August the lake absorbed it. The impossibly white sand drew children all through the long holiday afternoon and into the early evening of the picnic, freeing their parents to drink beer and yell at the volunteer softball umpire. Each year we dotted the little beach with toys and left it to do its job. That morning, like every other Fourth of July morning, Angie and I had gone to the toy store to buy pails and shovels, plastic dump trucks and front-end loaders. We'd been most satisfied with a little Ferris wheel whose seats were actually buckets that moved when you filled them with sand. She waved at me and flung sand in my direction with her rake by way of greeting. I waved back.

In our family I was the fair one, conventionally pretty, the only one among us who expected a smile and a little kiss to change Aunt Eleanor's mind about something. But in the larger world I disappeared where Angie stood out. Angie had muscle—a kind of physical authority whose power was magnified by her indifference to attention of any kind, be it praise or judgment. It was always a very interesting thing to watch.

Uncle Charlie gave up wrestling with the new grill attachment and was drawn into the house. I could hear the running water from where I sat so I knew why he'd been distracted. A Fourth of July overnight guest had been in the shower an unconscionable six minutes, ignoring the three-minute timer that Uncle Charlie had placed discreetly by every shower. Only Aunt Eleanor could ignore the timers with impunity. We all knew that though Uncle Charlie wasn't going to say a thing to the guest, he would pace in the hallway at the bottom of the stairs until the hot water was turned off. Sure enough, within two minutes I saw Charlie back on the lawn with Hank, puzzling over the mysteries of instruction booklets.

Uncle Charlie consulted on military defense contracts. His character and looks were shaped almost entirely by his years with the Marines, and people in the Pentagon trusted him. He had a high-security clearance, he knew the admiral or general to call, and these men returned his calls. Uncle Charlie got things done. Because so much of his work was in Washington our year-round house was just outside Arlington, but we lived at the Lake House summers as well as lots of spring and fall weekends. Eleanor's garden had a powerful hold on her, and Charlie took up hunting and fishing as we spent more and more of the year here on the lake.

The Lake House had been my mother's. When she died and Uncle Charlie and Aunt Eleanor became our legal guardians, they moved in here with Hank and took up my family's summer routine. Our father had gone through military school with Charlie. They met their future wives at the same off-base bar, courted them together and got married in the same June. The two couples had entered adulthood together. Their first dress-white balls, their first married-couple parties, their first children— they experienced these things as if their lives were firmly bolted into parallel courses. When Uncle Charlie and my father were both drawn into the earliest years of American involvement in a Vietnam that was still called French Indochina, our mothers accepted this as the natural order of things. They settled down into being best friends and waiting for their husbands together, expecting this strange parallel course to continue for the rest of their lives.

Then Charlie came back to Eleanor and my father stayed on, and what they thought was the natural shape of their lives was crumpled and restructured. My father accepted assignment after assignment that kept him away from us. By the time I was born he was merely the occasional visitor who dropped in when he was in the country.

Then our mother died and he stopped coming back to us. He settled in Paris and married a Frenchwoman whose family had roots in the Far East rubber trade. There were letters at first, birthday cards and false promises of visits. Then there was nothing. Finally Aunt Eleanor and Uncle Charlie informed us that our father had given them legal custody.

I hardly noticed the shift because I had always lived in their care and had few memories of the people that biological fact called my parents. I was happy with Eleanor and Charlie. My brothers and sister were older and less sanguine, perhaps, but Eleanor smoothed every path. She continued all the Sunnaret family traditions here that my mother had made. On birthdays, for example, we followed my mother's habit of giving the birthday child a cake upon waking and another one at night. The morning cake was accompanied by joke gifts, the evening cake by serious ones. The birthday child determined his own schedule and was free to cut school and request alternative activities. Requests made upon the birthday itself—particularly those made right after the morning cake—were much more likely to be granted than those made on any other day of the year.

That summer we celebrated Perry's twenty-first birthday—a significant day because it marked the year he became a soldier and changed his life forever. His wish had been to set out on a car drive with Eleanor whose path would be entirely determined by flipping a coin whenever they came to an intersection: right for heads; left for tails. She agreed. They got so far away they checked into a motel rather than try to reach home that night. He'd loved it. "When I get back from overseas we'll do it with Eddie, the very next birthday after I get back," he'd said when he and Aunt Eleanor returned. No experience was real for Perry until he had shared it in some way with Eddie.

For her birthdays, Angie used to choose extravagant shopping trips focused on clothes, but as she got older and the country's political climate shifted she made a point of scorning clothes and asking for trips to Georgetown's small radical bookstores. No cultural shift seriously interfered with her glamour. When the flips that dominated our middle school years gave way in the sixties to headbands and stick-straight sheets of hair, Angie could accommodate the changes as if they had been invented to suit her.

Hank had similar powers, but he didn't know what he looked like and had he known he wouldn't have cared. These qualities, of course, made him even more attractive. His senior class had voted him both "Best-Looking" and "Most Mysterious," which was a mystery to us, because in the family Hank was seen as a direct person, honest and quiet—a peace-maker at petty squabbles and the most reasonable among us on crabby hot days. I figured that he was voted most mysterious by the pack of girls who couldn't figure out why he wouldn't date them.

Hank became one of us—not exactly a sibling, but certainly an equal and a member of our tribe. He, too, was offered two cakes at birthdays, joke gifts at breakfast, an annual gift, a glass of champagne on his sixteenth birthday. He always asked for the same thing—a day with his father. He let Uncle Charlie choose the day's activities because they were not, to him, the point. The point was that he got Charlie all to himself with no interruptions from us clamoring adoptees or from his father's work. The two of them usually ended up on the air force base firing range, followed by a long lunch and a few hours hitting golf balls. I don't think Hank ever liked guns or golf. He fired off bullets and smashed little balls to gain access to his father's world, an entirely foreign country whose charms interested none of us but Hank, who hoped, like any diligent suitor, that if only he showed interest in what his father loved that he would be more lovable.

Uncle Charlie might be a stern man but I never doubted that he loved his son. After all, he loved me. His love was as much a fact of my life as gravity, so certainly he had to love Hank as much or more. Uncle Charlie had taken us under his wing like a small platoon that needed guidance and conditioning. My siblings sometimes chafed under his rules but I leaned right into them, happy with the way they built a kind of wall against confusion. Charlie made it clear that we could and should know exactly where he stood on everything. We were the troops. Aunt Eleanor was his partner, his lover, occasionally his Commanding Officer, so knowing where he stood demanded that we pay attention to her. To my mind, knowing Aunt Eleanor's views was a snap: she loved us, which made her, I thought, transparent to us.

That Fourth of July morning I had stepped around a corner to find Uncle Charlie seated at the kitchen table, smiling up at a blushing Aunt Eleanor as he lifted her hand from the kitchen table to brush it with his lips. They'd turned simultaneously when they heard me, their faces rearranging into more public configurations: parents again. Uncle Charlie's clear sense of his own authority and his belief in his responsibility to shield and guide what he called the fairer sex worked a magical tension, set as they were against Aunt Eleanor's own competence and intelligence. She made it look like she merely indulged him in his deluded, but charming, idea of her as helplessly in need of his protection. Had Aunt Eleanor been a different kind of woman, then my uncle's posture might have left a bullying aftertaste. But that wasn't the way it was. Their perspectives were different, but each of them faced every day knowing that the other stood at their back, as reliable as sunlight or rain.

Still, this year Uncle Charlie was a bit more impatient and baitable than usual because the boys were leaving soon. The boys took advantage of our uncle's more vulnerable state, Perry once going so far as to teach one of the family dogs to chew tobacco just because he knew it would upset Charlie. The dog drooled, of course, and got sick all over everything, just as Perry knew it would. But when Uncle Charlie turned sadly away from yet another doggy accident instead of losing his temper, Perry became sorry and kind, refusing the now enthusiastic dog any more tobacco and apologizing for days. "Charlie's just been so spring-loaded on pissed off this summer," Perry said to me, shaking his head. "He wasn't supposed to feel bad. I didn't want him to feel bad."

Aunt Eleanor was rattled as well, and I knew that because everything in the house was symmetrical. The order in her home increased in direct proportion to the degree she felt unsettled. All month the candlesticks had been set as if a ruler and plumb line were involved in their arrangement. Her beloved silver birds sat six inches each from the center of the front hall lowboy, and every boxed grocery item that entered the house had a place, an exact place, and if we put it elsewhere we were chastened.

After Perry told us he'd volunteered, she'd started wanting the foods arranged by nutritional content—all the carbohydrates clustered apart from proteins or fats. If her objects were pushed out of place, no matter where she was in the house or yard, she sensed it and became uneasy until she found the asymmetry and corrected it. In the last few weeks we'd all seen it—Aunt Eleanor lifting her head from the peony she was staking, hesitating, finally rising to walk inside to find that Eddie or Hank had knocked something six inches off center, correcting it and returning to her garden again. One night Angie and the boys pushed things around a dinner table she had just arranged and then set up a betting pool on the number of minutes she could stand it before rearranging them. I'd spoiled the pool by leaning forward and setting things back in their places just as she entered the room, timing my intervention with her arrival so they wouldn't have a chance to undo my work and upset her again. I loved Aunt Eleanor, and her distress only deepened my affection for her. There were lots worse things a person could do when she was upset, I knew, than put a couple of silver birds in a straight line.

The underlying anxiety in the household was held in check by the traditional patterns associated with the Fourth of July. The holiday spoke directly to all of Uncle Charlie's strongest impulses, providing special foods, explosions, military-style games and a large bonfire at its conclusion. It honored fidelity, pride and nationhood.

Aunt Eleanor made the table-sized tart she prepared every year, arranging strawberries and blueberries in the shape of the American flag's stars and stripes. Breakfast had been arranged on plates with little flag-stripes of bacon unfurling from a scrambled-egg square, studded with tiny sausage stars. Two years earlier, when the entire country was anticipating the moon walk, she'd presented us with a space rocket–shaped cake and Jell-O salad turned out of an American-eagle mold.

That year's Fourth was organized in the same fluid rhythm that began every Fourth. We scrambled to get bunting, barbecues, beach toys and balloons in position by mid-morning. In the early afternoon enough guests arrived for Perry to kick off the scavenger hunt. Then Eddie organized any willing participants for capture the flag. We reached the full flood of the day around five, when the meat was flying off the grill and the hardier guests floated in tire rings off the dock, beers in hand. The Jell-O molds were sufficiently savaged by then for Angie and I to start clearing them, and the last of the Tab and Orange Crush floated in melted ice at the bottom of the chests down by the dock. Softball and sack-race prizes were awarded, and we were finally called for the lighting of the shed-high pile of wood that Uncle Charlie and Hank had finished assembling at seven that morning.

The prelude to the fire was, as always, music. Neighbors and guests could volunteer to sing, but family members were required to stand and deliver a patriotic song. Some years this practice has been funny and true but that year the mood was more uncertain. Angie and the boys considered but rejected "Eve of Destruction" and "Ohio," and I had set off into the past to find more conservative alternatives. Hank had settled on "Oh! How I Hate to Get Up in the Morning" but switched in the end to "The Fleet's In."

Finally I stood beside Hank and the boys and heard him warble, "Hey there, Mister! You'd better hide your sister, 'cause the fleet's in. . . ."

I looked past Hank to Uncle Charlie, whose expression remained impassive. He was nervous with Angie's song still unsung and none of us sure what she'd do. But she stepped forward and swung loudly, enthusi-astically, into "Praise the Lord and Pass the Ammunition," and he beamed in relief. The tension vanished, and when Aunt Eleanor sang "When Johnny Comes Marching Home Again" and cried, we cried with her. Mr. Terindalle from next door stepped up to do "Dixie," and seven-year-old Petunia Anderson from across the lake did "My Country, 'Tis of Thee," which she said she learned this year in chorus. She remembered all the words and she got the most applause. I have the only voice with a big enough range to do it, so I closed with the national anthem.

That's always Uncle Charlie's cue. As the last note of the national an-them left my lips he leaned forward with his Bic lighter. It was a point of pride with him to have laid the wood so skillfully that gasoline was never necessary. Petunia passed out sparklers, and all in attendance stood in rev-erent silence as the whole thing blew into flame and ate its way up to the higher wood.

We had all been drinking beer. We had all sung songs in front of peo-ple we'd known and cared about for as long as we'd known anything at all. The bonfire licked up so high the lake caught its reflection and flung it away in loose arcs. I watched my brothers horsing around in the flick-ering light, my luminous sister raising an eyebrow at them and sighing. Uncle Charlie and Aunt Eleanor turned toward each other and kissed lightly, clearly satisfied with us and how this day had spent itself.

I thought my life was as knowable and open as a field of corn.

Hawaii

PERRY AND EDDIE HAD SERVED 131 OF THEIR 365-DAY TOUR BY the time Uncle Charlie managed to use his influence to arrange an R&R in Hawaii, a destination close enough to make a family re- union possible. Hawaii, I later learned, was the typical leave destination for married men in Vietnam because it was close enough for their state- side wives to reach. The other popular R&R destinations were selected for other reasons: Bangkok for sexual indulgences, Singapore for drugs, China Beach for food, showers and alcohol.

Eddie, Uncle Charlie was told, had already been on three China Beach R&Rs, and his commanding officer refused to let him accompany Perry to Hawaii. We had to settle for Perry alone.

Hank and I would return home from the University of Virginia so we could travel from Washington with him and Aunt Eleanor. I had entered the University the September that the boys shipped off, joining Hank, who was already enrolled there as a senior. Angie was flying from San Francisco, where she was in school. There was so much movement and pitched feeling that it was a shock to land in Hawaii and be finally facing the event itself.

The island's tropical brilliance gave me the unshakable sense that I was moving through a klieg-lit movie set. "It's just like being two-dimensional, existing on a screen with all these other shapes running along on either side of us," I cried as we drove from the airport to the hotel.

"You've just been in an airplane too long," Hank sighed.

"Mind the cab!" Aunt Eleanor exclaimed as it pulled to the curb. Because we knew her we understood this to mean that she wanted us to anticipate the cab jumping the curb, charging into the sidewalk pedestrians and crushing us. Aunt Eleanor hated leaving home. Only the promise of seeing Perry could have brought her this far.

"Yes, Aunt Eleanor," I said mildly. "It's under control."

Angie arrived the next morning. Then we all waited at the hotel for three days while Perry's arrival was redirected or delayed along his route from Southeast Asia. "That's bitter for the boy," Uncle Charlie sighed on night three. "Losing half of his leave to redirected planes and bureaucratic error."

But Perry did not look embittered when he finally arrived. He'd always been lean, but now he seemed made all out of angles and hinges. His walk was slower and more hesitant than I remembered it, and his head swiveled like a bird's every few seconds as he stood in the lobby with his duffel. When he looked right at me I was startled by his eyes: there they were, the same color and size, but they seemed flat instead of curved and they'd taken on a nacreous, bloodless look—even the irises. He put his duffel down and held out his arms to Angie, who reached him first. Then Hank, then Uncle Charlie and Aunt Eleanor, and finally me. He smelled of vanilla and diesel fumes, sweat and pepper with an afterwash of old beer.

"Little Iris," he said, actually patting me on the head, though I was a college freshman, and almost as tall as he. I drew back, startled. Over my shoulder he looked at Angie again. "God, Angie! You're a good-looking woman. How come I never noticed that?"

She smiled, but I could see that she, too, was unnerved by his apparently erased memory of us. Our eyes flicked together behind his back.

At dinner he ordered the filet mignon for two and drank five beers, speaking as little as possible. Every conversational hare passed him by, unpursued, and finally we settled into an unfamiliar and brittle quiet.

We parted for the evening, Perry heading to his room with Aunt Eleanor and Angie retreating almost immediately after. Uncle Charlie, Hank and I sat on the veranda overlooking the ocean.

"Don't feel rejected," Uncle Charlie said to us. "He needs time to shift from one world to another. He'll be fine. Well. I'm off to bed myself. You two don't stay up all night."

Three terrible and very polite days passed. We ate meals and went on island tours. We took boat rides and snorkeled. We played family games like "Most Memorable Ruined Dinner," which was pretty much exactly what it sounded like, and memory games like listing similar words and trying to trick opponents into "remembering" words that had never been spoken. "Sleep, bed, snore, rest . . ." we would intone, hoping the opponent would remember "tired" when it had never been said—only described. Angie was best at this game, Hank next best. Uncle Charlie and I were worst. We could summon up what had actually been said when somebody else was listing, but we couldn't make up a manipulative enough list to get our opponents to misremember. Things like this reinforced the family myth that Hank and Angie were very alike, and Uncle Charlie and I were very alike. The fact that these pairs shared no genetic makeup did not alter opinion. That's how we were seen.

Perry played along for as long as he could, pretty transparently looking for an opening so he could withdraw, pleading tiredness. When we were young, Perry was the most aggressive game player in the family, but I realized that week that Perry's chief pleasure in these games as we were growing up was engaging Eddie—struggling against or with Eddie. Now he was adrift, bored, unfamiliar to himself as well as to us. Each night he withdrew earlier than the one before.

When Eddie had enlisted, eager to go to war, Perry had been stunned. It was well after college deferments stopped in 1969. Johnson had begun withdrawing ground troops and using the lottery. If Eddie had just sat tight he probably wouldn't ever have been drafted at all, but he didn't sit tight: he volunteered. This changed everything for Perry. Chance and the government had issued him a high number so he would probably never have been called, and even if he had been summoned, the fact that he had a brother in Vietnam meant that military policy would have honored a request to serve in some other part of the world. No two brothers had to both serve in the same war zone. He could have asked for a German posting or a Californian one, for that matter, and gotten it.

Over everyone's objections, he made a special request to be in Eddie's unit. Aunt Eleanor was distraught, and we heard her arguing with Uncle Charlie behind their bedroom door almost every night. I heard my father's name marbled through this argument, and Uncle Charlie's protests that Oliver Sunnaret would have wanted his sons to volunteer where the fight was going on, even if it meant losing them. I could not hear what Eleanor said in response. It was only clear that she did not see the situation as Uncle Charlie did. She had been upset when Eddie left, but there had been no hissing and arguing behind their bedroom door. Perry had pushed her over some kind of line. Uncle Charlie kept his counsel right up until the week Perry was shipping out for training and then he told him that there was no shame in serving outside the Asian conflict. There was honor in serving anywhere, he said.

I loved Uncle Charlie, but certain questions had run through my head as day after day had gone by and he said nothing while the rest of us begged and pleaded. Why had he waited until the very last minute before offering an unconvincing speech about honor and alternatives? Uncle Charlie had never made a secret of his feelings about what should be done if a boy was asked to serve: no individual had any rights that superseded the state's needs. Uncle Charlie had served. Our father had served. Every man in his generation with a shred of intelligence and backbone had gone to war. Whatever Uncle Charlie said to him or meant when he said it, in the end Perry chose Vietnam; or, as we all saw it then, Perry chose Eddie.

Standing outside my older brother's hotel room door now I could hear shuffling footsteps. Something fell from a table. I knocked and hissed. "Perry? It's me, Iris. Can I come in?"

Silence.

"Please." This time I simply spoke in a conversational tone.

The shuffling moved toward the door then, and a hand scrabbled at the chain lock for a few seconds before getting it free. The door opened a crack and my brother's bloodshot eyes met mine. The room behind him was disheveled and smoky, full of room service plates and discarded clothes. He swung the door open just enough to admit me, shut it behind me and offered the joint he was holding. I shook my head.

"That's my unchanged Iris," he said. "Never touches the stuff. It's comfortable to come home and find things unchanged. Comfortable but tragic."

"When did you start using words like 'tragic'?" I flopped down in a chair.

"You're right. It's not a word I'd use. I meant to say something else but I don't know what."

"Reassuring?" I suggested.

"No. I wasn't going to say reassuring." He smiled thinly.

"I guess this isn't much of an escape for you. Sometimes family isn't what you need to unwind," I ventured.

"Maybe."

"Perry, are you mad at us?"

"Mad?"

"You avoid us. You look kind of mad."

"That's not my mad look. That's a misdirected attempt at looking existential." He coughed, set the roach down and picked it up again. "It's not working, is it?" He waved the joint in a general gesticulating way. "You know, back there I've stopped smoking this stuff. I don't know what happened to me when I got off that plane. Something, though."

"How are you, really?"

"God, am I as bloodshot as I feel?"

"Yes. Uncle Charlie says you're going to be pulled out of Khe Sanh soon. Is that good?"

"You can never know. It used to be the shithole of the universe. Now guys play a lot of softball and wait, which is maybe the same thing without explosions. When our guys started to get pulled out, the enemy started leaving, too. They were only there because we were there. Like we created them just by arriving—they pop out of the ground like the soldiers that sprang up from sown teeth or tossed rocks in that story. Then Rome is populated, or the world. What's the story?"

"There's a few like that," I said.

He waved the joint vaguely and lay back on some pillows. "The mountains pop straight up and then get wriggly on the tops like cartoon mountains. Very very beautiful. But scratch the surface, it's like voles have worked whole cities under the canopy. You can't see the paths or tunnels unless you know how to look. Those guys move through those jungles like there's subway systems in there. But you never see 'em. Or if you see 'em, they're the little kid you let inside your perimeter to help you fill sandbags for fifty cents a day or the girl selling Coke. We always know the road's clear if the little ladies with Coke carts come along with us, 'cause they know if the VC mined the road or not. I saw one kid we hired to lug rations take apart an M-60 machine gun when he was on break, clean it and put it back together faster than we could. Now where do you think he learned that? Sweet kid. Total VC. I don't know what happened to him after we got transferred back. I guess somebody shot him sooner or later. Or he shot somebody."

"So you can't see the enemy? Ever?" When I tried to imagine this literally, it didn't work; metaphorically it made perfect sense, though. Eddie tossed his roach onto the floor, where it sank into the carpet and began to smoke. I plucked it up and stubbed it out in an ashtray. He started rolling another joint.

"It's like fighting ghosts. You know when you know for sure that the North Vietnamese Army is around? I mean, besides when they're throwing mortars at you? The short-time girls won't hang around outside the perimeter, waiting for business. The VC are in another circle, farther out but all around us. The girls have to go through the VC to reach us and then again to go home. Everybody knows each other. The VC let the girls go through in exchange for a cut of their profits. But when the NVA sweep by—I mean, they're like a river moving through the woods all around us in the middle of the night, passing us to go on to some other battle farther south—then the girls are afraid the NVA will rob them or rape them. They ask us to let them in."

I got up and got a glass of water; returned and offered him some. "Do you? Let them in?"

"Yes," he said. He drained his glass. He coughed and rolled his joint between his fingers. "Being here, in this hotel, seeing you all . . . I need to go back. Isn't that weird? It's too solid here. Too shiny. I'm not acting like myself here."

"What do you mean, 'too solid'?"

"I met this guy who said he'd been through a firefight and that they were positive they'd killed hundreds, I mean hundreds, of VC. They'd seen the bodies before the daylight went. In the morning they moved in to count and they only found one corpse. The VC and the NVA vaporize in the night. They tell you to count any bloodstain wider than six inches and any abandoned weapon as a kill. The kill numbers are real important to them. Six inches: how ridiculous is that? I've seen a man get caught under a tank tread and the bloodstains from a full-grown guy stretch twenty feet in every direction. But there, people just get sucked up by the earth or evaporated into the mist." He stopped and stared blankly out the window.

"Are there good days?" I asked.

"There must have been," he said, furrowing his brow and concentrating. "If you could hire a mammasan to cook for you, that was good. Anything that fell off a truck or was seriously slowed down, they could cook. One night they served a dinner on these paper tablecloths with pink unicorns and teddy bears on it and 'Happy Birthday' all over it." He sobered visibly. "I liked that. I think about that."

"If I was there I'd think about home all the time," I said.

"Sometimes I think about fishing. You know that meadow near the little pool where Angie learned to cast? That girl's got a trout mind and a pitcher's arm. Knew exactly where to drop the hook."

"She was good at it," I said.

"She was. But you . . . " He actually laughed, and the sound was so unexpected that I was more startled than pleased. "If you were in danger of actually catching a fish you'd wait till Charlie and Angie weren't looking and you'd snip the line and then try to tell us the fish got loose on his own."

"Angie never threw anything back," I said.

"Nope. That wouldn't be Angie." He turned to look at me, still the glassy flat eyes but longing behind them now, just barely visible.

"You're at the end of your tour. Almost done," I said.

"At Lang Vei," he answered, as if this logically responded to my comment, "they came at us with a line of Russian fucking tanks. And napalm. Imagine that. They say some of the Lang Vei survivors came in to the Sanh insane—they came through the jungle right through NVA positions." His face shifted, reacted to something he saw in mine as I watched him. He leaned forward and slapped my leg. "But I'm not going to go crazy," he said. Then he smiled goofily before rising to shuffle to a pile of what looked like garbage by his bedside. "Though the same might not be able to be said for Eddie." He stuck a hand in it and pulled it out with a photograph clutched tight. "I didn't want to show this to everybody but I brought it anyway. I don't know why. There he is."

"I don't see him," I said at last.

"Yes you do. He's the middle guy with the dozen metal tags around his neck and the helmet that says 'Sucking wounds are nature's way of telling you you've been in a firefight.' "

"No he isn't." I looked again. Nothing there looked like Eddie except for the electric grin on the young man's face.

"He was born to do what he's doing now, Iris. Even if he comes back, he's never going to be back. It's gotten so he won't let anybody else take point position. He moves like the VC, I swear: a combination ghost and big bird, swiveling its head, stopping, stepping one or two or maybe four steps, stopping again. He can look at a whole bank of wet leaves and spot the one leaf that's got dew dripping in a different direction than all the others. He can see a trip wire or a tunnel entrance that's entirely invisible to normal people. And when there's incoming . . ." Perry shook his head slowly back and forth, thinking about this impossible thing. "It makes him alive."

"Not you?" I asked.

"No. Not me. It makes me something else." He stood up and walked in an awkward circle around the room. "He takes risks and he takes us with him. It's not lucky. He's playing games, seeing how far he can go. Or maybe he wants it all to stop for him, so he's just putting himself in positions that would make it all stop. I don't know."

"Isn't he just following orders?" I asked.

"Do you go fishing anymore?" he answered.

I nodded.

"Do you still go to that stream that empties out into the pool?"

I nodded again.

"Eddie talks about what Vietnam must have been like in the French years, the plantation life years. We found this abandoned mansion in the jungle once, a fucking swimming pool and a landscaped ten acres around it all going wild. Servants' quarters. Barns. What looked like a riding ring. And running behind this place was a stream that had a rock bed just like that one that empties out by a field."

"I swam by myself for the first time across that pool," I said.

"Me, too." He nodded. Then he said it again as if I hadn't understood him the first time. "Me, too."

Perry studied the picture he'd given me; jabbed at the figure next to the man he swore was my brother. "See this little guy? He mailed an ear home to his girl as a souvenir and then he couldn't figure out why she stopped writing. That's what it does to you. Not the ear—though I guess that's part of it. The not understanding why the ear has a different meaning back here than it does in country." His legs started jiggling, forcing his feet into a kind of tapping patter. "Maybe Eddie just knows that it's impossible to come back. Everything here looks so . . . flat. I mean, what's at stake out here? Getting to work by eight-thirty so you can write the Big Report?" He laughed a barking dog sound laugh, then coughed, waving the joint in my direction to tell me that he would be fine in a moment.

"You'll care about those things again, Perry. So will Eddie," I said.

My brother pointed to the man in the picture standing arm in arm with Eddie. "This guy, he threw himself on a mine to save the men behind him. You know, I'd do that. And what's interesting to me is that I wouldn't do it for anybody here but I'd do it for half a dozen guys back there. Even you, Iris. I wouldn't die for you. But I'd die for them. I got on the plane to come here and all the while I wondered if I'd feel differently when I actually saw you all. I was hoping for it. But I don't."

He rose, threw open the draperies and called over his shoulder, "Just look at that." There, spread out like a dream, was a twinkling harbor. Only a few hours before, candlelit dinners had been in progress on the hotel patios and moored yachts. Now in the early morning darkness, hissing sprinklers watered the landscaped grounds. In another couple of hours the hotel staff would be clearing palm fronds from the pool area and patios, clipping the bougainvillea and setting silverware on white linen. "It's ridiculous," he said, looking down on this scene. "How can you stand it?"

"Perry, you can transfer to a base in Germany anytime you want. You can get a posting in Saigon doing paperwork, or being a cook, or anything. You know that the fact that you've got a brother already there means that they'd let you leave the minute you asked."

"I can't leave, Iris."

"Of course you can."

"You don't understand. I can't change anything—not the stuff that got me there and not the fact that I'm there now. People here don't understand anything about people over there. It's like dropping through the rabbit hole. And I've been there so I can't, totally, come back, because I've seen it. Like, there's a series of mountains near us that the locals say are sacred. They're full of sorcerers, ghosts and holy men. They can cure cancer and talk to animals."

"You mean, people say they can cure cancer and talk to animals," I corrected.

"No. I mean they cure cancer and talk to animals. And on this mountain no guns can fire bullets. The VC carry machetes when they patrol on it and so do I when I go there." He looked at me, changing his tone when he saw my expression; laughed the doggy laugh again. "The wacky world of mountain sorcery, right? Where my destiny has led me. Sometimes I go over things in my mind and try to imagine things going differently, me not being there and Eddie not being there, but it doesn't work. It isn't possible." Perry sighed. He smiled suddenly, sat down and took out a small bag full of marijuana, started rolling another joint. "You know, when I first got there I had this dream all the time where I'm point man on a patrol leading nothing but a bunch of twinks and FNGs, fucking new guys, and then suddenly, in a real narrow patch, I see Uncle Charlie charging toward me with an M-16 in his hands and he's pointing it at me and telling me I have to get off the path 'cause it's his. So you know what I do?"

"What?"

"I kill Uncle Charlie. The last time I had the dream, it wasn't Uncle Charlie I killed. It was Dad. Weird."

I blinked. "Dad? Why would he even occur to you? I mean, he stopped even visiting when I was around seven."

"That's old enough to remember everything," he replied.

"Well. I don't."

"Weird," he said, rocking a bit where he sat and staring out past me into the harbor.

We sat in awkward silence for a few minutes. Then I said, "Bizarre dream."

"Yeah. I hated having that dream so much. But then it disappeared. And now that I don't have it, it's the strangest thing, but I miss it." He leaned back and drew in a long sucking hit, holding his breath, tears popping out in his eyes. "Smoke," he hissed, seeing me looking at the glistening eyes. He looked right at me again, struggling to explain something and clearly feeling like he was failing. "Eddie, man, he's . . . I mean, even the guys in the platoon are getting to be afraid of him. There's nothing he can do about it. I understand Eddie."

"You don't sound happy about it."

"It's an expensive proposition, understanding what he is. In the beginning I thought maybe we were both just trying to follow some deluded idea of being what Dad would have wanted. But in the end it was about Mom."

"You mean Uncle Charlie and Aunt Eleanor?"

"No. I mean Dad and Mom."

"How could you know what they wanted?"

"You're right, Iris." He laughed merrily. "I don't know shit. Just forget it. Forget it, okay?"

He set the still-burning joint down on the edge of the bed and fell almost instantly asleep. I got up, plucked the roach off the bed and extinguished it. I went to the drapes again and drew them halfway open. Over the horizon the orange glow had just begun to make the line between sea and sky clear. I could smell flowers and the ocean. Lights from the hotel kitchen flicked on, illuminating the tables and railing of the patio facing the breakers and beach.

The next day we hugged Perry good-bye and stood mutely watching the plane taking him back to Vietnam.

Jump

AUNT ELEANOR KNEW HOW TO DRESS A DEER BUT SHE ALSO knew how to serve it on Noritake china and end the meal with cheese and fruit in the European manner. She preferred Norwegian crystal to Irish but owned both. Any educated woman, she believed, could handle dead animals and finger bowls with equal confidence, and Angie and I had begun our education as soon as we could carry fine china without dropping it. I was a readier student than Angie, who was bored by table settings and disgusted by dead animals. As we left childhood and the lessons became more advanced, I found that I actually cared about the effects of candlelight and was interested in how to deal with ligament as opposed to muscle when butchering.

When the boys started growing facial hair, they were given what struck me as the harder path—they had to shoot the animals. Angie pointed out that they also got to run around outside on sunny autumn days while we set tables, but I was only pretending when I nodded and shook my head and made it look like I felt exactly as she did.

"This is just so disgusting," she said the year we were introduced to butchering. She was thirteen that summer and I was ten. Aunt Eleanor had called us out onto the porch to get a good look at a deer haunch that served as the manipulative for our next lesson. "So barbaric."

Aunt Eleanor was unflappable. "Just get that hook into the thing," she answered, "and help me get it up far enough to hose off the blood before I show you how to butcher it."

Angie sniffed. "You know, other people go to the store and there's these packages labeled 'Pork' or 'Sirloin tips.'"

Aunt Eleanor stopped struggling with the deer's hindquarters. "And just where do you imagine that sirloin tip was before it wiggled itself into that neat little package with the sticky label on it?"

"But we don't have to do this!" Angie protested. "It's not, you know, South Dakota in 1820!"

"Honey, it's just a good thing to know."

"We know where meat comes from, Aunt Eleanor," Angie grumbled.

"Not quite yet you don't. But you will. Now you go inside the shed and get the cleaver and the saw."

"The saw?" Angie gasped.

"Well, how else do you think you're going to get this thigh bone un-connected from the leg?" She drew herself up to her full height and ac-tually grinned. She put her hands, now bloody, at her hips. All her fingers left little red prints on the apron. "Go on, girl."

"I'm not eating one ounce of that damn animal," Angie hissed to me as we laid the oblong chunks of bloody meat into plastic wrapping. And she didn't. She sat stiffly upright, eating a circle around the meat on her plate.

I considered following her example, just for the sake of sibling feel-ing. But I found myself sawing at just the one end of the piece Uncle Char-lie had forked onto my plate, a little strip with a touch of fat sizzled up on the side. I popped it quickly into my mouth so that if I changed my mind and decided to stand firm with Angie, I wouldn't look like such a hypocrite.

But it was irresistible. Aunt Eleanor had finished it off in a sizzling pan of thyme and heavy cream dotted with new peas. I carved up the rest of the piece on my plate and later told myself that stands were very nice things but they could cost you an excellent dinner and not necessarily get you out of the messy job in the end.

Angie stuck to her guns, so to speak. All through the year that Angie was thirteen, then fourteen, Aunt Eleanor kept forking meat onto her plate and Angie kept leaving it there. The following fall we found ourselves once again on the porch with the slab of bloody carcass, a saw in my hand and a cleaver in hers.

Aunt Eleanor directed her opening comments specifically to Angie, though I was standing by her side with the sharp instrument in my hand. "Now. I showed you two how to go about this last year so I trust you'll do fine on your own this year." Then she left us to struggle in the slippery blood without adult supervision.

"Oh, come on, Angie. This is interesting," I wheedled.

"You are such a pansy-ass," Angie hissed at me. *"Oh, Aunt Eleanor, sure I'd love to go get the saw and the cleaver. Should I snap the ribs before I break the breastbone?"*

"I just do the job, Angie. You don't always get to pick your job. You know Perry told me he doesn't even like to go hunting—says he'd rather be in our shoes, even the cleaning-up part. You aren't the only person who wants to change things. You're just the loudest complainer."

She curled her lip at this but shut up—being called a complainer was strong language in our family. I'd surprised her.

"You know I don't think people should kill animals at all," Angie said to me that night. "But I can understand the attraction to guns."

"Well," I said. "Maybe you should ask for a gun." Personally I wasn't drawn to the idea of loading a chamber with gunpowder, laying it directly beside my ear and exploding it. My one experience on a shooting range had left me deaf for hours.

"Maybe I will," she answered.

As the boys got older Uncle Charlie wanted to take them farther afield, out of the familiar woods around our town and into wilder settings. When I was still in middle school he was taking them up into Canada, getting into rough country that you could only reach in a helicopter or a small plane, terrain that required guides and special gear. The year the boys got into trouble I was mostly obsessed with whether the agony of having braces at the advanced age of thirteen was worse than the agony of having a crooked dog tooth, and whether or not my hawk-nosed Spanish teacher was having an affair with the French teacher's husband. That's what everybody was saying, anyway.

Then Uncle Charlie called in the middle of their trip to say that both the boys were alive but in a hospital—there had been an accident. He told Aunt Eleanor that Perry had saved Eddie's life, and those were the words she'd used when she hung up the telephone and turned to tell us that Eddie had fallen off a high narrow path and plunged into a mountain pool below. Perry saved him, she told us. Perry leaped after him, pulled him to the surface and held him there until help could get down to them.

"Perry," she ended, "is a hero. A real hero."

I nodded in agreement but I was thinking something else. The scene she described was wonderful but I wasn't sure I'd call it heroic. Perry had only acted according to his nature, leaping after his brother without engaging his mind at all. The real heroic acts have to be the ones where the unfortunate person actually has time to realize that he's going to do something entirely contrary to his nature because he has to do it. If he does it in spite of the fear, that's heroism. I considered Perry's relationship to Eddie too pure to be the stuff of heroism.

I imagined Perry seeing Eddie's foot go out from beneath him on the path, watching helplessly as his brother's feet lost their hold on the pebbly scree, watching Eddie grab a branch, swing wildly to regain a hold, lose it and begin the terrible fall down into the water beneath them. There was no analyzing distances or angles or water depths when Perry jumped after him. He just gave up his own hold on the earth and leaped. He was young, still so young that the idea of death was like a cartoon image: Wile E. Coyote dropping an Acme anvil on Road Runner.

Which doesn't mean that it might not still be the real thing.

Staying afloat after he hit the water and held Eddie at the surface demanded courage, even if jumping in didn't. He saved Eddie's life, hanging on to the limp body and struggling with no inclined bank to make escape immediately possible and no help within the thirteen minutes it took the hunting guides to descend and throw him ropes. They were amazed he'd survived in such cold water, much less kept a muscular and unconscious fifteen-year-old body afloat.

Both boys were hospitalized with hypothermia, Eddie with a concussion and a broken arm as well. When the telephone rang that night I'd felt a kind of bad clang. I still remember the silence around Aunt Eleanor as she listened, a shiny tinny silence that frightened me even from the next room where I was arrested by the unusual quiet. I walked to the doorway to see her hand was on her chest, which it never was, and she was utterly still but it was clear to me, even at thirteen and suffering from extreme narrowness of vision, that something terrible had happened.

But in the end it wasn't terrible. It was, in fact, cause for visitors and cake and balloons. The local paper came to take the boys' picture and ran it with the caption "Local Hero," meaning Perry. In the photograph Eddie is beaming from his bed, dragging Perry over close so he'd be in the picture, too; Perry is ducking his chin and doing something like scowling. Aunt Eleanor was businesslike about sickroom care but also touched by that kind of giddy relief that hits when you discover, after terrible anxiety, that you are safe. We ate as much ice cream and cake as we wanted for days.

Hank was terribly quiet. He had been ahead of Eddie on the trail, directly behind the guide. Of all the boys he was the most athletic. Even at sixteen, though, that most careless of ages, he was also the most careful—not the kind of climber to rush on an unfamiliar and pebbly steep trail over a long drop. With all the bustle around Perry and Eddie in the days after they came home he was able to slip quietly away, going off to fish or walk in the woods around our house. He never carried a gun on these walks, even when the season began. He carried a rod around but never brought a single fish home. He avoided visitors who wanted to talk about the accident and had nothing to say about it himself when alone with the family.

The days following the boys' return were wonderfully irregular. Aunt Eleanor's order and routine were hustled into a corner and every guest was greeted cheerfully; cookies were eaten at all hours, often with ice cream, or in the case of older visitors, with bourbon; Elizabeth Smiley, an eight-year-old neighbor who had a terrible crush on Eddie, sprinkled confetti all the way between the front door and his bedroom when she came to visit, and Aunt Eleanor not only stood to one side and watched the girl do it, she left it there for an entire day, unswept. The general mood was festive.

So when I heard yelling from Eddie's bedroom on his third afternoon home I thought it was a playful exchange. Everyone but Eddie, Angie and me had gone grocery shopping, and I had just gone to his room to bring him a cup of tea, a pair of scissors and a pile of Sunday newspaper circulars that Aunt Eleanor had asked him to peruse for valuable coupons. I'd left him cheerfully mocking her frugality.

Now even from my bedroom I could hear him and Angie yelling, could make out Perry's name in their exchange and the word *parents*. Loud exchanges in our household were not uncommon, but they were generally high-spirited rather than seriously full of fight. What I was hearing between Angie and Eddie was toe-to-toe, brisk and bludgeoning. I dropped the sneaker that I'd been about to put on my foot and walked toward Eddie's bedroom, *kerthump*ing unevenly as one shod and one bare foot slapped on the wooden floorboards. The hallway before Eddie's room was carpeted, however, and they didn't hear me approach. I doubt that hearing me would have changed anything.

When I reached the carpeted hallway the voices stopped being simply loud and became something else. There were slapping and tearing sounds and then a wolverinish snarling. I couldn't make out words anymore. I stopped.

Then Angie burst from the room, her face mottled and her hair missing a jagged little clump just behind the right ear. She pushed past me and I kept going to Eddie's room; peered inside. He sat stiffly upright, holding a newspaper circular page in one hand and the scissors in the other, apparently scanning for the best discount from Winn-Dixie. His face was white.

"Eddie, what happened?"

He didn't respond. Rather than coerce and plead, I turned to follow my sister. I found her in our bedroom, sitting by the window. "Tell me," I demanded.

"He's just evil."

"Evil about what?"

She looked away from me, out across the lawn toward the lake. Her eyes brightened out of all proportion and then tears streamed down, but she still looked steadfastly away. She wasn't going to tell me what had passed between her and Eddie. I knew that and I accepted it. I picked up a brush and went to her, began stroking and humming. I brushed right through the chunk of missing hair, counted a hundred more strokes.

"You know, there's only about three inches gone here. I could even this out. It would look really nice a bit shorter," I murmured.

I was thirteen and she was sixteen and I had never before taken on the role of her comforter, though I had served as a diplomat often enough. She tipped her face up toward me and wiped away a line of tears. When she spoke she sounded actually grateful, which frightened me a little but I didn't back away. "That would be nice," she said. "Thank you."

There was only one really sharp pair of scissors in the house and they were kept in Aunt Eleanor's sewing chest. I went and got them, returned and trimmed the jagged little square from my sister's glistening hair by evening everything around it. She held a hand mirror up when I was done and declared the experiment a complete success. I left her to return the scissors and go to the kitchen, where I pulled down the family picnic basket. I sliced thick slabs of ham and fresh bread for myself, cheese and pickles for Angie. Then I ventured into the basement, pulled by an irrational and giddy impulse toward excess. There were always a few bottles of champagne in the house for special adult occasions. I knew where to look. I jammed a bottle into the basket and covered all the contents with a checked tablecloth. Then I trundled the whole thing into our room and spread the cloth out on the floor before the window. We weren't allowed to eat in our room, another fact that contributed to my intoxicated mood.

"I'm still not going to talk about it," she said, interpreting my actions as a bribe.

"I know." I nodded. "It's just a picnic."

We lay all my selections out before us, Angie grinning when she saw the champagne. "I don't believe it. Iris Sunnaret, lawbreaker. This is a momentous occasion." She handed the bottle to me, but I could not figure out how to open it. She took it, stripped the foil and wire and effortlessly popped the cork. I felt a moment of complete panic when it sprayed against the wall but Angie only laughed again and mopped it up with one of her sweaters. I buttered a piece of bread and passed it to her without speaking. Angie reached past me, picked up a thick slice of ham and popped it into her mouth. She sighed, arranged another two slices on her buttered bread and folded it over into a sandwich. I didn't comment. Together we only drank a total of perhaps ten ounces of the champagne, but I had gauged the value of the gesture perfectly. It entirely changed the afternoon's mood. In the end we poured the rest of the Louis Roederer into the garden bed outside our window, killing everything directly in the stream's path, and snuck the empty bottle itself out to the trash after dark.

But while we sat with our spoils before us on the bedroom floor, we had achieved a moment of perfect happiness. Even after Uncle Charlie, Aunt Eleanor, Hank and Perry returned home, we continued to sit on the checked tablecloth in a shaft of dusty light, surrounded by bread and ham crumbs, plum pits and cookie remains. I didn't ask why she and Eddie had fought. She continued to eat ham. When Aunt Eleanor called me to come help with the laundry I was brushing Angie's hair again, starting at the ends and working toward her crown, hard long strokes like the ones she had used on my own hair when I'd been very little. I was singing "Lazy Hazy Crazy Days of Summer" so quietly that only Angie could hear me.

"You should go," Angie sighed. "You know she'll just come crashing in here looking for you if you don't."

I was slightly tipsy and very pleased with myself. I had decided that I would think of the argument between Angie and Eddie as something just a little more extreme than the normal pushing and shoving among us—nothing important and none of my business. Angie was more sober.

"Thank you, Bear," she said. "Thank you so much." Then she kissed me on the top of my head.

By the end of that week, Eddie was back on his feet and he and Angie were behaving as if nothing unpleasant at all had passed between them. I found them sitting side by side on the piano bench one afternoon, talking gently, Eddie picking out the notes of "Knoxville, Summer of 1915." I saw that I was still so shallow that I continued to be distracted by the question of braces. I plotted out my most likely path and waited until my birthday to ask for an orthodontist right after the morning cake and joke gifts. Since it was my birthday, the wish was granted.

That year, on her seventeenth birthday, instead of asking for a trip to an alternative bookstore or a fashionable clothing shop, Angie asked for a gun. She, too, had her wish granted.

After the Visit

THE PERRY I HAD SPOKEN TO IN THE EARLY-MORNING HOURS BE-
fore his return to Vietnam was not a complete stranger to me, but
the life he described in Vietnam was new and terrible. I could imagine
the Eddie I'd finally made out in the cracked photograph: a person not
so much changed by war as intoxicated by it.

Thinking about my brothers like this was new to me and it revealed
things about myself I hadn't particularly cared to notice. For example, I
preferred Perry to Eddie and always had, though up until that week I
would have denied it confidently. Perry was dearer to me perhaps because
of the way he seemed in my new mind to always have fallen into Eddie's
shadow. When I considered all the dinner table scenes and slow afternoons on the lake rowboat, it seemed to me that Perry had indeed gotten less attention, smaller pork chops. He was also kinder than our other
brother, easier to lure into a card game he didn't really want to play or
to help with math homework when he'd rather go shoot baskets. It
seemed now that his gentleness, his willingness to pass up the larger
pork chop, had made him more invisible.

Angie didn't see things that way when I tried to explain my new perspective after our trip to Hawaii. She had always been on Eddie's side in

fights, had always agreed with him on what television channel to watch when there was just one television and five kids, had always said that Eddie was right in game rules or property disputes. This is not to say we didn't all love one another. Favoritism was a way of life among us, though to outsiders we were an impenetrable group.

When I returned to school after the Hawaiian interlude my picture of how things worked in general had been altered. At the University of Virginia campus, unrest had taken no more dramatic form than students refusing to wear coats and ties to classes in the Revolt of 1968. The bombings and occupations that were going on at places like Berkeley or Buffalo seemed as far away as Vietnam itself. On Sunday mornings as I walked across the Lawn on my way to the library, I still had to pick my way through white-trousered young people playing croquet and drinking mint juleps. It was Tradition, if you lived in a room on the Lawn, to play Sunday croquet and drink mint juleps.

Now approaching the end of his undergraduate days, Hank still seemed pointed toward law school. It was what his father wanted and we all knew that. If there were any expectations about me and my future, nobody mentioned them. Hank thrived here, playing on a varsity squash team, writing for the *Cavalier Daily,* debating on Friday nights with a plastic cup of Michelob in his hand among others crowded into Jefferson Scott Attic's room near the Rotunda. He had won a room on the Lawn the traditional way—peer votes.

I lived on the top floor of a rental house located only a few blocks off campus. Within weeks of moving in I discovered that my predecessors were famous on campus for their annual tiki lantern party. A cement totem figure holding a cement beer can sat directly before the house to help guide the revelers, and for months I turned away people who dropped by to check this year's party date.

Within this bubble in time and space I constructed yet another barrier between myself and war, between me and the assassinations and riots of the last few years of American history: I declared a major in classics and within a matter of months was devoting my evenings to chunky, graceless translations from Herodotus, whom I liked, and Xenophon, with whom I had no patience—endless flipping through the lexicon, only to be rewarded by the name for yet another obscure military tool or weapon. Would the siege of Plataea never end? Two hours of effort went into dribbling little paragraphs, not much different from what preceded or followed them:

> At this time the battle at Marathon had been going on for a great deal of time. The Barbarians in the middle of the army were triumphing, for there both the Porchians and Sakai made haste and breaking through the lines, they pursued them to the center ground: those in the outer wings overcame both Athenians and Plataeans.

These I offered at conferences with my Greek tutor, who sighed unhappily and scratched over them. "Not 'overcame,' " he would sniff. "Look up 'Temporal Clauses' again, please. You'll see that πρίν takes the infinitive when the principal verb is affirmative. With the infinitive it can only be translated as 'before.' With other constructions it can be 'before' or 'until.' "

Then he would sigh some more and sometimes chew a bit on his tie before rallying to assure me that if only I kept working perhaps someday I could spend my days with Sophocles, whom he suspected I would find a more interesting writer. Perhaps then, he suggested without much conviction, my translations would improve.

"I don't know why you would pick something like ancient Greek." Uncle Charlie had scowled when he saw my first-semester grades, and thus, my course selections. "What are you going to do with this, anyway?"

What I was going to do with this, I could have answered, was avoid instructors who wanted to know your opinions, or wanted you to draw parallels between 500 B.C. and A.D. 1971. My Greek professors only wanted me to get saddle girth correctly placed in my translation of the last armed assault.

So here I sat on Jefferson Park Avenue on an orange crate that served as my porch chair, watching the pickup trucks and semis and student

Chevy Novas stream by. This is where I read letters from my brothers, and two had arrived very soon after our Hawaiian R&R.

Iris:

I'm sorry I wasn't more sociable and cheery when you all saw me in Hawaii. I didn't mean to hide from everybody in my room. I was just decompressing. Back and forth—it's very confusing.

When I first got here it was just incredibly strange in reverse from how it was strange being in Hawaii. For example, part of the training we got before they sent us in country was how to search a village—smoke out Vietcong. They got these South Vietnamese people to actually let us practice on them.

We pretended to burn down their homes, capture them and interrogate them—whole families. So I pulled this little bitty thing with pigtails out of her house and I yelled right in her face, just like they told us to do it. I bent over to be more at her level, which was about at my belt, and I looked her in the eye and I tried to be mean-looking and loud but she was cute as hell. I said, "You Vietcong? You lying stinking Vietcong?" and I shook her just a little bit like they'd told us to but I was gentle because she weighed about as much as a raccoon. She gave me this killer smile, little bright face and her two front teeth just coming in and her big brother standing behind her, pretending to shoot her with a stick-gun and she said, "No fuckin' way, man. No fuckin' way."

I started laughing. Just couldn't stop at all. Kept it up for an hour. They sent me to the medic and he gave me a shot.

Don't worry about what I said about Eddie walking point all the time.

Perry

I thought about that one for a while, keeping the other thin envelope still closed in my hand until I was ready. Then I opened the other letter.

Dear Iris:

I thank you, and my platoon thanks you—packing the birthday cake in popcorn actually worked. It still looked and tasted like a cake when it got here. Perry says he loved Hawaii and I sure wish I'd been able to see you all there but it just couldn't be helped.

Did he look okay to you? I think he's been thrown off balance here, talking about fairy tales, monks, chickens. It'll probably be fine.

Eddie

I wandered back into my apartment's three rooms. I had met no one here who had a relative in Vietnam. My mailman always commented on the return address. "I deliver a few of these in town sometimes," he had said to me once, "and there's one boy on the Lawn who gets them."

"That's my sort of half brother. We both get letters from the same guys."

"Ah. I have a nephew in the Marines and I'm proud of him for serving—proud to death."

"Well," I had answered, wishing he'd phrased it differently. "I can imagine. Good luck to him."

I wandered into the kitchen and pulled the peanut butter off the shelf, carried it into what passed as my living room and threw myself down into the upholstered chair that had been too large for the last tenants to move. A Sophocles play already in translation lay on its arm and I flipped it open. I read: *I say to you at the very outset that I have nothing but contempt for the kind of governor who is afraid, for whatever reason, to follow the course that he knows is best for the State; and as for the man who sets private friendship above the public welfare, I have no use for him, either. I call God to witness that if I saw my country headed for ruin, I should not be afraid to speak out plainly; and I need hardly remind you that I would never have any dealings with an enemy of the people. No one values friendship more highly than I: but we must remember that friends made at the risk of wrecking our Ship are not real friends at all.*

I kept flipping, scanning for happier lines. I came upon:

*Numberless are the world's wonders, but none
More wonderful than man; the stormgray sea
Yields to his prows, the huge crests bear him high;
Earth, holy and inexhaustible, is graven*

With shining furrows where his plows have gone
Year after year, the timeless labor of stallions.

I could feel the happy response to this choral ode in my chest, which actually tingled as I turned the page. Then I reached the stanza's concluding lines: *He has made himself secure—from all but one: In the late wind of death he cannot stand.*

I closed the book and set it down on a flyer I'd ripped off a wall earlier that day: "NAUI Scuba Certification Course," it said. "Two Credits."

I could use two credits, I thought. I could use some old-fashioned physical activity. And how refreshing to consider a course that required no reading, no lexicons, no temporal-ablative irregularities, and yet still would never call upon me to offer a personal opinion on anything.

The next day I signed up, wriggling my way into the course a week after the deadline. That night I slept soundly.

Dive

I DECIDED NOT TO THINK ABOUT EDDIE'S DOUBTS ABOUT PERRY, but failed. What did his letters to Hank look like? Or the ones to Angie? One night after a dive class I was halfway home when I suddenly turned abruptly away from my apartment and toward Hank's. I could entertain him with stories about class, I thought, and then go home.

He had a fire going and books, as usual, spread over his entire room.

"Tonight was test night in my scuba class," I started, hoping he would pick up this innocuously amusing train of thought and make me more comfortable. "Got any tea? Will you make me a cup of tea?" I asked. I forged on despite his silence. "We swim around underwater and the instructors sabotage us—cut off our air or knock our masks off. And anybody who can't solve the problem underwater without having to surface loses."

"Loses what?" Hank was pushing boxes of cereal aside, looking for sugar.

"Loses the chance to go on the certification dive in the quarry."

"Very picturesque," he said, pulling a box of cubes from the back of a bookshelf. "Just like Jacques Cousteau."

"Right."

"You never drop by at ten at night," he said impatiently.

"I was thinking maybe you'd let me read the letters you get from the boys and I could let you read mine, so we'd . . . have a chance to share the letters."

"What's wrong?" he asked.

"I don't know. Nothing, probably. But I got like two lines from Eddie, asking me if I thought something was wrong with Perry."

"Do you think something's wrong with Perry?"

"Well, yeah. I think Perry's in a war."

"I think Perry's all right," Hank said. He'd seated himself in the room's rocker and now he shifted his weight forward and back, forward and back. "Or I think he will be."

"And what do you think about Eddie?" I asked.

"Eddie's a more complicated situation," Hank answered. "Eddie's not the same."

Hank went to his desk and rummaged around for a moment, returning with onion-thin sheets. My typical letter from Eddie contained three or four quickly scrawled lines. Hank's letter went on for three tightly compressed pages, describing a firefight in language that was exact, mesmerizing and thrilling in a tone that might be described as pornographic. *I've never felt like this before,* my brother had written, and *I'm afraid that if I come back I'll never feel like this again.*

I didn't finish the letter. Some kind of heaviness ran down my arm and made the hand holding the letter sag. It reached Hank's desktop and rested there.

"What does he say to you about Perry?" I asked.

"He says he thinks Perry needs his help; that Perry is out of his element and needs to be saved by him all the time. What does he say to you?" Hank asked.

"Nothing."

"Show me," Hank demanded.

"I don't have anything with me. He doesn't offer much, Hank. Really, just a couple lines that always say the same thing—he's fine. Everything's fine. That's the kind of letter I get."

Hank looked me over and considered before he spoke. "I didn't read you the worst ones."

I excused myself, and all that week struggled with an anxious, dark aftertaste.

It was with me on that weekend when the dive class drove out to the quarry where we would make our first and only open-water dive—our final examination. A freak snowstorm blew in as we were pushing ourselves into borrowed, rattily worn wet suits and checking oxygen levels. Once suited, we lined up on a ledge overlooking an eight-foot drop into utterly black water—a seamless unbroken sheet of obsidian that absorbed the snowflakes the instant they hit it. Five instructors swam in circles a few feet under the surface, waiting for us to join them. It was their job to get us started and paired off with our buddies, to monitor our progress, to sabotage us at appropriate moments, and finally to deliver us safely back to the surface.

I took my place in line and when I reached the edge I turned to face away from the water, fastened my hands to the mask and the tank, and fell backward into an element so cold that the muscles in my neck and throat clenched, making it impossible for me to breathe at first. I struggled to the surface, unwilling to submerge until my neck and chest admitted air. The instructor swimming underwater waited about two minutes for me to get my regulator sorted out and go under. When I didn't submerge myself I felt a hand on my ankle, tugging me down: the instructor, losing patience. I went under. Five seconds later my buddy splashed in above me.

Even at fifteen feet the darkness was terrible—so thick that I could not make out other divers if they didn't have lights. I waited for my partner to join me and began the short trip around the quarry's walls. As soon as my body warmed one layer of water inside the suit, it flowed out of the rips and was replaced by another entirely frigid supply. Then I felt it—a bump at the back of my shoulders followed by the oxygen being cut off. My first reaction was relief—I'd gotten my hand around to the knob during the pool exercise so I knew I could do this now even without a buddy. The rules dictated that before we addressed any problem we got our buddy's attention and access to his regulator mouthpiece if we needed it. I kicked my designated buddy with a flipper to get his attention, succeeded, and pointed to my mouthpiece. He panicked, pulled his own mouthpiece off and tried to force it into my mouth. A wrestling match ensued, effectively keeping me from getting my oxygen back on.

Before he'd let us out as far as the Lake House raft Uncle Charlie had given us all some "when you get in trouble" lessons. "When somebody panics and tries to climb on your head to save themselves," he'd told us, "don't waste your time trying to pry them loose. They'll be stronger than you because they're more scared. Push their heads under. Trust me, they'll let you go."

I reached behind my flailing "buddy" and turned off his oxygen. His eyes popped open horribly, the whites of his eyes now marbled with broken red veins. He grabbed my mouthpiece and released me, leaving me free to turn my own oxygen back on. I got both of our airflows on and our mouthpieces in, and I finished the dive.

When we got out I checked my tank meter—in a twenty-minute exercise I had run through the amount of oxygen that most adult males would use in two hours. I couldn't hear what anyone was saying, so the activity around me ran soundlessly—tanks hitting the ground but not clanking, suits coming off but no squishing or ripping noises—only the internal whooshing of fluid in my own head. Blood from a pressure-related nosebleed dribbled down my chin and onto my chest.

"Good dive," my instructor told me as I got out. He saw my quizzical expression, understood it immediately and spoke very slowly, exaggerating his lips and using hand motions. "You . . . will . . . be . . . able . . . to . . . hear . . . soon."

When I got home I was shaking visibly from the cold, thinking of nothing but the hot bath I was going to draw the second I got in the door. But there on my porch stood Hank. From the bottom of the steps I couldn't see his face and I thought he had come to congratulate me on my first dive. I squared off my shoulders and pulled my shivering lips back away from my teeth in the closest thing to a smile that I could manage, but when I got to the porch and saw his face it was clear that I had mistaken his purpose. He was not here to greet me.

He was here to tell me that Eddie was dead, and Perry missing in action.

Missing

PERRY HAD BEEN LABELED MIA BECAUSE HIS DOG TAGS WERE never found. Eddie's tags were there, and Eddie's body, which the government assured us would be sent to us immediately for burial. No arrangements were made for Perry, who had simply vanished. I tried to imagine Perry someplace on earth, still alive. At first I failed. I could not imagine my brothers' fates to be separate from each other.

Hank and I had driven home together from Charlottesville to wait with Aunt Eleanor and Uncle Charlie for the flag-covered box. Angie had been summoned as well and was making her way home from Berkeley. We would all be there together.

My aunt grew stonier by the day as we waited. Everything was the color of February mud: the mountains to either side of us, the color of the light that bounced from them into Aunt Eleanor's kitchen, the dirt beneath our feet as we wandered around the yard or from room to room and waited, not talking about Eddie.

A rift had opened between Uncle Charlie and Aunt Eleanor. According to the legal documents that passed us from our father into Charlie and Eleanor's hands, Aunt Eleanor was our nearest kin. And as such she had the right to tell the Marines that no military funeral would be held: no color guard, no taps, no rifles and bugles. She had agreed to let an escort come with the body and stand by our side when the box was put in the ground, but that was all. The government had sent a letter informing us of their sorrow and their confidence that Eddie was a hero. She burned it over a trash can one morning when Uncle Charlie was out, letting the ashes drift down into the eggshells and discarded junk mail. I watched her do it.

Uncle Charlie stiffened into a kind of stoic retreat. He seemed to absorb the news of the deaths as a terrible, necessary thing, but Aunt Eleanor's stand on the military honors the Marines wanted to give Eddie made him first angry and then miserable. Aunt Eleanor would not budge. Something in her was unleashed, and its visible parts looked like rage. I had been frightened one day to overhear part of an unhappy and increasingly loud conversation between them in the backyard, where they had gone to speak unheard.

"Oliver Sunnaret is wrong," I heard her say, "and you are wrong."

"If he told them that going to war was their obligation, he was right," Uncle Charlie said.

"He told them it was glory!"

"Oliver didn't use words like that," Charlie protested. "Perhaps 'crucible.' He might have said it was a kind of crucible. Eleanor, what's happened had to happen. There isn't right or wrong here."

" 'Crucible' indeed! I cannot even begin to tell you what you sound like, you and Oliver Sunnaret. We shouldn't have let Perry and Eddie visit him when Eddie asked to go to Paris. You know how vulnerable Eddie was to him. We should have kept the boys away from him, and now it's too late: too late and the man wouldn't even come to the funeral of his own sons!"

"He's bound to his work and he said he could not leave. We have to respect that." Uncle Charlie's voice rose on his last words and I started, snapping a twig underfoot. They whipped their heads toward the sound, both flushed.

My father had indeed declined to come to Eddie's memorial service. This hadn't upset me. I had long ago stopped thinking of him as having anything to do with us. I'd written him letters for a while when I was in elementary school, but when no replies came I stopped. As far as I knew, Angie had made no attempt to communicate with him from the day she crossed Uncle Charlie and Aunt Eleanor's threshold. Only Eddie had kept calling. Only Eddie had used his birthday wish the year before he enlisted to get on an airplane and go visit him. True, Perry had gone along because Aunt Eleanor had insisted upon it, but I had not envied them their visit. In my own mind my father remained frozen in the changeless twenty-two-year-old figure who stood in the only photograph I have of him, my glittering young mother's arm resting on one epaulette. The photograph was real and clear; actual memories of what he looked like or did during his brief visits were dreamlike and distant. I could easily have been convinced that he really had never existed. When we'd dropped the boys off at the airport I had not truly believed that there would be anyone in Paris waiting for them. He seemed more a part of Eddie's imagination than a part of my life.

Of course this wasn't actually true. He had come to our mother's funeral. But then he vanished again, back to Indochina and then, after that, to fulfill military obligations in Paris. He visited two or three times more but it became clear that we would never occupy more than the very smallest part of his real or imaginative life. When I was ten, Aunt Eleanor gathered us together in the living room in order to make what she described as an important announcement: our father had married a very sophisticated and important woman in France, and his professional responsibilities as well as his new marriage would keep him there. I understood this to mean forever.

Then she fed us warm dense squares of gingerbread with whipped cream, which I remember more vividly than the dramatic announcement. I could not see why this change in my father's professional or marital status would make any difference in our lives at all.

The marriage did change something in my relationship with my biological father: the birthday cards stopped; the wrapped box with his name on it at Christmas no longer appeared. Some cord that had served as a last connection had snapped. It was different for my siblings, who could remember his presence in our childhood more clearly. Even after my mother's death when we became Charlie and Eleanor's children, Angie and the boys spoke of him as if he were a real parent, living in real time. Not me.

Hearing Aunt Eleanor speak of him now in a way that made it clear that she had a telephone number or address for him and that she was actually in contact with him—this was a shock. In my own mind he had stopped having anything to do with us a decade ago.

"Iris," Aunt Eleanor said. Then we all stood there in a lumpy kind of silence.

"You asked him to come to the funeral?" I said at last.

"Eddie's his son, honey. He's your father."

The idea of this man standing by the grave with me, Hank, Angie, Uncle Charlie, Aunt Eleanor—it was jarring. It was wrong.

"But he's not coming?" I asked hopefully.

"He's very busy right now," Aunt Eleanor said. She added, "He was just crushed by the news. Devastated."

This certainly was unlikely, but I nodded vaguely. "You think Eddie and Perry shouldn't have gone," I said.

Aunt Eleanor sighed and pulled at a ring finger, her gesture of unhappy irritation. "I think it wasn't necessary for them to go," she said slowly, clearly listening to her words and editing as she ventured further out into an answer. "And I think they were brave young men who wanted to do what was right."

"Were you saying that they only went to please Uncle Charlie and our father?"

Uncle Charlie reared up and his hands got away from him, one jabbing the air and the other cutting back and forth briskly as he spoke. "Perry and Eddie made their own decisions. They were men, Iris—not boys to be told what to do."

Aunt Eleanor sat down slowly. "Oh, Charlie. You were the one making their decisions for them until just a minute or two before they got old enough to volunteer. They would never have been in such a hurry to prove that they were men unless they actually were boys."

"They did what was right," Uncle Charlie said. "Sometimes what is right comes with a high cost. That doesn't mean you shouldn't pay it."

"You tell that to Oliver Sunnaret, Charlie," Aunt Eleanor said, pushing herself to her feet and walking away. "The very next time you see him, you tell him."

THE SERVICE INCLUDED only the family, as if we hoped that by keeping the ceremonies associated with death as secretive and insignificant as we could, we might be able to take it all back and start over.

Angie, Hank and I were returned to our campuses, told that life was going to go on and that we would have to do the same. My family scattered as if propelled in different directions by some blast. Back in Charlottesville I felt at odds with everything around me. The smell of boxwood, the serpentine walled gardens full of plum trees just beginning to think about blossoms, the posted flyers announcing polo team tryouts hanging from the classics building bulletin boards—all, all seemed unnaturally bright and flat. My family had stepped into a war's path, but everywhere I looked there were people who seemed utterly untouched.

When my diving instructor called to ask if I wanted to go on a paid detail for the Washington, D.C., police, it seemed like a window into the real world had cracked open a bit.

"What kind of job is it?" I asked. "What are they looking for?"

"It's a car. Usually it's cars; sometimes bodies in the cars. But you find lots of other stuff down there. If it's an insurance company, they want the car body. If it's the police, they want the human body."

"But I don't have certification for that kind of work."

"No, and you never will if you don't get more experience. My boys will be along, and they'll be your master divers. You just follow orders. This is a perfect practice run for you because we won't be working at more than forty feet. Even if it goes to fifty, that gives you fifty-five minutes of bottom time. Room to look around and get used to things."

"I hear the visibility is so bad it gives you claustrophobia and sometimes you find stuff down there you wish you'd never found."

"Look. It's good money, Iris, but the real point is that if you don't dive, you lose the training. You're too green to be diving without more experienced people. So come on. You need the practice."

"I understand. But I'm going to say no."

"All right. I won't give up on you, though," he said. "I'll call the next time something like this comes up. Think about it."

I didn't want to think about it, so I didn't. But then I did. I imagined rusting cars standing on their noses on the river floor, side by side with old refrigerators, cracked rowboats and children's toys, oil sludge, tin cans. Bodies.

The first time I got a letter from the boys after their deaths was the most dissonant—the strange fold in time and space that sent a paper envelope that one of them had licked only weeks before right to my door. Reaching out to grasp the onionskin envelopes, I had the dissonant impression that the funeral had been a mistake. Here are letters after all, touched by them, written and folded and addressed by them.

But the dates on the envelopes were from before the day that Eddie had been killed and Perry disappeared. The letters had gotten tangled in mail systems, perhaps left sitting in a bag at an LZ for weeks before reaching my porch here on Jefferson Park Drive.

> Iris:
>
> Things here are totally under control. I am Absolutely Jim Dandy Fine. Everybody is Absolutely Jim Dandy Fine.
>
> Things are quiet lately. Boring even. Lots of mud and mosquitos and waiting, waiting, waiting.
>
> Eddie

The next day Hank showed me a letter he'd received on the same day. It read, in part:

> He's just sitting there with us and then he starts talking in gook. When he goes back to English he's still not making sense. Sometimes he talks like he thinks there are fairies and spirits in the trees. He disappears sometimes,

gone for forty-eight hours once. Comes back talking that way about trees
again. He'd be court-martialed but I'm the one who'd do the paperwork
on the AWOL so he's never going to be court-martialed for taking off to
talk to trees. Lucky him.

He doesn't understand that if you break off the ties with the guys who
are with you here, you risk everything. You can't stay alive here all alone.

"He's talking about Perry?" I asked.

Hank nodded.

I tried to imagine Perry like this and it was easy to do. I tried to imagine Eddie the way he'd looked in the photograph that Perry showed me, the words "sucking chest wound" running shaggily across his helmet. I summoned up his astonishing smile. Over the weeks since he'd first shown it to me I had been incorporating this image into my idea of him, and I found that it had moved further into my mind than I'd thought.

Yes. That was him.

You Don't Know Anything

ARLY SPRING IN THE BLUE RIDGE IS COOL IN ITS CENTER BUT pale green around the edges with enough sunshine in some afternoons to burn your skin if you let it. Hank and I had an academic break and all of us, Hank and Angie and I, were heading to the Lake House, which Charlie and Eleanor typically opened for this vacation.

It was the first time we'd gathered since the service for the boys. I had been letting things slide at school, losing track of deadlines and keys; putting the hot pot of coffee in the refrigerator when I leaned in to get some milk and forgetting where it was.

The first morning home I came down into the kitchen to find Aunt Eleanor slumped over something at the kitchen table, two brown grocery bags on the floor by her side.

"What's wrong?" I asked.

She raised her head and shifted just a bit so I could see what she'd been cradling in her hands: three cans of roasted cocktail peanuts. No one in our household would touch cocktail peanuts but Perry, who adored them. At her elbow was a package of dried apricots, Eddie's favorite treat.

"I don't think it was that I forgot," she whispered. "I don't know why I did it."

She stood, holding the three blue cans of nuts and the package of apricots before her like an offering, and walked to the trash can. She dumped them in one after the other. "Coffee?" she murmured, swiveling to get two cups out of the cabinet. But when she'd poured the coffee and sat down beside me at the table she couldn't stand it. She pushed the cup aside, walked briskly to the trash can, plucked the plastic bag out and went to the door. "I'll be right back," she said. I could hear her make her way to the side of the house, could hear the metal garbage can lid come off and clang back down.

"There," she said upon reentering. "We're fine now."

"Right," I answered. "Fine now."

When the drunken soldier knocked on the door the next afternoon and said that he had served with Eddie and Perry in their platoon and could tell us what happened if we wanted to know, I didn't notice his inebriation. I wasn't a drinker myself, though the smell of his skin and breath, the red in his eyes, signaled his condition to everyone in my family but me. If I'd noticed I would have let him in anyway. How could I turn him away? Here he was, our Pandora, lugging the trunk and holding the key.

He wore surplus fatigues and chains of all sorts around his neck. When he opened his mouth you could see a missing molar on the upper left and another gaping hole just below it. He limped but was also clearly a man who at one time in his life had been a natural mover. He couldn't have been more than twenty-three years old, though it was clear that all his youth was behind him. He came right to the point, and he addressed himself to Uncle Charlie, who seemed to be the man in charge. "Are you Charles Jackson? I'm here because I knew your sons, Pericles and Edward Sunnaret. I'm here because I was there at the end and I wanted you to know about it. If you want to know. I'll just go if you want. But if you want to know, I'm here."

I had never seen Uncle Charlie freeze up like he did then. The soldier waited for a moment and when Uncle Charlie still didn't move or speak, he went on. "I thought I should come because I owe your Perry a debt." Then he coughed and we stood facing him, frozen in place just inside the front door.

"What's your name, soldier?" Uncle Charlie finally asked.

"Thompson, sir."

The soldier straightened up as if the word "sir" had strings on it, reaching just above his head to an invisible authority that tugged him upright. Some of the rumpledness left his manner and his clothing, and I could see Uncle Charlie considering. "Come into the living room," he said at last. He stepped aside and the visitor picked his way past my uncle into the living room, where Uncle Charlie guided him into a chair.

"Who is it, Uncle Charlie?" Angie called from the kitchen.

"It's all right," he called back, meaning he didn't want her in the room—a sure draw. She headed straight in.

"Hello," she said, walking up to the intruder and extending a hand for him to shake. "I'm Angie Sunnaret."

"I knew your brothers," he replied. Angie responded by running to the bottom of the stairs and yelling up for everyone to get into the living room. Uncle Charlie had reached out to stop her but she was moving too quickly.

"This young man says he can tell us something about the boys," Uncle Charlie said to us when everyone reached the room's entrance. "Come in and sit down," he ordered, and we obeyed, arranging ourselves tentatively around the soldier, who was showing signs of reticent shyness now that he faced the entire family.

"Yes?" Hank asked, when a full minute had gone by in silence.

"Well," the soldier started, "I came mostly because I felt like I owed Robin—your Perry. That's what we called him. And Eddie, we called him Batman. I had to look at his dog tags to remember his other name, to tell the truth. Batman and Robin, see? Some of the guys called him Prince Robin."

"Why?" Aunt Eleanor asked.

"Your Perry had this knack for staying clean and eating with a fork, being our diplomat to the natives. He could talk history and law like they mattered, even where we were. He was like a guy visiting from another kingdom. But that doesn't mean he wasn't where he was supposed to be when you got in trouble. Not at all. That's what I came to say."

Then he ground to a halt again, sitting silently.

"Mr. Thompson?" Uncle Charlie prompted.

"I was trying to say that I'm here to say that your Perry saved my life, and I have a debt to him. He saved it more than once. The first time he did it I didn't see this trip wire. Perry had an amazing eye for booby traps. He and your Eddie both, almost like they thought like the Cong, but Perry was the one I stuck to. He saved my balls, man—literally—those things pop up right between your legs." Aunt Eleanor's expression caught his eye. "Sorry, ma'am. Pardon my language." He shifted around and settled into a new position. "If his aim hadn't been right or if he'd been a second slower, we both would have caught it and I know he knew that, but he did it anyway. When it's over, he just brushes himself off like he was clean to begin with, which none of us were but he was able to make it look like he had been once. He just keeps right on moving along at my side, and it's over. I saw him do that for two other guys. Saved our lives and risked his own. I wanted you to know that."

"Thank you, Mr. Thompson," Uncle Charlie said.

Then, after another few moments of silence, Angie prompted him. "What about Eddie?"

"Oh, Batman. For a long time there, everybody liked to be near him on a recon 'cause he had a real delicate feel for the landscape. We followed him wherever; I mean, really wherever, because he was lucky. We did whatever Batman said. But by the end we were starting to keep our distance from him because he'd been walking point so long we were all sure his luck was going to go soon. Nobody walks point out there in front as much as he did and lasts as long. Most units revolve the position. It ain't popular. But Batman, even when he was in charge and should have assigned it, he walked it himself. He had a good eye, but not as good as Robin. But then Batman started doing stuff that looked like all he wanted was to draw some fire. Like one time he has us use the road instead of moving through the jungle—I mean, only cherries walk on roads." He saw that some of us didn't understand. "In a road you're totally exposed. You never walk on roads unless they've been swept for mines and scouted for NVA. And he wouldn't tell us why. This kind of thing was making us crazy. He either wanted to die or his instincts had just gone kaflooey. Like he was trying, really trying, to get them to come out and fight."

"Isn't that the point of war, Mr. Thompson?" Uncle Charlie said.

"Not this war, sir. This war, if you want to make it to the end of your year, you keep your head down. But more and more that was not how your Eddie was operating. So I was sticking by Robin—your Perry—but I'm working just a bit ahead of him when all hell breaks loose—guys tossing missiles, real fire at us and we've got no place to go—no holes, no cover, no nothing."

He stopped again. No one prompted this time and there were an awkward few moments when it seemed Thompson had forgotten us. When he spoke again his expression had flattened and his words sounded recited. "This heavy, heavy mist closed us in, and the helos couldn't get to us. We just hunkered down there in the jungle for twelve hours, waiting for NVA to come back and kill the rest of us. They could have, easy. We made a circle, all of us back to back with our weapons propped on our chests, and we stood there all night like that listening for the sound of them coming for us until daylight burned off the mist and the helos could get in. I don't know why the Cong didn't come for us.

"Batman brought us there, and he got most of us out, but twelve guys never walked away from that. And he still couldn't tell us what he'd been doing, making us take that open road through an unsecured zone. Guys started being clear about doubting his judgment.

"It happened two more times—orders that were like he was just looking for a chance to die, and he was our CO so we had to go with him. Then the smoke grenade got rolled into his tent." He nodded and looked at us significantly, saw that we didn't know what was meant by this event, and added, "It's a warning."

"From who?" I asked.

"From whoever's thinking of fragging you."

He didn't have to explain this word. By 1971 enough vets had returned and spoken about commanding officers being killed by their own men in the field. "You're drunk, Mr. Thompson," Uncle Charlie said.

"Yes sir, I am. But that doesn't change anything."

Now that it had been pointed out to me I could see him swaying just the tiniest bit on the chair where he faced us, leaning slightly forward as if he were leaning into a wind.

"You can leave now, Mr. Thompson," Uncle Charlie said.

"No," Aunt Eleanor contradicted him. "Go on, Mr. Thompson."

"Time comes when Eddie orders another recon. By this time though, there's guys who don't want to follow orders from him, don't want to follow him at all. Nobody but your Perry would stick close to him if he had point—he was drawing fire now, see. That last recon, some guys trailed along but only your boys were in front. Then there was the shot. We hit the ground thinking it was a sniper, not knowing what else was going to follow. We waited but we didn't hear any more shots; no incoming or explosions. When we moved we were going like an inch an hour, looking for trip wires. We finally get to the clearing, though, and there's a bullet in your Eddie's head. And your Perry, no sign of him at all. I wasn't looking for sign. It was a kind of upsetting scene, you know. Later our best tracker said there was one pair of sign leading out of the clearing—a big footprint and broken weed like an American would leave. VC, they leave just about no sign at all. Little teeny guys, move like water or wind. So this sign, they figure, was Perry's."

"What are you saying, Mr. Thompson?" Aunt Eleanor's back was straight and her voice was steady but her face wasn't the right color.

"I'm saying your Perry and Eddie were ahead of the rest of the patrol, and your Eddie tried to put them in the line of fire again, so your Perry took care of things. Probably saved all of our lives, given how things were going."

"What do you mean, 'took care'?" Aunt Eleanor had reared up in her seat and now balanced rigidly on its edge.

"Stopped him. I'm only here today because of Perry Sunnaret doin' the hard thing. We figured what happened would come out even though we know the official letters don't tell you, and you should know how we all were behind Perry in ways that maybe pushed him, but we were still ripped up about it. I wanted you to see that it wasn't simple."

"You mean Perry shot him?" Angie said. I remember being surprised at her calm, the monotone in which she asked, the way she seemed to already know what he'd come here to say.

"Thank you, Mr. Thompson," Aunt Eleanor said then. "Now you may leave."

"I got the short straw, ma'am. That's all."

"Leave." My aunt rose up like a hot wind had lifted her, and seemed to expand until she took up the entire middle of the room and then more, pushing Mr. Thompson toward the door as she got larger and larger. But at the room's entrance he turned back to us.

"You don't have to tell me, or anyone who's ever been in a shithole of some kind, that the truth isn't always what you want to hear. But that doesn't change anything at all, just wanting something. I'm no happier to be here than you are to have me: nobody likes the man who brings bad news. But remember I'm standing here telling you that your Perry saved my life. Saved us all."

I sat there thinking that I wanted very badly for him never to have come; never to have changed anything. He shifted from foot to foot, frustrated, clearly feeling he hadn't made himself clear. "I had to come. I had a debt." He pulled a scrap of paper from a pocket and dropped it on a side table. "This is my telephone number if you want to find me again. And I wouldn't be a bit surprised if you decide you want to find me again."

We sat immobile, all of us but Aunt Eleanor, who took his arm and propelled him rapidly away. We were still in our places when she returned.

"He's gone," she said simply.

"He was drunk," Hank said.

"Thank you, Eleanor," Uncle Charlie said, "for removing that young man."

When I put my arms around her she stiffened but I didn't let go because I knew her and I knew she would relent and soften. She did, finally hugging me back, finishing the hug off with an officious little pat on the back, and then, as if changing her mind yet again, embracing me with real warmth before freeing me and stepping back to address her family.

She said, "The ridiculous little service we had for Eddie will not do. We didn't announce it, or tell anyone at all. We thought keeping it as small and quiet as possible would make it easier. It didn't, and it's time to correct that error. We need a bonfire at the Lake House, and I believe we can make it happen by next Saturday. A really big bonfire. And fireworks. Hank, you are in charge of fuel. Just go out and buy a few cords of wood—there's not time for the usual gathering up odds and ends. Charlie, if you go down into that old darkroom space in the basement you'll find a stash of fireworks I keep just in case we run short on the Fourth of July. They're there still, and it's time to use them." She turned to Angie and me. "Ladies, we have some shopping to do and then some work in the kitchen. We need to spend an hour or so on the telephone before we shop, though, because we need a lot of them."

"A lot of what?" Hank asked.

"Guests. Anybody who knew Eddie and wants to come to a good-bye party for him, they should be called. Friends of both of them, in fact. We should have done it before and we hunkered down instead. We are re-miss." She opened the secretary drawer and pulled out an address book and a legal pad. "Old high school friends. Neighbors. Teachers. All the people we didn't call when we had the small service. It's a good time to do it."

"But Aunt Eleanor, some of them know the boys had that small service months ago."

"And we made the mistake of not inviting them. Tell them we are correcting that error now."

I could see Uncle Charlie's imagination actually reaching this place—constructing this kind of telephone call in which he invited people to a service marking the end of the boys' lives. Aunt Eleanor saw it, too. "Charlie," she said, going to him and actually kneeling down before him as he sat. "We've just been pretending it's going to go away. We'll do it as right as we can. Then it can be done."

He nodded and rose, holding her hand and drawing her upright. He bent down to brush his lips to hers before facing us, pulling together his Big Dog self.

"We have work to do, men," he said quietly. "Up, up!"

We stood. Hank and I made the terrible calls, actually surprising some people with the news of Eddie's death and Perry's disappearance for the first time. My aunt and uncle had managed to move around this community for months, keeping the massive shift in their lives out of casual conversation, avoiding friends as well as acquaintances. The information seemed to have been contained to a very small circle. By the end of the day this had changed. Then we shopped for every food the boys had loved. Guests were told to bring something to burn and to come to the Lake House. Most of these people had been there and stood with us in the circle around a July bonfire. Not a single person said no.

In the end the assembled fuel included old desks and broken chairs, bundles of newspaper, odd lumber scraps and actual firewood. Our neighbor Mrs. Conroy's tax records from the last fifteen years went up in flames, and at least a half dozen people came holding packets of old letters. Estonia Wczecksi, who had loved Perry in ninth grade, brought a cigar box containing we knew not what. It was as if they came eager to destroy some little part of their own pasts and we had given them this opportunity.

Then it was the next morning and we were adrift again, even Aunt Eleanor sitting at the kitchen table for a full two hours with the same undisturbed cup of coffee. We were all due back at our lives of course, back in classes and in dorm rooms and apartments of our own, but we made no move to leave the Lake House and the blackened charcoal at the water's edge.

"Wednesday," Aunt Eleanor said to us at dinner on Sunday night. She could feel the way we were congealing here, getting stuck. "Nobody is allowed to stay here past Wednesday."

Monday morning at dawn, Angie, Hank and I found ourselves sitting in the kitchen around the coffeemaker, waiting for it to finish dripping: 5:24 a.m. If Uncle Charlie and Aunt Eleanor were awake, they gave no sign.

It was an unseasonable day, too early to know if it would be overcast but warm enough to stand outside with only a sweatshirt. Hank, Angie and I took our mugs of coffee and wandered in robes down the lawn to the dock, where a neighbor's rowboat still bobbed. As if by some prearranged agreement we had jammed our feet into old sneakers and walked out of the house in single file, heading for the little boat still tied to our dock. We climbed in and Angie pulled out into the lake. Steam rose up off the water, and within a few strokes we were invisible to the land, as it was hidden to us.

I sat at the stern; Angie in the boat's center; Hank before her in the prow.

"Let me help," he said to her. "Move over."

She shook her head from side to side, dismissing his offer. "He did it," she said, as if she'd been asked the question she was now answering. "Perry killed him."

I twisted around to face her. "How can you say something so ugly?"

"It isn't ugly." She stopped rowing. "He did what he thought had to be done. It was a moral act—saving the rest of the platoon from the risks Eddie was making them run."

"We don't know what happened at all," Hank said.

Now Angie turned on him. "Perry always acted on his conscience; always acted as an individual before he acted as a member of a group. What that Thompson guy said made sense."

"Made sense," I protested, "if you think Perry would hurt Eddie, which he never did in his entire life."

"You don't know the details of his entire life, or what passed between him and Eddie before they died," Angie replied.

I wasn't accustomed to fighting back at Angie, so I retreated a bit and did not say what I thought, which was that she seemed terribly invested in knowing more than anyone around her.

Angie might have had some power over Hank's feelings, but that never stopped him from correcting her. He did this now. "This is a bad time to get on a high horse, Angie," he said simply. "None of us knows the whole story."

"Some of us know more than others. They did write letters, didn't they? They didn't write the same things to everyone." She looked away.

"Why are you doing this?" he asked quietly. Lake water slapped gently against the boat. We could smell coffee from some other early riser's breakfast on the shore, making its way to us across an expanse of fog.

"What?"

"Angie," I said, "please don't be like this."

"This happened because Oliver Sunnaret is our father," she cried.

"What are you talking about? We haven't seen him since we were, like, seven and ten."

"Oh, Iris. The fall that Eddie signed up, do you remember what his birthday wish was that year?"

"Yes. He said he wanted to go to Paris."

"Right. He wanted to go alone, but Aunt Eleanor said that even if our father agreed to be visited, that he'd have to take Perry."

"I thought Eddie wanted Perry to go with him." I remembered the dinner table awkwardness on the evening that Eddie admitted that for years he had been asking our father if he could visit, but had never received a response. That year for his birthday, Eddie asked for Aunt Eleanor and Uncle Charlie's intervention. I remembered the event so clearly because it was the only time that Aunt Eleanor had asked one of us to change a birthday wish. Eddie would not change it, and she yielded to him. Aunt Eleanor had secured an invitation for him. Three weeks later we had driven them to the airport. Four days after that we picked them up, the visit's brevity dictated by our father. Both boys had new suits. Both answered questions about the visit monosyllabically.

Angie spoke to me in the tone she used with small children and the dogs, explaining the obvious. "Eddie was on one of those mythic seek-your-father-and-you-shall-find-yourself quests, and everybody knows you have to go on those alone. That's why he said he wanted it for just him."

"But Aunt Eleanor said he had to go with Perry."

"Yes. She said he had to go with Perry. And Eddie came back saying he wanted to be a soldier. Pretty ridiculous lengths to go to just to get somebody to love you," she finished.

"Getting somebody to love you is important," I said. "Important to me, anyway."

"I know," she replied. "That's why people love you." Her tone was more affectionate than condescending but it still made me blink. "But Daddy had the same effect on Eddie that he always had—made him cravenly eager to please."

"Don't be too quick to cast yourself as mind reader," Hank said to her, and his tone was not as neutral as Angie's had been.

They exchanged a heated, intimate, almost hooded look that took me by surprise. And what I saw as I looked at them was a new and more complicated sexual tension. Something had happened between them, something besides the funeral and the deaths.

The certainty that they had slept together felt so much like a tangible blow that I had to clutch the sides of the boat to keep myself from falling out. I felt adrift—utterly unmoored.

"What's wrong? Are you all right?" Hank leaned forward to examine my face.

"Sure. Yes." I straightened, struggling to get my head upright enough to assure Hank that he didn't have to look at me.

We rowed back, tied the little boat to the dock and marched back up the lawn, our feelings bristling unsmoothably over lunch, then the afternoon, then dinner. All that day I was unable to turn my eyes away from every interaction between Hank and Angie. I wanted to both stay right at their side and run from them and see nothing; hear nothing. What other secrets had passed between them that had been carefully secreted from me? I had trusted them utterly, my life entirely open to them; they had not trusted me at all, and even now they sat locked and tangled while I watched from a distance.

By dinner I had named the feeling that had almost knocked me out of the boat. It was jealousy.

Its Tomblike Feel

By the time Angie and I retreated to our bedroom that night, I felt flayed by the pictures I'd been constructing in my mind of her and Hank. I stood by her side in front of the sink just as I had stood on hundreds of other nights, brushing my teeth. I wore cotton pajamas with elephants on them; she wore bikini briefs and a clinging ribbed T-shirt. The contrast could not have been more upsetting to me. Uncharacteristically, we said nothing as we stripped back the twin beds in our childhood bedroom. I laid a copy of *Middlemarch* open on my lap. She had a *Rolling Stone*.

"So," I ventured. "We're all going back to our lives tomorrow."

"That's what they say," she murmured, reading on.

"Except that everything's different."

"Yes," she answered. "Everything's different."

"I don't think I mean it the way you mean it," I pressed on. "I know it's different because of Eddie and Perry. But it's different because of Hank as well—you and Hank."

She tossed the *Rolling Stone* onto the floor. "There's nothing between me and Hank."

"I don't believe you," I said sadly. I set down *Middlemarch* and wiped my sweaty hands on an elephant marching across my rib cage. "You slept with him, didn't you?"

"I have no romantic feelings about Hank," she said impatiently.

"So you haven't slept with him?"

"I didn't say that. What I mean is that Hank and I are not a romantic match. When Hank thinks about love, he goes straight to marriage and homemaking, diamonds and forever."

"That's not so terrible."

"That's a matter of opinion. Personally, I think even the word 'marriage' has a tomblike feel to it. I have no objection to sex but I don't want it to lead anywhere. I especially don't want it to lead to fidelity and dishwashers."

"But you . . ." I couldn't keep the alarm entirely out of my voice.

She sighed an exasperated sigh. "He's not my blood relation, if that's what's troubling you."

Angie slipped out of her bed and into mine. She pushed me over with a swing of her hip and pulled the covers up to our chins.

"It has nothing to do with you and me, Bear." This was my nickname from toddlerhood, given because of my then square features, thatchy hair and lumbering gait. "You and me, we're not changeable or interruptable. Nothing comes between us." My sister draped her arms around me and kissed my ear and I felt the old familiar happiness of being in her approving orbit.

It was true: for the larger part of our lives she had been my closest comrade. She was my memory as well as my playmate and confidant. She could describe all our mother's dresses and each piece of jewelry she had worn. *And it had a broken clasp so she never wore that string of pinkish pearls,* she would say. *Remember?* But I couldn't summon up the pearls or the clasp even after she protested that I had worn them myself, bobby-pinned to my head and wound around clumps of my hair. *Don't you remember?*

Even now in a decade when perfumes were unfashionable among the young, Angie wore our mother's scent—Shalimar. "She was like a queen," she told me again and again. "And when we grow up, we'll be queens, too. Because we're her daughters."

About our father Angie was less specific. There were no stories about what he had worn and how he had smelled and sounded.

When Uncle Charlie and Aunt Eleanor inherited us, Angie had a more difficult time than I, and so it was I who smoothed her way with Aunt Eleanor when the two arrived at one of their awkward impasses over a domestic chore or a disrespectful retort. Though I was three years younger than Angie, here I was the master and she the student. In Angie's service I was no longer the lumbering thatched creature who begged for stories and knocked over lamps: I took on the powers of the adored littlest child, more malleable and affectionate than my edgy sister and thus easier for Aunt Eleanor and Uncle Charlie to love very quickly. I was peacemaker and diplomat at about the same time I was learning to read and write, and I was good at it. I felt some gratitude to Angie for being so spiky that she needed me, and for her part Angie was grateful for my gentler habits. She didn't resent me my success with Aunt Eleanor and Uncle Charlie.

More important to understanding Angie was the fact that she wouldn't have resented my skills even if I had not used them to make her own way smoother. She would never have wanted to be the things I was—not for anyone's love—and she begrudged me the affection Eleanor and Charlie felt for me not one bit. My sister Angie was above jealousy. Even in childhood she was too large for such a petty and diminishing emotion.

We needed each other. I knew that. And here was the old, old happiness when she tapped her forehead against mine and called me by my nicknames.

Then I remembered Hank and confusion swept over me again along with an entirely new feeling in my dealings with Angie—something less happy. We were no longer us, the girls, together and apart from them, the boys. Angie had changed that.

"He's always loved you. But you don't really want him, do you? It doesn't seem even," I added.

Angie snorted and sat up, breaking the seal between our bodies. "Nothing's even. Hank knew what he was getting and he could have stayed away from me if it troubled him so much. He's old enough to take care of his own feelings, I think; and if he isn't, it's still not my job to take care of him."

"Maybe he couldn't."

"Couldn't what?"

"Stay away from you."

"Don't be ridiculous."

I blushed.

"We're just different, Iris," she said gently. "People love you for your discipline and loyalty. They don't expect those things from me. And every bunch of qualities comes with price tags as well as benefits. It all evens out."

But it was clear to me that no matter what she said, she didn't see our lives as even. She had chosen her own path because it seemed riskier and nobler than mine, and if I scratched the surface of those first unhappy feelings toward her, I would see that I agreed. Her way was the better way, of course, because it had produced this beautiful and persuasive creature who sat beside me now.

I thrust my head down on my pillow and told myself that I would sleep, and while I slept my feelings would fall into some kind of order that left me more peace of mind. But the next morning it was the same, and I could not look at Hank as we loaded the car and headed back to Charlottesville together.

"What is wrong with you?" Hank finally demanded after an hour's silence.

"Why should anything be wrong?"

"You aren't talking. You don't hear me when I say something. And you haven't looked at me since you got in the car."

"It hasn't been a particularly happy week, Hank."

"That's just it. When you're unhappy or confused you talk more. And here we are in the middle of all this terrible stuff and you're like a tomb. It's not like you."

"Maybe it's exactly like me," I replied.

"Are you mad at me about something?" he asked.

"It's not all about you, Hank," I said, startling him. I had never spoken to him like this, so distantly. I could feel my face warm up, feel him trying to get a sideways look at me as he drove.

"All of a sudden you sound like Angie," he said after a moment.

"That wouldn't be so terrible," I said.

"We've already got one Angie," he said. "I depend on you to be something else."

Once back in my apartment in Charlottesville, I went to bed, where I remained for the rest of the next day. I was roused at last by a telephone call from my diving instructor, asking me if I wanted to go on a dive into a lake about sixty miles from us. An insurance company wanted to see if anything could be recovered from a sunken boat that had been crowded with drunken, bejeweled New Year's Eve partiers before it went down. The celebrants had all been fished out, but a lot of their possessions hadn't come with them.

I agreed.

A week later I found myself in the backseat of the instructor's truck, surrounded by tanks and gear. He and two of his sons completed our group: we would be diving in teams of two. The company insuring the boat wanted us to examine the hull and engine and offer an explanation for its demise. Another insurance company, representing a passenger, hoped we could find her diamond bracelet. This was a shallow lake, and the instructor had mentioned that when he asked if I wanted to go along. My fee for the dive would be generous regardless of what we found, and that mattered, too. Suddenly I wanted money that my aunt and uncle didn't know about.

We found the boat, its starboard side still sporting a hunk of the cement piling it had rammed into fifteen minutes before it went down. My instructor had descended with lights and a camera to record this story for our employer. I held one of the lights while he captured images of the hull. Then we left the relative bright world outside the craft and flippered into its dark interior. My diving partner saw me breathing rapidly and moved to intervene. He plucked what had once been a woman's sun hat from its resting place on the remains of a cabin dining table and jammed it on his head, striking watery balletic poses until I actually laughed, larger glubby bubbles floating up from my equipment along with the tiny ones. He patted my arm, saw that I was now at ease and signaled for me to help him force the little door into the sleeping quarters.

There the flashlight's searching beam actually, to both our amazement, picked up an answering sparkle, and we swam eagerly toward it. My partner reached it first, plucking a piece of shattered glass from the luxurious wreckage. He shrugged, miming disappointment, but I had not moved my own flashlight's beam from the corner and the answering sparkle continued. I reached into the column of light, pawing gently in what I assumed was glass-riddled trash to pluck out the largest sparkle and lift it up to examine. I held a band of diamonds.

It wasn't until I surfaced that I knew what I wanted to do with the money I had earned on this dive. It would help me rent a car or take a plane, talk forever long distance—it would help me reach the other men whose names could be provided by Private Thompson, and give me other stories about my brothers' deaths besides Thompson's. After all, he'd dropped the card on the lowboy on his way out, and I felt sure that Aunt Eleanor hadn't destroyed it.

SHE HADN'T.

"I wouldn't use that if I were you," Aunt Eleanor had said to me as soon as she'd read the numbers over the telephone. "But I guess it's yours as much as mine."

I used it immediately but I kept getting people who weren't Thompson. Each person who answered the telephone when I dialed the number he'd left claimed to know him. Each promised to leave him messages saying I was calling. None of them identified themselves or clarified their relationship with Mr. Thompson. Just as I'd reached the point where I was admitting that I was a teeny bit relieved not to have actually reached him, I picked up the telephone one afternoon on the first ring and heard what could only have been Thompson's voice.

"You Batman and Robin's sister?" the voice said.

"Mr. Thompson?"

I could hear him pull on a cigarette and exhale. "So you called." There was so long a silent pause on the other end that I thought the line had disconnected. Then I heard breathing.

"I wanted to ask you to describe what happened again, Mr. Thompson."

His voice narrowed and thinned. He said, "How do I even know if you're who you say you are? Maybe you're just a friend of my ex-bitch-wife who's playing games with me."

"No," I said calmly. "I'm Iris Sunnaret, Mr. Thompson. And you gave my family this telephone number yourself. You know me."

I could hear his breathing, then something like a deep sucking sound and a cough. He said, "Don't worry, honey. I was just jerking your chain a little. Foolin' around." I heard rapping in the background and a woman's voice singing.

"You know your Eddie, just before he got it, said he was tired of waiting for them."

"For who?"

"VC. NVA. Anybody who was trailing him, watching him, trying to find a way to kill him. You can go crazy waiting. He got real tired of it."

"I guess you could," I said.

"The day he died nobody wanted to go out with him on recon. Guys knew he was looking for fire. Your Perry went, and maybe five guys who trailed along behind for old times' sake, backup for Batman. But they wanted to keep their distance. Only Robin stayed next to him."

"Were you one of the guys following them?" I asked.

"Yeah. I was one of the guys following them. We were about twenty yards behind when I heard a shot. One shot, man, just one shot."

"Were they being attacked?"

"We thought so. Hard to tell with your face in the dirt and your blood banging in your ears. When we got into the clearing, Batman was there waiting for us with a bullet in his head. There was no Perry around. But there was sign, broken branches, leaving the clearing. We hit the dirt fast, sure a sniper'd gotten Batman and was still in range. We stayed like that for, I don't know, maybe an hour."

He stopped talking. "And?" I asked. "What did you find?"

"We didn't find Perry," he said.

"But, he had to be somewhere. Something had to happen to him."

"I told you, we didn't find your brother. Not even parts of your brother. He was a good man in the jungle—could slide out of sight and away in a second. He spent a lot of time in the jungle. Knew a lot of things."

"Why would he disappear like that?"

"Maybe because he'd just blown away his brother the platoon leader. Maybe because he had a girl stashed somewhere. There's thousands of American guys still there. There's beautiful women there, nice women. You try dipping your toe back into this country, being who you've turned into over there. What did he have to come back to, anyway?"

"Us. He had us."

"Who are you to him?"

"That's not for you to say, is it, Mr. Thompson?"

"Right you are, girlie. Not for me to say. But I can say what I knew, and that was that your Perry knew a whole lot of *mammasans*, and I know that I heard one shot, and when I walked into that clearing I saw your Eddie with one bullet in his head and your Perry just completely vanished."

"Who else could talk to me? Who else was there, Mr. Thompson?"

"I'll give you Geronimo's number. I got it ready because I figured you'd call."

"Did he see and hear the same thing you did?"

"You ask him yourself, but if he doesn't say the same thing I did, you just remember that Indians lie." Thompson finished off this announcement with a bray, which I ignored. I could hear an uneasy shifting as if Thompson were deciding whether to go on. "When I was there, I loved your brothers," he said in a rush. "I was also a little bit afraid of them. Now, I don't think I love anybody. I can't even remember what that felt like, to love them. The faces, the voices, the way elephant grass cuts and won't lie down when you move through it—all as crystal clear as if it were rolling on a movie screen in my head right this minute. But the feelings aren't so clear. Have you ever seen a little bird go from alive to dead?" He didn't wait for an answer. "Like one minute it's this lively, shiny little thing all full of itself and so colorful and quick. You break its neck and it just vanishes. The body's still there, but all the color's gone and you can't explain why but it's not even recognizable anymore even though, feather for feather, it's the same bird. That's what it was like looking down at Batman in the clearing. I can't tell you what it costs to love somebody and then look at that. I can't tell you."

My throat had closed on the words "feather for feather" and then there was a raspish hacking for a minute before he continued.

He said, "You try to talk to Geronimo. He was there. You might have to actually go to the guy to talk to him. He headed back to the Iroquois Nation as soon as he got back. Not a telephone or return-your-call kind of guy."

"Iroquois Nation? But you call him Geronimo. Wasn't Geronimo an Apache?"

I could hear a quick inhalation of a cigarette; a shrug. "Yeah, maybe. What the fuck."

I scratched down the telephone number and ended the awkward silence with a hesitant thanks for his help.

"Good luck to you," Thompson said. "You tell Geronimo I said hello." There was the mucousy cough on the other end of the line, and then a click.

Of course I went to Hank, banging on his door at ten o'clock that night and finding him sitting in front of a fire, papers and books radiating out in a circle on the floor around him.

"It doesn't matter," he said.

"But Hank, it's important!"

"This Thompson guy's a drunk, and probably nuts," Hank said to me. "As far as I'm concerned, they both died in battle, both on the same side."

"But Thompson was there. We weren't."

"Iris, eyewitness accounts are like the old memory game—you see what you're looking for like you hear what you're listening for."

"You don't want to know what happened. That's what's going on, isn't it?"

"You're right. I don't." Hank bent back over a paper and examined it so carefully I knew he wasn't reading a word on it.

"I'm going to call this other guy, the Indian guy they called Geronimo."

"Your friend told you this Geronimo person probably wouldn't even come to a telephone."

"If he won't come to a telephone, I'll rent a car and drive to upstate New York, or wherever he is, and I'll talk to him." I hesitated. "You can come with me if you want."

"No thank you."

"Well, then at least wish me luck."

"Good luck, Iris." He continued scrutinizing the pages fanning out on the floor around his body and I turned on my heel, clicking the door behind me before stalking off across the lawn.

It took me another week to pick up the telephone and dial the number that Thompson had given me. Geronimo, as predicted, would not come to a telephone, and his other name, I was informed by the aunt whose telephone number he used for emergency contacts, was actually Ulysses Crooked River. On five subsequent calls I set up telephone dates, to which he would not come. I set up new dates and was ignored some more.

"You sound like a nice girl," his aunt told me on the seventh call. Her voice was cartoonishly feminine—kittenish. I imagined her lounging in silk pajamas with long hair that looked windblown in the fan-driven way of perfume commercials. "It's nothing personal. Crooked River does things his own way, and you know, you are calling from the Vietnam days, and he doesn't seem too interested in them."

"Would he talk to me if I came to see him?"

"I don't know, honey. I don't know if I'd do it if I were you. It's a long way to come for a whole lot of nothing and other people on the reservation may not be happy to see a white girl bothering Crooked River about the Vietnam days."

But in the end the aunt told me how to reach her own home and promised to tell Crooked River I was coming.

Once again I approached Hank and asked if he wanted to come. "Don't you have any papers to do?" he said mildly. "Reading to get done?"

"I'll take that as a no," I sighed. "But it's up to you, of course." I was standing by his desk. Angie's handwriting was as familiar to me as my own, and when I saw a small stack of envelopes addressed in that familiar loopy roll I felt another kind of unfamiliar jealousy: my sister never wrote to me, yet here were at least a dozen letters for Hank, sitting by a discarded coffee cup.

He hadn't noticed my attention focusing on the desk. He said, "I had no idea you were so irrational and melodramatic. It's kind of interesting." His eyebrow lifted.

I made a conscious effort and succeeded in turning my face away from his desk and the letters. I said, "I'm leaving at five tomorrow morning and I'm going to drive straight through. Call me before then if you change your mind."

He didn't change his mind and I left in cool darkness, wending my way over the mountains to Route 81 and pointing the rental car north. By afternoon my concentration had frayed so completely that I didn't recognize the snowflakes hitting the windshield for what they were. It was a temperate sweatshirt day in my native Virginia—but not here, and within an hour I was so rattled by the thickening storm that I pulled over at an orange-roofed Howard Johnson's and checked in for the night.

In all my life I had never stayed in a motel—never stepped into a roadside restaurant alone and kept a waiter standing while I weighed the relative merits of the cheeseburger and the fried clam roll. Following the chipper hostess to a table I had felt tired, lost and sodden.

The waiter set down my clam strips with a cheerful little rap and asked if I wanted a cup of coffee. By the time it arrived my deep-fried sandwich had kicked off a second wave of energy. My face relaxed back into its normal configurations and I managed to look around me, noticing that no one in the restaurant seemed to know or care that I didn't do this every day. I was invisible. The coffee tipped me further into a kind of giddy euphoria. Here I was, doing exactly what I wanted and what Hank (and, I'm sure, Aunt Eleanor and Uncle Charlie, had they known) did not want me to do. This was fine. I was fine.

Crooked River

I T SNOWED MORE THAT NIGHT, AND MORNING FOUND ME STRUG-
gling to reach the middle of the back windshield to wipe it away with
my bare hands. The rental car didn't have a scraper in its trunk; I didn't
have mittens or a heavy coat. But I was close to the turnoff just south of
Syracuse that would take me into the Iroquois reservation, and by mid-
morning I was off the thruway. The sun had come out and the temperature risen enough to begin melting off the newer snowfall. The landscape
was Dalmatian: white snow sprinkled with patches of dark earth.

The moment I turned into the reservation the concrete gave way to
mud road. I stopped at the first public-seeming building—a wooden
store whose porch actually held rocking chairs and a woodstove. The
scene wasn't charming, however. The building had been painted once,
perhaps, and a good deal of the wooden porch had been rendered unreliable by years of exposure to snow, rain, sun and the ravenous insect
world. The men on the porch resembled the building itself, sagging a bit
like the roof's central beam. They didn't move or greet me as I pulled in
front of the store and got out of the car.

"I'm looking for Ulysses Crooked River," I said. "Or his aunt Jenny."
The men sat on, only one turning his face to me with the same level of

attention he might have given a bag of nails or a passing feral cat. "Could you tell me where they live?"

The store's front door banged open on its hinges and a stout woman with black eyes and hair chopped off at the nape stood wiping her hands on a towel and looking me over. "You're the Sunnaret girl?" Here was the owner of the kittenish voice, which I now saw was entirely at odds with the rest of her.

"Are you his aunt Jenny?"

"I am." Aunt Jenny sighed audibly. "He made no promises to talk to you. But I think it impressed him some when I told him you were driving all the way up here. He said to tell you where he lived but not to say for sure he'd be home. Come on. I'll show you." She whipped the dish towel over one shoulder and stepped off the porch. "You follow me in your car. I have to get right back, and you'll want your own locomotion out of here in case he isn't feeling friendly enough to give you a lift back to the store. Now when we get there," she said, stopping and turning to be sure she had my full attention, "you just be patient and stand on his porch as long as you need to. He takes his time and he might not be done considering."

We passed clusters of wooden buildings. Trucks and cars stood on cement blocks in front of perhaps half of them, with the occasional washing machine leaning to one side in the yard as if dropped there from a passing plane. Children called out and waved at Jenny and then at my own unfamiliar car, but no adult greeted us. Crooked River's aunt stopped before a flaking wooden cube with small porches at its front and back, stuck a hand out and pointed to indicate that this was it. Then she drove away.

I stepped onto the porch and knocked. No one answered, but I was almost sure I saw a movement at a front window. I knocked again, and when no one came to the door I settled into a rusting iron lawn chair on the porch. I rocked there for about ten minutes, flicking green paint away from the chair's arms where it stood up in rusty rows. Then the door opened, revealing a meticulously groomed man with a pocked young face and entirely white hair. There was an ironed crease in his jeans and even from across the porch I could smell starch in his white shirt. His hair was parted in the center and tied at the nape, every strand shining.

"Mr. Crooked River? I'm Iris Sunnaret."

"I know. You've cut your hair."

"Pardon?"

"Your brothers had a picture of you. You cut your hair."

"I guess I did."

"You still have those blue shorts?"

"Blue shorts?"

"That you had on in the picture. With a plaid shirt."

"No. I don't have those anymore."

"Well you might as well come in." He disappeared back into the little house but left the door ajar. The interior smelled of gunmetal and what I thought was abandoned Chinese takeout. I wrinkled my nose.

"It's the rabbits," he said, seeing me react. He turned and I followed him through the little kitchen at the back of the house and onto a porch. I stepped down onto the indoor-outdoor rug and found myself standing between walls of stacked cubes that had apparently been stuffed with large balls of fur. But the fur moved, and from cube to cube it varied from piebald to chestnut, clipped smooth surfaces and long silken coats, floppy ears and spoonlike erect ears: rabbits.

"I show them at the state fair and I do real well with them, too. I got a reputation as a killer rabbit man." He shrugged a shoulder toward the one wall that was free of cages to indicate the blue and red ribbons hung there. He opened a cage and plucked its resident out by its nape. "This one's my primo best gold-minted champion Belgian."

I stepped forward to stroke the blinking little animal, which endured my attentions without a murmur or movement. "What's its name?"

"She's Handsome Lake." He swept Handsome Lake back into her cage and opened another. "And this one, if he wasn't so evil-tempered, I'd show more. But he bites. Pees on you, too, on purpose. He's Tadodaho."

"What does that mean?"

"To us Onondaga, it basically just means son of a bitch."

"That's what the word means?"

"Nah. Tadodaho was Hiawatha's enemy—a snake-haired evil wizard who never wanted the Iroquois to form our federation." He pulled a cage down and set it on the floor beside Tadodaho, who responded to the sight of another rabbit by springing just far enough up in the air to get his hind feet under him so he could kick the unoffending rabbit's cage right over on its side. "See?" his owner said sadly. Crooked River plucked Tadodaho up by the ears and pulled his face back to avoid the thumping blow the rabbit aimed in his direction. He swung the uncooperative animal gingerly back into its cage, but still Tadodaho managed to get his feet under him fast enough to twist around and sink his teeth into Crooked River's palm before the hand could be withdrawn.

"That's why he's Tadodaho." He closed the punctured hand into a fist, reached into his pocket and pulled out a handkerchief, which he wound around the palm.

"Why do you keep him?" I asked.

"He's a warrior rabbit. He can't change what he is, and maybe a new owner would just think he was only good for stew. So we're stuck together in this world, Tadodaho and me."

I set the tipped cage and its resident back in their place and surveyed the entire wall of bunnies. "They're really beautiful, aren't they?"

"Eyeh. When I was a kid I did chickens. They're beautiful, too. And I miss the eggs. But then I went to the rabbit show and I never looked at another chicken. Beer?"

"What?"

"Want a beer?" He stepped back into the kitchen.

It was eleven o'clock in the morning and I would probably have a long drive ahead of me after I left here. "All right," I said.

We settled into two chairs facing the window in his living room, which offered a view of a fallow field, two abandoned trucks and the muddy swath of road winding back toward the outside world. The house was cold and I shivered in my thin coat but Crooked River seemed entirely comfortable in shirtsleeves. "So," he said finally. "I guess you're here about Batman and Robin."

I had made my way through only half the beer and it had set off a disorienting but pleasant buzz. I went straight to my central question. "Thompson says that one of my brothers killed the other one."

"Well, what can anybody know, eyeh?"

"Everybody who was there knows more than me. You, for example, know more than me. Thompson knows more than me."

"Thompson's a crazy son of a bitch. Also, I've never seen him straight."

"But did what he say happened really happen?"

"And what was that?"

"He says that Eddie—Batman—was getting unreliable and dangerous. He says he was starting to do things like go out and stand in the open, in clearings where VC might be moving, and see if he could get them to shoot at the platoon." I stopped talking, watching his face closely, but it remained impassive. "Did he do that?"

"Your brother liked walking point. He may have stepped into an open clearing or two."

"Alone? Knowing he'd maybe attract fire?"

"Who can say what's in a man's mind when he stands in a clearing? VC were all around us. Always there. To invite them to kill you when you stand there alone is not the same as to call them down on your friends."

"But stepping into an open clearing—what was he doing?"

"I said I knew of a time he stood alone in a clearing. Can't a man stand alone for a minute in the open?"

"I guess from what I've heard, no. He can't."

"In that jungle, always crawling and digging holes, you could want a little clearing very bad. Rainy season, the air almost liquid, felt like you were breathing water, all closed in and like you were drowning. Only way to breathe and not get a mouthful of mosquitoes and water was to smoke. You had to keep a cigarette lit all the time just to feel like you weren't underwater. Now if the sun came out for a minute or two, and the mist cleared, a man could want to step out in a clearing for a minute. I felt it myself, and I didn't want to die."

"Thompson said that Eddie wanted to kill things."

"Well, that was why we were there, wasn't it?"

"But what he meant was that my brother killed because he liked it."

"Some men do."

"Did my brother?"

"Why do you want to know these things? I can tell you what you think you want to know, but you don't want to know them."

"Yes, I do."

"That's what they all say. Then you tell them and they call you a liar or a son of a bitch. I don't know why people ask these questions."

"They ask because they really do want to know."

"If that were true then I'd say yes, your brother Eddie liked killing. And maybe yes, maybe he wanted to die. But that feeling your brother had about death might have been a kind of backblow caused by the killing. You can't step toward it and not get burned yourself. You know?"

"No."

Crooked River stood up restlessly, fingered his bottle, went and got a new one, came back and fiddled some more before finally sitting down again. "That's why you talk to men like me and Thompson? You think we can help you know?"

"Yes."

"Well, we can't."

"But you can tell me what you heard and saw the day my brothers died."

"I heard a shot. Maybe more than one shot. Two, or maybe a half dozen. Then what sounded like bouncing bettys going off—booby-trap explosives—things that could have left your brother Perry in little pieces if he'd gone into the jungle after a sniper and got unlucky. You hear that, you don't know if it's incoming missile fire or mines or what because you got your face in the mud and a lot of things aren't terribly clear. We lay there for a long time before we started crawling toward your brothers. Your Eddie was dead when we reached him. Your brother Perry was who knows."

"Thompson said he only heard one shot. He said there was a clear trail out of the clearing, fresh sign, like Perry had walked away just before you got there."

"Like I said—Thompson was stoned and his face was in the mud. Got to consider those variables. You ask me what I know, I know your brothers died that day whether we found one body or two. Bodies that step into some of those mines, you got to shake the trees to find the dog tags. Just because there isn't a nice corpse left behind that doesn't mean a thing. They both died facing the enemy like they were supposed to."

"Thompson said there was sign leaving the clearing."

"Did Thompson see that himself?"

How could I not have asked this question myself? I shrugged. "I don't know."

Crooked River snorted. "See what I mean? Why are you trying so hard to believe that guy?"

"I'm not trying real hard," I protested. "I'm just listening to him."

"You watch out, girl. People tend to find what they're looking for. If you're looking for your brother Eddie who loves to kill, and your brother Perry who murdered him, you'll find them. The same with looking for your brothers the heroes, the men who died to keep America safe. You can find them, too. Going looking, that's the best way to find out what you want—which is a quick way to finding out who you really are."

"I'm just looking for the truth about my brothers. Just for that."

He settled deeper into his chair. "The truth about your brother Perry is that he was a diplomat and a thinker, a man with some healing powers. He pulled guys through at least five times I saw that they should have been dead before the helo got there, but your brother kept them alive. He knew a little western medicine—where to get your fingers to stop bleeding, how to deal with shock. And he was learning about other kinds of medicine. Plants. Magic. He knew how to talk to a man in a way that kept them alive." Crooked River popped the new beer and set it gently down directly next to his first bottle. "He talked to sorcerers. Monks. The other guys didn't listen to him, but me, I'm Iroquois. We have sorcerers. Made sense to me."

"Like what made sense?"

"Oh. Like when he was practicing the spell to make a bush eat chickens. Every month you chant. Start the fucker up with an egg, and when it can handle that, you move on to chicks. Takes ten months to get to the whole chicken. I knew a Huron had a spell like that."

I watched him carefully as he said this. He didn't seem drunk, though he had had two beers. He didn't seem to be making fun of me. "Why would you want to train the bush to eat chickens?" I ventured.

"You can make some very powerful medicines from the leaves of a bush like that. I told Robin—your Perry—to watch himself around sorcerers and wizards. They're low-class types. Very likely to get you in trouble. You should only talk to real medicine men and monks. But he talked to all kinds. That's what maybe happened to your Perry, I've thought—he got in trouble with magic. He was very interested in that first sorcerer he found in the cave, and I warned him off. I told him to look for another teacher, somebody respectable—an abbot or monk. You know?"

"What sorcerer in a cave?" I tried to keep my tone neutral.

"He found a sorcerer. Went looking for a monk and found a sorcerer."

"Why would a Vietnamese monk help an American?"

"Holy men don't take sides. They take students. Same with sorcerers, but they play with you—they're not reliable."

"What did Eddie make of all this?"

"Your Eddie? He pretended it wasn't happening. Just kept walking point and killing things. I think that's what pushed your Perry the opposite way. Perry really wasn't interested in killing. But Eddie was a very good killer—got him lots of leave at China Beach. All the good killers got leave time at China Beach—partly I think 'cause what the hell are you going to do with them when they're not busy killing. Batman could get the platoon to do anything in the days they trusted him. I tell you they trusted his little plastic Batman, too. It got to be important. We wouldn't go out without it. Maybe being up in those mountains got us more superstitious, but most platoons that were out there for a while got superstitious. That little plastic Batman took on some kind of power—it was our lucky talisman, and we were sure that your brother had survived so long walking point because it was lucky. One month he decided to look like Batman, and he put on a black cape and little ears on his helmet—bat ears. A mask. That's where the Batman name came from. And every man in the platoon put on a cape and little ears and a mask. That's leadership."

"I sent him that Batman plastic toy," I said.

"I know it. Some of you was in that Batman, I'll bet. I myself would not go out on recon without that Batman. And we stuck close to it."

"I bought that Batman when I was ten—too old for that kind of thing, but he was just so . . . perfect. Perry and Eddie made fun of me for buying him, but they liked him, too. They had all the comics." I had a very clear memory of the toy. He'd been standing in a row of identical Batmen on a drugstore shelf and I'd found them all mesmerizing—obsidian flared capes, square jaws, Episcopalian noses under egglike hoods. They stood in a line, feet squared directly beneath the wide shoulders, all their arms crossed over their little chests, each and every one of them Saviors of Humankind. "Batman was an orphan," I said. "I liked that about him. Perry and Eddie made fun of me, but they stole him to play with themselves the first week I had him."

"So you lost him?" Crooked River asked.

"Oh, no. I stole him back and hid him from them. They'd say, 'What's that Batman up to now?' and I'd say, 'Just last week he stopped the Russians from blowing up the Eiffel Tower,' but really I'd married him to a plastic princess I had who came in her own carrying case. Then I got a little older and I forgot the Batman. I found him in that case a few months after Perry and Eddie left."

And then I had sent Batman off to Vietnam all by himself—no explanatory note or card. I told myself that I only hoped Batman would amuse them, but in reality I expected him to shield them against evil. Off you go, I'd said to the little square package with my brothers' names on its front. Good luck. Then I let myself forget him.

"That's odd, about the Batman stuff," I said.

"Nah. I heard of a guy who went his whole tour with a cookie his wife baked him and sent—his lucky cookie. Believe me, in that climate a wrapped-up cookie is much odder than a plastic Batman but this son of a bitch had it with him still when he got on the plane to go home. And he lived to get on the plane so it must have worked. Guys had lucky cards and pins and enemy souvenirs. Your Eddie was a leader, and he had Batman. And we were in these spooky mountains, ghosts all around us. So we all did the Batman thing."

"And after Eddie died?"

"The whole damn platoon went to the place we found him and we combed over every inch of the ground looking for that Batman. We never found it, and our luck was not so good after that. Thompson, me and this other crazy guy who joined the platoon the next month—we're the only ones alive. Only ones to come back."

"Do you think that Perry killed Eddie?" I asked him.

"Why would he do a thing like that?"

"Thompson says he did it to save the other guys in the platoon from being ordered into a dangerous situation by Eddie."

"Well, there's a reason for you if you want one. But me, I would never want to wipe out the guy who was carrying our Batman. And I was there." Crooked River cocked one eyebrow at me over his beer bottle.

"Were Eddie and Perry fighting with each other at the end?"

"Oh, eyuh. It doesn't mean anything, though. Not necessarily."

"But Perry vanished, which matches Thompson's version of what happened. You say there was other incoming, other explosions, but nobody found Perry's body afterward."

"That doesn't mean much. Lots of bodies just vanished in those mountains—living ones and dead ones. Sometimes it was just because the bodies were in so many parts you couldn't put together enough to say it was a man. Sometimes it was more mysterious than that—you'd be in the dark, in a firefight with what had to be twenty guys. You'd get backup missile support and you'd blow the entire world away in their direction, and you'd go in at daylight to do a body count and find nothing. Nothing. Just the remains of a fire or two, some tins and thousands of used shells—enough shells to make it clear that there were fifty men there only last night, just like you thought. But in the morning—no bodies. The Cong could move like smoke. Could take things in and out of the jungle like they didn't weigh a thing—like all they really transported was just the essence of the thing. Like they put a spell on the bodies, or themselves. Or we'd been fighting ghosts and not men, so there really were never any bodies to begin with.

"Your brothers were almost as good in those woods as the Cong. They were better off in that kind of country than anybody else in the platoon. Guys would look at me at first and think, Well, he's an Indian so he has to be good in the woods, but Christ, look where I come from." Crooked River's arm swept before him, taking in the cars on blocks and the crooked little shelters, the dusty packed road and the clear absence of wilderness. "Your brothers—they'd spent time in the woods for real. They could both head off and just become like fog. But not this time. I saw what was left in that clearing, and I'm telling you to forget what Thompson said."

"So you're saying, kind of, that Perry wasn't found because of something to do with sorcery?"

Crooked River shrugged and looked out toward the remains of a Dodge truck and what was once a red Mustang, now teetering on cinder blocks and home to mice and raccoons. From what I could see of the activity around the car carcasses, they also served as playthings to wandering children who made forts from them after chasing the animal residents away.

What would be better to believe—that Eddie needed to be killed, and Perry followed him and shot him dead before vanishing into the jungle himself? Or perhaps it would be easier to think that they had both simply died the traditional way, destroyed by the enemy. The sorcery theory was strangely attractive. Sorcery might even leave Perry still alive, perhaps in a shaman's cave deep in a sacred mountain?

Perhaps nothing at all I'd been told was even close to describing the actual scene.

"It seems to me," I said at last, "that you didn't really want to talk to me at all."

Crooked River shrugged. "You came to me, remember. It's good to see the girl who sent the plastic Batman." He looked me over, clearly considering. He said, "Perry kept something that I kind of inherited when he vanished. It's a book he wrote in."

"Why didn't you give it to his family?" I demanded.

Crooked River's civility fell away with stunning speed. "Don't talk to me of what the family should have had. Your family wasn't there. I was there." Crooked River rose stiffly. "I can't explain the things you don't know." He shook his head, as frustrated at his own limitations as at mine. "I tell you what. I'll look for this book he left. And if I find it, I might send it to you later."

"Why can't you just let me have it now?"

"I've told you what I'm willing to do. Go home now, little sister."

He walked me to the rental car and stood by it as I started the engine. I rolled down the window. "Crooked River, why did they call you Geronimo?" I asked.

His shoulders hiked upward in the gesture that turned his entire body into a question mark. "Maybe because the Iroquois never took scalps," he said. "But the Apache did." He stepped back and waved. He was still standing there when I reached the first turn, a quarter of a mile of dirt road away from his little hutch of a house.

Being Cassandra

BACK IN CHARLOTTESVILLE I THREW OPEN MY WINDOWS TO listen for the sound of the creek that ran behind my little house. The rain swelled it into an audible plashing background that accompanied me into sleep all through that season. The first warm night after my trip to upstate New York it sounded less like a continuous soothing flow than like rocks banging up against water. When I woke to see a flurry of white stuff blow past my window I was sure that the blossoms were upstate New York blown snow. Then I remembered that I was back in the Blue Ridge and I sat up and rubbed my eyes, throwing open the window to discover that it was a beautiful spring morning.

My downstairs neighbors were three pragmatic engineering students from Danville. I could smell their brewing coffee and hear their Labrador retriever, Square Root, barking to go out. Then the familiar creak on the steps that meant that Danny, largest and most gregarious of my neighbors, was making his way up the front steps to my door.

"Iris? Iris, you want to try one of my momma's favorite recipes?" he called from the porch.

"No," I yelled. The most casual of Danny's invitations could lead to a two-hour chat.

"It's fried squirrel brains!" he called happily, ignoring my refusal. A window next to the front door looked into my living room, and I could see Danny's nose pressed against its screen as I walked to open the door. "Real fresh," he assured me. "Rootie brought it home just this morning. This might be your only chance, you know. Rootie's a good boy but retrievers are used to bringing back what somebody else killed—not killing it themselves. Surprised me to death when he actually caught this squirrel. Isn't going to happen again soon. Y'all go visit your folks? I haven't heard you for a day or two."

I blocked the doorway as one of Danny's feet lifted and threatened to cross the threshold. "I'm taking a rain check on the squirrel, thank you though, Danny. Got a class."

"I could set some aside for you in the Rubbermaid. It's good warmed up, too."

"Very kind. But no."

"What're you up to this weekend?" he asked. I shrugged noncommittally and he shook his head at me. "Last weekend my date had these white kneesocks on that just knocked me out. I don't know what it is about white kneesocks. But this girl . . . whoooeee." He looked at me sadly— I was wearing sweatpants and a T-shirt. Danny shook his head. "You shouldn't be so shy of things, Iris. Bye now."

Shy? I was surprised to find that I felt a bit stung, and almost called out after him to protest, to say that not only was I not shy, but that I was the kind of person who would drive eight hundred miles to introduce herself to an Iroquois known as Ulysses Crooked River and Geronimo, depending upon who was speaking to him, which didn't sound either dull or shy to me. Why, I had drunk a beer before lunch just this week!

But I didn't call out. I went back inside and boiled the same three-minute egg I ate every morning, made instant coffee from the hot water I'd used to cook the egg, and slammed the back door on my way to my first class.

I LEFT A NOTE shoved halfway into Hank's mail slot on my way and when I walked past it later that morning the note was gone. No answering note was taped to his door. I left another one. Mid-afternoon saw that one taken as well, but he didn't telephone or drop by.

The next day, Friday, passed as well with no word from him but I knew that most Friday evenings he could be found sitting on one of the folding chairs between the podium and the keg by the door to the Jefferson Literary and Debating Society. There was a guest speaker so the hall was packed and loud, the room's predominant scents sweat and Michelob beer. I scanned the crowd of about sixty faces, searching for Hank's. There were only a handful of women in the room. The pretty ones were pinned like the bull's-eyes in targets, surrounded by undulating circles of young men. The plain ones sat in ones or twos in seats at the front of the hall. Most people held plastic cups of sloshing beer and talked very loudly.

Then at last I found Hank's familiar face, isolated it among a throng of blue and khaki against the fireplace on the other side of the room. Yes, he was wonderfully good-looking, clearly popular yet reserved, holding himself and his plastic cup at a bit of a distance from the young men around him. Standing here in this room on the West Range I was experiencing a visceral, nearly abstractly impersonal reaction to the muscles in his forearms that moved as he lifted the cup and to the heft of his legs and shoulders. Was this the way that Angie saw him? It was both the Hank I knew and not. Now my picture of Hank included a new idea of his relationship with Angie—he wasn't just one of us. He was something different, as was my sister. Their sexual involvement had changed them to me as well as to each other. He had shifted the balance of our family, disrupted my unchallenged primary place with her and the nature of my affection for him. Directly behind this unpleasant realization lay a whole line of new reactions, ready to fall like dominoes as soon as I flicked over the first.

I turned on my heel without speaking with him and left the room. I found myself walking to a convenience store, buying a quart of ice cream, walking home, eating the entire thing while listening to the sounds of a student party going on across the street. I tossed the dripping carton into a trash can and headed out the door again, walking toward Hank's room with no real idea of what I would do when I got there.

I didn't get there. I stopped by a patch of lawn that lay in enough shadow from the bright moonlight that I could lie in it and remain unnoticed by passersby while I watched Hank's windows. There I settled in, struggling to pay no attention to what I was doing. Parties of students swept by either side of me through the night without seeing me, couples clearly on their way to make love; packs of drunken young men clearly not; once a single meandering figure whose gender wasn't clear, perhaps also on a night walk like myself. I lay there as the temperature cooled and the blades of grass beneath me felt more and more damp. Spring had progressed enough for the night insects to begin their rattling and sawing, and the night was actually noisy until somewhere in its very middle, perhaps three or four a.m., when all noise stopped and there was only total silence and a bright moon. I even fell asleep.

Hank's window had lit up at around midnight but he'd drawn his shades. No one had entered or left his rooms. The light went out perhaps two hours after I lay down in the wet grass but still I watched, the dew soaking through my jeans and my sweatshirt, the elbows of my coat. The first suggestion of lightening gray in the air pushed me to my feet and started me home. The grass was so damp and dense that I left a clear set of footprints behind me, a little stream of them flowing away from the larger impression of my prone body in the lawn.

At first when I'd lain there I'd thought of Angie and Hank as lovers. Then I'd thought of Crooked River and Thompson, and of how much clearer my thinking would be if I could just talk this over with Angie. By the dark middle of the night I wasn't thinking of anything at all. I was just becalmed.

My neighbor Danny, most unfortunately, was in the yard when I got home, standing by Square Root, who had clearly woken him in order to be taken out for a walk. The dog was urinating in a thick stream on another roommate's car tire.

"Well, well," he greeted me happily. "I've got the hangover cure for you—much improved on the old tomato-juice thing."

"I don't have a hangover, Danny." I had begun to shake on the way home and the idea of a hot bath was pulling me faster and faster up the stairs to my apartment.

"Whatever you say, Iris." He grinned.

I walked directly from the bathtub into my bed, fell almost instantly asleep, but woke feeling stiff and anxious. Then I remembered. I had to tell Angie and Hank what Crooked River had said to me. I would leave out the parts about the chicken-eating bush and the rabbits. But when I actually reached Hank and told him the story over the telephone, all he had to say was, "So one man says that Perry and Eddie both died in the same attack, and one man says that Perry killed Eddie and then vanished into the jungle."

"Yes. That's right." I was nodding furiously on my end though he couldn't see me.

"Iris, why are you doing this? Stop this. These people are not reliable sources of information."

"Wouldn't Uncle Charlie and Aunt Eleanor want to hear what another guy from their platoon had to say?"

"No. Momma and Daddy have already dismissed this Thompson guy as a fool. They have no interest in hearing about him, or his friend the Indian. It's over."

"Angie would want to know," I said stiffly.

"You haven't called her recently?"

"The last few times I called her there was no answer," I said. "Why?"

He hesitated a moment, then said, "You won't get her at that number anymore. She just goes back to pick up mail so it won't come to Momma and Daddy's attention that she's moved."

This was a surprise, and for a moment I struggled with the impulse to lie and pretend I'd known all along. I abandoned this. "So where is she?"

"She's way off campus—someplace on the beach north of the city."

"Is this some boyfriend's apartment?" I was dismissing this possibility even as I aired it. Angie was not the move-in-with-him kind of girlfriend.

"I don't think it's a boyfriend kind of move."

"What about her classes?" I asked. "What about graduating this year?"

"I don't think she's worried about that," Hank said.

"She's not going to classes? Is she still paying tuition? Uncle Charlie thinks that money he's transferring is going to tuition." Our father and Uncle Charlie had set up a fund in our names that would be in Uncle Charlie's legal hands until we were twenty-four. Uncle Charlie transferred enough cash out of these accounts into our checking accounts so we could pay all our own bills—even tuition.

"I don't know exactly what she's doing," Hank said. "But I think she considers it her money and she figures that what she does with it is her business."

"Well, what's she spending it on if she's withdrawn from school?"

"Ask her yourself. I'll give you a telephone number."

As soon as I hung up on Hank, I dialed the new number. An answering machine picked up, the message tape playing Jefferson Airplane in the background and a male voice saying, "If you want to leave a message do it now. If you don't, we don't give a fuck."

"I'm trying to reach Angie Sunnaret," I said, trying not to sound tentative. "This is her sister, Iris. Call me, Angie."

All that afternoon and into the night the telephone rang only once, and it was the scuba instructor asking me if I wanted to step in to help his new students on their first pool dive. His sons had fallen in love with distant women and temporarily abandoned him, he explained. "And I need one more set of hands to help get students into the gear the first time they try it. What do you say?"

I said yes. Then I resumed my vigil by the telephone. At one in the morning it finally rang.

"It's me," she said.

"Hank gave me this number."

"I figured."

I felt the same sting I had when I'd seen the stack of letters in her handwriting on Hank's desk, knowing that she never wrote me. Even in the telephone silence she could feel the hesitation, the sharp intake away from her.

"I wasn't trying to deceive you or hide from you, Bear. Especially you."

"Do Uncle Charlie and Aunt Eleanor know where you are?"

"Probably."

"How would they know if you haven't told them? You mean you think Hank told them?"

"Charlie keeps closer tabs on us than you might think, Iris. He knows what we do. He knows where I am."

"What's going on, Angie?"

"I can't talk on the telephone."

"Why not? It's working."

"I just can't talk. I think the line's tapped."

"You've got to be kidding," I snorted. She didn't respond. "Well. Can you talk in person?"

"Yes."

"Then I'm coming to visit you."

"There really isn't much room here, Iris."

"What? What did you say to me?"

She sighed. "All right. I'm living in sort of primitive quarters. No telephone yet. But I have running water."

"But you're talking to me on a telephone. I left a message."

"You left a message with some people I know. They get in touch if there's a need. They have sort of a commune thing going on—something I didn't have a lot of patience for. You know: people staying up all night smoking hash and debating whether or not refined sugar should be banned from the household on political grounds."

There was something in her voice I had never heard before. I tried to keep her talking until I could identify it, and now, on the word 'political,' I had it.

"Angie, you sound so bitter."

"That's allowed. In fact, I could say it's a more informed response to things than banning refined sugar. Look, Iris, you'd have to ask Uncle Charlie for airfare. He'd know where you're headed and I don't want that."

"I wouldn't. I can get my hands on some cash."

I could hear her eyebrows lifting. "Really? Well, you'll have to explain that to me when you get here. But there's a condition. You can't tell Charlie, or Eleanor, or Hank you're coming. And if I say that something is only between you and me, it stays between you and me."

I hesitated. Then I said, "All right."

"Look, Bear. Don't worry about me. I'm perfectly fine. When you get a date and arrival time, call the number Hank gave you and leave it there. I'll meet you at the airport."

I nodded into the receiver and she must have heard the bob of my head. She hung up.

The Fate of the Body

I COULD GET USED TO THIS FLYING AROUND, LEAVING THE COCOON of my little square room with its desk pushed up against all the space that wasn't occupied by my bed. Fly to California? Why, I had the cash in my pocket right here, and a bag I could pack as well. I could call a taxi-cab and use it to get me to the station in time to catch the six a.m. stop of the Southern Crescent on its way to Washington, and an airport. Why hadn't I understood that airports were so easy to get to, portals through which I could step into any kind of place in the world: the Alps, the jungles of Central America, Laos, my sister's home!

I delighted in the long flight, pleased with my courtesy tomato juice and peanuts, marveling at the way it could actually become boring to hurtle along in space at hundreds of miles per hour. Sometimes I didn't think about Angie at all—only about the fact that I was moving in an utterly unaccustomed way.

But then there was my sister at the other end of the journey, standing by the gate to meet me the moment I stepped out of the walkway. I never forgot the fact of her physical appearance—I just forgot its visceral power. She wore the uniform of the attractive girl of the times: a black leotard and jeans cut at the hips and flaring at the ankles, hair hanging in a curtain around her shoulders, broken only by the little tangle of glass beads swinging below her ears. She ran to me and kissed me on the lips and I laughed, perfectly delighted with my reception.

"We'll stop for lunch in Berkeley. Then I'll take you home," she said.

"Who are these people?" I asked in amazement as we drove through the streets of this new world. "Are they students?" The people in question were bedraggled, thin teenagers lounging in doorways and clustered in parks. They wore headbands and feathers, beads, tie-dyes and jeans. The effect was glittering and grungy at once. I rolled down my window and the breeze from the park carried the sound of guitar music; the smell of marijuana, hashish and frying meat.

"They're runaways, some of them. A few of them are actually students. That little cluster over there," she said, pointing, "I think are vets. They look just like the runaways, some of them. Most of them have part-time jobs but more of them are living on handouts or cash from home. Parasites."

"Well, we live on money from home, Angie."

"The money we get from Charlie is our money. He only manages it for now. I am not a parasite. Neither are you."

"Okay. What are these people hanging in the park doing here?"

"Looking for the Summer of Love, which was over years ago," Angie said dryly. "If it ever existed at all."

We ate in a vegetarian restaurant where I mistook the bottle of tamari on the table for maple syrup and poured it into my tea, thinking it was the institutional replacement for refined white sugar. I took a sip, pushed the cup away and hoped Angie hadn't noticed. I'd ordered all the wrong things: a gelatinous pile of overcooked brown rice accompanied by crunchy vegetables that had barely been passed over a flame. Angie had an elegant salad of crisp greens and seared salmon. She insisted on paying the bill.

"Where did you get the car?" I asked as we pulled into traffic. We were in an Alfa Romeo.

"A friend lent it to me for the semester, or until he gets back. He's traveling."

"What friend? A boyfriend?"

She ignored this question. "Let's stop at a café for coffee. Then we'll pick up some staples and be off."

She found a place on Telegraph Avenue and deftly maneuvered the little car into a space with about four inches to spare at either end. "Well, come on," she said, swinging out of the driver's-side door. "Stick with me."

Ten minutes later we were in a crowded café at a sidewalk table waiting for espressos. I had never drunk an espresso. All around us people hunched over empty cups and gestured emphatically. The occasional corduroy sport coat broke up a sea of T-shirts and worn jeans. That, Angie explained to me, indicated a teaching assistant or untenured professor.

Directly next to us were a couple who had clearly chosen the wrong café. They wore polyester pantsuits and looked down at their espressos with clear dismay at what they'd been offered when they asked for coffee. The man wore a striped tie and the woman a little bow at the neck. They twirled their miniature spoons silently, unhappily, swiveling their heads like owls. A woman with a dirty seven-year-old walked up to the outermost café tables and greeted the first clump she saw enthusiastically. Then she saw Angie and turned, waving and calling out. Now that she faced us I could see that the woman was actually young, though several of her front teeth were missing and she clearly hadn't bathed in a while. Neither had the child with her. "Hello, Annie," Angie said. "How are you?"

"Cool. Groovy. Couldn't be better," the toothless creature replied. She sat down at the table nearest us and plunged into conversation. The child stood listlessly at her side, swaying a bit.

"Why do you talk to them?" the polyestered woman beside us said to Angie.

"Who?" Angie asked.

"These street people. Hustlers. Hippies," the man replied.

Our espresso arrived. Angie lifted the little cup to her lips and arched her eyebrows over it, turning just enough so that our neighbors could see as well as hear her. She spoke slowly and clearly: "You are the 'they' to whom I do not speak." She tipped her cup upward and sipped. They looked away.

"You could have been kinder," I said to her as we drove away. "They were out of place and felt uncomfortable. Maybe a little frightened. And the street lady didn't hear what they said so they didn't hurt her feelings."

"Don't think I like Amphetamine Annie any better than I liked Mr. and Mrs. Nebraska," Angie said to me. "I particularly dislike the fact that Annie's seven-year-old kid gets to live on the streets because he was unlucky enough to have a drug addict for a mother. All this romanticizing of street people, calling them 'free,' " she snorted. "But worse than I hate the beggars who drag their kids around in the streets I hate the people who treat street people like vermin."

"But Angie, you treated Mr. and Mrs. Nebraska like vermin."

My sister focused more single-mindedly on the road ahead and pursed her lips.

"I do too understand!" I protested, knowing exactly what she wasn't saying to me.

She grinned and glanced over at me as she turned onto an expressway. "Okay," she conceded. "Fine. I'm about thirty miles north, so settle in."

She popped in a Doors tape and accelerated. "It's just a car that somebody I know doesn't need right now." Then she said something else that couldn't be heard over the press of air through the open windows, the engine cylinders and the radio playing "Light My Fire." We made our way up and down supermarket aisles, where she tossed what looked like five weeks' worth of food into our carriage. And it was extravagant food: triple-crème cheeses and tenderloin, out-of-season vegetables and tropical fruits. I picked up a package of shrimp she'd tossed into the cart and looked for the price sticker.

"You were expecting tofu and seeds?" she said dryly.

"Well, no. But I guess I was expecting something more vegetarian."

"Not me," she answered. "The meat here comes like it should, wrapped neatly in plastic. And I never liked the raw-seeds-and-tofu thing."

I backpacked my groceries from the nearest store in Charlottesville or caught a ride with Danny, and I had never spent more than fifteen dollars at a time in a grocery store. Angie spent three times that amount and pushed my efforts to contribute aside. "Forget it," she said. "You have to earn your extra cash wearing a silly rubber suit and goggles while I just don't pay my tuition. You're my guest here, Iris."

We drove off, Angie taking me more and more deeply into uninhabited landscape. The city fell away, and then we were skimming past larger houses, then mansions, and finally we were beyond the reach of paved roads. We drove on gravel and then packed dirt and finally on sand.

Then I saw it. The cottage itself was miraculous, rising up like a little mushroom directly out of the sand, its crooked roof and pink door like pretty details from a children's book illustration. I balanced my own bag with a sack of groceries and followed Angie inside, expecting the kind of dark square of space I'd known from hunting cabins in the Blue Ridge. Instead I found myself stepping into a kind of jewel box whose entire interior was lit with moving reflections from the waves almost directly beyond a glass wall. No more than a hundred yards separated this barrier from the edge of the ocean, its booming laced through with the hiss of the successive waves against the sand, rising and sinking back into the sea. The air itself was a mild blue-green.

I pulled my attention away from the glass to turn it on the room itself, which was cleanly designed and simply furnished with polished maple. Its rugs were the only clear luxury besides the view. I set my toe in the largest and dug it into the weave. "Iraqi?" I asked.

She shrugged. "I don't know. It's a friend's place. Not a boyfriend," she added.

"Gone traveling and left you to take care of it while he's away?"

"While she's away."

"I thought you said the car's owner was a 'he.' "

"He is. This is a different owner."

"How did she get her hands on a place like this?"

"Hollywood money. Her mom's kind of a hippie and bought it thinking she'd like isolation and nature. But it turned out she couldn't stand either one, so here we are. She just hasn't gotten around to selling it yet."

"You met this person at school?"

"Exactly."

This was a lie.

"Now," Angie said, "we'll get the perishables into the refrigerator and then we can go."

Angie worked as she talked, slamming things into their places so quickly that I couldn't have helped had I tried. "Throw your stuff down and come out here. We'll walk and talk and catch dinner." She had rifled through the groceries as she talked, putting some in cabinets and others on the counters. "Come on." She walked back to the door, opened a small closet door and pulled out two enormous fishing rods. "You won't even need waders here. Just go barefoot."

Angie equipped me with a shirt and shorts more appropriate to spray, sand and hooks. She led me about a mile down the beach before finding a place she decided was right and told me to cast my line. Then we buried the long wands in the sand and strolled away. As we walked I told her everything I could remember that Thompson and Crooked River had said to me. I didn't edit out the sorcerers with the chicken-eating bushes or the beer as I had with Hank.

We gathered driftwood as we walked back to the fishing lines. Angie set and lit a fire just as the sun sank down to the horizon line. The cooling evening air at our backs pushed us nearer to the fire.

"Well, say something," I demanded. "Which story do you think is true?"

"How could I know?"

"I didn't ask what you knew. I asked what you thought. The day Thompson came to the Lake House you told us you thought that he was telling the truth."

"I did. I'm sure Perry shot Eddie. Just like Thompson said he did."

"Impossible. Perry loved Eddie."

"I know that." She was looking out at the waves, her face turned from me so I couldn't read it. "Haven't you ever wanted to kill something you loved just because you loved it? It makes a kind of basic sense to me."

"What do you mean, 'just because you loved it'?"

"If you've felt it, it makes sense. If you haven't, it doesn't."

"So you've felt it? Wanting to kill something just because you love it?"

"Yes." My sister gave me a quick look, searching at first and then evasive. She said, "Almost everybody does, Iris, despite what you'd like to think."

I stuck a branch into the fire and dislodged a piece of wood, sending it hissing into the flame beneath. I said, "Hank told me not to talk about this with Uncle Charlie or Aunt Eleanor."

Angie pitched her hair from one side to the other, the effect making me think of a horse refusing a bit. "What right does Hank have to tell you what to say to anybody?"

"Angie, tell me why you told Hank you were here but you didn't tell me. Why did Aunt Eleanor and Uncle Charlie know but not me?"

"I didn't tell Eleanor and Charlie."

"But you said they knew where you were."

"Charlie applied for a higher-level security clearance. In the process of investigating him, they also investigated us. The FBI reported my new address to him."

Her tone made it clear that in her opinion the FBI, and Uncle Charlie, had no right to her address. I said, "That kind of investigation is standard. They just check out our addresses and schedules."

"And sexual behavior, supposed political orientation, friendships . . . Iris, these guys started showing up at places where I knew people, asking questions. They actually wear black suits and sunglasses and travel in twos, just like in the cheesy television shows."

"Oh." I was stunned, but I wasn't sure by which part of what she'd told me. "But . . . you knew that Uncle Charlie did work that required security clearances."

"And who asked me if I would enjoy being investigated by the FBI?"

"It's just routine."

"Charlie didn't think so. He apparently was given the impression that some of my acquaintances were undesirable, unpatriotic persons. He also discovered that Hank and I had a more intimate relationship than he'd thought we did."

I waited.

"I lent some money to some people," she finally offered.

"What kind of people?"

"Some people who are politically active, and opposed to some things that Charlie accepts."

"Things like what?"

"Things like the war that ate Eddie, and Perry, and our parents."

"Uncle Charlie didn't tell them to go to war, Angie."

"Yes he did. And our father did. And now he wants me to see them as heroes and accept war as a noble activity." She blew a little gust of air out of her nose. "I've spent lots of time, Iris, thinking about what it looked like, what was around Eddie when he died." Angie turned to me and got me level in her gaze, not continuing until she knew I was look-ing back. "Think of the bodies lying eviscerated by the sides of roads, mu-tilated and abandoned in a burning city's alleys, exploded into red vapor by a bomb. Think of the fate of the body. Do you know where animals start eating corpses? Their eyes, their genitals. Birds like to pick out the soft flesh in the mouth. That's what we do to one another. There isn't any reason to fight a war that's as compelling as the idea of a bird pecking away the rotting insides of Eddie Sunnaret's mouth. There isn't any evil that's more evil than that picture in my head. Any act that opposes a war is a moral act."

"You make it sound so simple, Angie—just one side and the other, and that's all."

"It is."

"I don't think so. How can you stand there and act like you understand everything so perfectly?" I protested.

"You don't have to understand it perfectly to understand it. Pretend-ing it's complicated is just another way of rationalizing it. And look at all the scum that war attracts—dogs to the corpses. Think of the CIA planes flying heroin to Marseille for the tribes in the mountains that it wants to seduce into fighting on our side. Our government, helping dealers in Marseilles get the raw goods to distribute to America's hopheads. But it's worth the price, it seems, because we buy Montagnard support with it, and they'll kill VC for us. That's what this is: one kind of animal eating the other kind from the inside out. Start with the soft tissue. How can anything I do be evil if it interferes with that? No. I'm right, and Charlie and our father aren't just wrong—they're evil. Perry shot Eddie through the head, Iris. That's what happened."

"What did Uncle Charlie and our father have to do with that? What are you talking about, heroin addicts?"

"That's always been your privilege and your charm, Iris—your rosy, unchallenged worldview."

"Angie, what have you done to 'interfere'?"

"I moved out here to get some distance from some people I'm helping do some things that are technically not legal—things that mess up draft board records. My moving out here gave me a bit more anonymity. And these people might be doing something I support, but I'm not exactly one of them. That's all."

"What do you mean, 'mess up' draft board records?"

My sister shook her head vehemently. "You aren't involved."

"But I am involved. You're my sister. And Uncle Charlie's involved. He's your guardian—our father. And Hank is his son. We're all connected, Angie."

"I'm not his daughter. I don't even live under his roof anymore. And Hank can't always be what his father wants him to be."

"Tell me what Uncle Charlie said."

"He told Hank to have nothing to do with me again. Ever."

"He didn't!"

"Jesus, Iris. You still see Charlie as a sweet guy who gets cranky sometimes. Why don't you have any idea how things really are?"

"Are you in trouble, Angie? Hiding from the police? Is that why you're here?" I waved an arm around to take in the surf, the miles of sand.

"I will not be watched and judged. Not by Charlie. Not by Hank. Not by anybody." She took my face in her hands and I let her. She said, "Bear, in my whole life you've never judged me; never betrayed me. That's why you're the person I trust more than anyone on earth. I can be entirely myself with you and know you won't tell anyone anything about me that they could use against me."

I made a mistake. I said, "Uncle Charlie raised us, cared for us, protected us!"

The hands were withdrawn from my face. "Controlled us! Monitored us, parceled out the money from our mother's estate! I'm not a child anymore. I live apart from them, and I don't ask them for anything that isn't mine."

She was fully lit now, entirely enraged.

"Angie," I said, "you just sound angry with everybody."

"Not you, Bear." She calmed. "Never you." She stood up and looked me right in the eye with her arms at her sides and the last of the sun reflecting off the caramel skin at her collarbones. "You're the one we all love best," she said.

I felt a little thud-like bump in my chest—a detached, anxious kind of thud.

"I'm not going to talk about this any more with you," she said. "It's not the right time." Angie pulled her T-shirt over her head and kicked her pants to one side in a single seamless gesture. "Come on." A sand devil twisted up into her shirt and carried it, flapping and gesticulating, down the beach. I pursued. Angie ignored it.

I caught the runaway clothing and turned to see my sister, entirely naked, quite perfect, poised at the edge of the surf. Then she charged: three, four, five strides and a plunging dive into a swell. She vanished. I stood waiting for her head to surface and found myself counting. I entirely forgot about the little anxious thud in my chest. The beach itself was in deep shadow but the sun illuminated the horizon line at the level of the sea, and when I'd reached eighty-nine a dark bobbing ball popped into view in a wave about a hundred yards offshore.

"Angie! Angie, is that you?" I screamed, but the booming waves carried the words directly back into my face. I dropped the clothes and pulled off my shirt and shorts, feeling more exposed in my underwear than my sister had looked when entirely naked. I made a note to consider following her underwearless example next time I swam and ran into the sea, calling her name.

The dark shape broke through the surface again, still about a hundred yards from me. Two brilliant eyes flicked open—my familiar sister once again. I swam to her.

"Look at how the light has turned red." She raised one arm out of the water and pointed in the direction of the setting sun, and I looked. Angie flipped onto her back, floating with only her face and breasts visible now. She said, "We'll come back later to see the stars from here."

About to protest that we could see the stars from many, much more accessible places, I was stopped by my realizing, for the thousandth time, that my sister was right. This was the best place. I flipped onto my back and looked up, considered the growing darkness, then twisted to look back to the beach where our fire burned.

"In a minute," Angie said, "we'll need that fire to find our way back."

"There's stars tonight. And the moon," I countered.

"But the swells get like hills that you can't see over. You ride up and down, and you lose your compass—stop knowing for sure which way is back. We'll need the fire. You'll see."

I thought of the mandatory lecture we'd gotten in diving class on currents and beach-front ocean entries—the most treacherous kind of dive because of the real likelihood of being carried out beyond the limits of your oxygen supply. Angie felt my shifted mood. When she spoke her tone was flirtatious and playful, reeling me back to her.

"Stay a little with me. I know you like this."

Of course I did. I always did. I smiled at her and she smiled back, rolling onto her back and reaching out to grasp my hand as we floated side by side.

One late spring night when we were in high school, Angie had come into my room in a black mood, her hair like a tangled pelt hanging to her shoulders and her whole face dark. Come for a little drive with me, she had said. At thirteen and sixteen, we were both too young for a night-time driving license, but she plucked Aunt Eleanor's car keys from the hook without breaking her stride and I trotted along. The only thing on my mind was keeping up and finding out where she thought we should go. An hour later we were at the Lake House, stacking wood in the stone-and-cement barbecue that Uncle Charlie had built at the water's edge. Angie pulled away the lattice woodwork along the porch's base to get at more wood.

"That's too high," I'd protested when she kept stacking, remembering every rule about safety and economy that Uncle Charlie had taught me.

"Good," she answered, tossing a match. Miraculously, it caught and began working its way up. Angie then turned her back on the fire and walked briskly to the end of the dock. She paused at its farthest end only long enough to get a good grip with her toes and then she sprang into the water. I followed, setting my toes exactly where she had placed her own and hitting the water within an inch of where she'd gone in.

In the minutes between our arrival and our launching ourselves into the water, the stars had vanished. A light rainfall sprinkled down around us while Angie paddled contentedly, singing "19th Nervous Breakdown." The sprinkle thickened into a downpour so dense it was difficult to draw a breath without getting water in my nose, my mouth. I treaded to get my head upright, struggling a little to breathe as the rain seemed to be moving sideways as well as down, into my mouth and nose no matter how I twisted away from it. Through the hissing water I could hear my sister still singing, laughing now as well, and all the boundaries of the world merged into a single hissing liquid gray, the lake's surface indistinguishable from the air itself. I hadn't been able to see her anymore.

I had called out to her, anxious but exhilarated, in the minutes before the downpour softened and thinned enough for the boundaries of lake surface, air and tree-lined shore to emerge. The fire still burned in the pit by the lake's edge, miraculously clinging to life even through the soaking rain. Angie and I bobbled side by side, watching the rainfall move over the now entirely flattened lake surface in tessellated sheets and squares.

She stopped singing. I began, picking up the chorus and repeating the first verse.

We floated there for perhaps thirty minutes; perhaps ten; perhaps a hundred. I felt like I was somewhere in Angie's mind—that the warm rain and the silent lake ringed by woods and empty A-frames had sprung from my sister's head like Athena had sprung from Zeus's—the invention of a divine imagination.

Then we went to shore, broke into the Lake House and threw our clothes into the dryer, falling asleep wrapped in Uncle Charlie and Aunt Eleanor's flannel robes, lying side by side before the fireplace.

The next day we were grounded for a month as punishment for staying out all night and frightening them half to death. I was sincerely sorry to have caused them grief, but I would have followed Angie back to the Lake House, or anywhere else she wanted to go, in a heartbeat.

I'd never asked her what caused the black mood that set that evening in motion. I had forgotten all about it by the time we were a block away from home, flying along in Aunt Eleanor's stolen car. The feeling I'd been most aware of was gratitude—gratitude that she had shown me what it was to be in the middle of a lake in a rainstorm, everything around me borderless darkness. I could never have discovered this on my own.

"Angie," I said, floating by her side now in the Pacific Ocean, remembering the way it felt to be so entirely under her influence, and happy. "Angie, why are we here?"

"Because I want to be here," she said.

I spent three days with her, and for the first two and one-half of these days the list of what we did not speak of was brief but pointed. We did not speak of our brothers. She did not speak of Vietnam, of drugs and planes, or draft boards. We did not speak of Hank, or of her abandoned studies, or of Uncle Charlie and Aunt Eleanor's feelings. We spoke of swimming, eating, fishing, windburns as opposed to sunburns, short hair as opposed to long hair, Christmases and July Fourths, particular fishing trips or birthday wishes.

The second night I was with her she drove us to a beach-side restaurant that catered to movie industry people. She wore a clinging black lace pullover and leather pants. Combinations like this were entirely foreign to Charlottesville and our own small high school before that, and until we stepped into the restaurant they struck me as almost humorously, aggressively sexual. But Angie had gotten it exactly right: every head in the restaurant turned to watch her swing across the room to our table. I wore black slacks and a cotton shirt, the definitive Dowdy Presence.

"Where did you learn to dress like that?" I said wonderingly. "No one back home in Virginia ever dressed like that."

"I'm not in Virginia," she said coolly. "And neither are you, thanks to me."

"Yes," I said, raising a glass of wine that she had selected for us without being asked her age. "Thanks to you."

She drove me back to the airport in the borrowed Alfa Romeo. I turned to her at the gate and said, "You know, Uncle Charlie and Aunt Eleanor love us. It won't compromise your integrity to put yourself in their position now and then when you think about all this."

"Iris," Angie said to me slowly. "The time is coming when you won't be able to be the peacemaker or the bridge-builder. You're going to have to choose sides."

With that she was gone, leaving me to a long flight that I spent reassuring myself that my sister was wrong, and that nothing, really, had changed: that I would not have to change.

We Were All Happy Together

Y OU'RE THE GIRL WHO LAY ALL NIGHT ON THE LAWN."

The speaker was goggled and flippered, clipping a weight belt and standing by the pool before his qualifying test for an open-air dive. I was yanking the back of his wet suit vest into place as he spoke.

"Pardon me?"

"I have the room two doors down from Hank. I could have saved you the worry—he doesn't date anybody seriously."

"Take the goggles off," I said.

He flipped the mask up over his head and smiled at me. "Vito Signori." He held out his hand and I took it gingerly. "You actually met me the last time you helped with class—the night we got introduced to the wet suits and tanks."

"I'm sorry, I don't remember you."

"No offense taken. These oxygen tanks we're wearing make everyone look alike."

He looked over one shoulder to check an air hose connection, straightened again and smiled at me. "You know, you're very good with people in this class. Very calming. You make jokes."

"I hadn't noticed that I did that."

"Oh, yes." Vito pointed to someone just getting into the water. "You told Elena a joke about a duck, but you told Jack over there"—here he pointed to a handsome young man flirting with another student by the oxygen tanks—"a joke about drowning. I get the impression you don't like Jack."

I didn't, in fact. The man he called Jack habitually tossed equipment on the cement apron and walked away from it, confident that someone else would put it away. He brightened out of all proportion around the two pretty female students and went dark and empty around the plainer women, waking briefly only to slap the rear ends of the two fraternity types who were enrolled. With these men he made barking noises. "Why should it matter what I think about Jack?" I said.

"It doesn't, really. What do you think about the guy you lay awake all night to watch?"

"I didn't lie awake all night." I could feel the heat in my face as I imagined this man standing at his window watching me lie on my belly in the darkness, unaware of his presence; ignorant of his state of mind.

"Of course. That was a presumptuous question and you certainly don't owe me an answer." He pulled his mask back on. "I watched you all night. You were remarkably still."

About to protest that I hadn't been watching anybody, I stopped. Pointless, given how baldly obvious was the lie.

"You look too old to be an undergraduate living on the Lawn," I said.

"I am too old to be living on the Lawn. I was gone for a couple of years."

"Gone where?" I asked when he didn't volunteer the information.

"Vietnam. I was a Marine."

"A tour of duty's just one year," I said. "You look, what . . . twenty-six?"

"I'm twenty-three. I served two tours. What else can I tell you?"

"Tell me how you got the room on the Lawn." These coveted rooms were awarded by student votes, and people who transferred in or entered late were seldom well known enough to get them.

"My congressman asked the housing office to give it to me."

I laughed. A joke. I said, "If you don't reclip that weight belt, you're going to lose it the second you get in the water." I tapped the belt.

"Thanks for the tip." He fastened the weights more securely, turned away and stepped over the lip of the pool, slipping beneath the water's surface and paddling off, his bubble trail tracing an unevenly discursive pattern of circles behind him.

I made a point of not giving Vito another thought until the end of the class when I noticed the usually close-packed circle of students making a space around one of their number, backing away from him as he peeled off his suit. Vito stood at the thinning center of this crowd, and it seemed that what had made his fellow students back away was a massive angry scar that tore all around his left flank. Nobody actually looked directly at it but their positions made it clear that they were viscerally repelled. His body frightened them and he knew it. He stood his ground and smiled, toweling himself cheerily and continuing to chat with whoever was closest.

I was a hundred yards away from the gymnasium doors when I heard his footsteps, then his voice. "Iris! Slow down there."

I stopped and watched him struggle to catch up, noticing for the first time that he had a scrambling wind-up-toy kind of walk—a pain-accommodating gait. I shifted from foot to foot and wondered if I should just keep going.

"Stop shifting like that," he said when he reached me. His breath was even and light: he hadn't really hurried. He had just wanted to see if his voice alone could stop me. "You look like you're deciding whether or not to take off again." He fell into step beside me, reached into a pocket and pulled out a pack of Blackjack gum. He offered me a stick.

"No thank you."

"We seem to be going the same way. Let me walk you home."

"I know the way. There's no need." I smiled a civil smile.

"Of course," he said, shaking his head. "I'll just tag along until you're past these partially lit paths."

I considered simply leaving him behind—he limped so I could manage it easily. But when I imagined what that would mean, me striding ahead and this stubborn man bouncing along behind me, probably call-ing out loudly as he ran, I rejected the idea. Vito Signori was making me uneasy. He stopped talking and I got more uneasy.

"Is something wrong?" I asked.

"Probably not. But somebody's following us," he answered.

"Really?" I didn't believe this. We were on a narrow path running alongside the serpentine walls of the East Range. This was the heart of the campus—no one would be "following" us except some student mak-ing his way home. But as I was making this point to Vito, clearly audible steps broke out behind us and we found ourselves overtaken by a stranger. He actually wore a ski mask on his head. For a moment I won-dered if this was some prank arranged by Vito himself.

"Wallets," the man snarled. He held something that glinted but was obscured.

Vito said, "Fuck off, buddy," took my right elbow and guided me past the robber, jostling him in the process. I saw the man look Vito up and down. Vito was a head shorter, probably sixty pounds lighter, and limping.

"The purse," the man said, jumping ahead of us again to block our way and gesturing at my bag with something that glinted. I stepped back, away from what I assumed was a weapon. "Your wallets. Hand 'em here."

"Asshole," Vito said. His tone conveyed more disappointment than anger. He took a shockingly quick step directly into the assailant's chest and pulled one knee up into the man's crotch, then he swept his elbow down onto his nose. I could hear breaking bone and the squishy, liquid sound of ripping cartilage and soft tissue. This was not a prank.

"Get up," Vito said evenly. He drew back his arm and it was clear to me that he was going to break the man's nose in a new place. The mug-ger gasped, struggling to wipe the blood from his mouth and breathe. Vito's strategically placed blow caught him entirely unaware, and he screamed in pain. Wincing, Vito vigorously shook the hand he'd just used to strike this blow. Then his other hand gathered the assailant's collar, choking him and lifting him at the same time. Vito pinned the struggling, bleeding man against the brick wall and delivered another blow.

"Stop!" I cried, pushing Vito away from his victim. But Vito seemed to have gone deaf and dumb and partly blind. He swatted at me without turning his attention from the mugger, who looked as if his windpipe were being crushed, and the casual arc of Vito's hand took me backward off my feet and into a bed of ferns. I grunted and the sound finally caught his attention. The mugger took advantage of the distraction to wrest free and dart into the darkness. Vito looked after him almost longingly, and as he leaned forward to offer me a helping hand I saw a good deal of light go out of his eyes as the man he was about to strangle slipped beyond his reach. But he didn't leave my side.

My T-shirt had been torn and the seat of my jeans was orange with Virginia clay. Vito's hand reached out to brush my rear end and I slapped it away, noticing the blood on his knuckles and wrist as I did so.

"We should go to the campus police and report this," I said when we'd fallen in step again.

"Why?"

"The man had a weapon! The police can check the emergency room at the hospital for guys who come in with broken noses!"

"He didn't have a weapon," Vito sighed, "and people who get their noses broken like he did don't go to emergency rooms."

"But I saw something shining." My tone was more hesitant now.

"Watchband," Vito said. "The guy was bluffing. That was just his hand under his coat—not a gun."

"Well, I should find someone to report this to. Campus police can use information like this to make the grounds safer."

"Well, if it makes you feel better"—Vito shrugged—"go ahead and refer the problem on to our protectors and leaders. But in your position I think I'd just carry pepper spray."

"You don't need to make me feel naive," I said sharply, "just because I assume that people do their jobs."

"I didn't mean that," he said.

"Yes you did."

"All right. I did mean that you were naive, but I didn't mean to make you mad at me." He smiled apologetically. Suddenly he looked very tired.

"I'm reporting what happened," I said grimly.

"I'll walk you over."

This he did, but he left me at the door of the security office. I strode in purposefully, only to find a dozing lumpy man behind a telephone who, woken, pawed through his desk until he found some forms, which he pushed across the counter and asked me to fill out. "Are you going to call the police?" I asked the security guard.

"He didn't manage to actually steal anything, did he?"

"No."

"Well. We got no crime to report."

"How about assault?"

"The friend of yours who beat off this robber, he didn't want to come in and report it with you?"

"No."

"Well. We'll follow up. We got the description of the guy from you, and we'll inform everybody on campus. We take every report very seriously." He reached under the counter and the hand came up holding a Hershey's bar. He unwrapped it dreamily and broke off pieces while we talked, a seamless flow of chocolate rectangles from the brown wrapper to his mouth. He offered to drive me home. I declined.

Thirty yards away from the security office door I heard footsteps. When I slowed they accelerated. I decided the best thing to do was turn and face whoever was there immediately. Halfway through my reversal something familiar about the footsteps calmed me even before I consciously knew why. They were uneven, scrabbly steps.

"Iris! Wait up!" Vito's voice.

"What do you think you're doing?" I demanded, furious at having been frightened.

"I'm sorry. I did give you some warning by yelling, didn't I? I was waiting for you to come out but got distracted and missed you when you first stepped out the door."

"Leave me alone, Vito." I turned on my heel.

"No. I'm going to walk you home. The cop offered you a ride, didn't he?" He was struggling a bit to keep up with me and I wasn't making it easier by slowing down.

"Yes."

"And you refused the ride."

"Yes."

"I thought you would." Vito continued to keep up though I accelerated. He made casual attempts to reopen conversation but I walked grimly along without responding. "I have a question," he said when we reached the steps to my apartment. "It's actually why I wanted to talk to you after class. That night you just lay on the lawn, why didn't you just knock on the guy's door? You visit him a couple times a week so it's not like you don't know him."

The question actually stopped me in my tracks for a moment, but just a moment. "I have no idea." I looked at Vito and found myself thinking about how his face had looked as he broke the mugger's nose for the second time; about how it should have alarmed me but didn't.

He turned to go, twisted around for a last word. "Look, I'm exactly two doors down from your friend. We know each other as neighbors. If you ask him about me he won't have anything disturbing to report. You would be very welcome if you happened to drop by the next time you come to see him." He waited just long enough to hear my hesitation and interpret it as a positive sign. He added, "I would love it if you would."

I made a point of going to Hank's room the very next day, knocking and calling as casually as someone who had never considered the romantic life of the room's occupant and, had they done so, wouldn't have cared enough about it to form any opinions. I swung his door open and stepped in without waiting for an answer to my knock. With the exception of the typewriter on his desk and the titles of the engineering texts beside it, Hank's room probably looked very much as it had a hundred years before.

"That doesn't matter," he was saying, cradling the telephone with one raised shoulder as he paced in the narrow circle permitted by its cord. "Not to me." He jerked his head impatiently toward the door as I entered, clearly unhappy to be interrupted. His mouth was set in a straight little line like a dash at the bottom of his face—an entirely uncharacteristic look. I stood, refusing to make the polite retreat he clearly wanted. With some effort he softened his facial expression and said into the telephone receiver, "Your sister just walked in. Want to say hello as long as you're on the line?"

He handed it to me and I took it gingerly. "Angie? Are you using the phone at that commune house?"

"No, I'm on the beach. I got a line hooked up. There was an underground line that the owner didn't even know about—I stopped a telephone truck in town and found out that it ran right down the dirt road to this place but the owner before last didn't hook it up! I've sworn Hank to secrecy about the number—just you and Hank. That's all who'll know it."

"Why?"

"For me, Bear. Don't be stubborn. Look. I don't see things being ironed out between me and Charlie before Fourth of July, and I was just calling Hank to tell him that I didn't think I'd be coming east this summer. I can't see how it would work. Charlie was pretty clear about how he felt."

"Angie, people say things when they're angry and shocked, and then they have time to think about it and they want a way to take it back. Give it to him."

"It's not just the way Charlie feels about me, Iris. It's the way I feel about him."

"But Angie, Uncle Charlie is not the only one who'll be looking for you here at home. What about me, and Aunt Eleanor and Hank? It's the first Fourth of July since Eddie and Perry. I don't understand this."

"I know you don't," she said. "Let me talk to Hank again."

I handed him the receiver and he nodded into it for another three or four minutes before hanging up.

"What?" I said to him. "What did she say?"

"Nothing. She just repeated what she'd already said to you."

"You're going to work this out with your father, aren't you, Hank? Find some way for things to be all right again?"

"Iris, things are what they are. My father should never have asked for a copy of the security report on us, but he did, and I don't know why they gave it to him. It isn't standard procedure to share information on someone when that person is supposed to be the subject of the review."

"So why did they do it?"

"I don't know. Sometimes I've thought that explanation about the security clearance upgrade was just the story he invented to cover up the fact that he had Angie followed."

"Angie said the same thing," I told him.

"I know." He sighed. "Finding out that Angie and I are involved— sexually involved—just pushed him off some kind of a ledge. He's crazed about it."

"Hank, if you think the security clearance story wasn't true, then why do you think he had her followed?"

"I think someone at the Bureau was investigating bank statement trails and they found one that led back to Angie—money going from my daddy's account to hers to other accounts that the Bureau was watching."

"She told me about giving money away but that's not a crime."

"There was a shooting at a draft board office in Virginia."

"What does a cash donation have to do with a shooting?"

"A policeman died, Iris. The people she gave the money to were the group who claimed responsibility for trashing that draft board. They killed a policeman who tried to stop them from vandalizing the records. The man was shot in the face. He was twenty-nine years old and he had two small children."

"What does that have to do with Angie?" I was suddenly aware of my wet palms, the tremor in my hands.

"You've never been stupid, Iris. There's a cash trail that runs from my daddy's bank to Angie to these people. What conclusions do you think are being drawn?"

"Who are these people that the FBI says are Angie's friends?"

"The letters S-D-S are being used. You know what that would sound like to Charlie Jackson."

"Well, are they SDS? Did Uncle Charlie actually speak to her directly about this? Don't you think this is all a misunderstanding?"

"They spoke. Speaking made it worse."

"How could that be?"

"They *were* SDS, Iris. They *did* make bombs and carry guns and shoot people. She did give them money, and she did know who they were."

"How do you know all that?" He turned his face away from me. I said, "That's not possible. That's not who Angie is." My palms were slick.

"That's not who Angie was," he corrected me. "But then Perry and Eddie died. That was her ledge, and over she went."

I could hear my sister telling me that I would have to choose, that it was no longer possible to claim simply, naively, that I was on the side of my family. We had splintered into different factions that could not peacefully coexist, and if there had been a moment when I could have stopped it, made it all better, it had passed me by unused. I retreated to an illogical windy internal height and let my hopes blind my wits. "Your father loves you enough to try to make all this right," I insisted.

"To make all this right, Iris, my father would have to agree that lending money to terrorists is a legitimate activity. He would have to accept that I'm in love with Angie and that I'm going to marry her. When I told him that, he said that she was an enemy of the state; that as far as my attraction to her went he thought she was just a piece of tail and that I could get over it and find better elsewhere."

"He didn't say 'piece of tail,' " I protested.

"I'm afraid he did."

"That's not Uncle Charlie."

"It is. You've known him almost as long as I have, Iris. You've been a child in his house. But you still only see what you want to see. He said I was just too young to understand what a manipulative woman could do to my judgment. It's not just a matter of his being the kind of man who's used to getting his own way, which he is. He was completely beside himself—utterly repulsed. You know, he's not bothered by the fact that we were raised together. He doesn't think of us as brother and sister—it's something else about her that disgusts him. Her alone. I don't know what."

His eyes glistened. I could not remember ever having seen Hank cry and I could feel my chest respond, constricting until I had to actually think about it to get a deep breath. All I could say was, "Oh, Hank." Then, because I couldn't think of anything else to say, I repeated myself. "Oh, Hank," I said. "I'm sorry."

"Sorry for what? Sorry that I fell in love with somebody like Angie?"

"I'm sorry that you're unhappy. Sorry that you and Uncle Charlie are at odds when you love each other so much."

"He'll have to learn to live with this because I'm going to be with Angie. I can't be what he wants this time."

"Have you actually talked with Angie about marriage?"

"Yes."

"Really?" I tried to keep the disbelief out of my tone.

"She probably didn't talk about it with you when you went to see her because she wanted to spare you from getting in the middle of it." He saw my eyebrows lift. "She's told me about your visit—she tells me everything."

I wasn't sure why I was so certain that this was not true, but I felt sure that Angie didn't tell Hank everything—that she didn't tell anyone everything. Until a matter of weeks ago I would have sworn that she told me everything. I was her Bear, her intimate confidante, the best-loved among all her people on the earth. Hadn't she told me this countless times? Wasn't I the one she would have told if she had fallen so in love with a man that she was planning to marry him?

Or maybe not.

Certainly the unhappy person who stood before me now was not that man. I knew this like I knew the configurations of Hank's sober, intelligent face, like I knew every root and stone on the path down to the lake, like I knew the taste of Aunt Eleanor's Triple Threat chocolate cake—

things I couldn't remember not knowing. And because there were things about my sister Angie that I knew in this way, I knew that Hank loved her in vain.

I made some excuse and I left him, standing for a moment in the veranda to get my bearings before starting lamely in the direction of the rotunda. I hadn't covered a dozen yards before Vito Signori was at my side, holding my elbow, guiding me back to the veranda that connected the West Lawn residences. He was wearing a torn T-shirt, jeans and a white apron, brandishing a wooden spoon as he walked.

"I saw you cross the Lawn and I've kept half an eye out for you. It almost cost me my risotto to do it."

"Not now, Vito. I'm not . . . I can't chat now."

"Yes you can." He guided me to his own door, releasing me just long enough to open it and sweep me in. "I told you my room was only a few steps down from your friend's," he said. "Here. Stick a fork in the beets and tell me if they're done." He handed me something and I took it though I don't remember actually feeling it—only being guided by the natural authority in his manner.

Vito Signori's room might as well have been in a different universe from Hank's, though the two were identical boxes in a line of identical boxes. Two walls were covered in industrial steel restaurant shelving. The first wall held a toaster oven, cookbooks, a KitchenAid processor, an espresso machine, and a spice rack took up its center shelves. Bottles filled the rest; pots and pans hung from either side of the racks. The second wall was full of books, little hammers, bottles with dropper caps, bottles filled with what looked like dirt, and rocks of all sizes and types. Thousands of things, all in their places.

"You can't get a decent meal at the Corner, and cafeteria food . . ." He shrugged. "Here." He handed me a fork. "Poke the beets that are in the toaster oven and tell me how much longer they need."

"I can't stay," I repeated, but I kept doing what he told me to do, holding the things he pressed into my hands and poking the things he told me to poke. I opened the little toaster oven door and jabbed the blood-red globes.

"Well?" he asked.

"Well what?"

"How much longer do the beets need?"

I didn't have the slightest idea.

"Guess," he demanded.

"Another fifteen minutes," I said.

"You look like you're near tears," he observed matter-of-factly, taking one wooden spoon from my hands and replacing it with a larger one. "Stir this." He placed his hands gently at the back of my waist, a whispery kind of suggestive touch, and I walked in front of his open palms directly over to the hot plate that held the risotto. As soon as he said the words, I could feel the tears myself, though I couldn't have sorted out if they were for me or Uncle Charlie and Aunt Eleanor or for Hank or for someone or something I hadn't even considered. He said, "I have to slice some pancetta." He waited for just a moment until he was sure I would actually begin stirring, then he went to a tiny refrigerator, poked around in it until he found what he wanted and slapped it down on the cutting board that sat on top of the miniature appliance. I was aware of him watching me and withholding any reaction: just watching. He chopped, talking rapidly about prawns and mushrooms, and I stirred on without speaking. Vito filled two glasses with wine, handed one to me and sipped from his own, staring down into the pot I stirred. "Getting there," he observed, and then he tipped his wineglass over it, dumping the contents directly into the pot. "Keep stirring." He plucked another bottle from his windowsill, opened it and refilled his glass. "Cooking is the ideal distraction. Demands just the top of the mind—perfect undemanding distraction."

"What?"

"I don't mind people crying if you want to cry."

"I'm not going to cry."

"All right. Give me that spoon. You're letting it stick." He pushed me gently aside, taking the spoon from my hands. "You chop the beets into little cubes." He waved his wooden spoon toward the toaster oven. "While I finish this and then throw the pancetta into a skillet."

I obeyed because every time I'd considered leaving I'd had a terrible prescient vision of myself at home, alone in my three rooms. And besides, there was the interesting new sense of being someplace entirely unpredictable, and the good food. Staying here with Vito and his risotto was the clear superior alternative to going home. I held out my glass and he refilled it again, and when he served the meal he'd made on cracked plates decorated with military insignia, I stayed and ate.

"Don't you have classes this afternoon?" I asked.

"None that I need to actually attend." Vito looked up at me. "My, my," he said. "You look like you did when you first came in only a little worse."

I looked around the room feeling as though my chair were a small raft in a large body of fogbound water, no clear way to shore. "I'm just a little drunk," I said, holding hard to the chair's arm. "That's all." And I was. "I should go home. I've got twenty lines to translate before class tomorrow."

"Sure. That's a good idea."

"Where did you learn to cook?" I asked.

"My mother. I swear the hardest part, for her, of my being overseas was that she couldn't mail me my favorite meals."

"Like what?"

"Oh, lamb shanks in polenta. I used to love that, and it drove her nuts that she couldn't find a way to mail lamb shanks to Saigon."

I laughed. "You don't love it anymore?"

"Yeah. But I lean more vegetarian lately—I got so I didn't like to see the bones sticking out of what I was eating. Better not to cook something that can make eye contact."

"That's pretty restrictive. You know, I can do a few things in the kitchen with deer shanks."

"Really? I didn't know anybody did that anymore."

"They do if they grow up in the hills with Aunt Eleanor and Uncle Charlie."

"Aunt and uncle? They're not your parents?"

"No. They're Hank's parents—that guy who lives three doors down from you."

"You and that guy are cousins?"

I had clearly amazed him, which pleased me. "Not my blood relation. His parents are my guardians." Then, for reasons I didn't bother to examine, I added, "Hank is in love with my sister."

Vito shook his head slowly. "Really. I'm sorry."

"Why would you be sorry about something like that?"

"Because I think it's possible that you're in love with him."

"I'm not in love with anyone. And I'm going home now." I struggled to my feet and walked purposefully, slowly, to the door. "Thank you so much for the lovely lunch."

"You're really not in love with him?" he asked.

"Really not," I said. Then I leaned forward and kissed Vito Signori directly on the lips, a more forward gesture than I had ever made in my life. More surprising, I felt an actual buzz move from my lips and through my torso. He very distinctly kissed me back.

Once outside his door and on my way I made a conscious decision to pretend that the kiss never happened. I made my way back to my three rooms on the second floor of the little cape on Jefferson Park Avenue. There beside my mailbox was a book-shaped rectangle wrapped in brown grocery bag paper. Crooked River's return address was in the corner.

I held it, unopened, and planted myself in the hole-infested chair left by the previous residents with the package balanced on my lap. That night I set the book under my bed, still unopened. I could wait. I'd waited this long, after all. It would be there for me in the morning.

Moon Fairy

I PERFORMED ALL MY MORNING ROUTINES: BOIL THE EGG, USE THE water to make instant coffee, pull the soft-boiled egg out right when the toast pops and give it a good smack before cracking it over the bread. I set the brown paper–wrapped package by my coffee cup and felt happy. Also not happy.

This could only be Perry's diary, and when I opened it perhaps I would lose the Perry that I had always known to some other Perry—the Perry who sat on the edge of a hotel bed in Hawaii with a roach singeing his fingers, asking me how I could stand it. I left it in its place on the table and went to two morning classes, the feeling of having a secret both charging and darkening everything in my routine.

It was night before I opened it, folding the brown paper away from the rectangular box, lifting the lid and finding a small pile of papers that had clearly been torn from some larger book. I smoothed the paper carefully and removed a letter that had been jammed between some of the pages.

Little Girl, it read. *This is part of your brother's diary. The rest is here with me and the rabbits, and someday it may come your way. I can't say for sure but it might. I will talk to you if you want. I have also enclosed a leather bracelet. If any of the pictures here make a story for you that you wish to keep, tie it to your wrist and it will seal the story inside you so you don't lose it. I've tried it. It works. No baloney. Sincerely, Crooked River.*

I shook out the loose pages and a strip of leather tumbled into my lap. I set it on the table beside the pages and began to leaf through. The first sheet looked like a drawing of a snowstorm, but on closer examination it was a foggy mountainside sliced through with tracers and the after-effects of what must have been shell explosions. The next ten pages were exact sketches of bugs, often being eviscerated and eaten by other bugs or small, opossum-like mammals; women cooking, plates piled with noo-dles; and then, over and over on the last pages in the group, a woman flowing upward into a moonbeam, clutching a child. Beneath her in the bottom right-hand corner of the page stood a furious man letting loose a barrage of arrows aimed at her and the infant. She paid him no mind, but kept her upturned face tipped into the moonbeam. The pages after that were full of pictures of things being sucked up into moonbeams: chil-dren, banyan trees, arrows, women, even the occasional man.

I stopped turning pages. The rest could wait. I didn't understand the little bit I'd seen.

I was confused but relieved not to find what I had to admit to myself had been fears of finding loopily violent and unbalanced prose, or draw-ings of bloody corpses and piles of skulls. I flipped back to look at a drawing of a furry little creature clutching a frog; a small girl pouring a beaten mixture through fork tines and into a cooking pot. An M-16 sat by the little girl's side. In the next drawing the same little girl cradled the M-16 over one shoulder and grinned out happily from the portrait. I sniffed the paper and felt its edges, but could not determine the draw-ing's age. It might have been done a year ago—or last month.

I went to the last drawings and was embarrassed to find portraits— graphically lively and fleshy portraits—of a naked Vietnamese woman. Sometimes the woman, like the little boy, held weapons and smiled. I kept flipping, and the graphically exact naked Vietnamese woman began to ap-pear floating upward into more moonbeams, spiraling trails of guns sucked in her wake, accompanying her. The final picture was of Perry himself being pulled into space, reaching upward toward what looked like the woman's feet yet looking back down toward the earth as he rose. The face was obscured.

I found myself wanting to share these pictures not with Hank, not with Angie, but with Vito. The very next day I did. I sat beside him and watched him flip from page to page, growing quieter as he did so.

"Your brother had friends," he said, stopping at the pictures of the little girl cooking with the M-16 at her side.

"How does that picture prove he had friends?"

"This is a particular girl, at a particular moment—not a generic 'girl cooking' kind of thing. Look at how she's looking at the person drawing her. They know one another."

I looked. The girl in the picture looked directly back, and I tried to imagine myself being the person she was looking at while he drew her. From this perspective it felt very much like this girl and my brother knew each other very well. "Did you have friends?" I asked. "Over there, I mean."

"Depending on where you were posted, it could be very easy to have friends," he said.

I let that evasion go by, assuming he meant that he had indeed had 'friends.' "Vito, do you know what's going on with all these moonbeam pictures?"

"The stock Vietnamese fairy tale has a mortal falling in love with someone from the fairy kingdom—which is forbidden, of course. There was a story about a man named Hau Nghe who would fit these pictures." Vito turned to one that I hadn't paid a great deal of attention to—enormous birds with shardlike feathers—sweeping around a lone man who held a bow and took aim at a bird whose talons stretched into the air directly before his face. The man's face was my brother Eddie's.

"Yes." I nodded, answering his unspoken question. "That's my brother. One of my brothers."

"This particular story started with the hero battling evil spirits who'd taken the form of enormous, powerful crows who swooped down on villages and ate all the people's crops. A beautiful Moon Fairy looked down and saw him killing these evil spirit crows left and right, and she fell in love with him right then and there. She came to earth, helped him defeat the evil crows and promised to stay on earth to live with him forever."

"But she couldn't?"

"Hau Nghe had a bad end. As soon as the grateful people made him king, he changed—bled them dry to build himself palaces, that kind of thing. This picture looks like the end of the story. The Moon Fairy left him, and as she flew up in the moonbeam she told him that he'd changed; that the man she fell in love with didn't exist anymore."

"What about the baby?"

"The baby's the detail that makes me think it's his story. Hau Nghe let himself be convinced that if he only boiled down a bunch of babies into an elixir, it would keep him alive forever. His own daughter was going to be the last one in the pot. Moon Fairy drew the line there and packed herself and her baby up to leave him. I think that's what's in this picture, her clutching the baby and ascending in the moonbeam."

"So he was left all alone with his palaces?"

"No. The parents of the other babies that he was intending to turn into elixir finished him off."

"That's not very believable," I said.

"People from different worlds falling in love? Fathers cannibalizing the next generation for the sake of their own interests? Marriages coming apart when parents don't agree? Of course not." He smiled. "It's a fairy tale." He ran his finger over the edges of the picture and said, "It's been torn out of something larger."

"The man who sent it told me that I didn't deserve the whole thing, and that he'd think about sending the rest of it later, maybe."

"What do you have to do to deserve the whole thing?" Vito asked.

"I don't know. I think that's why I wanted to show the book to you."

"Because I'm a vet, too, like this Geronimo Crooked River, and I might know about some secret handshake that only vets know about?"

"You've seen the world he's drawn. I haven't. Did your Vietnamese 'friends' tell you the story about Hau Nghe?"

"Yes. And those friends would look at these pictures and tell you that a Moon Fairy was your brother's undoing. Moon spirits are the ones who tie you to the person you love with their magic threads. They often accidentally fall in love with mortals, which causes a lot of trouble. If I were Vietnamese, I'd maybe say that your brother's particular Moon Fairy wouldn't give him up, so the Jade Emperor sent Thunder and Lightning spirits to destroy him. That's the usual method."

"Yet another useful theory on my brother's fate." I straightened the pictures as if preparing to go. "I can add that to the others."

"Iris. When you get other pages, if you get other pages, you'll show them to me?"

"I will," I promised.

"The man who sends them to you is named Crooked River?"

"Yes. But his nickname in my brother's platoon was Geronimo. He raises beautiful rabbits that he takes to the state fair competitions. He wins. I've seen the ribbons."

"You're sure that what he's sending you is actually what he says it is?"

"Perry drew all his life. He never drew the things I see in these pictures, but then, he'd never been to Vietnam. These pictures look like his work to me."

"What about the way they feel?"

"They don't always feel like what I thought he was—but people change. Or maybe I didn't know him as well as I thought I did."

Vito shifted position, curving around me to look at the picture from just behind my own head. I could feel the heat of his chest and legs for an instant, and then it was gone. He'd stood. "Just asking," he said. "I don't want to seem nosy. I mean it to be more like watching your back for you," Vito said.

"I know," I said. I stood up myself.

He hadn't touched me but I felt as though I'd been firmly handled. He smiled, crossed the room and raised one hand to say good-bye. His uneven steps going down the porch stairs had a broken wind-up toy sound.

Everything about the way I reacted to Vito was unfamiliar to me. Perhaps he had purposefully created this effect, but I couldn't tell. I was too inexperienced. The same social climate that had nurtured Angie's inclinations toward sexual experimentation had deepened my natural reserve. I had stood to one side and watched while a good deal of my generation plunged into what was colloquially known as free love. So now, when another girl might have been sure of Vito Signori's intent and mood, I was at sea.

An ungenerous eye would have called me prudish. Certainly girls with this kind of attitude didn't attract young men by the bucketful. Yet I seemed to have attracted Vito Signori.

LATER THAT DAY, I walked right past Hank's door without so much as a knock. I knew I'd seek him out within the next day or two, and I wanted a few buffering days between the conversation I'd just had with Vito and contact with Hank.

The next few nights I dreamed dreams full of Vito Signoris: they wore goggles, they ran in jungle grass, they stirred pots full of babies that rose up, when they were done, in moonbeams that carried them out of his little room. They made love with me. In one or two dreams the Vitos became, without explanation or transition, Hanks. I woke with a ringing sensation in my entire body and a pervading, amorphous anxiety. Also happiness. The happiness I was aware of only because the feeling dogged me into my first class, and I'd found myself singing. I'd stopped mid-bar in "Take Me Out to the Ball Game," one of Aunt Eleanor's favorites, suddenly aware of what I was doing because I'd attracted a little cluster of stares.

When Hank showed up at my apartment, the strangeness of his face in the porch window reminded me that he'd only stood on it perhaps a half-dozen times in all the months I'd been in Charlottesville. He accepted a cup of coffee, which he clearly had no interest in, sat making small talk for perhaps four minutes and then got to his point. "That conversation we had about Uncle Charlie's feelings about me and Angie?" he said. "I didn't mean to burden you."

"You didn't."

"What I mean is, please don't talk with Angie about it. I said a few things to you in ways that are maybe more direct than the ways I've said them to Angie and to Uncle Charlie. I need some time to get things clear with them before they say anything else about Angie and me to you—or you say anything to them."

I assumed that this speech was Hank's way of correcting the lie he'd told me when he claimed that he and Angie had actually spoken to each other about marriage.

"So. You just don't want me to talk to them about . . . what?" I said at last.

"Just don't talk with Angie about me. I guess that's what I want."

"I understand," I told him. If he noticed that I had not promised him anything at all, he didn't argue.

Paper Trail

THE NEXT GROUP OF PAGES ARRIVED ONLY A FEW DAYS LATER. They weren't bound or even in a sequential group. Like their fellows they had been torn out, set into a pile and jammed into a brown envelope. No note accompanied this second shipment. This time I didn't wait but sliced the envelope open immediately and shook its contents out on my living room floor, arranging the dozen pages in three rows before me.

The drawings were all of bodies: eviscerated bodies; bodies that betrayed no visible explanation for their deaths, bodies splayed on the ground before wooden houses and chopped into pieces on the jungle floor or leaking in gooey disarray from black body bags piled beside a helicopter. Every one of them had Eddie's face.

I put them all back in the brown envelope. In fifteen minutes I was sitting on the rocker outside Vito Signori's room, waiting there for him with the brown envelope full of drawings on my lap. Then, not wanting Hank to cross my path and see me at Vito's door, I tried the latch. It gave way. I swung the door open and sidled into the room, settling gingerly on a stool between the metal grates holding restaurant equipment and a little cluster of oxygen tanks.

Vito found me there twenty minutes later when he bustled in, a newspaper in one hand and the remains of a cigarette in the other. I had never seen him smoke. He saw the envelope and sat down next to me on the floor, taking it from me without a word of greeting and gently shaking the drawings out between us, arranging them so he could see them all at the same time. We sat there studying them together for a full five minutes before I spoke.

"Vito, these dead people are all my brother Eddie."

I told Vito everything I knew about Eddie and Perry; everything I knew about our parents and Eleanor and Charlie. I talked for an hour without interruption and then I stopped, waiting for some reaction from him.

"You want to know," he answered after he'd thought a few minutes, "if these are pictures of what your brother was afraid of, or pictures of what he wanted. You want to know if I think that your brother Perry could have killed his own brother—if Vietnam was the kind of place where those things happened."

I nodded.

"You could answer that question as well as I could," he said, setting the drawing down on the floor.

"But I wasn't there. I've never been in a place like that."

"But you knew your brothers."

"Like you say, Vito—people change." I lay right down on the floorboards, all my bones suddenly feeling as though the marrow had turned to lead. "The stories about fragging, about mutinies, about accidents are true, aren't they? I know that. What I'm afraid I see in the pictures is the inside of Perry's head."

"Almost all stories are true for somebody. Remember that your brother didn't expect these drawings to end up in a brown envelope in your mailbox."

"I don't know why but I feel sure that he did, and that's why he gave them to Crooked River. He did it so I'd be looking at them now." I stood up. "It's so frustrating not to know what happened. Vito, there has to be some official record of the event; some official file on my brothers."

"There's the records at the Quartermaster's Office, Disposition Branch. Anything the service had to say about lost veterans, anything it knew, it'll be there."

"Who uses this branch? What's it for?"

"It was set up initially to track POWs and MIAs in the Second World War. If there's an official story on your brothers that's more extensive than the one they've shown you already, that's where it will be."

"You mean what they tell the families isn't automatically the whole story?"

"I'd guess it almost always automatically isn't. That doesn't guarantee that the whole story will be in any one place, but the military files could have another piece."

"Why should they tell me something they haven't said to the family before if I show up in person?"

"I can make a telephone call," Vito said. "My congressman friend." He shrugged. "He can make a telephone call or two of his own."

"You mean there really is a congressman friend?" My mouth hung open. Vito nodded. "If you'd help me," I said, "I'd be grateful."

"All right. But keep in mind that right now you're free to imagine anything you want. The more you find out, the less of that freedom you'll have. Trust me on that."

"I do trust you," I said.

"And you still want to know more?"

I nodded.

"Good," he said.

Suddenly self-conscious, I turned away from him, nodded at the tanks in the corner.

"Diving alone?"

"No, no. Just putting it on and submerging myself regularly in the pool between classes."

"Why?"

"I seize up. I can't get over expecting the air line to collapse like a bad straw." He shifted his weight around, turned his face away from me and then back before adding, "I spent a few hours underwater breathing through a reed once. Anyway, the instructor told me to just put in some time with the equipment."

I stored this image of Vito and the reed away to consider later when I was alone. I said, "You don't trust the equipment yet. That's all."

"Could be." He didn't seem in the least embarrassed by this admission; nor did he offer it in so ironic a manner that I wasn't supposed to take it seriously. "You're going to be one of the teachers going on the open-air test dive, aren't you?" he asked.

"I'm not a teacher. I was just an assistant."

"Tell you what, Iris. I'll get this appointment at the Disposition Branch, and you promise to be in the water when I go in for the open-air dive."

"I'm not experienced enough to go as a teacher diver. Besides, you'll do fine. The boys have been managing this test dive for years—they're very calm people."

"I've already asked the instructor and he said it was a good idea to have a newly graduated student along as an example." Vito grinned. "I offered you already."

If he had looked the least bit triumphant I would have simply refused. "Come on," he said lightly. "It'll be fun."

"It'll probably snow again."

"That will be more fun."

I hesitated another moment. "All right," I said. "I mean, now that I know that it'll be fun."

"So. That's settled." To my surprise, he looked relieved. "Shall I make us lunch?" he asked, turning to me.

"No, thank you. I've got about forty more lines to translate before my three-o'clock Greek class."

"I see." It was clear to me from his close scrutiny that he wasn't sure if I was lying. I wasn't sure myself.

"Herodotus," I volunteered, knowing that even a small detail would dispel most of his doubts; discovering that I wanted to dispel his doubts.

"All right. I'll make a few calls. Then we'll go together to the Disposition Branch."

"You don't have to come with me, Vito. I can do it myself."

"You can walk point if you want, but I'll tag along at your back. It's better that way." He interrupted me as I was about to protest again. "I want to," he said. "Indulge me."

That afternoon I arrived at class with none of the translation done, hoping against hope that I would not be called upon. Of course I was.

"θαρσέω," Miss Sunnaret. Meaning?" The instructor wasn't even looking at me. I thought I heard him sigh when he called my name.

"A brave death," I ventured. Then, seeing the stricken expression on the teacher's face, I stopped and pretended to inspect my notes again.

"The word is θαρσέω, Miss Sunnaret. Not θάνατος. *Bravely confident,* Miss Sunnaret."

For a moment I thought this critique described my manner as I guessed the translation; but no, he meant that the word's translation was "bravely confident." He continued: "Though they do rest side by side, no doubt, in the lexicon you consulted, the words have no real relation. The Persians come to Marathon, Miss Sunnaret. The Athenians ask for help at Sparta. They are granted assistance, and they press on *with great confidence, though before this time even the name of Mediken was fearful to the Hellenes*—meaning the Greeks." He sighed again before adding, "A brilliant and heroic confrontation, a definitive moment in establishing the most cherished values and characteristics of what we now call Western civilization."

Only a few weeks ago such a lapse on my part in a class would have left me jangled—uneasy until I had found a way to undo the false step. But now it didn't matter. I had larger things on my mind; larger plans and intentions that made my shabby grasp of Herodotus irrelevant.

TWO DAYS LATER we were seated in the dining car of the six a.m. Southern Crescent, ordering eggs and toast, me feeling like I was actually going somewhere. Vito drank eight cups of coffee before we pulled into Washington.

Though we reached the Quartermaster's Office ten minutes before our appointed time, we found ourselves sitting for two hours in a dark waiting room piled full of two-year-old magazines and an atmosphere of defeat. A civilian secretary had greeted us, gotten us six more cups of coffee as we waited and explained that we were fortunate to speak to anyone at all on such short notice and the reason that this miracle had been accomplished was a call from a congressman who had asked for this meeting as a very special and particular favor. She also noted that typically visitors asked for information on only one relative, and there had been some scrambling and confusion because my paperwork had named both my brothers and my father—very irregular, but once again, the congressman had asked for forbearance. The colonels assigned to this office, she had sighed, revolved every three years, and learned how to handle the public and access the records, as far as she could see, only moments before they were transferred away. She was so sorry, so sorry.

It was three hours before the colonel himself ushered us into the luxuriously private inner rooms. We sat on deep leather chairs facing his desk, a behemoth with brass detailing in the legs and clawed feet. "I'm so sorry about the loss of your brothers, Ms. Sunnaret," he began. "I'm sure you know that they died bravely, doing their duty for this country, and that we are all profoundly grateful for their sacrifice."

"But only one set of dog tags was recovered," I began.

"Miss Sunnaret." He waved a hand gently in the air to stop me; to indicate the futility of my naive hopes. "It's our business to handle information like this, and sadly, we have done it thousands of times. Given the testimony of those in the platoon and the evidence gathered on the scene, we are entirely confident that both your brothers died that day within seconds of one another. Again, I am so sorry, ma'am." He snapped a manila folder shut and swiveled to one side: meeting over.

I leaned forward. "I've spoken to two members of the platoon, and one believes that my brother Perry Sunnaret survived."

"And this soldier's name?"

"Thompson."

He rooted through the folder before him, settling on a paper that he didn't show us. "Yes, I see that a Private Thompson was interviewed at the end of his tour. And as to Mr. Thompson's reliability, I am willing to share with you that his medical records include drug abuse, possible alcoholism and paranoia."

"And my father? I asked about his service record in Vietnam. Your secretary had me present identification as his next of kin."

"That's because Oliver Sunnaret is still alive, and serving in a diplomatic post in Europe. It's very irregular to have a relative ask about an officer still on active duty. We called him to ask his permission."

This was news to me, and it left me vaguely chilled. "And?"

"He informed us that he'd prefer his records remain entirely confidential." The officer shrugged. He picked up another folder and opened it.

"Excuse me?" My first reaction was irritation—then something darker set in. "I am his daughter. And I'm only interested in knowing more about his service in the late fifties and early sixties."

"Oliver Sunnaret wasn't even a member of the armed services between 1955 and 1961, Ms. Sunnaret."

"Impossible. He was in Indochina the whole time I was little."

"Our record systems are quite exhaustive and impeccably accurate," he replied. "There is no doubt."

I reached over his desk and touched the folder with my family name on it. The officer slid it gently away. "If you don't have any more questions, I'm afraid I have to move on to my next appointment."

I was too stunned to respond quickly, and by the time I managed to say, "But I do have more questions," the colonel was halfway across the room, turning and sighing extravagantly to indicate exactly how patiently indulgent he was being.

"You're a disgrace to the uniform," Vito said quietly, standing to go.

"Pardon me?" The colonel flushed and compressed his lips.

"This is the man's daughter. If you feel you've got to feed her this crap, you go ahead and do it. I pity you."

The colonel said nothing more as we brushed by him on our way out. He opened the door, tilted his head stiffly in our direction to hurry us on our way and swung it shut behind us.

"Oh, I hope he was very helpful to you," the secretary said as we walked past her desk. "I'm sorry for your loss."

The words sounded sincere enough to set off a salty taste in my mouth and some rapid blinking, even though I knew intellectually that these were the same words she said to each of the hundreds—perhaps thousands—of people who filed past her.

"I didn't know what to say," I said to Vito. "I just wasn't prepared for that kind of . . . He was so absolute."

"It wouldn't have mattered what you asked," he said. "He wasn't about to help you. I was afraid this would happen but I figured better for you to see it yourself. Look, I know a place with phenomenal strawberry pie on the Number Ninety-two line, and I just happen to see a Number Ninety-two coming down the street at us as we speak."

I got on with him, rode the fifteen blocks and suffered myself to be guided into a cavernous cafeteria and set onto a stool before a slice of strawberry pie. There was a choice: baked or refrigerated. "I think we need to order both," Vito said to the counter clerk. "For comparison's sake."

"My father never left the service for a second. I'll go to Charlie and get this cleared up."

Vito speared the last triangle of pie, dredged it through the red residue of crushed strawberry. "Some things don't clear up," he said.

"Everything clears up if you scrub hard enough," I insisted.

"Iris, there are such things as people who don't officially exist. They volunteer to become invisible—their records disappear or they have no official records to begin with. Then they go on the kind of assignment that if something goes wrong, the military doesn't know who they are."

"Now you sound like my sister Angie."

"What does she say?"

"She said that war attracts vermin and thugs and immoral compromises."

"That's a fact. And probably the other stuff she said is right, too. There were lots of rumors about things that happened over there, officially and unofficially, and what I saw was worse than the rumors."

"How do you find out if a rumor is true?"

"You don't want to." He saw my expression and modified his answer. "You can't—not without help from people who have more influence than I do. I'm sorry, Iris."

"Don't be sorry. I'm grateful to know whatever I know, and it's clear to me now that no one in that office would have talked to me at all if you hadn't gotten the appointment. So how do you get to be personal friends with a congressman, anyhow?"

"You become part of a large Italian family with a father who grew up next door to him and gave him his first bloody nose and his first campaign contribution. You and your brother grow up with his son, who is your best friend."

"Is he still your best friend?"

"We enlisted together. He didn't come back."

"And your brother? Did he go, too?"

"No. I went instead. Two brothers don't have to . . ."

"Yes. I know the rule," I interrupted.

"He sold cars on Cicero Street in town and did quite well, thank you very much, and is now the dealership manager. Lovely wife and a beautiful little two-year-old named Rosemarie."

"I'm glad," I said.

"I am too."

"But you went to college?"

"I had the veterans' benefit. My brother didn't. So, I go to college. What are you going to tell Hank and your sister?"

"Probably nothing."

Vito just nodded.

"But I'm going to talk to my uncle Charlie," I added suddenly. "He went to military school with my father. They served together in the fifties. It's impossible that he wouldn't know exactly what my father was doing."

"Don't you think that if the man had anything to say to you that he would have said it already?"

Had Vito asked that question of me nine months before, it would have caused me no unhappiness, secure as I'd been in the idea of Uncle Charlie and Aunt Eleanor as openhearted protectors and guides, and my-self as living in the happiest of all places—their family. I would have said that the prices people paid were somewhat commensurate for what they got and the idea of paying for something with your own life wouldn't have even occurred to me despite the fact that I read about it in the papers every single day and one at least and possibly two of my brothers had given their lives in warfare. Now I was amazed at how much I had never bothered to be bothered by. "I don't know," I said. "I'll probably ask him anyhow."

We caught a 5:48 back to Charlottesville.

Easy to Love

I RENTED A CAR AND DROVE HOME WITHOUT WARNING AUNT Eleanor or Uncle Charlie that I was coming. I left right after a nine-o'clock class. Sophocles again:

> We heard his shout of triumph high in the air
> Turn to a scream: far out in a flaming arc
> He fell with his windy torch, and the earth struck him.
> And others storming in fury no less than his
> Found shock of death in the dusty joy of battle.
>
> Nothing you say can touch me any more.
> My own blind heart has brought me
> From darkness to final darkness. Here you see
> The father murdering, the murdered son—
> And all my civic wisdom!

This time I had translated it as easily as if I had written the passages myself a long time ago and then forgotten them, and then as the first words of the lines were exposed everything else opened up like a recalled scent or taste. "Very good, Miss Sunnaret," my instructor noted with visible surprise. I nodded at him. Yes, I thought—those are very good lines indeed.

I reached Uncle Charlie and Aunt Eleanor's city house by noon and let myself in with my own key, calling out their names as I moved through the empty rooms without expecting any reply. Uncle Charlie would be at work; Aunt Eleanor's car hadn't been in the drive. I headed directly for the study. I had lived in this house for almost all the autumns and winters of my life, but I had not been farther in this room than the doorway. I had stood here at the edge of the rug and summoned Uncle Charlie to dinner thousands of times, but never stepped into his sanctuary. Now I stood squarely in the center of the room and looked around me. Drawings of the Lake House, portraits of Hank, Angie, me, Aunt Eleanor, were framed and hanging on the wall facing my uncle's desk. Most of these were Perry's work. My uncle had loved his drawings, and Perry, I saw now, had lavished them on my uncle. I couldn't remember if they'd been there all along or were newly hung. I looked at them now with the other drawings in my mind. They'd been shaped with the same hand but perhaps a different mind than the ones I had in my brown envelopes.

Three oak file cabinets stood in a stiff line behind the desk, so bulky and scarred they might have been drifting from owner to owner for a century or more, making their way from some distant fly-infested colonial office of a great empire to more modest settings and, finally, of course, to this house.

Pictures of us as children hung in the hallway leading to the study, anchored on one end by a landscape with horses and a storm. Uncle Charlie had worked in Wyoming on a ranch the year before he went into the military and he said he had fallen in love with this picture because it reminded him of that time. The photographs on his desk were more familiar to me—the first one was the birthday Angie had gotten her gun. It sat side by side with the shot from the year I dropped Perry's cake on the way to the table. I'd cried, and Uncle Charlie had captured my misery on film. There was Eddie, aged about nine, standing uneasily on a foam surfboard in the middle of the lake. He'd been entirely possessed by the desire to surf that summer and he'd made us all line up behind him and cup our hands, pushing as much water toward him and his little foam surf-board as we could to provide him with waves. This photograph had been snapped, I knew, only a second before he fell into the water, the surfboard plunging down beneath his scrabbling feet before shooting up from under him as if launched, twisting in the air and narrowly missing his head on its descent. I didn't know if I actually remembered that or if I had been told the story and absorbed it as my own. That's the trouble with pictures, I thought—they shape stories to fit their own configurations rather than reality's. I remembered the photograph of Eddie on the surfboard as being funny, but as I walked past it today my nine-year-old brother had an unhinged kind of look that made me uneasy.

I had never opened the file drawers before—never been curious, in fact. Now I yanked the one holding family records open and flipped through the titles: Taxes, Car Insurance Policies, Instruction Manuals to Appliances. *Jacqueline Sunnaret.* I yanked this last folder out and opened it. *Marriage certificate. Dental records.* Dental records? Were there no personal letters, no keepsakes?

I started reading—turned out Sunnarets had impermeable enamel. My mother had had no more than a few fillings in her entire life. The marriage certificate held no surprises: Jacqueline Ariadne to Oliver Sunnaret, May 21, 1949. Then a surprise—a cracked envelope with the local police station address on the outside. I opened it and read: *Drowning, possibly related to drug overdose. Apparent suicide.*

"Iris?"

Aunt Eleanor, one hand on the door frame and the other arm still cradling a bag of groceries. "Iris, what are you doing home? Is anything wrong?"

"No, Aunt Eleanor. Nothing's wrong."

"You're white! What are you looking at?"

She saw the folder in my hand. I'd pushed the individual sheets back into it at the sound of my name, and the file label was invisible to her from where she stood. She set the groceries down and approached me, so distracted by my face that she didn't see the name on the file I'd just jammed back into place. Then I changed my mind and pulled it out, held it toward her.

"Aunt Eleanor, why has Uncle Charlie kept my mother's dental records?" I was surprised to hear anger in my voice as well as anxiety.

She stood her ground and looked at me carefully. "I don't know. He's an orderly man. And things like that," she added, trying to make this sound like a casual afterthought, "help identify bodies." She coughed and shifted to a sober, admonishing tone. "You shouldn't be in Charlie's records. You know how he feels about anybody being in his study."

I laid the folder down on top of its fellows. "Where's her death certificate, then? You said it was an accident, Aunt Eleanor."

"Her body wasn't found, so there is no death certificate. Only a police report. Iris, we told you the truth. Your mother drowned—a terrible accident."

"It says here, 'Probable suicide due to a drug overdose.' "

Eleanor pushed the file back down among its fellows and shoved the drawer shut. "You come to the kitchen and start dinner with me. Get that second bag of groceries," she commanded, picking up the first where she'd set it on a chair. I obeyed. Once in the kitchen she unpacked with grim determination, talking as she worked.

"The doctor who wrote the police report only used the words 'drug overdose' because he didn't want anyone to think he hadn't given her clear instructions about the pills."

"What pills?"

"The pills he'd given her to even out her mood. People taking them can get confused and forget when they took the last one. Their judgment isn't very good. They can go swimming when they're too tired, really, to do it. That's what happened to your mother—a terrible, tragic accident."

"What was wrong with her mood? What did she need relief from?"

"How can anyone who wasn't her know that? Your father was away so much, and when he did get home he was changed. Distant. Hard. I don't know how to say it. They loved each other, Iris, I'm not saying they didn't love each other. He couldn't have made her so desperately unhappy unless she was in love with him. But it looked to me like they might not have gone on together. Your father was disappearing into whatever he was be-coming in Indochina. When I first met him he was so . . . brilliant. And then he left for Indochina and every time we saw him or heard from him after that he was dark. Then darker.

"At first she was proud of his work, but then they started fighting about it. She was so fiery when they started out. He loved that in her. But she changed—they both did. He'd come back from Southeast Asia and you could see him getting silent and hooded, and her getting more colorless. Maybe he stopped loving her then. She got so terribly sad," Aunt Eleanor continued. "She started doing odd things—leaving you places. When you were younger, one or two, she used to put you in that little baby swing we'd hung from the big maple and wander off. It got worse. And it just kept on and on. Once she left you in a store and came home without you. Perry was the first one to notice you were gone. He got me to come over because she couldn't remember where you were and he was frightened."

"I don't remember that."

"Well, that might have happened when you were four. Five, maybe. You were just six when she died. When we retraced her steps we found you sitting outside the five-and-dime store on the mechanical horse."

"I remember the horse. I had three dimes and got three rides."

"You don't remember being frightened?"

I had been frightened sometimes, certainly. I could remember that feeling. And I remembered the horse. I tried moving backward or for-ward from the memory of the horse and my dimes, my pink purse and the little zipper pocket that held my dimes. There had been the candy aisle and the aisle with plastic soldiers and cowboys, holsters and cap guns, assemble-your-own bow and arrow sets. How I had loved that store. But I did not remember being left there all alone.

"Wasn't I with Angie or Perry or somebody? Wasn't I all right?"

"Is a four-year-old left alone in a store all right? Maybe. If she's lucky. And maybe not if she isn't. That day she left you at the store was when I knew we had to do something. You were a wanderer. A thunderstorm had started during dinner and she'd put the meal on the table but you weren't there—not in your fort in the backyard or on the swings or in the house. She didn't say a word—just kept laying down the silver while we got more and more frantic, asking her to tell us where you were. Perry kept asking her and she was just shrugging. He was practically hysterical by the time he showed up on my doorstep asking for help. It took us another hour to track back through her afternoon with her and figure out that she'd driven away with you and come back without you."

"Where was our father?"

"Overseas."

"So you all just went looking for me?"

My aunt nodded. "We looked at all the bags and receipts she had to figure out where she'd been. That's how we got to the five-and-dime. She knew something terrible was happening to her, Iris. She tried to explain it but I didn't really understand. She died the month before your sixth birthday. She called me just the day before it happened, but I didn't understand."

"What did she say?" I asked.

"She said she was afraid she'd hurt you," Aunt Eleanor said. "But I think I knew that already. So that day when she came back without you, imagine what was in my head! That was when I asked her to make up the papers—the ones that gave all of you to Charlie and me temporarily in case something happened and your father so far away . . . I told her she could count on me and Charlie and she signed them. But she wasn't in her right mind when she did it."

"You mean she didn't really want us to come to you?"

"No, no. I only mean that she was in a terrible state. She trusted us completely. She knew we'd love you."

"Why didn't someone contact our father and tell him to come home?"

"You can't just come home from some kinds of places, dear. Your father was in one of those places."

"Did Angie and the boys know about the pills?"

My aunt nodded. Yes.

"But I didn't?"

She shook her head from side to side. No.

"Why not?"

"They were older and can remember your mother, Iris—they remember the way she looked and what she did. You don't have the same memories. And I swear I'd never thought of it as selfish until right this instant, but we didn't want you to change. You were so exactly right just as you were: open and happy and always with your eye on the next good thing."

"That makes me sound like a simpleton, Aunt Eleanor—like a child."

Aunt Eleanor flapped a hand at me impatiently. "Well, you were a child, for God's sake. And you should have been allowed to be a child. Iris, some people are very hard to love. It's your gift that you're easy and that gift deserves protection. If you don't see it that way now I'm sure you will in the future."

"How could knowing a little more about my parents have hurt me?"

"It might not have. It changed your brothers and your sister, though. It made Perry more worried, more protective of you others. It made Eddie more detached." She stopped and then she added, "Made Angie more . . . I don't know. But you were the sunny one, always."

"And then," I added, "then later our father gave you and Charlie full legal custody."

"Yes. Then you were ours entirely."

Aunt Eleanor approached me; put her arms around me. I didn't think. My own arms lifted thoughtlessly and I embraced her as I always did, and felt a sharp little pang when relief flooded her face. Suddenly I recognized why I'd felt the house was different: things were overly symmetrical. It wasn't the pictures that had changed; it was the evenly placed candlesticks beneath them on the lowboy and the bowl, no longer sitting comfortably but pushed into a military kind of line. I noticed, finally, that as we'd unpacked she'd pulled out three or four things to rearrange by expiration date and chucked a protein that had made its way into a group of carbohydrates right into the trash.

"Aunt Eleanor, do you have any other pictures of her? Of both of them?"

She nodded, stepped out of my arms and indicated that I should fol-

low her back down the hallway and up the stairs to her and Uncle Charlie's room. I hesitated at the threshold, trained from toddlerhood to regard this space as forbidden. "You can come in," she said. "If you're old
enough to ask about them, finally, then you're old enough to come in."
She turned her back on me and opened a jewelry case on her dressing
table. I could hear the clinking of earrings and pins as she rummaged.

"Here," she said, holding a silver frame out to me. "It's all of us. I kept
it because it was such a happy night."

I reached out my hand. There in the photograph were two shining couples at a formal military affair, Uncle Charlie and my father in dress
whites; Aunt Eleanor and my mother in floor-length gowns. They held
champagne flutes. My mother was laughing, her head tossed back and her
white throat exposed.

"She's so beautiful," I breathed.

"That's the least of it, my dear. You were too little to remember her
like this; maybe too little to remember her at all, but your mother was
magnetic—playful, a wonderful dancer—seemed to make up the rules
for wherever she was just because she could. Your father had to elbow
aside quite a crowd of young hopefuls to get his first dance with her."

"Angie remembers sitting and watching her get dressed. She said she
was a queen, and that made us princesses."

Aunt Eleanor took the frame from my hands and examined it carefully, holding it close. "Yes. She was a queen."

"And my father?"

"The brightest of the bright. He probably had the highest scores on
code-breaking skill assessments of any man who's taken the tests. But he
didn't want to work in an office on codes." She touched the picture's
frame, examined the portrait again. "Your sister is right: they were a
kind of royalty."

"Why didn't you show me the picture before?"

"I know it sounds like a simplistic explanation, Iris, but you haven't
asked about them. And I've always thought that the best way to know
when to say things is when people ask you to say them."

"When was this picture taken?"

"The year that your mother got pregnant with Perry. You can't see it in this black-and-white photograph, but my dress was a kind of robin's-egg blue. Your mother's was red—that was her color. Dark hair, black eyes, white skin. You know the story, honey—how your father and Charlie were at military school together and then they met us, and your mother and I were just, instantly, best friends. I had never had a best friend." Aunt Eleanor stopped for a moment and ran a finger over the picture. "We had this romantic idea, like we were going to make ourselves the four musketeers or something. What did we know?"

"And then our father and Uncle Charlie went to Indochina together. What were they doing there, Aunt Eleanor?"

"We learned not to ask. Wives kept the home a place to retreat from all that—that was our job. I didn't care for the fact that a lot of what they did was classified. I never cared for secrets. But your father and Charlie—secrets were their lifeblood."

"Secrets like CIA planes flying heroin in and out of mountainous country?"

"Angie's been talking to you, hasn't she?" Aunt Eleanor snorted just a little.

"Yes."

"Angie doesn't understand, Iris. She tries to bully very complicated information into simpler shapes. Lots of people do that when they're young. She'll outgrow it eventually."

"But it's true?"

"I can't answer that," she said.

"Could Uncle Charlie?"

"Perhaps. But I doubt if he would."

"Aunt Eleanor, is it true that Uncle Charlie told Angie not to come home again?"

"She shouldn't have told you that."

"I would notice if she wasn't here sooner or later, Aunt Eleanor."

"That's why you've come, then." Aunt Eleanor shook her head and sat down heavily on her bed. "Iris, you can't make things right between your sister and Charlie. Time will do that. Don't interfere."

"But if it isn't fixed between Angie and Uncle Charlie, then things can't be right between me and Uncle Charlie; between me and you."

"If that's the way you see it, then perhaps you'll have to tolerate that."

She didn't sound blaming or frustrated: she was sad; sorry to have to say these things, sorry to have to endure the mess brewing in her once orderly and smoothly operating household.

"Aunt Eleanor, Angie's only taking a simple moral position that a lot of other people hold as well."

"And what would that be?"

"That war is bad. That's all."

"If everyone believed that war was bad then there would be no wars. Unfortunately, a lot of people like war. Your sister is ignoring history as well as a good deal of current information."

"It's not just how she feels about war. I think that, in her way, she's trying to stand up for Perry and Eddie."

Aunt Eleanor's face seemed to suddenly fly apart right in front of me. "How is giving money to people who kill police officers, people who break the law and dismantle civic life, standing up for Perry and Eddie? How is seducing Hank honoring the memory of her brothers?"

"Aunt Eleanor, that's not fair!"

"What's this?" Uncle Charlie stood in the bedroom doorway, a briefcase in one hand and a glass of water in the other. "I called when I came in but no one heard me. What are you girls up to?" His smile faded as he saw that we were, actually, up to something. He set the briefcase and water down and crossed the room briskly, and even through the unfamiliar anger and anxiety in my conversation with Aunt Eleanor I could feel the familiar happy lifting in my chest when he walked toward me, smiling again and holding out his arms. He kissed the top of my head and folded me into his arms. When he moved to slip his suitcoat off and toss it into a chair I saw with a pang that he walked with a crooked hitch as if trying to avoid pain in his hip. I sought out his face and found a new papery quality to the skin. "I knew there was some reason I felt I had to come home early today," he said. "And what's the reason for this unexpected visit?" he asked.

Aunt Eleanor and I blinked and stared. Uncle Charlie's face lost its happy animation. "It's the Angie thing, isn't it?"

"That has come up," Aunt Eleanor said dryly.

He turned to me. "I'm afraid it's really not your business, Iris. It concerns my son and your sister. Not you."

This was, of course, patently ridiculous. "But Uncle Charlie . . ."

"Please, Iris. Please."

I felt a little panicky jolt. Uncle Charlie pleaded with his children no more than he would plead with one of his dogs.

"Uncle Charlie, Angie was only doing what thousands of people do—giving money to a cause they think is just. That doesn't mean a lot. And is it so terrible for her and Hank to go out?"

" 'Go out'? Is that what it's called now? And as to the rest of it, Iris, I don't think you know enough to form an opinion."

"How can you condemn Angie, and say nothing about Hank?"

Uncle Charlie didn't look at me when he spoke now. "What we've said or not said to Hank isn't part of this conversation. You make assumptions, Iris, that may not be accurate."

I charged ahead, heedless. "Angie can't control how boys react to her. She didn't pursue Hank. She isn't responsible for how Hank feels or what he chooses to do about how he feels."

"Perhaps, but she's responsible for how she herself acts," my uncle said. "And when I look at her I see a young woman who does what she wants. Period."

"Uncle Charlie, Hank was the pursuer. You know that."

"Young men will tend to pursue. But young women don't need to be provocative," he said stiffly. He clearly wanted the conversation to change direction. He had gotten his tie off and now he went to the closet, hanging it in the tie rack in the same place he'd found it that morning.

"You mean how she looks? She can't change her looks. And what Angie wore, everybody wore. It just looked different on Angie. That doesn't speak to her moral fiber."

"You don't understand. You're too young." He shook his head sadly.

"Angie didn't do anything to encourage him!"

Uncle Charlie's voice rose and cracked. "How can you be so naive, my dear? I doubt if you saw the half of what she was."

I was too shocked by the bitterness in his voice to speak for a moment. Then I was angry. I said, "Well, Uncle Charlie, they say people only see what they look for."

"Iris!" This from Aunt Eleanor. Her husband, standing beside her, had gone white, and then pink.

"You will apologize for that," Aunt Eleanor said.

"I'm sorry," I said. "I'm sorry for this whole mess. It would be better if I didn't stay."

"I'm going to wash up," Uncle Charlie said, turning heavily. "Iris, of course you'll stay. Please. We're going to find a way through this."

He lumbered through the door and off in the direction of the bathroom.

"I'm going, Aunt Eleanor."

"Honey, you can't walk out that door after saying something so sharp and hurtful to your uncle. Not until some kind of peace is made. Come on back down to the kitchen and help me with supper."

I sat miserably, peeling vegetables and weighing my desire to bolt against my love for Uncle Charlie, tempering both of these considerations with a terrible fear that I had been right when I suggested that he had looked for provocation when he looked at my sister. I had thought I'd spoken in defense of Angie. But I had simply said what I thought instead of saying what might reconcile the parties involved.

"Aunt Eleanor," I said, raising my head and speaking softly enough so someone coming down the stairs could be easily heard. "How did you and Uncle Charlie first learn that Hank and Angie had become involved?"

"Charlie was going through a routine security update at work. It surfaced as part of the family check."

"If it was a security clearance check, though, its contents would never have been passed on to him, would it? I mean, he was the subject of the check. It doesn't make any sense that information gathered in that process would be handed to him."

Aunt Eleanor stopped what she was doing, looked at me quizzically. "I don't . . ."

My heart sank. The security check story was simply a story.

"Here," she said, holding out a peeler, wiping at her eye with a forearm as she held it out to me. "That's enough history. Enough for me, anyway. Pick up that potato there."

We peeled more than we needed, lulled by the comforting useful dipping strokes.

Deeper

THAT NIGHT I SLEPT UNEASILY ABOVE THE FAMILIAR SOUNDS OF my aunt and uncle talking softly, moving around the kitchen, closing down the house just as I had heard them closing down the house a thousand times before: the sound of a bolt being thrown, a door handle jostled, a light switch flipped. I knew that I would wake to the sound of a pot hitting the stovetop and the smell of coffee, and I did.

By the time I got downstairs, Uncle Charlie had left for work. Aunt Eleanor sat alone with a cup of coffee smoking on the table beneath her nose. "Eggs?" she asked.

"You sit, Aunt Eleanor. I'm big enough to make my own eggs." I smiled as I said it and she smiled vaguely back.

I opened the refrigerator, retrieved the eggs, pulled a pan down from the rack. I let a pat of butter hit the bottom of the pan when it was hot enough to spit and dropped the eggs onto the bubbling fat. I stood at the stove with my back to her as I beat and poured and stirred.

Aunt Eleanor rearranged her weight in her seat. "You have to get back to school this morning, I know," she said, "but before you leave I just need you to hear me clearly because your feelings for your uncle Charlie, and me, too, I guess, are getting sharp—and I'm asking you to be fair. Charlie didn't change things. Hank and Angie did, and they can't be put back the way they were."

"You could make it better," I said, turning to face her now.

She spoke briskly. "The biggest thing you'll ever need to learn growing up is that not only are there consequences to the things people do, but that the doer has got to face the consequences. And I have no magic wand to make it all fixed."

"But what do you have against Angie? You love her. You know her through and through, Aunt Eleanor."

"I do." She turned her face away from me and made a huffing noise. "And I wish I didn't. Sometimes I look at that girl and see your mother."

"But that's a good thing. Our mother was your best friend. That's what you said."

"She was until the end. Then she wasn't anymore."

"I'm my mother's daughter, too, Aunt Eleanor. Just like Angie."

"I don't see your mother in you, baby. You were different from the others right from the get-go."

My initial, unthinking response to these words was happiness—the response of a child who understood from the parent's tone that she was loved. But then came shame: this infant narcissism would not help me navigate the choppy surf I faced now, the slapping scend of one value slicing across another; the deep undertow of history and something else I couldn't name yet. I finished my breakfast, kissed my aunt good-bye and trudged out to the rented car to begin my trip back to the university.

On the drive home, I found myself trying to imagine what had passed between my guardians and their son when Hank last visited them. Surely the same things that had been said to me had been said to him. Had he tried to use his parents' love for him as a lever to move their position? Had he come to Angie's defense, or had he simply fallen back into propitiating gestures?

And then there was this new vision of my own mother, and my family's silence about her. I tried to imagine Hank knowing all this when he was nine years old, being told it at the breakfast table as his parents explained why we would be living with them. I imagined my aunt and uncle watching us, going home and talking about what to do from the privacy of their bedroom after Hank had gone to sleep, deciding to step forward and care for us. I was not only used to thinking of them as supporters and guides—I loved thinking of them that way. I was deeply unwilling to challenge these old feelings. Yet now I could imagine them repudiating a child, judging and choosing to sacrifice the child rather than give way and forgive. They would not concede that Hank could be right, or that right and wrong were not always so important. If I admitted this less happy picture of Aunt Eleanor and Uncle Charlie into my ideas about them, what else would have to shift?

There in my memory was Aunt Eleanor's face shining with happiness in the rowboat, lifting the oar and hooting on the occasion of my courageous first dive from the tippy little board on our lake float. There is Uncle Charlie on one knee, offering a dandelion he had plucked on his way into the house where I sit, weeping because I was not asked to the prom, asking if I would honor him by escorting him to the most extravagant restaurant within a hundred miles. I had been so sure that I would never for the rest of my life forget the way I felt about that prom, but by the time my veal Oscar arrived, I had. Not entirely—but enough.

There was the terrible power to make them unhappy as well—the terror I'd seen on Uncle Charlie's face when Perry accidentally clonked me on the head with a baseball bat backswing, Aunt Eleanor's real anxiety when I'd lost a pet hamster and cried for four hours straight into the night. There was a profound gentleness in their attitude toward me and there always had been. It could not have been shaped by duty alone. They had to have loved me—really loved me.

And I had always assumed they loved Angie and the boys. Now I found myself confronting a naked revulsion toward her, and her certainty that they had betrayed my brothers by lying to them about what war really was.

Had I been loved as I'd thought myself loved?

I tried to resume my life when I got back to Charlottesville but couldn't make sense of what had been absolutely routine only a week before. I opened the grammar book to the optative mood, a psychological distinction acknowledged by the Greeks but basically lost to modern speakers. Page 398: "The optative functions as a past tense to the subjunctive. Invent examples for the following moods":

Exercise question number one: "Offer an example of a past general conditional statement with the optative." I penciled in what I hoped was translatable as, *If anyone was ever abandoned, she was helped.*

Question number two: "Offer an example of the past contrary-to-fact condition." I tried, *If she had been abandoned, she would have been likely to lie about it.*

In the end it didn't sound terribly Greek to me, or to my professor, who wrote in the margin: "ἄv is never used with the protasis of a past contrafactual condition."

I swore I'd remember that, but I didn't.

Her Perfect Body

THE LIBRARY STACKS IN THE UPPER LEVELS WERE LIT BY narrow windows at the ends of each double column of shelves. The windows looked out directly at the setting sun on one side of the stacks and the rising sun at the other. Nestled into each of these beautifully lit corners was a desk, an electrical outlet and a chain link door barring all but the holder of its key. Graduate students tended to hold these keys, but in some instances enterprising seniors got one—as Hank had. He was one of the selfish extravagant kind of keyholders, leaving his little cage unused most days while other applicants, trapped in tiny apartments with loud roommates, applied for a gated cubicle in vain. And so when I wanted to find Hank, this little corner of his was the last place I looked—but after I called his room, went to his door in person, peered in the windows of his favorite diner and walked through the student union, I climbed the library stairs and made my way past an eighth of a mile of books on every war in which the United States had ever been engaged. There he was, at the end of the row of spines relating to World War I.

I should have been at my own desk. I'd tried, but my efforts to understand how the Athenian fleet under Alcibiades had fared in its attack on the Spartan fleet under Mindarus near Cyzicus had been fruitless. I looked down at the gnarled, stumbling translation I'd managed and ripped it up. Who could make sense of "Being hidden along towards the Aklesean so as the ship put out to sea while it was raining for Cyzicus"? It was probably just a matter of time before my advisers recommended I find a new major. In the meantime here I sat, defeated by the optative conditional and descriptions of battles that had taken place four thousand years before I was born. I closed my lexicon, flipped my text shut and went to seek Hank.

Hank had to know more about my mother than I did—perhaps he even knew more about her than my sister did. He had been so much older than I when we were folded into his family, and perhaps he'd had greater access to what his own parents knew than we Sunnarets had. Thus my satisfaction at finally seeing his silhouette against the narrow window of his study carrel.

The cages to either side of him were vacant except for the forty or so books piled in each. One of them held a small pantry's supply of cereal, soft drink cans and Frito-Lay chips. The other one held only books. Food was technically forbidden here, but library staff had never been sighted up in the deeper recesses of the stacks, which loosened any tendency to worry about rules.

Hank's cage was spartan: only the books immediately before him and his backpack at his feet. He didn't see me approach and he jumped when I spoke his name.

"God! Don't do that!"

"I'm sorry, Hank. I wasn't trying to frighten you."

"I don't think I've ever seen another human being up here in daylight hours. The other people on this floor all work at night. And I've never seen you up here." He closed his book.

We were talking through the chain link gate but this barrier suited us at the moment—kept us enough at a distance that either of us could make some excuse and disengage; claim to only have been in the library looking for a book; claim to need to study and be unable to stop for conversation. Hank seemed aware of this, but after a clear moment of consideration he leaned forward and unlatched his little door. He nodded at the second chair in his cage and I stepped in and sat down.

"I went home yesterday," I said.

"You were trying to fix this thing with Angie, weren't you? God, Iris." He shook his head.

"I looked in Uncle Charlie's filing cabinet and opened one of the folders labeled 'Sunnaret.' I found a copy of a police report on my mother's drowning."

"Why would Daddy have that in a file cabinet?" Hank was sincerely surprised. He swiveled in his chair and faced me squarely now.

"It said she overdosed on pills and it was a probable suicide."

Hank's posture stiffened and his face lost much of its human animation. It was as if he'd turned certain internal knobs that controlled his vitality—his connections to anything outside himself. "Really?" His voice had flattened and cooled.

"Uncle Charlie and Aunt Eleanor said it was an accident. That the doctor had prescribed the pills because she was depressed and she hadn't understood how dangerous they could be if she didn't follow instructions."

"Well, that makes sense," he said. His face remained puppetlike.

I leaned in a bit to scrutinize. I had seen that look on Hank's face. I remembered it, but there was something odd about the memory—something that couldn't have been accurate. Then it struck me. The thing that was inaccurate was my father, who should not have been in the memory yet who was very much there indeed.

"Hank, did my father come back, ever, after my mother died?"

"Yes. Sure."

"Do you remember him punishing Eddie for something? Arguing with Aunt Eleanor about something Eddie had done?"

"He punished Eddie all the time. Eddie could be hard to handle. Defiant. Why? Why are you asking?"

"No reason." But the word "defiant" had spun the memory out into completion. Now I could see Hank's puppet face—not the one I'd just seen now but the one in the memory where he stood frozen in the kitchen doorway watching my brother Eddie fall to his knees and lie on his belly in the middle of the linoleum expanse.

"What's the matter?" Hank asked, leaning toward me. "Your face just got white." I shook my head vigorously from side to side.

"Nothing. I'm not sure. Nothing," I said to Hank.

But I was remembering Aunt Eleanor in the pink dress she wore all through the summer of 1962, standing with a blue bowl in her hands. She was speaking to my father, who sat at the kitchen table with a cup of coffee in his hands, and she was upset. She was saying, *"He's just hard to control. Since Jackie died he's just so . . . defiant." She is talking about my brother Eddie, who is not in the room. Aunt Eleanor says, "I hate to burden you with this as soon as you walk in the door, but you have so little contact with them . . ."*

"Eddie!" This from my father, a trumpeting, authoritative call. Eddie appears in the kitchen. "Well?" my father says to him. Hank and Perry have drifted toward the call, too, and come to rest at the room's periphery.

"Well, what?" Eddie says.

"You say, 'Yes, sir,' " he is told.

Eddie hesitates. He drags one flappy little-boy foot in a circle and says nothing. My father gives him a look that makes up his mind.

"Yes, sir," my brother says.

"Lie down," my father says.

"What?"

"I said lie down." My father speaks in a different voice this time—a scary, quiet voice. Eddie drops to his knees. My father fixes him with a steady directing eye, and Eddie sinks farther, his belly hitting the linoleum and his knees sliding out behind him, until he lies entirely facedown on the floor.

My father then returns his attention to the cup of coffee on the table before him. "See?" he says to Eleanor, not even bothering to look at her as he speaks. He picks up his cup and sips. "He isn't so hard to handle."

"Get up," Aunt Eleanor says angrily to my brother. "Don't you lie on that floor, Eddie Sunnaret!"

My father turns to her. "He's mine, and he'll always be mine. You have him on loan. And I say he lies there."

I am frightened. My aunt Eleanor's face is white with fury, and my clear sense is that she is going to do something that will tip the balance of this scene in dangerous directions. Eddie, in this memory, does not seem as rattled as Hank and Perry, who stand in the doorway and watch. Eddie accepts his position: he has his place. We, on the other hand, do not.

Then the memory stops. Where was I in this memory? I can see my aunt, my brothers, Hank, but where am I? Why do I know what Hank's face looks like at this moment, and how Eddie's pants bunch up so his ankles are exposed above his socks as he lies there, but I don't know where I am in this picture?

"He made Eddie lie down on the floor," I said.

"Are you all right?"

Footsteps and then the metallic scrambling of a key in a metal lock— one of Hank's neighbors was arriving for work. "Why didn't he take us away with him when he remarried?" I whispered, a vain attempt at privacy in an environment where every mousy chewing away at a book spine could be heard.

"It wouldn't have made sense. You all were in school, settled with us, my folks already running your lives. It would have been too disruptive for you to have been shipped off to a stepmother in another country. Right?"

"Everybody agreed? That's how your parents explained why we stayed with you?"

"Hey, Hank! Got anything to eat?" This from the neighbor without supplies.

"Nope," Hank yelled back. Then, to me, in a hissing whisper: "Don't waste your time, Iris. Worry about something that matters."

"Maybe he's the reason our mother died."

"Your mother drowned. How could he be the reason your mother died?"

"I don't know." I sat back with my spine pressed against the chair rungs. "It just occurs to me."

But Hank was back to my sister again; my mesmerizing sister. He said, "Iris, you understand how I feel about Angie. I know you do."

"How do you know I do? What have I ever said that would make you think that I'm particularly able to 'understand'?"

"You can put yourself in other people's situations. That's all I meant."

"Maybe I'm not so good at that as you think," I said.

He continued as if I hadn't said anything. "The first time Angie and I made love was the night that drunk came to the house to tell us what he claimed happened to Eddie and Perry."

"I don't want to hear this." My kiss with Vito came joltingly to mind, tasting of salt water and grass; the smell of his starched shirt.

"Please. Please listen."

I looked him in the eye, intending to deny him what struck me at the moment as a selfish indulgence, but our history laid down the present moment: between us, he had always been the indulged and I always the indulging. Now I didn't want to indulge him.

Had the kiss with Vito made me different? I could imagine this scene that Hank described in ways that only a short time ago I would not have understood. Had I simply been told that I would develop this acuity I would have been naively pleased; now that I indeed had the ability to understand him, I hated it.

Hank kept talking. He said, "I was stunned, actually. I'd begun to get used to the idea that Angie would always reject me, but that night after that Thompson guy left she asked me to go for a walk. I said yes. I would have said yes if she'd asked me to eat Borax, probably. She led me to this little meadow I'd never even known about."

"I know that meadow," I said.

"How do you know it?"

I felt irritation at his surprise, his insulated idea that his relationship with Angie was entirely exclusive and unique. "Wildflowers and grasses on one half," I went on. "Moss and shallow pine roots on the other. Scrub oak on the side opposite the pines."

"That's what it was."

"Angie and I had our castle in one of the trees at its edge," I murmured. "We were princesses there. Eddie and Perry weren't allowed. I could go show you where we buried our jewels the last time we played in that spot together. I think I was seven."

He nodded but his disinterest in my childhood memories was clear. "It was late in the season—cool but sunny. The grass was yellow and the summer flowers gone to seed except for a few purple gay feathers. She told me to turn around, and I did. She told me to turn back again, and she was lying there naked on this thick green moss, all framed in that green with the purple and brown behind her. Her body was perfect. Perfect."

He stopped speaking and I could see that my sister was in his mind now just as she had been that day, and this image commanded him entirely. Her perfect body. I had been in the kitchen, probably, brewing coffee and wandering in little circles while my sister had led Hank farther and farther from home.

"We made love. Then she said that she wanted me to think of it as something that had happened once but would never happen again—an aberration. We walked back together and there was the house, and you all, and dinner. I can remember being amazed that everything for me had changed and all around me nothing had changed. There you all were sitting behind your plates eating salad. I couldn't believe it."

"But it did happen again," I said.

He nodded. "I became this kind of monster. I have actually felt glad that Perry and Eddie died because I'm sure that otherwise that afternoon would never have happened to me." Hank's face sank into his hands but he didn't stop talking. "I knew even then that she wanted some kind of release and I was just . . . there. I could never have persuaded her to be my lover, just me all alone. Something had to happen to help me. And Perry and Eddie happened. Then I realize what I'm feeling and I try to take it back but it's too late, you know? You can't do the impossible. And I haven't told anyone about that feeling but you. You know what it's like, wanting to take back a feeling but it being too late."

"What do you think I've wanted to take back?" I asked, surprised.

"Being jealous of Angie," he answered without missing a beat.

It was clear to me that he didn't mean jealousy of Angie's dominion over him. He meant jealousy in more general terms: jealousy of the way she moved through the world.

"Even if I were, that's not exactly being glad that my brothers are dead, is it?" I said sharply.

"Don't be mean, Iris."

He was right. I wanted to hurt him. "If only you'd said no, Hank. If only you hadn't let it happen."

"I couldn't control what happened!"

"Of course you could have! What kind of excuse is that?"

"It wouldn't have stopped this, though, Iris—all of this. It would just have delayed it." Hank's arm swept his little cubicle and the stacks beyond it as if the destiny he imagined included even the Chee-tos in the next cage, even the rows of books beyond his little cage with names of wars running up their spines.

"Angie was heading out of her old life into something else. Sleeping with me was kind of a swinging door leading out. I think she knew that if she slept with me she'd never be able to walk back into my daddy's house the way she last walked out of it. And she wanted so badly to leave."

"You're afraid she doesn't love you." I didn't pose this as a question.

"Of course I am. But even if she didn't love me I'd still stay with her if she let me."

I asked the question that I knew was what I'd wanted to say all along but had managed to withhold. "How long do you think she'll stay with you, anyway?"

"I can't control how long it lasts but I'm going to be there for the whole of it," he said grimly.

"What will Uncle Charlie do?"

"I can't make all my decisions based on my daddy's possible reactions, Iris. It's too late, anyway."

"You mean too late because he already knows about you and Angie?"

"Oh, it's more too late than that. How do you think he felt when I didn't enlist?"

"I didn't think about it," I said.

"Momma was just as happy to see me stay out of it but he wasn't. If he could have handpicked his son instead of just getting him from simple biology, he would have had Eddie. Eddie was born to go to a war. And Perry was loyal. Those were the things Daddy valued. When he looked at me, he saw somebody who was easy to push around. The thing with Angie just confirmed his ideas about how easily manipulated I am."

"I don't believe that. How many squabbles did you smooth over between your father and Eddie when nobody else could? That takes authority, and generosity."

"Well, there's something that's different between you and my daddy. What you see as a kind of power he sees as a weakness."

"Aunt Eleanor didn't want anybody to go to war. Not even Perry and Eddie."

"I know that. But your father was a military man, too. And he wanted them to go to war."

"How do you know that?"

"Things that Perry and Eddie said when they came back from that trip to see him just before they enlisted."

"Things like what?"

"Maybe it was more what they wanted to hear than what he said. How would I know? I wasn't there. But Eddie came back with this romantic vision of the soldier hero in his mind."

"Did Perry come back talking the same way?"

"You'd know as well as me," Hank answered. "But offhand I'd say not." He flipped open a book and bent over it, his gaze entirely too fixed for him to actually be reading.

"Did they say anything about us?" I asked.

"Who's 'us'?"

"Angie and me. Do you know of anything that my father ever said about what he thought was important for us?"

"You're girls," Hank said simply. Then, after an awkward pause, "Well. I've got a lot to catch up on."

I nodded, dismissed, and padded away down the long narrow aisle that stretched from Gettysburg to Pearl Harbor on either side of me.

Trying New Things

TUPPERWARE DID INDEED KEEP FRIED SQUIRREL BRAIN relatively fresh, and Danny tossed it into a little pan with some butter to reheat it for me.

"I knew you'd try it. I had faith in you." He beamed.

Squirrel brain, it turned out, was creamy—the crunchy fried exterior made a pleasing contrast and butter, in my opinion, never hurt anything it came into contact with.

"Not bad, Danny."

"I only know this one thing. Otherwise I just live on Cap'n Crunch, salami and Denny's pancakes. But I do love squirrel brains."

Danny had been, as he so often was, the first thing I'd seen when I walked up the dirt path that served as a driveway to our house. There I found him at the other end of Square Root's leash, waiting patiently while his bearlike companion peed on a car tire. Rootie dropped his leg and wagged his tail furiously when he saw me.

"So," Danny said. "Your love life has clearly not taken a turn for the better, given what your face looks like right at this moment."

"My love life hasn't changed since the last time you saw me," I answered.

"Well, you come on in. I've got a cure for that mood of yours."

I followed Danny into his dark little first-floor apartment and sat at his linoleum kitchen table. He moved among the piles of unwashed dishes, purposeful and serene.

"My great-grandmamma and my grandmamma were both Welsh," he said, pulling down plates and tossing butter into a pan. "And they believed in having a real tea—sandwiches, or fried-up whatever came in that afternoon with the boys. You and me'll have what she called a proper tea." He rooted through his freezer, popped open the Tupperware and revealed all that was left of a squirrel's mind.

"But it's frozen, Danny," I protested.

"Don't you worry. Put it in a plastic bag, run some cold water over it a few minutes, drop it in poppin' grease and you got yourself something almost as good as fresh. You wouldn't believe how happy my grandmamma was when these freezer bag thingies got invented. I tell you, it's gonna be heaven."

It wasn't heaven, but it was marvelously soothing: the fussing Danny, Rootie's cold nose pressed into the palm of a free hand, the brains themselves giving way through a crunchy exterior to a custardlike center.

"A person can go a long, long way on nothing but this," he sighed, forking more onto my plate.

"Really. How long can you go on eating squirrel brains?"

"You can go just about forever on something if you've convinced yourself it's enough," he answered. Danny set the beer he'd been lifting back onto the table. "Do you think I could shape a romantic evening around this dish?"

"Maybe. But you should widen your repertoire."

He sighed. "I don't have so much interest in cooking as I do in romance." He eyed me carefully. "Now you're a girl whose mood can be swayed by a man with a spatula in his hand, aren't you?" He picked up a spatula and demonstrated a gentle little arc over his plate.

"You've been very sweet, Danny, but remember you just told me you basically live on Cap'n Crunch and salami."

"That's true. I shouldn't have done that." He grinned. He took the last remaining bit of organ meat and crouched down at Rootie's level. He held the treat a few feet from Rootie's nose. "Wrestle me for it, dog!" he said playfully, and the command must have been familiar for Rootie launched himself directly at Danny's chest, twisting his head as he rose through the air to snap at the tidbit that was held just beyond his reach. Danny laughed and let the Labrador's weight carry them both onto the floor. Rootie got the meat between his teeth but before he could swallow it Danny pinned the dog against his own side with an elbow and took a firm hold of Rootie's snout, twisting it at an angle and pretending to snatch the treat from between the dog's jaws. Something about the angle of the dog's head made my stomach drop.

"What's the matter?" Danny said, looking at my face and getting very still.

"Nothing," I said brightly, setting my hand firmly on the counter because I'd noticed that it shook some. "I just, for a second there, it looked like Rootie was going to get hurt." I stood, suddenly very eager to get back to my own apartment, my familiar rooms. "Thanks for the tea, Danny. I'm heading back upstairs."

I hurried out Danny's door and up the stairs to my half of the house.

I RECEIVED a C on the last ancient Greek examination before the term's end, a C on a mythology writing assignment, and I seemed to be heading directly into an Incomplete in a psychology course. I had slept through two solid weeks of this last class, missing a paper due date and an exam. But it was a large lecture class on a fairly large campus and no one noticed. At any rate, no one came to my door, outraged, insisting that I straighten myself out.

The real revelation to me was how deluded I had been about how important my own failings were in the general scheme of things. I was actually surprised to find that the natural order of the universe was not disrupted when I slept through classes, missed deadlines, mistranslated "stirrup" as "end-iron" and set an entire trireme of enemy forces off at the wrong island. No men ran through the street with their hands ablaze as a result of my failings, no terrible and unseasonable storms blew through the capital city, no owls or lions hunted in the streets by daylight as they did in Shakespearean plays when people challenged the natural order of things.

As to psychology, I was done with it. I'd been fooled by the tweedy ivy look of the lecturer for this course, but when I seriously sat down to consider what he was saying to us it was clear to me that he made no sense at all. Every kind of human experience had been reduced to categorical systems that bore their originators' names and were subgrouped into levels and stages that closely resembled the "Are You Really in Love?" quizzes that Angie had showed me in teen magazines when she was eleven. We had filled them out from the perspectives of Daffy Duck or the Lone Ranger, and then compared results for our own amusement.

I had let Easters Weekend pass me by, that three-day drunken transition into the last weeks of the academic year celebrated by not only Virginia students, but hundreds of fraternity brothers on campuses up and down the East Coast. Fraternity first floors were literally awash in beer and tracked through with mud carried in by revelers who had flooded the athletic fields and then pushed passing cars and pedestrians into the viscous new-made ponds. I stayed inside and pretended to read while parties flared up in houses and apartments nearby. Hank offered a half-hearted invitation to a few relatively sedate events on the Lawn, but I refused him. A scrofulous, cheerful Danny invited me to parties to which I would not go.

Instead I found myself sitting in the light of my living room windows making lists, comparing events and stories and time lines. Three or four times I picked up the telephone and began dialing the last telephone number I had for Angie. Angie could tell me where I'd been when I saw Hank's blank face and Eddie prone on his belly at our father's feet. She could tell me about pills and toddlers left to swing in trees until her siblings went in search of her. I put the receiver down every time before I finished dialing.

Whenever I ventured out of my apartment I thought I saw her on campus. A swinging sheet of hair seen through a closing door and then the look of someone's retreating back sent me twice running in pursuit before I stopped myself. I told myself I must want to see her very badly to have invented these false images. In the end, however, these chance sightings proved to be quite accurate.

I was relieved to return to routine after Easters Weekend ended and the student body pulled itself together for the last few weeks before final examinations. My daily routine always took me across the Lawn and therefore past Hank's door. I had worked very hard to restrain myself from my old habit of dropping in, trained by both Hank's reticence when he was home and the infrequency of finding him there at all. But on this particular morning I veered to walk directly past his window and I peered in. A brassiere lay draped over his chair. Women's sandals lay where they had been tossed at the foot of his bed, one askew and over the other, as if their owner had tripped and left them where they'd been planted directly before the fall. I had been with Angie the morning she'd bought them.

I rattled the door that I found uncharacteristically locked. I gave it a vicious yank before I turned on my heel and began hunting all over the campus. She was here—the distant retreating back I'd seen could actually have been her and that was, what, three days ago? She had been here perhaps three days without letting me know.

My practical mind told me to do what I'd been told to do whenever I was lost: stay put. Don't move. Someone will come to find you, I'd been told a dozen times before venturing out into the woods. Or in this case, someone would have to return here sooner or later and then I would find her. If I crisscrossed Charlottesville looking for her I might pass her by a dozen times without seeing her.

Finally I decided to retreat into the gardens directly behind Hank's rooms. If Angie did not want to be found and she saw me waiting for her, she was quite capable of disappearing again, so I was better off approaching from behind than standing in plain view. I could concentrate, as I waited, on the plums and the cocoa bean scent underfoot. I made my way along a twisting pea-gravel path, planting myself finally on a bench set into the side of a mammoth rhododendron. There I waited for perhaps an hour before walking deliberately back to Hank's room. The door was open, and she was sitting on his bed waiting for me.

"A guy two or three rooms down told me you'd been here," she said. "Big guy. Sexy. Italian name."

I sat down on the opposite end of the bed. "How long have you been here?"

"Not long." She stood up and went to a hot plate, set a kettle to boil and reached up onto a shelf to move a tin aside, revealing another tin that she lifted down. I hadn't known either tin was there until this moment and I'd been here dozens of times. It struck me that I didn't know Hank's habits or habitat all that well, while she was entirely intimate with them.

"You've come before," I said.

"A few times."

"And I never knew it."

"I'd come on business. I didn't want you to know it."

"What 'business'?"

"None here in Charlottesville. In D.C. Other places."

"Why couldn't you have let me know you were here?"

"Because I don't want you involved in what I'm doing. It could cause trouble for you."

"What about for Hank?"

She didn't answer.

"If it's just that you wanted privacy with Hank, you know, that's not, I mean, that's something you could have. I don't have any opinions about that."

She walked briskly to a backpack and rifled through until she found what she wanted. "I have something I want you to keep for me. You can't ask me how I got it because then if you're ever asked you might feel compelled to tell. All you know is that I gave it to you. All right?"

She held out a manila envelope. I didn't reach out an answering arm. "Come on," she said. "Come on, Bear."

"Isn't it kind of contradictory—wanting me to stay out of your business but then wanting me to hold on to something for you that you don't seem to want to keep yourself?"

"Yes. I'm doing it anyhow."

"I'm not taking it unless I know what it is. And I'm not amused by the cloak-and-dagger stuff." I sat back and stared blankly ahead of me. If I'd looked at her I would have simply held out my hand and slipped the envelope into my own backpack.

"It's Hank's draft papers."

"I don't believe you." I wouldn't look at her.

"Fine. Don't believe me." She kept the hand extended.

"Okay. Let's say I believe you. Where would you have gotten Hank's draft records?"

"Draft records are usually filed at draft offices. His were in Virginia, of course—his home state."

"These are from that office that got vandalized? And the policeman shot?"

"Maybe," she said.

Meaning yes, they were, absolutely.

"I don't want them."

"Yes, well, sometimes we get given things we don't want," she said.

"Why would you be treating Hank's draft papers like some cold war secret? The draft has slowed down to a trickle, and Hank's not likely to get called. There's no reason to take chances for something so unlikely."

"He'll be out of college in a few weeks and his number's low."

"But he plans to go on to law school. That would keep him in a 2-S classification."

"That's just what he says to some people. He's planning on deferring law school and letting himself get swept up." I hadn't known that and she saw this. "Iris, Iris, Iris," she sighed, meaning poor-Iris-never-knows-a-thing-does-she?

"He never talked about it. Nobody in the family talked about it," I protested. But as soon as I'd said it I knew that this was not true—that nobody had talked about it with me, but that it had been discussed. "Uncle Charlie wants him to serve, doesn't he?" I said.

"Yes."

"And Aunt Eleanor doesn't."

"Right again."

"What about Hank?" I asked.

"Hank doesn't know I have these," she said, tapping the envelope. "He's a good boy and wouldn't approve, so I'm doing what he won't do or can't do. But now the United States government will have experienced a bookkeeping lapse. They have misplaced the paper trail that leads to Hank." She saw me considering. "Look at it as a kind of trade, Iris. They got Perry and Eddie and our father. We get to keep Hank."

"This is pure melodrama, Angie. Hank's 4-A, an only son. He already has a way out. And as for your burning draft records, remember when that draft board in Minneapolis got vandalized and the records were burned? They replaced them in three weeks. The same thing's going to happen at the draft board in Virginia where you got these papers. You haven't changed a thing."

"Protesting is changing things! Every little thing, every thorn in their side, adds up."

"Hank wouldn't want this," I told her.

"I don't care what Hank wants. And he doesn't have to know anything."

"I won't take that envelope. And I'll tell Hank that you were involved in vandalizing the draft board where the policeman got shot."

"Of course you won't."

"You don't expect me to fall for that 'for me or against me' crap, do you, Angie?"

I'd surprised her, which pleased me for a moment before it depressed me.

"Iris, you don't understand how things are. Charlie is not on your side. I am. I've been on your side since before you even had a memory. When you were a baby, and a kid. And now."

"Why do you think I needed somebody on my side?" I protested. "I was safe. I was not surrounded by the enemy."

"So you've told me."

"I know that you've spent all this time thinking of our mother as a kind of beautiful ruined queen, and you probably think of our father as the person who ruined her. Angie, that's a fairy tale—stock figures from a bad psychology lecture. Maybe Mom was just a pretty, sad woman. Not a queen. Maybe our father was just a responsible man doing what everyone in his generation said was the good thing to do. And the boys, the same, and Uncle Charlie . . ."

"So reasonable!" she flared. "So blind." These last words in a more gentle tone—almost pitying.

"Angie, I think you've invented some save-the-world job for yourself, and you're dragging Hank along in with you in ways that hurt everybody in the family. That's what I see."

"I see fathers who sent their own sons off to rot in mud holes and jungles, doing it and congratulating themselves for having shown their children how the world really works."

"Does it make you feel better to blame somebody for Eddie and Perry?" I asked, wonderingly.

"Yes," she said after a moment. "Considerably."

"Well, do it then. But I don't have to."

Hank walked in the door, stopping dead for just an awkward instant when he found us together but recovering and greeting me cheerfully. I struck a false cool pose myself and we stood in a triangle in the center of his room, pretending to be at ease. I let him stumble through some transparent lie about how Angie had just surprised him and appeared at his door unannounced, had come to surprise us both! I could hear the rationalizations in his mind, hear him reminding himself that indeed Angie did surprise him every time she came, so it wasn't such a lie, really.

I invited them to dinner at my apartment and they agreed; mostly, I felt, to find some way to end the awkward standing around in Hank's tiny room. I said please. They said thank you.

Angie arrived alone at my apartment that evening, explaining that Hank was coming directly from a lab and would be there soon. She wore jeans and an embroidered cotton tunic, her hair braided in a thick column down the center of her back and silver hoops at her ears. As I opened the door she was fingering open the braid, loosening the whole mass so it fell in waves below her shoulder blades.

"I'm glad you came alone before Hank," I said. "I have something I want to show you." She shrugged, asked me if I minded if she smoked, sat down and lit a Marlboro without waiting for my reply. I went to my room and opened the T-shirt drawer, whose bottom was lined with the envelopes from Crooked River. I extracted the Moon Fairy pictures and brought them into the living room, where she sat looking out over Jefferson Park Drive. I laid them on the floor by her side.

"Look," was all I said.

She stiffened. "They're Perry's," she whispered. "When did he do them?"

"I don't know. A friend of his sent them to me."

"Why didn't you show them to me before?"

"That's a ridiculous question coming from someone who hides from me when she comes to Charlottesville." I gave her a moment to make some conciliatory gesture. None came. "Somebody who knows Vietnamese fairy tales told me that these images tell the story of a man who fell in love with a fairy. They had a child." Here I pointed to the baby who floated upward in the moonbeam with her mother. "But the fairy's lover was corrupted by power so the fairy took their child and returned to the fairy world."

"No," Angie said. "That's not what it is at all, Bear. This"—here she pointed at the child, brushing my own fingers away—"is you. And this"—here she touched the ascending woman—"is me. And I'm trying to save you."

"From what?"

"The grown-ups," she said simply. "Who want to destroy us."

"So if you're the woman, then who is the man shooting arrows?" I expected her to name Uncle Charlie, or perhaps our father.

Before she could answer we heard Hank's sharp rap at the door. I rolled up the picture as if it were a piece of pornography and hurried to put it away before he came in, knowing the entire time I did this that I was behaving illogically.

We three had an awkward dinner together that night at my apartment. Hank took pains to be appreciative and talkative. Angie did not. She cut the evening short and made it clear when she stood up from the table that she was spending the night not with me but with Hank. He tried to hide his own eagerness to leave but it was clear.

"You'll show me more of your pictures, Bear," she whispered to me when Hank left the room for a moment. "No secrets. United front."

She meant that I could have no secrets from her—not that we would have no secrets. Angie left the next day. I congratulated myself on intimidating her into dropping the subject of the draft papers but I was premature. Two weeks later I found them propped at the back of my closet where Angie had hidden them. I let them sit there, unable to bring myself to throw them away, and that is how they became mine.

Take the Goggles Off

ALL SEMESTER I HAD BEEN ASSISTING AT FRIDAY-NIGHT DIVE classes. They were calming, demanding just enough of my conscious mind to keep me from thinking about anything but what I was doing—rather like the way that Vito described cooking. I also found that I looked forward to predictable contact with Vito Signori in a setting that precluded intimacy but made it easy to observe each other.

"If you know why you want to dive and actually have some goals for yourself," the instructor started class one night, "you're much more likely to stay in the sport and not be one of those people who go to the Cayman Islands, put their big-bootied feet all over some fragile coral, scare the shit out of some poor octopus by trying to pet it and declare themselves at one with nature just before they drop diving entirely for some half-assed thing like bowling."

"So do you have a goal?" I asked Vito that night. I was checking the air pressure on a line of tanks, getting them ready to be strapped onto students. He was helping, moving the heavy filled tanks to one side as soon as I weighed them.

"Look at rocks," he replied.

"You can do that without taking a dive class."

"Not if you're a geology major studying the Virginia Tidewater shoreline," he said. "I guess my immediate goal is to dive along the coast here in Virginia and then do the same along the African coast to get more data on how they match."

"Sounds like a hopeless venture," I sniffed.

"It's not. They used to be attached to each other. Virginia was on a continental mass that geologists call Laurentia; Africa was called Gondwana. Gondwana collided with us and just kept going—squashed the edge of the continent up into the ridges that make up the Adirondack Range. That's why the Blue Ridge have all those pretty folds—Africa crumpled them into place when it collided with us. That's not even the ancient history. The Blue Ridge sit on about four older mountain ranges."

"So why aren't we still attached to Africa?" I asked.

"The tectonic plates that the continents float on shifted. Africa was pulled southeastward. A lot of what it left behind in the Tidewater is submerged, which is why I'm in a diving class. I have to go underwater to get at it."

"But don't geologists all hang out in, like, Nevada—or Kuwait?"

"The oil guys and the basin and range guys do. I don't know yet where I'll end up. If I don't get this diving thing down, though, I won't be concentrating on any kind of work that'll take me underwater. I started out thinking it would be great to see the USS *Wilkes-Barre*. Maybe the USS *Monitor*. My goals have been readjusted since then."

The *Wilkes-Barre* and the *Monitor* were the gold standard destinations for wreck divers, and I was suitably impressed. "Well," I said, "the *Wilkes-Barre*'s at two hundred and fifty feet. This class only certifies you to sixty. And wreck diving—that's a whole different certification program."

"Yeah, I know. There's a club in New York called the NYC–New Jersey Wreckers and all they do is dive wrecks. I've seen pictures of them. They jump right off the docks into the Hudson with air-powered impact hammers, chisels and wrenches hanging off of them. Tides, cold water, oil slicks, rats and wrecks. They carry double everything because their equipment gets slashed and crushed so often: two regulators, two watches, two knives, two masks."

"Air-powered impact hammers?" I ventured. I was trying to imagine the effect of this kind of silhouette at the end of a city dock. "I think I can understand the appeal."

"I'm not surprised." He grinned.

The following Saturday the class members convened at the gymnasium pool to drive to the quarry together for the open-air dive. The day began bright and cool, ideal conditions, but got grayer as we approached our destination. It had been a dry winter and spring, and the drop from the lip of the quarry to the water was more than ten feet: a difficult entry for even an experienced diver and a situation sure to end in lost equipment for beginners. I helped the students struggle into their gear before putting on my own, and then I preceded them into the quarry along with the master divers. My certification level gave me just enough authority to function here as moral support and equipment backup.

Vito was the first in. The water temperature was still almost winter-cold so he registered a general state of shock when it flowed into his wet suit: popped eyes, spasmodic gasping until he got the few voluntary muscles involved in breathing to cooperate. The master diver in charge of the first four students waited just below the surface for them to gather around him before descending. I followed.

The dive plan began with one revolution of the quarry at fifteen feet. Then a master diver would offer some kind of challenge to each student, just as they had done to my class. Assuming they solved the problem the instructor created, students would drop another fifteen to twenty feet, where the next master diver would meet them. Vito had cheerfully replaced the mask that his master diver knocked askew when he was about twelve feet down, got it cleared, gave his partner the okay sign and began to sink to the next testing level. I followed.

Suddenly the world we were in darkened dramatically. The clouds drifting thousands of feet over the quarry had obscured the sun, dimming the light at the surface but plunging us, at about forty feet, into almost total darkness. We went from being able to see one another to being suspended in a kind of impenetrable liquid fog. The master diver beneath us flicked on a flashlight so we could find him. Something collided with my thigh and flank—Vito's shoulder. He was heading up—too fast and entirely out of the dive plan. I grabbed one flipper to stop him but he slid past, minus the flipper I'd dislodged. From this depth, Vito was unlikely to get nitrogen poisoning on his ascent, but he was clearly moving faster than his air bubbles.

The master diver was busy with another student and I went after Vito alone. I shot out a hand and grabbed—it clamped around his ankle. I made my way up his body hand over hand and when I reached his torso I settled one palm firmly on his chest. His heart banged out a furious thudding staccato. I kept my hand still and flicked on my flashlight, shining it at my own face and my hands, which were signaling that he should ascend with me, slowly. He grimaced but nodded, and started up with his one remaining flipper. Two master divers, seeing us swimming out of the expected pattern, approached. I nodded furiously and gave them a thumbs-up. Vito jerked his thumb downward, indicating that he wanted to descend again. We got a round of emphatic no's and gestures making it clear that our dive was over.

For a moment I was sure he was going to swim directly away from me and go down, but he hesitated. I set my palm on his chest again and he covered it with his own hand. He followed me up, still holding my hand against his chest.

We popped to the surface simultaneously. "What happened?" the instructor called from above the ladder on the other side of the quarry. We hadn't been down long enough to finish the dive and he knew it. "Everybody all right?"

I nodded and slapped Vito until he nodded, too. We swam to the ladder and heaved ourselves up.

"Equipment problem? Breathing problem? Panic?" the instructor asked as soon as we reached him.

"I dropped a flipper," Vito said.

The instructor nodded, pursed his lips. I knew what this meant: no certification for Vito Signori. When the master divers got back he would grill them for the rest of the story. The panicking and risk-taking would be added to this small admission and that would be that.

Our teacher turned away to meet the next dripping student, whose shining face made it clear that she'd had a happier dive than we had.

Vito and I stripped off our gear, turned in our tanks and sat side by side, waiting for the rest of the class to finish.

"What were you doing?" I demanded finally.

"It was the breathing thing. Something about the light dimming made my throat close and then I swear the regulator openings all got smaller."

"But you didn't panic at all in the practice dives. You didn't panic when somebody jumped out of the bushes and tried to rob us. I don't get it."

"The water's different," he said. "I can't explain."

"Vito, maybe this is just the wrong sport for you. Your heart was going so fast. Like you were on amphetamines or something. You weren't, were you? On amphetamines?" I hadn't thought of this until I'd said it, actually. Then I did, and all the warnings about not even taking an antihistamine within twenty-four hours of a dive came flooding back.

"I'm not interested in hurting myself, Iris. Really."

I turned away so he couldn't see my face, which registered some doubt. He reached forward and took my chin, not gently, turning my face around so he could examine it. I slapped his hand away.

"I'll tell you some stuff because I want you to know it. Okay?" he said. I nodded.

"You come back from Vietnam and people walk on the other side of the street because they figure you've got problems and you're a problem. I hated that, especially since in my case I did come back with a bad habit. But it's gone."

"What made it be gone?"

"My mother put me in detox. Told me she'd kill me if I didn't clean up."

"Your mother could do that?"

He nodded. "She could and she did, and that's not even the limit of her powers—you should taste her lime ricotta pie."

"Really? Well, then, I hope to."

"It can be arranged," he said.

"What about her cakes?"

"What?"

I'd confused him. "Your mother's cakes," I said.

"She's not a cake woman," he said, shrugging. "Pies. Calzones. Chicken. Gnocchi."

"Lucky you," I said. "To be born to such a woman."

"Yes," he agreed. "Lucky me."

THAT WEEK I was fussy and restless, angry when I couldn't wring a fluid line from Sophocles, whom I knew to be fluid; angry when Danny trotted upstairs to ask me if I wanted a beer (no); angry with Vito for I wasn't yet sure what. This mood persisted until only Rootie the dog greeted me with unaltered enthusiasm and Rootie was, when all was said and done, only a dog.

At the end of the week, another packet arrived from the Iroquois Nation.

You aren't saying not to send more, so I send more, Crooked River wrote. *I think of you quite a bit. Perhaps this year Tadodaho will go to the fair because he'll have finally gotten too old and tired to want to kill other rabbits. I will let you know.* This envelope contained four tattered sheets. In the first, Perry had drawn us before the bonfire at the Lake House. He had rendered the fire's animal-like heat and energy in a way that gave the entire scene a hostile look. It was very beautiful. Standing directly before the fire and about to stick his hand in it was a grinning Eddie, with Angie scrutinizing him at his left, her back slightly curved to accommodate Hank, whose body clung to hers, wrapped against it from behind with his arms crossed over her breasts—a posture I had never seen in actual life. The figure representing me sat on the ground at a slight distance, the only one looking directly toward the person drawing this imaginary scene. We are all in our late teens and early twenties. Only Perry himself was missing. We had been drawn sympathetically, lovingly.

The second drawing was another fire, this one consuming the kind of large paper house that Vietnamese make to offer up to their lost ones on the anniversaries of the deaths. A woman stood to one side, watching as it burned. Paper furniture filled its rooms. Small clothes hung in the house's windows and a larger set of paper clothes hung on a separate line in the house's front yard. They too had been lit. But it wasn't a Vietnamese house: it was our house—the Lake House.

The third drawing was of my mother and father. They faced the artist and looked directly at him. My mother's face in this drawing was suffused with rage. My father's was somehow both blank and threatening. His image seemed to have come from some primitive folk art school while hers seemed to have been cobbled together by Gustav Klimt and Edvard Munch.

The last drawing was of water: it was our languorous crescent-shaped lake, but drawn from some perspective that I couldn't place. There was the burn mark from the fire in '68 on the south shore. There was the old Macaby farm to the east. But the water stretched out like an inland ocean where reality gave it only a three miles' length, and a perfectly cakelike island bobbed in the center, not at all like the lake's actual tree-lined chunk of granite. There was a diminutive castle on Perry's island, full of turrets and faceless people poking out of every window. They were waving—not a hello kind of wave but a come-save-me kind of wave.

I looked up, uneasy, feeling watched. The feeling drew me to the window and when I reached it and looked out I was greeted by the sight of Vito Signori standing in front of my house. I withdrew out of sight. The next time I looked he was gone.

His Last Visit

Uncle Charlie and Aunt Eleanor's home had always had dogs. When Angie was ten she'd been given a Rhodesian ridgeback named Otto, who was, in general, a willing animal but inconsistent. One day he was the model dog, obedient and careful of your feelings. The next, he might forget himself and growl if you sat too near him when he was napping on the sofa. If he growled at Angie she just laughed. If he growled at the boys they'd curl their lips in disgust but give him some room. But once he growled at Uncle Charlie, who stood right up, took hold along the bristly chestnut mohawk of fur along Otto's back, and shook the animal until its teeth literally rattled against one another. "Do that again," he said grimly as he put the dog down, looking him right in the eyes, "and it'll be the last thing you do." The dog never growled in Uncle Charlie's presence again. When Angie cried and raged against his cruelty, he said that an animal that doesn't know its place is no good to anybody. Otto's place, he reminded her, was beneath that of any human in his household, and if he didn't understand that, he had no place.

There hadn't been any vindictiveness or even anything I'd call personal in Uncle Charlie's reaction to Otto. He was merely reminding the dog of where it stood in the order of things, as a member of his household and in the world at large. The reminder had been violent, but then, the dog had been bred to kill lions so perhaps that was merely speaking to it in its own language.

There was also a Jack Russell named Pinocchio, who was in charge of clearing the property of rats, and a whippet named Skinny, who was the acknowledged master of squirrel removal. Everyone at Uncle Charlie's had a job.

Pinocchio did indeed have a pointy nose but he was Pinocchio to us because Uncle Charlie was convinced the dog knew how to lie. "Did you chew this rug up all to hell?" he'd ask the dog, who would stand his ground and look right back at my uncle—except his drooping tail and quivering rear leg gave him away. "Liar," my uncle would sigh. "I can't believe you're looking me right in the eye. Smile and smile, and still be a villain."

"The dog's rear leg is shaky because he's afraid he's going to get whacked with a newspaper, Charles," Aunt Eleanor would break in, exasperated. "Dogs cannot lie."

"They can lie all right, but they're lousy actors. Look at that animal's tail," Uncle Charlie would say.

I never took to that Jack Russell terrier, because I honored my uncle's judgment and distrusted the dog's character. Pinocchio continued to earn his keep by laying rat corpses just outside the kitchen door, where Otto would have to be forcibly reminded not to eat them, but Pinocchio never won Uncle Charlie's trust or affection. This my uncle reserved for the delinquent and apologetic Otto, who was always sincerely sorry for leaving rat parts on the porch or curling his lip at the smaller humans on the property. Otto was in charge of border patrol, and his responsibilities brought him into contact with some of the larger members of the Blue Ridge animal kingdom. He tackled skunks, who should have been left, by rights, to Pinocchio. He once tackled a big cat, probably a mountain lion, and came home mauled, matted with dry blood, crusted over from the mud hole he had rolled in before dragging home. We found him lying on the lawn like a toy that had been left out in the rain and then run over with a lawn mower. Uncle Charlie wept as he lifted the 105-pound Otto gently in his arms and carried him into the house. He stitched the bigger gashes up himself. The dog recovered and continued his night patrolling duties.

I could see the attraction to Otto.

Skinny was the beloved of Perry and Eddie, mostly because of his speed and agility and willingness to chase any moving object. Balls, Frisbees, sticks—the animal was a brilliant runner and he had eyes like satellite tracking devices. Throw anything in any direction and he would return to you in a moment with the object between his teeth. I never liked Skinny. He slavered, for one thing, in a skinny-dog way—not the necessary kind of panting that a big thick-coated animal like Otto might do but something that managed to look cold and slippery at once. Skinny was a distant, preoccupied kind of dog, interested in catching thrown objects and thus in the people who threw them, but interested only as far as he had to be. No more. There was no doggy fidelity or companionable warmth about Skinny that I could see, though my brothers adored him.

The second memory I had of a visit from my father involved these dogs, and it was a dog who rattled the memory finally back into plain sight. I was taking care of Rootie for a few days while Danny went off to Dartmouth for a weekend party. His roommates would be going to the same party, he told me, so I would be alone in the house and would certainly want some company, wouldn't I? I moved the Labrador's bowl and stuffed monkey toy up to my living room.

Rootie was an affectionate creature, very attached to his owner, and Danny's absences made him anxious and then listless. He sagged at my feet like a small black bear, sighing. "Oh, come on," I urged, stroking his back with my bare foot. "Buck up, Square Root." Rootie's tail thumped dutifully to show me he was listening, but his head stayed down and he sighed again. He brightened a bit when I stood and got his leash, and we headed out for a stroll and perhaps a dash at a squirrel or two.

I fell into my usual path and within ten minutes Rootie and I were crossing the Lawn, where we found a softball game in progress. A keg sat on a chair behind home plate and I saw to my surprise that both Vito and Hank were playing, albeit on opposing teams. I stopped to stare at Hank. He was running, which I had always regarded as his most beautiful state.

I only heard the crack. We were on the Rotunda side of the game at the back of the outfield when the impossibly low and fast ball came straight at us. I was still tracking Hank, vaguely aware that I'd heard a sound that meant maybe I should be ducking. Rootie wasn't much faster but he had a dog's magnetic attraction to balls and he had moved toward it rather than away. Too late I saw the ball coming, and I jerked Rootie's leash in an instinctive but ill-advised effort to get his head out of the ball's path. Instead, it brought the resisting dog's forehead directly in line with the ball and he went down in a furry, apparently boneless heap. His tongue flapped out of his mouth to one side as I slid a hand under his face, his seal-like nose and whiskers so blameless and helpless that I could taste the salt in my mouth that presaged tears.

Within a minute three people who'd been on the nearer team were at my side. Before I could stop him, a young man scooped Rootie up and tucked the dog closely against his chest. Rootie's head dangled at an impossible angle and I felt the same ground-falling-away-beneath-me kind of drop that I'd felt in Danny's kitchen when he teased Rootie with the fried squirrel brain, twisting the dog's head at an awkward angle.

"Don't touch him! Don't move the head!" This was Hank, who now ran furiously toward us.

The young man set the dog gently back down on the ground. Square Root's eyes fluttered open and his legs scrambled in an effort to get beneath him. Advice rained down on us from all sides as the other ball players reached us. They were flushed from running, all of them except Hank, who was ceiling-paint white.

"Hank, take a deep breath. He'll be all right," I said, addressing the color of his face rather than my own fears about Rootie's condition. I had laid my hands on the dog's head but I let him sit up now. He licked my hand. "See? Rootie's going to be all right."

"Watch his neck," Hank insisted. "Don't twist his neck. Or his head . . ."

All the while I had cradled the prone Rootie, the words *My fault! My fault! My fault!* rang in my head. Why had I yanked at the dog's leash instead of trusting his own superior evasive powers!

I looked up at Hank's white face and was stunned to find that Skinny had popped clearly to mind—Skinny, tucked into my father's flank, his ribs held flush against the man's with an elbow while the two hands held the dog's jaw and the back of his head. Then the hands twisted, the part of the animal connecting its head to its heart snapped, and Skinny became a muddled heap of gray parts where a dog had been only a moment before.

I shook my head and stood up as if I could literally shake the image out of my mind and back away from it. Vito offered the keys to his car to Hank and I, and the game resumed while we called a local veterinarian, got an appointment, and urged Rootie into the backseat. The Labrador had a fairly clear idea of the connection of car rides to veterinarians and his entire body drooped as we shoveled him in and slammed the door.

We were silent for the first mile and then I said, "I was thinking of Skinny."

He nodded. "I thought I'd forgotten the way it sounded and what it looked like."

I said, "I remember those things, but I don't know why it happened. How old was I?"

"You were about seven. I was ten," Hank said.

"You and Perry and Eddie were playing Frisbee," I continued for him. "You were tossing it to Skinny and teasing me—throwing it over my head or just out of my reach. And my father was visiting."

"It was his last visit, in fact."

"And the dog wouldn't give it to me to throw—he'd circle around me and give it to one of you," I went on.

"Yes. And I threw one too low and you got it, but Skinny lunged for it just as you got your hand on it and the two of you collided."

"I fell on the dog and he bit me!" I cried, jubilant at having retrieved the scene so perfectly and then uneasy when it rolled in its entirety through my mind. "He bit me on the forearm." I rolled the forearm over now. There they were, the little ridged white keloids I had lived with for so long I had stopped seeing them. Skinny had given them to me. Of course.

"Remember, we told you to stop crying and we tried not to let the parents know," Hank said. "We washed you up and tried to wrap some bandages around you but you kept bleeding through them and Perry said we had to take you to the grown-ups. They were on the veranda and we brought you to them and told them it wasn't Skinny's fault, exactly, that you had collided with him and then fallen on him. Any dog, even a good dog, would have reacted like that."

I knew why the argument had been thought out before the boys presented it. We all knew what happened to dogs who bit people, who forgot their place in the world and made nuisances—even dangerous threats—of themselves. They were of no use anymore. Hank and Perry and Eddie had known that if they had to show our parents what Skinny had done that they must follow this with a plea for his life.

They lost. Everything that followed was clear in my mind.

My father had glanced quickly at Uncle Charlie, who merely nodded and remained where he was, but my father had risen and gone in search of Skinny, who knew full well that he was in danger and had gone to ground in the barn. Aunt Eleanor had risen to go into the house for antiseptic and more bandages, calling to me to stay put. I ignored her and trailed along after my brothers and Hank, all of us refusing to be turned away when my father told us to do so, all of them but me knowing essentially what was going to happen.

When my father ordered Skinny to come to him, the dog slunk forward from the corner of the empty stall where he had been waiting. My father ordered us, once more, to leave, and we retreated to the doorway of the barn. Standing there close enough to see and hear but wanting terribly to do neither, my brothers turned their faces away. Hank and I did not. We hung by the last stall and looked as my father swept the animal up, gripping him firmly against his own body with his arm while he took a quick deft hold of the head. He snapped the neck with the proficient economy of a man who did this every day, and then he simply dropped the body to the ground. When he brushed by us in the doorway he told us not to go in there. He'd come back and deal with it later, he said. We filed back into the dark interior as soon as my father was out of sight and circled the little body. I didn't remember what we said or did then but I remembered what I'd been thinking: *My fault! My fault! My fault!*

"There was blood at his mouth and nostrils," I said wonderingly. "I remember the smell."

"It's just the way it is in the country," Hank said to me now. "You know—like hunting and butchering your own meat. Every creature in its place, serving its particular function. And if the animal doesn't function, you take care of the problem yourself. No running off to a vet to put him down, or to obedience school to try to set him straight. You take care of it yourself."

I had no answer to this, and I remained silent through Hank's greeting the receptionist and the veterinarian, through the brief exam, the questions, the reassurance that given Rootie's presenting balance, pupil sizes and good cheer that he was probably fine, the list of symptoms to watch for and the advice to return if he showed any of them. The bill was an astronomical twenty-five dollars—a month's spending money.

"You didn't like my father," I said when we were clear of the parking lot and headed home.

"I don't know if I disliked him or was afraid of him. The two can get confused. You weren't afraid of him. Neither was Angie."

"But the boys were?"

"Well, I was."

"But what about my brothers?" I persisted.

"Eddie adored your father. Imitated him when he could. He and Perry always got into fights right after he left. Eddie would try on the big-dog act, try pushing Perry around. Perry would start off tolerant and all but then there'd either be a fistfight or Perry would keep away for a while. One or the other. You know, I thought your father hated Perry."

"Why did you think that?"

"Maybe he didn't hate Perry. I just thought he did. Your father and

Eddie were sort of on the same wavelength. Eddie resisted him. But that was what was expected of a boy—to resist, and carve out your own space, and push back when you got stepped on if you could. But Perry just folded under the guy every time. Every fucking time."

"What times?" My hands had gotten suddenly clammy.

"Just times. You know what I mean, Iris. Boys had to be things, do things, that girls were not supposed to do or be. And there were consequences if you weren't those things. Everybody had his place."

"What was your place?"

"Under Eddie. Same level as Perry. Above the girls. Then the dogs on the bottom. That was the order."

"But you didn't always stick with Perry," I insisted. "You argued with him. Sometimes Eddie took your side."

"Only when it didn't matter. When it really mattered it was us against Eddie. Your father hated me, too. That was another thing that made it me and Perry together and Eddie alone. Eddie didn't mind. He'd have rather been your dad's favorite than be anything else. I think he almost went crazy the last time your father left. He didn't think your dad was ever coming back, and as it turned out, he was right."

"What about us girls? Were Angie and I side by side, or one before the other? To you guys, I mean."

"I don't know. You were like our pet, and Angie was like our opponent. But you girls weren't playing the serious games with us—the ones with hunting and being out in the woods."

True. We had been left behind. "I liked staying behind when you'd go out on those trips," I said. "And Angie hated it."

"I know. She hated all of it—the being kind of not in the game. Getting left behind. We all had something to hate, didn't we? All of us but you. It was all right, though. I mean, everybody in the world hates something. It's just being human. There were little rough patches but we were happy enough. Right?"

"Yes. I guess we were."

We'd reached my own dirt drive and he pulled in. I got out, opened the rear door for Square Root and waved good-bye. Hank offered a thin little dribbling wash of a wave in response, almost all fingers. He didn't look at me as he pulled out and drove Vito's car back to the student lot.

I tied an ice pack onto the top of the poor retriever's head and kept it on for ten minutes; off for ten; on for ten. He protested at first but then bore it because I put him in my lap and held him while I balanced the pack.

I sat there with him for a full hour. I tried to pull my train of thought back to what Hank had said but no sooner had I summoned up the picture of one of the dogs or Angie or Hank in the barn and my mind would slide right off that image. Ten or fifteen minutes later I would find myself aware of nothing but the feel of Rootie's silky muzzle and the pleasure of sitting quietly with a warm amiable being. When the telephone rang I considered letting it go unanswered, but I had never been good at that. So I repositioned Rootie, freed myself from his weight and picked up the receiver.

"Did you get the pictures all right?"

"Mr. Crooked River?"

"Eyeah. I just wanted to make sure you got the pictures all right. I didn't hear from you."

"Well, you don't have a telephone and you didn't seem eager to hear from me. I'm sorry if you expected a note or something. I guess I should have sent one."

Long pause.

"Well," I said at last. "How is Tadodaho doing?"

"That rabbit is calming down. We're headed for the state fair for sure this year. I'm gonna test-drive him in early June at a smaller fair, in the 4-H show. See how he does."

"Don't you have to be in the 4-H to enter your rabbit, Crooked River?"

"I kind of am, seeing as I advise Mary Beaver Dam's club on rabbits. I help with goats, too, since I know something about goats. Cows I want nothing to do with. She's got two little ones raising calves. But I give any of her kids who wants a rabbit a starter rabbit, and I make sure they know what to do to take good care of them."

"Oh."

"So you could come see Tadodaho at the 4-H thing. June third, all afternoon. Not on the reservation. At the high school in Pompey Center. Not Pompey. They're different towns."

"Oh."

It was clear that this invitation had taken me by surprise. "See, I wanted to talk to you about the pictures," he added, as though this were an afterthought.

"Well, you could just talk to me now, couldn't you?"

"You think about it. You call my aunt Jenny and leave me a message."

He hung up.

For some reason this open-ended exchange cleared my mind. I opened my books and found myself able to concentrate for the first time in a month. With finals only two weeks away this was a bit late—but better that, as they say, than never.

The afternoon that Skinny died we'd sat in a little clump around Aunt Eleanor's dinner—the children anxious and the adults sullen. The body had been bagged and put with the trash. Otto and Pinocchio discovered it just as we finished our salads. Uncle Charlie, Aunt Eleanor and the man who was my father did not acknowledge the ghoulish echoing howls that broke in as Aunt Eleanor passed the pepper to the children's end of the table. It was clear what we were supposed to do: nothing. We were supposed to accept what had happened to the little dog in the same way we accepted our own punishments.

This was harder to communicate to the dogs themselves. Otto lost half his fur in the succeeding weeks; Pinocchio became a cringing idiot. Our visiting father was gone in a matter of days.

What He Really Wanted

I DIDN'T THINK THAT WHAT CROOKED RIVER REALLY WANTED WAS to get me to come to the 4-H competition, but I was drawn all the same. I told Vito about Crooked River's invitation. I was falling into this habit, telling Vito whatever was on my mind and showing him whatever came into my mailbox.

"I'm driving up to Geneva to go to a festival," he said after a moment. "I can drive you. It's only like a half hour out of my way. Nothing at all."

"I was going to rent a car. Besides, I don't want to trouble you." Nor did I necessarily want to be dependent upon him for transportation.

"I'll point out the obvious," he replied. "Rental cars are expensive. It's a long trip and company will keep me more alert. We can split the driving. And you don't even really know why you're going to see this maybe-alcoholic clearly unemployed guy and his yard full of rodents. Besides, if you come with me, you get to come to the Feast of Saint Dorothea."

"And I get to meet your mother," I added.

He nodded. "That's correct."

The fact was I wanted to meet his mother. I spent about twelve seconds imagining myself left with the 4-H'ers and Crooked River, all by myself; then I imagined the same scene with Vito in the background. The latter scenario looked better.

"I don't know why you're trying to make me nervous about this," I said. "I've already met him. I met the rabbits. He was perfectly polite."

Vito's playful tone fell away. "Look, Iris, you haven't spent much time with guys who've just come back. I have. These guys can have good days and bad days."

"He didn't 'just' come back," I said.

"If you got back this decade, it's 'just got back.' " He saw me thinking. He added, "I like rabbits. Maybe there'll be a stump-pulling competition I can drop in on while you talk to the Indian. I like those."

I agreed.

I scrambled my way to a C in Psychology 101, did a flat-out running finish to a B in the two reading courses and was awarded a C– in Greek. "It's not that you don't work, Ms. Sunnaret," the professor said in the end-of-year conference he liked to schedule with each of his students. "I'm just afraid this might not be the way your genius lies." My final examination lay on the desk between us, tiny red-ink notations pockmarking it considerably. He looked sincerely troubled as he fingered the edges of the test paper. "I just don't understand how you could have gotten 'We forget when we have help and the dreadful is well' from the lines I gave you to translate. It doesn't even make any sense."

I looked down at Teiresias's actual words, which my professor's assistant had scribbled in below my own as he was grading:

How dreadful knowledge of the truth can be
When there's no help in truth! I knew this well,
But made myself forget.

We both shook our heads sadly, equally discouraged by my mediocre performance. The Classics Department had shrunk terribly as students abandoned it as irrelevant and I knew my professor was seeing another potential major falling away, his department drying up and vanishing. "I won't stop you from continuing next year, of course," he said, "but I ask that you think about it and perhaps look for an alternative if things don't improve."

I had lied to Aunt Eleanor and Uncle Charlie, telling them that I finished the semester with one incomplete and that I needed to stay on to wrap up an outstanding paper. The truth was that I didn't want them to know I was going to the 4-H show in Pompey, New York. I would stay in Charlottesville until the 4-H weekend, leave from there with Vito and go to the Lake House upon my return. At that point I would take pains to look relieved about all my coursework being successfully completed and I needn't say anything at all about my trip to the Onondaga Nation. To my surprise they didn't question me any further about the course or my plans when I called to say I wouldn't be home right away.

Of all their children I was the one least likely to finish a semester with an incomplete, and still they did not challenge me. Every other year of my entire life I'd been adamant about being the first person in the lake when the summer house was opened. "Well," I'd said, giving them one more chance to tell me that I could certainly finish the paper at home and be there with them at the lake, "you don't need me opening weekend anyway. Hank can handle getting the boat in, right?"

A moment of silence greeted this before Aunt Eleanor said, "Well, Hank is looking at a graduate program on the West Coast and he's talked to us about a couple of different summer jobs, or maybe even not going straight to graduate school out there. We aren't sure of his schedule."

I took this to mean that Hank had headed toward Angie the moment his last exam ended and that my uncle and aunt were at a loss. So I was surprised when Hank turned up at my door in Charlottesville two days later with a backpack, looking and smelling like someone who had driven nonstop across the country. He had gone to her. They had fought and she'd asked him to leave. He'd hitched a ride with a Berkeley student whose name he'd seen on a ride board.

"I've already turned in the keys and checked out of my room on the Lawn for the year," he said. "Can I stay here for a while?"

"What about the Lake House? Charlie and Eleanor?"

"They aren't expecting me. We've already talked. So. Yes or no?"

"Yes. Of course, yes. They told me you were looking at graduate programs and job hunting," I said.

"They're lying," he said briskly. "They know I went to see Angie, and what my daddy had to say about that to me was that I'm a fool. We continue to be threats to his professional well-being and if we want to be welcome in their home we should just sort ourselves out."

"But it's your home, too. You can't fire somebody from your family." Hank raised an eyebrow and didn't even bother to respond. "What did you and Angie fight about?"

"I can't go into that with you." He looked at my face and changed his mind. "The truth is, I don't really know what we fought about." He stepped into the kitchen and opened the refrigerator, took out a quart of milk and brought it back into the living room, where he drank directly from its spout. "I think maybe we fought because she's tired of me and she wants me to go away but she wants me to be the one leaving. So she tries to make me miserable enough for that to happen." He looked at the container of milk in his hand as if he had no idea how it had gotten there. "Got any ham?"

"No. How did she make you miserable?"

"The usual way. She said she didn't want us to be lovers anymore."

"Well, maybe that's best."

"No. She didn't mean it. She was just upset."

"About what?"

The milk carton rattled and splashed when he put it down. "I don't know," he said.

"You mean that, don't you?" I was incredulous. "You have no idea."

He shook his head from side to side. He didn't. "What made me leave, though, was the way she was looking at me when I was eating dinner. I could tell that there was something about the way I chewed that was bugging her. Really bugging her. If you can't stand the way somebody chews, what does that mean?"

"Hank, why are you in love with her?"

Hank looked at me carefully, a little up-and-down sweep from my hairline to my lips, twice. "You don't like her, do you?"

"Don't be a jerk."

He stood up. "Look, I'll find somebody else to put me up tonight and maybe I'll try going home and seeing if I can't make things better with my folks. That's what you think I should do, isn't it?"

"Don't be like that, Hank. Stay here."

He hesitated. He was clearly lost. Even if he had someplace else he might go, he was too stunned by recent events and exhausted by the long trip here to plot his way to any other shelter. "All right. Only one night, though. I promise."

No matter where we stepped in the kitchen as we prepared dinner together, we were in each other's way. Any harmony that had ever existed between us had evaporated in the last few months. I opened the refrigerator to take out an egg and blocked his way just as he was trying to get to a dish towel. He reached for a chopping board at exactly the same time I pulled open a cabinet door that met his face and stopped him with one hand stretched out, nothing in it at all.

"You're heading home in the next few days?" he ventured as we sat over a burned meal.

"No. I'm staying put for a little while after my last exam and then I'm going to upstate New York. I've told Aunt Eleanor and Uncle Charlie that I'm just here finishing a paper, though."

"Upstate New York?"

"Vito Signori's giving me a ride."

Hank set his fork down, clearly surprised. "Is this about Vito Signori or about that Indian guy who says he knew Perry and Eddie?"

"He did know them."

"So it's about him, then? The Indian?"

"His rabbit's in a 4-H competition. I said I'd go." As I spoke I could hear how this sounded—how much it fed into Hank's worst fears about me. "He says he has things of Perry's."

"He's still stringing you along? Iris, think! What kind of man would play games like this with you? What is he up to?"

"I don't know. I don't think he's dangerous, though, Hank. He really does have things of Perry's—pictures Perry drew. He hasn't told me a single lie."

"Not one that you've caught him at yet."

"You seem to want Crooked River to be lying to me. And you don't want me asking questions."

"What does it matter? We can't change anything. You think asking Crooked River about Perry and Eddie will do anything? It won't. You think asking my momma about your parents will make anything better? It won't."

"I have the right to know more about my parents. It's natural."

"Why would you need to know anything more than you know now? You were lucky to get given to my momma and daddy. Your father was so . . . Even Daddy toward the end was afraid of him."

I nodded.

Hank was agitated, scattered. He tapped a fork up and down. "I could imagine him doing it over and over, not just to animals. He knew exactly what he was doing. I hated it when he came. Perry would do his best to hide from him and Eddie would be at his heels like a dog. And I don't know that the man cared for either of them. Don't you remember?"

"I remember the day with Skinny. And I remember the day he made Eddie lie on the floor."

"God! God, he did that kind of shit every time he came! And it was Eddie he did it to—never anybody else. Like pulling one man out of line and shooting him to keep everybody else in his place. That's what it felt like, watching it. But the big mystery to me was that Eddie adored him, and the next time the guy showed up, there would be Eddie, imitating the way he walked, trying to talk like him."

"But our parents were best friends! Why would Uncle Charlie be friends with this thug you're describing?"

"There were things between them I didn't understand. There was all that shared history. And people change. My daddy got out of the field work and settled down. The only time I ever saw the old part of him was when we went hunting."

"What old part of him?"

"The part that liked being in the woods with a gun, away from rules. I don't know what it was like to be in the field in the early U.S. years in Indochina, you know, the fifties, but I know what people say about the guys who liked it, and other guys were afraid of them. They were total maverick lone wolves—lots of times they were guys who couldn't live in civilization anymore even if they wanted. They didn't talk about what they were doing and if it didn't work they understood that they'd signed on to have never officially existed. That's not a part of my daddy I see a lot of now that he's in Washington—my daddy made a choice in his life and it was to come home to us and be our father. But I'd see it peeking through sometimes. I know it sounds kind of weird, but he'd get so excited and happy when he killed something. It didn't cross his mind that the bird or doe we were trailing didn't have a chance against a semiautomatic weapon with a sighting device. Then the butchering in the woods. He liked that, too."

"How do you know what they did over there? Why are you imagining it this way?"

"It doesn't matter."

"Why did you go hunting with Uncle Charlie if you hated it so much?"

"I wanted to be with him. I could go with him sometimes and have him all to myself." Hank poked a pine nut in the remains of his meal. "I don't want to make you unhappy, Iris. Look—Momma and Daddy made us a wonderful life and I knew it all the time. I still know it and I'm never forgetting it. I loved the Lake House and the order and the affection and the way there was room cut out in that family for every single one of us, the funny foods at holidays and the steady way they lived. And you—I think they loved you the best of all of us. But things are falling apart now. I don't know how to stop it but if I could I swear I would."

"Make peace with Uncle Charlie, then. Why can't you just do that?"

He slapped one hand down so sharply that I jumped. "Because it costs too much! My daddy's still rooted in the moral landscape of the last world war. The Vietnamese are just Japanese playing dress-up to him. Try to imagine what Angie looks like to a man like that."

"What does what she's doing look like to you, Hank?"

"It looks like what she's got to do."

"Oh, Hank! When did you become such a romantic? You think all those people going to marches are doing it because it's their political responsibility? Half of them are blowing the cash from Mommy and Daddy on dime bags or sitting around in serious rap sessions trying to decide what to do with their own personal feelings about racism and whole grains, smashing windows and closing down buildings in their spare time, or worse. The people she gave the money to killed a man. Angie was part of that."

He stared at me quietly for a moment before he spoke. Then for the second time in as many weeks he said, "You're jealous."

"Jealous of what, exactly?" I could hear what I sounded like, and I didn't sound like a nice person.

"I don't understand you, Iris. She's your sister. She didn't intend for anybody to die. She had no idea it was going to get violent."

"How can you be sure of that?"

"You're saying you think she expected someone to die?"

"I don't see how an intelligent person who even reads the newspaper regularly much less somebody who did things with SDS guys could convince herself that nobody would ever get hurt. It's not tiddledywinks."

He pushed himself away from the table and walked over to his backpack. "I can find someplace else to crash."

I got up and followed him. "The truth is that Angie doesn't mind some kinds of people getting hurt. Think of that policeman." He didn't respond and I heard myself say, " Think of yourself! She didn't mind you getting hurt, did she?"

"Don't tell my folks I'm back," he said, slinging the bag onto his back. "Please. I'll talk to them myself, I promise."

"Look, Hank, you don't have someplace to stay, really, do you?"

He hesitated. "No," he said. "But I can find something."

"Here." I held out my key. "I have another one. Take it, for Christ's sake. I'm leaving in two days, and then the place can be yours. I never found a subletter. When I get back from this trip to New York, I'm going to the

Lake House like I always do. I'm only going to be breezing through to pack my bags. Stay here. It would be stupid for you to go try to find someplace when this one's empty."

He took the key. "Thank you," he said. "I can find someplace else tonight."

Then he was gone.

I spent the next days in waiting, occasionally walking Rootie for Danny. Though his roommates had left for the summer, Danny remained in the apartment on the first floor because of a summer interning position at a nearby engineering firm. During the daytime, Rootie was my only companion, my confidant, the one who listened to me wonder aloud what we had done.

Door Swinging Open

VITO AND I HAD SET OFF BEFORE SUNRISE AND REACHED POMPEY just as the children's heifer competition was beginning. Trailers that had hauled in the summer fair rides and games lined the streets leading to the high school. Vito and I parked the car and made our way past the haunted house and the beer stands, the cotton candy and fried dough carts. A merry-go-round's tinny siren call blended with the pings and clangs from carnival games, hawkers and crowd conversation to the relative calm of the other half of the fair: the equestrian competitions, the stock-raising shows, the displays of baked pies and handmade dresses.

A little tumble of bleachers huddled under a rental tent in the middle of the school track. Flatbed trucks and trailers bordered one side of the football field; tents the other. As we neared the exhibition area we could hear the judges calling the next event into the ring: children's calf competition. A line of bleating calves and anxious children were stalled at the entrance behind the first contestant, a worried blonde moppet in cutoffs who hissed and struggled and yanked, but could not persuade her animal to move. The judge sat in the center of the track's field on a tipped-over wooden crate, looking a bit like a sluggish shark and offering very little encouragement. Even from the twenty yards that separated us as we walked toward them we could see that the tiny blonde was about to cry. The six other contestants were banging up against one another behind her in a raggedy line, their own calves apparently happy to go where led. Finally the lead contestant dislodged her little animal. He bleated, farted, and stepped into the cordoned-off ring. The audience in the bleachers sighed in relief.

A soccer field stretched out behind the track, and 4-H'ers in formal riding attire and English saddles posted solemnly in circles, destroying the grass. Mixed in with this group were riders in cowboy hats and boots, western saddles and jeans. This latter bunch of riders whooped and hustled, chasing one another across the field and annoying the more formal equestrians.

The calf contestants were still walking in circles as we reached the first tent, where canned goods, baked goods and chocolate candies were carefully laid out for inspection. The rabbits, we were told, were waiting for their judgments in the last tent along with the chickens.

"Why, here she is!" I was greeted as I stepped into this last shelter. "Come to see Tadodaho bring honor to us at last!"

Crooked River was surrounded with nine- and ten-year-olds, all milling in front of a bank of rabbit-filled cages that were labeled with the inhabitant's breed, owner and 4-H club affiliation. Most cards identified the contestants as representatives of the Iroquois Nation, Onondaga People.

"This here is Mary Beaver Dam," Crooked River said to me, stepping forward and taking my arm. "And these are her 4-H'ers: Peter Brushfire, Janey Big Tree, Tom Smith and Arthur Weaver." Each child smiled and nodded. "Their rabbits, they're each and every one of them Tadodaho's babies, and we're entering him, too, just to see what happens. Everybody, this here is Iris Sunnaret, who is sister to some buddies of mine."

They nodded and smiled, waved. This cheerfully gregarious Crooked River was a bit of a shock—not the man who waited behind blinds to consider whether or not he would answer the door to a stranger standing on the flaking paint of his porch; not the man who refused to get a telephone and made his aunt the go-between connecting him to the world.

"This is my friend Vito Signori," I offered in kind. The group flicked little shy waves at Vito, just as they had to me. "His family's in Geneva and he gave me a ride up here."

Two members of the group brightened at the mention of Geneva and began describing relatives of theirs who had gone there to work construction.

"Where were you?" Crooked River broke in, interrupting a story involving an unfortunate poker game and an AA meeting. It took me a moment to realize he was addressing Vito, who had understood this immediately.

"The Delta. What about you?" Vito said.

"Khe Sanh, partly in the worst of it. Middle of my tour."

"Well, fuck," Vito responded, and this seemed to be the appropriate thing to say. I could see Crooked River soften, see Vito make similar adjustments in his mind that left both men instantly familiar.

Just then three ponytailed men in their mid-twenties drifted by, walking unsteadily. "How!" one yelled out to our assembled group, which clearly included Iroquois. He raised one palm in salute. "Me friend to Indian. Hey, Chief! I said, 'How!' "

Vito stepped sideways briskly, cutting the young speaker off midstride. He reached behind the young man's neck, balled as much hair as he could wad into one fist and pulled the kid's face directly into his own. The little 4-H'ers got blank expressions on their faces and became very still—the reactions, I imagined, of children who had seen men get into nasty confrontations before and had some idea of what could happen next.

"That was not very polite," Vito said quietly. "It would be a civil gesture on your part to apologize to my friend Crooked River and his 4-H club members."

The ponytailed man spit in Vito's face. Vito kept his grip and bore down, forcing the young man to his knees. With his free hand he lifted the young man's shirt up to wipe his face, tearing it as he went. One of Ponytail's group of friends stepped forward, and Crooked River moved between him and the unfolding scene. Crooked River was large and very quiet, and the combination stopped Ponytail's friend in his tracks.

"Let him the fuck up, man," Ponytail's friend protested from where he stood. "I'll call the fucking police."

"You do that," Vito suggested. "Crooked River? Don't you think these young men are stoned? Look at their pupils. And didn't you see this guy take a swing at me? I think that one over there was carrying an open bottle, don't you, before he tossed it in this trash can? I think that's against the law. I think if we pointed that out to a policeman, it wouldn't be good for this boy." Vito nodded at a nearby trash can, which did indeed have an empty beer bottle poking up at the top of its greasy contents.

"The fuck, man—there's more of us will say you're lying," the friend sputtered.

"The fuck right back, man—you're stoned and slightly drunk. I'm sober and totally straight," Vito continued. "You're a hippie. I'm a clean-cut citizen. Where do you think Mr. Blue Uniform is going to come down?"

"Jesus, you are a total asshole!" This from Ponytail, still held firmly down on his knees before Vito. "You're ripping the hair out of my head, man!"

"You could be right," Vito answered. "I'm a total asshole. I think one of you should go find a cop to stop me before somebody gets hurt. Of course, I am acting in self-defense against this drug-abusing young man who attacked me."

"I didn't attack you or anybody," the kneeling young man protested. He tried to struggle to his feet but Vito held him firmly down and turned to speak to the victim's friends.

"I'm afraid this man you've been hanging out with is more dangerous than you realized," Vito said sadly. "You never know when someone under the influence of drugs is going to just lose his mind and come at you."

The largest of Ponytail's friends walked up to the trash can, pulled one of the three empty beer bottles out and smashed it against the rim, leaving half a shattered bottle in his hand. He took a step toward Vito and Ponytail. His second step unfroze me from where I'd been standing. I walked briskly up to Vito and his victim and struck the hand that held Ponytail down, taking Vito entirely by surprise and breaking his grip. Ponytail leaped to his feet and scrambled backward. I didn't say anything.

"You crazy fucker! I could charge you with assault!" Ponytail cried as he retreated farther, his friends closing around him.

Vito started after him and I rushed to place myself between him and the little group he seemed intent on hurting. He was moving with a great deal of mindless energy so I braced myself when I got directly in his path, only to be knocked entirely off my feet and into the group of Ponytail's friends by the force of our collision. They fell away as if I had been purposefully thrown at them. When my rear end hit the dirt it made a surprisingly loud *brummpp* noise followed by a higher-pitched rip—a pocket giving way. This sound rather than the collision itself seemed to stop Vito, recalling him from some distant place inhabited only by him and his victim. He bent down to take my hands and pull me up onto my feet. Ponytail and his retinue took this distraction as an opportunity to rapidly retreat.

"What were you doing?" I sputtered.

"He didn't apologize yet," Vito said grimly. But he was looking at me and his eyes were clear now. Perhaps Hank had not been so wrong to warn me against traveling with this person.

"That's all right, man," Crooked River said. "I know in his heart that hippie was sorry before he left." All the little 4-H'ers behind him nodded solemnly. "And in my heart, I accept his apology, for myself and on behalf of my 4-H'ers here."

Vito sighed. He looked suddenly depressed and a little confused. He sat down abruptly in the dirt. Mary Beaver Dam hustled up, brushing 4-H'ers to either side as she made her way through them to his side. "You stand up, Vito Signori, and come with me," she ordered. "I have a nice cool drink that can calm you considerable."

Vito stood and let himself be led away, leaving me with Crooked River, the rabbits and the 4-H'ers.

"Don't you worry," Crooked River said to me. "Mary, she can calm anything down." Crooked River let me sit silently for a few moments. "What's the matter?"

"You saw him," I answered.

"I saw."

"That's not normal," I insisted. "That's not right."

Crooked River shook his head. "He didn't hurt anybody."

"I don't know," I said.

"I have a good feeling about that man, little sister. You don't worry about that man."

"But look what he did," I protested.

"I looked. I saw when he put his hands on that skinny hippie, the hippie went down like a house of cards. Now Vito saw the same thing, and it could have gone either way for the hippie. He could have been hurt, or not. I saw him not get hurt."

"Vito was willing to hurt him, though, wasn't he, if things had gone just a little different."

"It's a wicked, wicked world, girl. Being willing to hurt somebody is maybe not the worst way to walk around in it. Now come look at these rabbits. What do you think of this rabbit, ayeah?"

I peered into Tadodaho's cage and met the animal's eyes. He sat quite placidly, chewing on something.

"See how happy he is?" Crooked River insisted. "He hasn't bitten me in two months."

"What do you think happened to him?" I asked.

"Mary Beaver Dam fixed him with a spell. Made some medicine. Said an incantation. Then she gave it to me and Tadodaho together. Now we're both calm."

"Why did she give it to both of you?"

"She says we're linked in the spirit world, and that's why I was drawn to Tadodaho and all the rabbits. It's probably why I never made him into stew. Good thing, huh? Mary Beaver Dam's from a long line of healers. Her mother and her grandmother were medicine women."

"How did she know you needed healing?"

"My aunt Jenny sent her to me for rabbits. Jenny told her to come talk to me one day because she knew Mary needed pets for her 4-H kids to raise. She's got herself a 4-H group with about twelve kids, all Iroquois— some Seneca, some Mohawk, some Onondaga. Got them together at a powwow. She comes to see me and I show her Tadodaho and she pets the damn rabbit and he's happy. Polite as can be. She puts him in my hands and he bites me. She asks me how I came by him, and where I'd been. I told her—every minute of it. It took ten hours and she stayed for the whole story. By the end of that day she knew all about the string and Batman and the night in the hole I was sure I was going to die and how I told all my family stories to the Batman, waiting for a helo to come in. I told her about the five other guys who weren't with the Batman and didn't make it. She used my stories to figure out what kind of medicine I needed and she used the string to make it. Remember I told you once that if you tie a string around your wrist when you're told a story, that the story keeps?"

I nodded.

"She asked me for the string I'd tied around the Batman to keep the story whole. She burned it, and mixed it with crushed dry corn, said an incantation. Then she rolled it into a ball and fed it to me and Tadodaho. And now we're calm."

"Why did you still have the string if you say that the Batman was lost with Eddie?"

"The day your Eddie died I found the string folded into a square of paper and set into my gear careful so I'd see it."

"So somebody else had the Batman? Who left the string?"

Crooked River shrugged. "Somebody who knew I'd need it. It was a powerful medicine, for sure, when I finally got around to using it. Something in me shifted, just like Mary Beaver Dam said it would. I know some people wouldn't say that. Aunt Jenny says I'm just in love with the woman and that's what's calmed me down. I don't think so, though."

"Well. That's good," I said. "If you're in love, I mean."

Crooked River twisted to open a cage and pull out its resident. He offered it to me to stroke. "Now you look at these animals and tell me those aren't the prettiest coats you've ever seen in your life," he said, gesturing to two other rabbit contestants behind the fellow in my hands. The rabbit I held had Tadodaho's dark rich coloring and full ruff. The two others were piebald chestnuts with very round ears.

"They're real nice," I concurred.

"They're all alert. But so calm. Feel the coat."

It was as dense and fine as mink and I said so.

Crooked River didn't look at me. He opened another cage and reached in to pet its occupant and said, "Iris, that Vito, he's not bad for you."

I looked up from Tadodaho's great-niece. "How would you know that?" I demanded.

"Mary Beaver Dam was pretty sure you'd be coming with someone," he said, as if that answered the question. "She was real curious about you. Asked me questions. I can tell she likes that Vito of yours."

"She met him an hour ago. And he's not mine."

"She's never been wrong as far as I know and I can see she likes him. I should tell you maybe that Mary's the one said to call you."

"Why?" I kept stroking the rabbit.

"She says it's time for me to pass on the rest of what I have of Batman's. She said I needed to give you the picture of your mother and the pills because you'd need it soon."

My hand froze halfway down the little animal's back. He twisted away and I realized that I had started pressing on him very hard. Crooked River took the rabbit out of my hands and popped him back into a cage. He moved away toward the opposite end of the football field, waving to me to come with him past the chicken tent and into the line of pickup trucks. He stopped before a blue Chevrolet and reached inside the driver-side window to yank up on a bent coat hanger that served as its latch. He reached in for the waiting manila envelope and twisted around to put it in my hands, then stood by my side waiting for me to open it.

"I think I'll keep them for later," I said. "Thank you for giving them to me, Crooked River."

"You should open them here," he insisted. He sat right down in the grass and patted the johnson weed beside him. "Now."

"Is this the end of the pictures? The last of them?"

No. There were more.

"But didn't Mary say I should have everything you've got left?"

"Soon." Crooked River nodded. "You will. My time with them is just about done."

Despite my spoken protest that I would wait and open them later, I dropped down onto the weeds and slipped a finger under the manila envelope's flap. Three drawings slid out onto the grass before us.

Angie had told the truth about my mother—she had been a queen. Perry had drawn her lying sprawled across a bed in a tidy square room. She was enormous: her image spilled far beyond the boundaries of the page, the arms thrown up over her head and the curve of her flank and hip flowing beyond their actual limits. Something was uncoiling in this woman, passing through her and moving on. The picture made me think of the way a rainstorm looked hissing away from you over a smooth body of water that's been stunned into mirrorlike smoothness by thunder.

The woman was clearly dead. Crooked River sat silently.

"Do you know what this is?" I demanded. I felt heat radiating off my face. The visceral sense of my own open capillaries and the plunging sense of dropping, dropping, dropping was being caused by the image's eerie familiarity. I could not have ever seen this myself yet it felt as if I'd seen it a hundred times.

I set this drawing to one side and picked up the second one, working to steady my hands. In this picture a woman lay adrift on a river of what looked at first like millions of bubbles but proved, on closer examination, to be riplets made of pills. She was being carried toward the horizon and the look on her face was the way I imagined the sounds the dogs made when they found Skinny's body would look if they were a face instead of howls.

This was not a Queen mother. It was her companion, her double, her other self—a person I also knew but had somehow managed to banish from my idea of her, and how it was to live with her—she was the Animal Mother, and despite my confidence in my own happy childhood, I knew for a fact that this woman was also familiar to me.

This drawing was spare, minimalist—only the feathering surface of pills and the woman borne along—and in the corner, tucked into a ripple, was a child who looked very much like Eddie, who looked stoically and directly at the river of pills as it carried him.

I shook the envelope to get its last sheet free. This one was reminiscent of Perry's comic-book days. A toothless Vietnamese man in a patched and faded black robe stood on a mountainside, wind lifting his thatchy beard and scrim of hair. He held a chicken upside down, clutching its feet.

I looked up at Crooked River, who watched me attentively.

"Well, this is interesting," I said, sliding them back into the manila envelope. I saw Mary and Vito making their way across the football field to us. Vito raised an arm and waved. I waved back.

As soon as they reached us, Mary said to Crooked River, "Tell her."

I tipped my face in his direction, waiting to be told. "What?" I asked. "What?"

"It's only that your brother asked me that if anything happened to him he wanted me to destroy those three drawings. He didn't want those passed on."

"Why did you keep them?"

"Your brother could be wrong sometimes. These pictures, I could feel that there was some kind of medicine in them but I didn't know what kind. You have to be careful with things like that. I figured that underneath his wanting me to destroy them, he wanted me to give them to you."

"To me in particular? Not my sister?"

"He talked about your sister, but not in the way he'd talk about you. And you were the one who gave us the Batman. Something was different about you."

Mary nodded. I turned away from her, irritated. What did she know, anyway?

I said, "I think you should give me anything else he left. He was my brother. Not your brother."

"He was mine, too," Crooked River said, shaking his head in a way that looked like he was sorry about it. "I've told you before—what's from there is more mine than yours. It was only Mary who convinced me to give you these." He patted the manila folder.

"Why did you do that?" I asked her.

"Crooked River had the string to keep, to give him back his story. You don't have a string. You have papers, like other white people—certificates and records and sometimes, like these, you have pictures. A person has a right to her kind of string, whatever it is. Those papers the white men send to you, they won't do it."

I thought of the visit to the missing persons bureau in Washington; about not having a string or even, sometimes, certificates and records. Less than a string.

"You should forgive your brothers," she said. "They weren't bad men."

"Forgive them for what? I don't need to forgive my brothers for anything."

Mary only shrugged. "It's hard to imagine what it was over there."

"How would you know?"

"Oh, I was there. I was a nurse at a MASH station on the Delta. Then on a carrier. I have an RN but when I was there I learned a lot about healing plants."

"From who?"

"A monk. I never went near the sorcerers. You have to stay away from sorcerers."

"I've been told that," I murmured. Mary stood looking at me, waiting patiently for I knew not what. "Well," I said awkwardly. "We should be heading on."

Vito heaved himself to his feet. "I hear a corn dog stand calling to me," he said simply. "Anybody else want something? Then we'll head out." This last to me. He sauntered toward the food stand.

"You shouldn't waste that man," Mary said to me when he was out of earshot.

"What?"

"That man," she said, pointing again to Vito, "loves you pretty good. He's a little spoiled, crushed and bent right now, but he can be smoothed out. I know you're worried about what he did with the hippie. But you know, he could have hurt him and he didn't."

"It doesn't matter."

She sighed. "All right, girl. You go ahead and ruin your heart."

Crooked River broke in. "The ribbons get handed out in five minutes. Iris, you come and rub his cage for luck; come pet his children, then watch us whip their little butts. I'll show you that you have the touch." He winked, the first playful gesture I had ever seen from him.

I did what he asked and passed the few minutes before the judging announcements petting rabbits and hearing stories of the particularly heroic, warm or dull-witted animals who had passed through the lives of Mary's 4-H kids. Vito stood fitfully by, holding a corn dog.

The ribbons came down on the side of the Onondaga, Seneca and Mohawk Nations. Tadodaho took second place to a brindled daughter of his who hopped away with the blue ribbon. All the other winning places were held by his offspring, and the representatives of the Iroquois Nation announced that they were going out for pizza to celebrate. We were invited.

"Vito has to get on to Geneva," I said awkwardly. "A religious festival."

"Really?" Mary asked. "What kind of religious festival?"

"Honoring a Catholic saint," he said. "Sausage-and-pepper sandwiches, fried bread, statues, parades, dancing."

She nodded. "Like a powwow."

Vito nodded back. They had hit on some mysterious rapport but I remained at a distance, cautious. It occurred to me that this was another new behavior, this Angie-like reserve and suspicion of mine. That was not me. I was the open one, the sanguine thoughtless affectionate one.

Wasn't I?

We headed east toward Geneva and for two or three towns we said nothing.

"I didn't hurt him," he said at last.

"I know. I was there," I replied.

"I maybe should have just let it pass by and waited for them to move on."

"Maybe."

"Then again, maybe I did exactly the right thing. Sometimes things like that have to be done."

"That's ridiculous. Nothing 'had' to be done."

I stared out the window.

"Look," he said, "think about it. Let's say I'd sat there and done nothing. Let Crooked River and Mary and the kids get mocked by those idiots without saying a word. Would that be ideal?"

I shook my head no.

"Fine," he continued. "Let's say I'd tried to chat with them in hopes of making them understand that their behavior was rude. Would that have worked?"

I shook my head no.

"All right. Let's say I'd actually hurt the kid."

I shook my head no again.

"There you have it," Vito concluded. "Don't think I didn't run all those alternatives through in my mind before I picked the route I took. Personally, I think it went very well."

"Why did you just kind of sit down in the dirt afterwards then, if it was all so ideal?"

"What's ideal isn't always so easy." He cleared his throat. "So, was your trip to see Crooked River what you wanted?"

"I don't know yet. What did you think of him?"

"Liked him."

"What Mary said about sorcerers and monks and healing herbs . . . did you see that in Vietnam?"

"Didn't see it. Heard about it. There were lots of Vietnams, Iris. Even in the same platoon sometimes, guys were in different Vietnams."

I pressed my head back into the headrest, hard. "What's the worst thing about it?" I asked. "What's the worst?"

We drove in silence for so long that I thought he'd forgotten the question. Then, almost fifteen minutes after I asked it he said, "The ones you kill yourself."

"What?" I wasn't sure I'd heard right.

"I said the worst of it is remembering the ones you killed yourself. And if you were there for long, and in country for long, you did kill them. You didn't let them get near you. You warned them off and if they kept coming you shot them. All kinds of them—old people and kids and teenagers, people coming at you with guns and people coming at you with baskets of fruit. You could see their faces and what they were wearing. Never what they were thinking, though."

"How often do you think of them?" I asked.

"Oh. Maybe every ten, fifteen minutes."

"Every day?"

"No. Some days it's every half hour. It's been changing recently—getting better. My personal best was five hours."

"When was that?"

Now he looked at me. "Today." He smiled.

I didn't smile back. "And when you do remember, what's it like?"

"It's like a dual-screen experience. I'll be tossing a skillet of mussels and seeing a little boy rolling down a hill. Or I'll be sitting in a lecture and see a woman holding a toddler just before her chest kind of explodes all over the place. The two things, both at once, side by side, all the time."

"Is it like that for everybody?"

"Like I said, different Vietnams for different people. Some guys, it never touched them. They were just made like that or maybe they were lucky and had an easy tour. Others, toward the end of their year or when they got back, they didn't feel particularly interested in living with themselves anymore. When you told me about your brother, I thought about that."

"You mean you thought he killed himself?"

"Yes."

"That doesn't fit my brother. That's not him."

"I'll tell you a story. I was a sniper. Most of the snipers in my class were country boys who'd hunted their whole lives. I was an anomaly—a city kid who didn't meet a rifle until boot camp but just had this gift. I was psychically, physically connected to whatever was in my sights. I never missed. Then one day I got shot out of a tree. Shattered one ankle when I landed. Ripped open my side on the way down. That's where the scars come from, and why I limp." He stopped talking.

"You're telling me this story to explain your limp or to convince me my brother changed?"

"I'm telling you this story to explain how you can't predict when this idea that maybe you should be dead yourself will happen to you. I sat in trees killing people for months and all the feeling was slowly leaking out of me. I got to the point where I didn't think I'd feel anything again for the rest of my life. Then it changed: it got worse. What changed it was this scout with our platoon, one of the country boys who should have been good with a rifle but wasn't. What he was good at was moving through the bush without making a sound. He had real nerve—would go right out on perfectly black nights—he liked the rainy season nights best because the sound of the rain made him totally invisible. He called rain his magic cloak. He'd come back with the kind of information you had to be close enough to see faces to get right and he always got it right. He volunteered in dangerous situations—saved all our lives at least three times. Then he went out one night and didn't come back. I'd been posted in a tree just outside the perimeter. At dusk we'd heard mortar fire and gunshots moving closer to us from the west. Sometimes the VC could get within yards of you and you'd never see them. The tops of grasses just to the west of me moved. I waited. They moved again. I shot. They didn't move anymore."

He stopped talking.

"Vito? Then what?"

"The next day we moved out and there he was. Everybody but me assumed a VC sniper got him. Maybe a VC sniper did get him. But he was so close to where I saw the grass moving . . ."

"Did you tell anyone?" I felt cold. My back teeth were chattering though it was a humid eighty degrees. I suppressed a terrible nervous impulse to laugh.

"No. I've only told you. Just now. After that I started taking these ridiculous chances. I tried for a while, but I never got killed."

"I'm sorry, Vito." I was still very cold. I stifled the temptation to offer up the obvious platitudes about doing one's best, doing one's duty, the tragic confusions inherent to war zones.

"Don't be sorry. I've been afraid that I couldn't feel anything anymore."

I looked at him. "And?"

He lifted his right hand off the steering wheel and took my left hand. He opened it, rotated it palm upward and aligned my pointer and index finger right next to each other before drawing them to his throat and laying them along the jugular. The steady *ca-chug* of the pulse beat out rapid and fervent. He met my eyes thoroughly before turning them back to the road. "Feel that?" he asked.

I could feel the skin of my face change, heat up and flush. I turned it away and looked out the window. He set my hand down.

"When I got out of detox I tracked down some information about that scout. He lived in this town called Uppity Falls in the Virginia Tidewater. Uppity Falls has a hundred and twenty residents, one Pump and Pantry, a feed store, two traffic lights and a gun store. He had six sisters and two brothers, got straight A's in school and represented Virginia in a national science fair competition during his junior year of high school. Earth Science was his favorite subject. His favorite food was Blackjack gum. He could tame squirrels as fast as shoot them. Nobody in his family had ever gone to college but he got a scholarship to the University of Virginia and he had plans. When he finished his tour he was going to be a college boy and major in geology."

"Blackjack gum is not a food."

"I know."

"How did you get all this information? Did you call his family?"

"No. God, no. I went to his military and school records with some help from my congressman friend. I called other guys who'd known him. I found myself applying to the University of Virginia as a geology major. As soon as I got here, the moment I stepped onto this campus, I stopped wanting to be dead. But I didn't start feeling. I was in a kind of limbo but I could stand it."

"What was his name?"

"Proover Davies. His mother's family were Proovers."

Vito was actually sweating. The truth was that this look on Vito Signori drew me like gravity. I'd had no experience with it or it might have affected me very differently.

"So," I said, "if you turn yourself into the person you killed, you're cured?"

"I've met guys who were there who think they're turning into Vietnamese. But me, I got Proover. And you. The night you lay on the lawn until sunrise, I noticed you around two in the morning. Watched you for hours until you left."

"So?"

"All I saw was you—no dead people. It felt like a door swinging open. I thought you were the most beautiful thing I'd ever seen, lying there waiting in the dark."

He said it simply and then he turned his attention back to the road.

Birthday Wish

ON MY SEVENTH BIRTHDAY I MADE A REQUEST, RIGHT AFTER THE morning birthday cake, that my birthday dinner take place on the raft that floated about a hundred yards off our dock. I had an August birthday so this wasn't entirely unreasonable, but I also wanted control of the menu and I wanted roast pork and biscuits. The temperature that week hovered in the nineties, a situation complicated by unusual humidity. Still, I clung to the idea of roasting a large piece of farm animal and paddling it out at sunset. My father was supposed to be there and I had the idea that roast pork was something he liked. Though the thought of my father visiting made my stomach hurt, it was also thrilling—like the circus coming or a big storm.

Most of the year leading up to my seventh birthday had been scoured out of my mind by my mother's death. Within a matter of weeks I had begun to have difficulty summoning up her face or the sound of her voice. Only Shalimar brought her clearly, jarringly to mind, and I would go to her room and sit in her closet where the scent lingered for months. There were no pictures of her in the house. I never asked who removed them any more than I asked questions about her death or my father's absence.

These were the simple facts of my life: my mother had died in a drowning accident. My father's work took him far away. My brothers were Perry and Eddie and I had a sister named Angie. We lived with my parents' dearest friends and their son, Hank. They loved me and kept me safe.

I had stopped going to the closet to smell my mother by this time, and we were all at the Lake House waiting for my birthday to come, my perfect birthday that would be crowned by a visit from my father and a seasonally illogical hunk of pork eaten on a bobbing raft. I had learned to tell time and held out hopes for a watch, pink, with a gold buckle.

The morning opened in a foggy haze. A cake was delivered to my bedside and I blew out every one of the candles, unassisted. My siblings had pooled their resources and wanted me to open their gift right away and not wait until dinner. They set their lumpily wrapped offering at my feet—a stuffed Dalmatian dog! I had watched him sitting on the shelf of our local five-and-dime for months now and was convinced that no one in the world had paid any attention to my mooning over him. But they had—they all had, and they had bought him weeks ago and hid him away under Perry's bed.

There are few pleasures as keen as receiving a gift that you want very badly and thought you would never receive. The misery you feel if the new gift is damaged is just as keen, which I learned when my dog's ear was pulled from its socket within the hour as I tried to forcefully take it back from Eddie, who was pretending to offer it to one of our real live dogs as a chew toy. I cried, of course, and Eddie said he was sorry. He was actually sorry, I think, but he was also impatient with my tears and told me to grow up. This suggestion brought a rain of criticism down on him from Hank, Angie and Perry, who said he should shut up and stop making stupid suggestions and he shouldn't have been offering my new toy to Otto to begin with. Exactly what did he think a Rhodesian ridgeback was going to do with that stuffed dog, anyway?

I had three wishes coming because it was my birthday morning. I had only used two of them with the first cake and I had been thinking carefully about my third because I didn't want it wasted. But now in the heat of the moment I forgot all my care and I threw the third wish away in a petty little spasm of rage. I wished Eddie was dead. Then I wished I hadn't wished that—after all, it was only play and he was only teasing and he didn't really understand about stuffed animals. I wished that last thoughtless wish unwished over and over but I knew that I had used up the three allotted wishes and I was only throwing away more feeling on a situation over which I had no power. It was done and that was that.

In the end my father didn't come that birthday. We waited all day and began the birthday dinner without him. At around eight that evening he telephoned and asked to speak to me. He was in some foreign country, speaking on a military line. "Now every time you stop talking you have to say 'Over,' and when you're done you say 'Roger, out,' " he instructed. But I couldn't get the hang of it, so the conversation was halting and lumpy, its real content overshadowed by shouted *Overs* and *Roger, outs*. And I was only seven, without much to say of interest to a man in my father's position. I was holding my new dog and his ripped ear as I spoke and I tried to say something that would make my father understand that I had made a terrible mistake that had something to do with Eddie but I was old enough to know that he didn't believe in birthday wishes, though I still did myself. So I was evasive and distressed at once, and the *Overs* and *Roger, outs* defeated me.

The same was not true for Eddie, who got to talk after me and settled into the rules of military conversation as though he had invented them for his own amusement. He blushed happily at something my father said to him, and spoke briskly and coherently about his hopes for tackle football in the coming year. Angie and Perry took their turns and nodded into the telephone. I don't remember them speaking though they must have.

"Wasn't that fun?" Uncle Charlie said when the connection broke off. "Your very first military hookup!"

"Where was he, Uncle Charlie?" Eddie asked.

"Oh," he was told, "very hard to say."

I imagined this meant that wherever my father was, its name was unpronounceably foreign. I didn't think, *Military secret,* because that thought would have been carried by the anxious undertow of politics and war. Whereas I was safe here on my birthday in the care of Uncle Charlie and Aunt Eleanor, who were never going to leave or change or be so distracted that I fell out of their minds. And I was surrounded by my brothers and my sister and by Hank, all of whom I adored. My brother Eddie had apologized for the incident of the ear, and my brother Perry had gotten a needle and thread and reattached the thing more or less so the damage barely showed. True, I had wished Eddie dead and that troubled me, but I had not been in my right mind and certainly whatever power controlled these things would see that and sift the mistaken wish out of the pile before it was granted. I was more troubled, actually, about having thrown away a perfectly good wish.

Someone was wearing a cape at my birthday dinner that year, so it must have been around the time the boys discovered the *Knightfall* episodes where Bane cripples Batman and leaves him for dead, and Jean Paul Valley, aka Azrael, an initiate into the ancient order of St. Dumas, is summoned by debonair playboy Bruce Wayne to replace the fallen hero, who is actually Bruce Wayne himself in disguise. Perry would tell me the stories, though I didn't like the pictures and wouldn't read the comics themselves. They were too full of stomach-dropping graphics and giant "AAAUGH" noises. The imitations that Perry drew absorbed whole summer afternoons and showed him his own talents as a graphic artist. And though the original comics alarmed me, I loved looking at Perry's versions of heroic events—renditions that incorporated him and Eddie into the action. Angie neither read the comics nor listened to synopses, considering the whole thing dumb.

Part of my charm, I can see now in retrospect, was my fascination with everything my siblings liked, and my willingness to do whatever they told me to do. There were the minor useful ways these characteristics played out: I was always free to run and fetch them water when they were in the tree house and coming down seemed like too much trouble; I was the first to try eating anything we found that might be good but whose poisonous qualities were as yet untested; I was first to step into a creek and see if any leeches rose to the occasion. I was happy to pop the chrysanthemum petal in my mouth and trot into the stream because my brothers suggested it and it made me proud to do it when Angie refused and told them they were stupid. They were my brothers: they wouldn't let me come to any harm. No significant and lasting harm, anyway.

I spent the afternoon of my seventh birthday holding my Dalmatian dog and waiting for my birthday dinner. I waited mostly in the backyard, where the boys got a badminton birdy stuck at the end of a tree limb. Perry climbed up but couldn't get far enough out to shake it loose.

"Iris, you go on up and shake that thing, will you?" Eddie asked.

I was a good climber, and the lightest of us all, thus the best candidate to get close to the birdy. I might even be able to pluck it from the branch. I agreed and set my dog down on a rock so I could see him while I climbed.

"Nah. Too high for her," Perry said, shaking his head.

"She can do it," Eddie contradicted him.

"But she's not going to," Perry said sternly.

"What are you going to do? Tell Uncle Charlie?"

I remember the way Eddie said that to Perry, and I remember realizing that I had become invisible to them. Even at seven I knew that something was out of whack. There was entirely too much heat in this brief exchange between my inseparable brothers. I had one foot on the lowest branch and my arms around one above it and Perry strode authoritatively up to me and peeled my hand away. He wasn't rough. He was just firm, like a grown-up who wasn't mad yet.

"Fine," Eddie said, shrugging and turning away. "Momma's boy. Maybe you've forgotten that Momma isn't here anymore."

Perry didn't reply. He kept my hand in his and led me into the house, stopping to pick up my dog, and delivered me to Aunt Eleanor in the kitchen. Whatever had passed between my brothers troubled me only in a seven-year-old way, meaning that if it didn't interfere with my birthday dinner I didn't see any reason to pay it any mind.

I was happy: I had heard my father's voice for the only time in that year; I got my stuffed Dalmatian dog as well as my first two wishes, which concerned all of us being safe and being able to go on living here with Charlie and Eleanor. The third wish I decided not to think about.

My seven-year-old-birthday day ended, as I'd hoped, with all of us eating corn on the cob and roast pork on the raft. I had sparklers on my second cake and a swim with a flaming orange-red sunset backdrop.

I could hear my brother Perry crying in the bathroom just after I went to bed that night, but when I got up to go to him I found the door ajar and the room empty.

Vito's World

Vito and I got back on Route 20 and headed toward the Finger Lakes, through Marietta, through Auburn, over the tip of Cayuga Lake and on past Waterloo. Vito had told me that he lived just on the other side of Waterloo, and I'd said that sounded like a country-western song by a person with a weak grasp of European history.

"That's it exactly," he said to me. "That's the part of the world I come from."

Geneva itself was not a pretty place, and the streets Vito turned down were nothing like the domestic settings of my own life. I kept looking for Seneca Lake, which according to my map should be running in a dramatic blue strip downward from the place on the map labeled "Geneva."

"You said you lived on the lake," I protested when we pulled into a street marked by nothing but an ownerless dog and a green storefront with a board nailed to its front that read "Private. Gerome Street Men's Club."

"There." Vito pointed, jabbing at a narrow space between two peeling gray buildings. "You can see it, can't you?" Indeed, there was a tiny patch of what might have been water. "This is home," he said, pulling abruptly to the curb beside one of the flaking buildings.

It was after eight o'clock and the tiny patch of blue that Vito had pointed out was framed above by an effulgent strip of pink sunset. Crowd noises and the smell and sound of popping fat, ground meat and blackened oil drifted between buildings from the next block. Vito pulled in to the curb and in a seamless series of perhaps three distinct movements got himself and our two bags out of the car and to a door at the side of a convenience store. The front of the building bore a sign that read "Joey's Spa." I followed him through the door and into the narrow bottom landing of a flight of stairs.

"Ma!" he called up.

"Vito!" A woman with the physique and coloring of a robin popped open the door at the top of the stairs. She was gray-brown except for her apron, which was red: brown hair, losing its luster to gray and dirt tones; brown eyes and brown features; gray dress. The front of her body swelled out in proportions that seemed to have nothing to do with the tiny little legs that supported the whole structure. She held her arms out and called his name again.

"This is Iris Sunnaret, Ma," he said when we reached the top of the flight. His mother hugged him, hard, and then stepped away from him to give herself a clear view of me. I could feel her take in my khakis, the white cotton shirt, the lack of makeup. I saw that I confused her somehow.

"Well," she said at last. "Welcome, Iris." She hugged me with the same vigorous energy; released me. "You'll excuse me while I see to the chicken. Vito, your brother said he'd be here for dinner but I think that wife of his has some other plans for him."

"Ma, come on. Would you have wanted Pop heading off to eat at his mother's once a week after you got married?"

"Your father did head off to eat at his mother's once a week after we got married. And I understood, knowing that a mother would miss her son. But not this woman."

"Ma, they've got a kid now. Be reasonable."

"I invite them all but do they come?"

"No. They don't come," Vito said, tugging at her apron playfully. "They rip your heart out of your chest every week of your life."

"Do you have brothers, Iris?" Vito's mother demanded suddenly.

"Yes," I said without thinking.

"So? Do they behave like this to your mother?"

"Her brothers served overseas, Ma. Didn't make it back," Vito said for me.

"Oh, my dear. I am so sorry." Tears sprang to Mrs. Signori's eyes. "So, so sorry." She stepped forward and touched my arm. Her hand was very warm—almost hot. I drew away.

"It's fine," I protested. I smiled to prove it.

"I know how a question can catch a person by surprise," Mrs. Signori said. "I'm sorry. You know I didn't intend any hurt."

I nodded energetically. "Don't even think about it."

She reached up and pinched my cheek hard enough to make me have to struggle not to squirm out of her grasp. "It's a good thing, being tender," she said. "It's nothing to hide." She released me. "Now." This to Vito. "That brother of yours, I don't care if he's here or not. We're eating. Go get your father out of the garden, Vito, while Iris and I put the lasagna and gravy on the table."

"Gravy" proved to be tomato sauce, and lasagna proved to be just a first course, followed by roast chicken, escarole with white beans, salad, and broccoli studded with fried garlic. We were clearing this last when the downstairs door opened and a man's voice called up to us.

Mrs. Signori rose with more slow dignity than I would have thought she possessed. She reached behind her and took a second, perfectly roasted yet uneaten chicken by the legs. She and the chicken went to the door at the head of the stairs.

"You're too late for dinner!" she shouted, and the chicken whipped over her head and downward. We heard a greasy thud.

"Ma!" her target protested.

She shut the door and resumed her seat at the table. "I don't understand how people act today," she said, looking imploringly to me for support. "Does an invitation today mean nothing? Is it acceptable now to let someone who has cooked for you wait, and wait?"

I looked down at my white beans and escarole. Vito pushed his chair back and reached for my hand, pulling me up and out of my own seat. "Got to go, Ma. We meet at the club. Great dinner." He bent over her and pecked her cheek.

"When'll you be back?" she asked. "You know Gerry and Anna want to see you and I told them you'd be here!"

"Don't you worry. We'll be back."

"Your father didn't say a word all through the meal," I said when we were on the street again. "Your mother threw a chicken at your brother!"

"Doesn't that woman make a phenomenal roast chicken? And Dad, he stopped talking about eleven years ago."

"Why?"

Vito shrugged. "Mom talks for him."

"Does she throw chickens a lot?"

"If she appreciated her own genius with chickens a little more, then she would throw fewer of them."

In the next hour I was positioned outside the men's club of Vito's patron saint, left under the protection of his friend Mikey while Vito took his place as one of the statue's bearers. I followed the icon's slow progress toward church, Mikey showing me how to pin a five-dollar bill to her robes in order to protect Vito's good luck and to show respect. The saint was plastered in small bills by the time she arrived at her destination. Vito reappeared ten minutes after she had been put on her pedestal, and dismissed Mikey.

"Come for a drink," he said. "Meet some of the neighborhood."

We waded through nearly impenetrable waves of sticky, yelling people. Half-eaten fried dough, wadded hot dog buns and weeping toddlers blocked our path in every direction. "It'll clear out in an hour," he yelled back at me, "when the kids get sent home to bed." He led me to the local under-fifty drinking hole: a Sheraton Hotel bar. The bartender greeted him by name; about a third of the patrons greeted him by name. It was clear that these people had made certain assumptions and that I was getting assessed as a new girlfriend. The faces looked as puzzled as Mrs. Signori's had looked.

An explanation for this confusion sat down beside Vito within ten minutes of our appearance: collarbone-length black hair, enormous kohled eyes, a leather miniskirt, bangles on both wrists and a gold crucifix clearly visible between two perfect and very tanned breasts. This woman was the kind of person who had sat in the back row of my eighth-grade typing class sighing, already very much in command of information that would be forever out of my grasp.

They were high school's romantic alpha girls, indifferent to grades or the future beyond next weekend, quick and brutal and glamorous, desired by boys of all cliques and academic strata. Angie had been the only girl in our school who was both like and unlike them—someone both heading for college and bumming cigarettes and gossip from the hairdressing school girls. Angie had had a broad kind of glamour, something these girls could recognize and honor just as my sister could see and love their own brand of erotic messaging. They'd liked one another. The more khaki-ish and bespectacled among us had anxiously avoided any mixing while Angie straddled the two worlds.

"Got an extra?" I nodded at this young woman's cigarette, half closing my eyes and pouting just the tiniest, smallest bit.

"Sure." She looked at me for the first time.

"Iris, this is Carla," he said, leaning back so I could see her face. The girl shook a cigarette out of a box for me and I took it, trying to channel my sister's spirit as I balanced it between my fingers. When she turned her attention back to Vito I leaned across him, cigarette in my lips and breasts in his lap. "Light?"

I took one drag, didn't inhale, didn't cough and then held the cigarette in one hand and watched.

"I'm a girlfriend from his past." This she said directly to me. "And maybe the future." This she said to him. She flicked his chest lightly at about the place his nipple would be and slid off the bar stool.

"She liked you, I could tell," Vito said to me.

I said, "Now I know why everybody's looking at me like that."

"Yeah. You're not what they'd expect."

"Any more recent girlfriends here tonight?" I craned my neck, looking past him to a buzzing little crowd at the door.

"Nah. There's the ex-wife, though."

I twisted around to see where he was pointing. "Really?"

"Really and truly."

"That one with all the gold? White pants?"

He nodded.

"Who else?"

"There's been nobody since I got back. My friends are starting to get worried about me."

"What'll they say now that you've shown up with me?"

"That they're more worried." He grinned.

"Until you tell them I'm not a girlfriend."

"I'm not going to tell them that," he said.

Two men Vito's age broke away from a group and approached us, asking Vito to introduce them to me. He did, and they hustled in closer, arguing the case for Brandy Alexanders over white wine, beer over Brandy Alexanders, a simple roast chicken over puttanesca. "His mother!" one of them said, jabbing his finger in Vito's chest and then bringing his fingers to his lips in the universal sign of acknowledged perfection. "Have you eaten his mother's roast chicken?" I said I had, and this set them off in another flurry of praise for various foods and cooks and restaurants they had known. The argument over arugula, Vito assured me when they left us for a moment to go to the bathroom and to collect on a bet, respectively, was a form of flirtation.

It was one in the morning when Vito led me away from the Sheraton. His house was about a mile away from the bar and since we'd gotten there on foot we set off the same way now toward his family's apartment. "The first friend of yours, Johnny, was very good-looking," I observed, stepping carefully around the debris in the street left from the feast. The remains of the feast crowd blew through the early-morning streets, some still shutting down food stalls and others settled onto stoops or folding chairs on the sidewalk. "Don't they have girlfriends?"

"Afraid to," Vito answered. "That's why they think talking about puttanesca is hitting on a girl."

"What are they afraid of?"

"To put it baldly, they have problems in bed. Since they got back from 'Nam. It makes their enthusiasm for salad greens and roast chicken get a little out of hand."

"But still, they flirt."

"Flirting's easy," Vito said. "They do it to reassure themselves."

"Oh."

"I don't flirt," he said, trying to head off the question and the challenge. "Not like that, anyway."

"What about your feelings for polenta and lamb shanks?"

"Sometimes a polenta is only a polenta." He stepped in front of me and bent down, one hand behind my waist and the other cradling my head.

I had been kissed in high school by boys who didn't have any idea what they were doing, and by boys who had come looking for Angie's attentions and turned to me when she ignored or rejected them. None of these kisses had felt directed only and entirely at me. They were experiments and play. This one was neither. It had the force of Vito Signori's complete attention. His physical mass seemed to expand behind and around it, dwarfing mine.

I had kissed him briefly before in his room at the end of the long and somewhat drunken meal we'd shared that spring but on that afternoon I had taken him by surprise. Now he was the initiator and the effect was very different. This kiss was like moving through salty dense water— warm but shot through with cold currents. It lifted me straight out of whatever I'd been and put me in a different state, washed me along and then, as the kiss ended, deposited me back on this dark street in a corner of Geneva, New York.

I'd had no idea.

I didn't want Vito Signori to know that, however, so I smiled brightly and took a step away in the direction we'd been moving. "Come on," I said.

He fell into step beside me. "I'm not going to pretend that didn't happen," he said to me lightly.

"Fine," I said. "Don't."

I was tired all the way into the center of my bones when we reached Vito's walk-up. A tangle of sounds rolled down the stairs: glasses, pots, knives and voices all clinking against one another. "I hear your brother," I said. "Your mother must have forgiven him."

"She was mad at him?" Vito asked. I looked at his face to scan for irony or sarcasm. There was none.

While the younger members of the community had been cruising one another (or not) at the local hotel bar, the generation above them, it seemed, had been in rooms like this one all over the neighborhoods in Geneva that observed the holiday. The Signori kitchen was crammed full of middle-aged neighbors, most sitting around the kitchen table with spoons in their hands and coffee cups at their elbows. Latecomers leaned on the counter with a spoon in one hand and a coffee cup in the other until a place at the table cleared. As we entered, two people were leaving and someone else was yelling up from the bottom of the stairs. The group now in residence ate communally, leisurely, from a rectangular pan full of polenta that was almost as long and wide as the table itself. Pitchers of tomato sauce and a chunk of ungrated parmesan were passed around the table along with the grater. Mrs. Signori stood at her post by the coffeepot, which she emptied and re-brewed twice in the forty minutes that I was able to keep my eyes open and my face out of the cornmeal.

"Ma!" Vito finally protested, intervening on my behalf when a plate of leftover salad greens was wedged between the polenta pan and the tiny bit of table allotted me. "Let the girl go to bed!"

"But that's the way you like salad best!" she argued. "Wilted a little, on bread." She was brandishing a loaf of Italian white and a knife in our direction as she spoke.

"She is not me. I'll eat it for breakfast. I promise," Vito told her, standing and kissing her on the cheek. "Now I'm showing Iris where she's sleeping. Say good night," he said, the order seeming to be directed at everyone in the room. And they all turned to me and sang out a simultaneous "Good night!"

"Here," Vito said, propelling me gently into an entirely plaid room. "This was my brother's room." A twin bed took up most of the floor space, and rock band posters still hung from the walls.

"How long has he been married?" I asked, amazed to find an essentially undressed image of Sophia Loren still hanging on the closet door.

"Five years. Sometimes when he and his wife fight he tries to hide out here, but Ma sends him packing. She says no married man is going to sleep away from his wife in her house."

"But he can come to eat without her?"

"Eating's a different category. All comers welcome there."

When he'd left I opened all his brother's drawers, dug into the back of the closet. I wasn't looking for anything in particular—just some sense of secrets, perhaps notes or mementos hidden in corners and left behind at marriage. Two baseball trophies had been jammed into the closet on a top shelf. The rest of the closet was given over to a dismantled weight-lifting set. A jewelry box on the dresser still held a plain gold chain. The room was simple, free of photographs, books, paper. I shed my clothes and fell into a dreamless sleep. The next morning I woke to the smell of coffee and voices in the kitchen only eight feet and a thin wall away from me. For a few moments I didn't know where I was, and the unfamiliar sounds, the scent of garlic still in the air from last night's meal, left me disoriented but calm. Happy.

"You have such a noisy house," I said to Vito during the long drive back down Route 81 to Virginia. "It's snug. And it feels simple."

"Families look that way to people who aren't in them." Then he switched the subject quickly back to my own family. "You didn't show me the pictures you got this time."

"I guess I didn't."

"You know what I'm asking."

"One was of me and Eddie and my mother. The other one was all of us and our mother." One was the Queen, I wanted to add but didn't, and one was the Animal. Anyone with eyes could see that.

"Okay." He kept his eyes on the road but he was clearly attentive; clearly not satisfied with this answer.

"I didn't understand the pictures, Vito. So I can't explain them to you."

He pulled the car over to the breakdown lane and snapped on the flashers. "Show me."

I protested that they were in my bag, in the trunk, and he climbed out of the car directly into the backdraft of a three-segment semi, popped open the trunk and rifled through my underwear until he found the envelope. I didn't stop him. He got back in and handed it to me. "Show me," he said again. Larger vehicles passing by sucked at our car, successive shaking *swchwwp, swchwwp, swchwwp*s. I opened it and handed the three drawings to him. I explained about the drowning, about the pills the doctor had prescribed, about her state of mind.

"Is this little kid you?"

I nodded. "And that boy holding me is my brother Eddie. But why we're there I don't know. I told you I didn't understand it."

Vito started the engine again and pulled into traffic. He accelerated.

"We need some perspective," he said. "We need a long view. I know half a dozen good trailheads right off the Blue Ridge Parkway. Right in our path."

I didn't take him literally until he started adding up the weights of various food items and asking me how many pounds I thought I'd be comfortable packing into the mountains. We wouldn't be troubled for lack of a tent, he said, craning his neck out the window and looking up to the sky. Years of driving in a snowbelt had left him with the habit of traveling with blankets in his car trunk and some were there now. When he began to describe particular trails I told him I wouldn't do it. I hated camping. I had to get home.

But I didn't have to get home and he knew it. I was curious about the mountains, and he sensed that as well. By the time we reached the first trailhead that he'd named, I was discussing our options with clear personal preferences. I voted on the third one he'd described: streams along most of the path, outcroppings at regular intervals giving unimpeded sixty-mile views. All the years Uncle Charlie had gone into the mountains with the boys I had been confident I didn't have a shred of curiosity or envy. Now it seemed that I'd been wrong.

We stopped at a small grocery store and Vito, more experienced at knowing what would carry, what would work over a fire and what wouldn't, did the selecting. He bought food that could last three days if it had to last, and when I protested that we would be gone no more than one night he said that leeway was important in mountains. We bought two backpacks in the stationery supplies aisle and divided the weight between them. By the time we actually got to the small dirt parking lot off the Blue Ridge Parkway, I was giddy. The fact was, I probably hadn't done something simply because someone suggested it since the days when my brothers would set me to digging holes to China or jumping from trees with capes because they said I would fly. I felt the same mindless exhilaration now that I'd felt then, hoping for an updraft or looking forward to my first glimpse of a pagoda.

We locked the car, adjusted the packs and began. The path seemed to lead endlessly upward. Here in the woods themselves the Blue Ridge were not blue at all but mossy grays, fern and pine greens, orange clays, black irons. We followed a stream that flowed like a glycerin rope, me looking up every ten minutes hoping to see flat terrain, only to discover that the apparently flat meadow I'd glimpsed from below was only the beginning of another upward rise over loose rock. Twice I made Vito stop because the relentless slow incline left me staggering and nauseated. The thick underbrush gradually gave way to house-sized boulders and upheaved sheets of limestone and sandstone. The varied trees yielded to pine and then the pine itself thinned. Vito stepped off the main trail onto a side path that deviated off toward the edge of the mountain we climbed. When I followed I found him sitting peacefully on a rock outcrop watching the declining sun light fifty miles of mountain folds like a purple and orange flare. A beautiful round oasis of moss lay between the woods and the outcrop, flat as a table and four inches thick.

"Now you can see it," he said. "From Charlottesville it looks like layers on a cake—blue hill, then fog, then blue hill. But from here . . ."

Yes, from here you could see the patterned effect of some incomprehensibly large force. We dangled our legs over the side of a two-hundred-foot drop. Before us the land rolled out like crinoline wedding gown folds. The more distant ridges looked, again, quite blue. Vito elbowed me gently and tipped his head to the left. There on the next boulder sat a bird the size of a nine-year-old human. I gasped, and the creature swiveled his head to regard me impassively for a moment. Then it opened what seemed to be a fifteen-foot wingspan and simply fell forward into the downdraft, tipping its glide to mirror the angles of the valley walls in his descent.

"That's metamorphosed basalt flow," Vito said to me, pointing at the outcrop where the bird had stood only a moment before. "Basalts come up to the surface still molten, squeeze between cracks in the granite and then freeze into shapes like that. Basalt outcrops mean a volcano eruption happened here. And limestone"—here he pointed at another horizontal stripe along the range beneath us—"always starts out at the bottom of a tropical ocean."

I tried to imagine these things.

"As long as it's not moving now," I said.

"But it is—just slowly. Even the moon has enough gravitational pull to move the ground a foot or two in waves. Like tides."

The bird had not finished his journey downward through the valley. He tipped, lifted the end of one wing and tipped again. He rose and fell on the invisible currents as if they were roller-coaster tracks arranged over the earth's skin, invisible and irresistible at once.

"What do you think?" he asked.

I reached over with my left hand and took his right, aligning his pointer and index finger and drawing them to me, setting them at my throat along the jugular where he would feel the pulse.

He pushed himself back onto the table of moss and lay down, pulling me along. I shifted and twisted suddenly so that I was above him and looking down at him where he'd arranged himself along my hip and flank. He raised one eyebrow, just a quick check to make sure that I meant it. All the signals were clear, but did I mean it?

"Yes," I said.

I thought I was ready. We didn't leave the moss tabletop for two days.

Willing

I WASN'T READY. THE THINGS THAT MATTER IN THE END ARE THE ones that happen to you when you're not ready. Nobody remembers the advanced swimming lessons your mother signed you up for after you passed the intermediate ones; everybody remembers being pitched off a dock when they hadn't yet mastered a dog paddle. Surprise and ignorance are key.

So I was caught unprepared, and what I learned was that if you let this kind of thing touch you then the world is never the same again. It's much bigger, and you're much happier, except for the inevitable times that come along when you know it's bigger but for some reason you've just lost sight of it. Then you're miserable.

By the time I got back to Charlottesville and stepped into my apartment, I could not clearly remember who I'd been before the two nights and one day on the table of moss. Before, my body had been a casual companion; after, it became the lens through which I saw everything around me. I made the neophyte's error of assuming that this new richness of sensation was something that had come entirely from Vito instead of from my own capacity to respond to him.

I felt like I had a great secret, and I didn't want to talk to anyone until

I'd had it to myself for a while. I didn't want to be told that I was very young and that my inexperience placed me, perhaps, too much in Vito's power. I knew I would receive advice like this as if my critic were speaking Swahili or encouraging me to invent cold fusion. I would assume they had no idea who I was or what had happened to me.

There was the obvious imbalance. He was sexually experienced; I was not. Vito took this in stride, showing a depth of imagination and flexibility as a lover that surprised both of us. And I was as much a revelation to him as he was to me. Instead of hesitancy on my part and authoritative confidence on his, we found that I was aggressively curious, jarringly responsive. Vito conceded, shifted, followed, changed. I scared him some.

In the first weeks after we became lovers I found myself using his vocabulary in my head, receiving my accustomed physical surroundings through his eyes. I could raise my head from a book and look out a window at the Blue Ridge and be as stunned as if I'd never seen them. Before Vito, they were an immovable and apparently constant bunch of hills. Now they were the uneasy responsive skin of the earth, shifted by the plates beneath them; spiked through by molten stone—one force always rising up, another always washing down. Now I saw that all things moved and changed because I had. Now I knew that if you reach the crest of Mount Everest you find marine limestone under your feet. It made perfect sense—the floor of an ocean sits on the highest peak in the world.

My perspective had been recalibrated to contain both a minutely close focus on the feel of a finger on a nipple, and the enormous distance from which one continent slowly reshapes another by the force of collision and explosion. I'd lost most of my middle ground. To the casual and more experienced observer, I'm sure I looked lost. I could see this, but I saw it from the same kind of distance that someone under the influence of codeine sees pain: it's there, but it doesn't matter very much. It occurred to me at one point that this might be why my aunt Eleanor had always said that teenagers were too young for sex.

Well, what did she know? If she had a prayer of having this for herself, she'd take it. Anybody would take it.

The first, immediate experience of this shift was joy.

The second was fear. Now I looked at Hank and saw his helplessness before my sister as something I understood much more intimately. Was I as helplessly in Vito's hands as Hank was in Angie's? And if so, was I in danger? These were merely rhetorical questions. I wouldn't retreat now regardless of the answers.

Had my mother felt this for my father? Perhaps this would explain why she was destroyed by his absences, his indifference, his more secret, more important life in Indochina. I saw now that love itself might have been the force that shaped her into what I now remembered as the Animal Mother as opposed to the Queen Mother.

And my sister, who took Hank and then left Hank, only to return and take him again—did she feel like this with him? She couldn't have and continue to behave and look as she did. Impossible. Now that I knew the sensation and had seen it in my own mirror, felt it in my own body, I could review my memories of her with the young men who pursued her openly. I considered her behavior through the time I knew she had been Hank's lover.

No. I had never seen a flicker of what I thought of as love. I concluded that though love probably wore differently on different people, what I was experiencing was something that Angie did not know. My first reaction to this conclusion about Angie was like my first reaction to the knowledge that I was in love: first joy, then fear.

When Vito and I returned from the Blue Ridge I passed through my own apartment just long enough to get some clothes. Hank had moved in during my absence, as I'd expected, and though he wasn't in the apartment the rooms were full of him: underwear, damp towels, books. I took some clothes, left Hank's debris untouched and went to Vito.

He had sublet rooms for the summer in a tired Victorian behind Rugby Road, owned by a woman whose neighbors claimed that she was the last living survivor of the assassination of Czar Nicholas's family. Rumors claimed she had been the baby in the line of brothers, sisters and parents who had been propped against a wall and shot, and had survived by falling beneath the body of one of her siblings and left for dead. The lady herself had never bothered to deny or confirm these stories but in her smaller habits she did indeed look a bit like someone whose family had been executed before her eyes. She puttered in her rocky garden behind the house during the day and read Russian newspapers at night, apparently friendless. She kept lodgers and answered the door if she had an empty room and the visitor might be a potential renter. Otherwise she answered neither door nor telephone.

For days Vito and I ate and slept when hunger or exhaustion forced us to do so. There was no other rhythm to our activities—no morning, afternoon or night as people whose lives were in calmer waters would have described them. We might leave the house for a walk at three in the morning, or three in the afternoon. We picnicked on his bed. Once the telephone in his room rang and when he made no move toward it, I stood to pick it up myself. He stopped me. "No intruders allowed," he said. "You don't have to answer a telephone just because it rings." He brought steaming coffee to me and flowers, waking me at dusk. We told our stories about our siblings, our homes, our ideas about how we'd come to be here together. We talked about geological theories, we wondered about Oedipus, we improvised scenes from the Peloponnesian War, we offered impressions of people who mattered to us and of people we had seen only once. We made love.

On the sixth day something altered this little encapsulated universe, cracked it open and admitted the other world again. The conversation had turned to Angie and Hank, and Vito brought me up short by observing casually that he had known all along that the boyfriend in California wouldn't hold her and she would come looking for Hank. Or someone else, he concluded lazily. I lay between his legs and against his chest.

I sat up. "What boyfriend?"

"The college professor," he said. "But Mr. College Professor's politics are too centrist."

"And you know this because . . . ?"

"I'd talk to her sometimes when she'd visit Hank," he explained. He was alert now, watching me.

I imagined Vito and Angie talking in his room, on the Lawn, in Hank's room; imagined the way she looked and moved; remembered her referring to Vito as the sexy one with the Italian name.

"Breathe," he said sharply. I started breathing again. "What's wrong?"

"I'm fine." I smiled but I slid away and around so I could get a clear look at his face. "I didn't know you and Angie were close."

"Who's close to Angie?" His shoulders and eyebrows glided upward. *Who indeed?* the shoulders said.

"I am. Hank is." An illogically defensive tone colored this assertion, given how little I wanted Vito to describe her as someone with whom it was easy to be intimate. I cleared my throat and adjusted to a warmer, more merely conversational sound. I said, "She seems to have gotten your attention."

"If Angie wants you to pay attention, she can get your attention."

Only a moment before, I had been as happy as I'd ever been in my life. Now Angie intruded, and clanking along after her like tin cans on strings came Perry and Eddie and Uncle Charlie and Aunt Eleanor. It occurred to me that I'd promised Uncle Charlie and Aunt Eleanor that I would be back at the Lake House by . . . was it yesterday? I hadn't even called them.

This wasn't like me. It wasn't fair or kind or even civil, and suddenly it mattered again. I imagined Aunt Eleanor bent over a roast, looking distracted and troubled; Uncle Charlie slumping a bit in his seat on the rowboat with a rod dangled indifferently over the side. They were waiting. They'd been left behind, and they were in a bad place. "Vito, I've got to go home and check in," I said. "Just check in."

He said he understood, which I believed. He told me he would cover the room in flowers when I returned. We promised to call each other. We talked in open-ended terms about when I would return; when he would visit at the lake. He reminded me that the summer was only another eight weeks, which startled me. Eight weeks? Look what had happened to me in the last two weeks. Anything at all might happen in the vast, nearly geological expanse of two months. Vito seemed unconcerned and breezy, confident that when we saw each other again we would be nothing but pleased.

I didn't have his perspective. I didn't have any perspective. I was nineteen years old and nothing like this had ever happened to me. It might go away in an instant. A few days separation might break the spell entirely and it would be gone and perhaps it would never happen to me again. Perhaps I should stay—just pretend that Aunt Eleanor and Uncle Charlie didn't exist and I had never looked at their troubled faces and told them that I'd be back soon.

Vito said, "Invite me for the Fourth of July at that lake place. I want to see the Jell-O molds in the shape of the Lincoln Monument."

I told him that he would see that and more and kissed him. I looked carefully for anything in his face or posture or voice that might reveal a man with anything on his mind that would hurt someone who loved him. Then I smiled and told him that I loved him, which I did.

Following Her with So Much Hope

MY APARTMENT ON JEFFERSON PARK WAS CLOSE ENOUGH TO Vito's that I could walk from one to the other. I could pack a few things and ask Hank to give me a ride to the train station—catch a cab or call Eleanor when I arrived. I climbed the steps to my apartment so preoccupied that I didn't think twice about the unfamiliar car in the drive. I let myself in the front door without any ceremony and dropped my keys on the table. A slamming door at the bedroom end of the apartment startled me. "Hank?" I called out.

Angie appeared in the kitchen doorway wearing a white cotton shirt that I recognized as Hank's and a pair of worn jeans. Silver dangled from her ears. She raised a hand to brush a strand of hair from her eye. Her nails were a pale enamel as reflective as tiny mirrors.

"God, you scared me!" I said. "How long are you here?"

"I come and go. I still have the beach house in California." Her tone was cool.

I didn't realize I was angry with her until I heard it in my own voice as I suggested she come to the Lake House with me. "Give me a chance to present a united front with you," I pleaded. "Come home and thrash it out. We mean too much to Uncle Charlie not to move him if we all stand together."

I could hear Angie take in a sharp, exasperated breath before she began. "All right, I'll speak plainly here, Iris," she said. "You had your chance to stand with me and you didn't. You kept talking about all of us understanding one another. The truth is that you didn't want us to understand each other—you only wanted us not to disagree and make you uncomfortable."

"But I do take your side. I have taken it."

"I don't want your help, Iris. I don't want you standing on my side."

"But I'm already there. I've always been there!"

"Really?" she said coolly. "Well. No need to do it anymore, then. Look, I'm sorry that Eleanor's upset." Angie pulled a pack of Marlboros from her hip pocket, shook out a cigarette and lit it. She sat at the kitchen table and waved her free hand toward the chair opposite. It had taken her very little time to make this apartment her own. "But you don't have to be their official spokesperson, Iris."

"How are things with Hank?"

She smiled thinly. "I've taken him back temporarily. He's happy." My sister sat back and stretched. She crushed the cigarette out. "Don't worry. I'm quitting. It smells bad and wreaks havoc with your skin." She looked up at me. I was probably staring. "You know, Iris, there's an ugly judgmental opinion in your look right now."

"He's in love with you," I said.

"I'm not responsible for that."

"You slept with him."

"Sex isn't a binding contract, and it's not my job—or your job—to take care of everyone's feelings."

"I'm not talking about everybody. I'm talking about Hank, whose feelings should matter to you—his and Aunt Eleanor's, and Uncle Charlie's."

"Look at Charlie closely, Iris. Tell him that American napalm is burning the flesh off noncombatant civilians, and he shrugs and tells you that's just the way it is—war is tough, he says, like he's reminding you that spring follows winter. Totally calm and accepting. But tell him I've had sex with his son and he becomes apoplectic—his language gets ugly and, I will add, sexually creepy. Do you know what he called me when Hank told him we were lovers? I went in an instant from being a human being to being a body part—a singular body part at that. If I can make that kind of man unhappy, I will, and I'll consider it a good day's work done. If I was about to put Hank at arm's distance before, all I had to hear was what kind of manipulating cunt I was to change my mind. I quote him. I'll sleep with Hank just to enrage Charlie, now."

"That's not doing what you want. It's doing what Uncle Charlie doesn't want."

"I'm not playing semantic games with you, Iris."

"It's not a game."

"You're right." She leaned forward. "It isn't a game—it's very serious. Because if I don't take what I want I'll get what I'm given."

"What would be so terrible about that? What horrible things have you been given?"

She stared blankly, an uncharacteristic reaction that stopped things quite dead. When she started talking again she had changed subjects, clearly saying not the first thing that had come to her mind but the third or tenth.

"You know, Iris," she said, "you were the one person I didn't think would judge me."

I didn't say anything to that, which amounted to our both acknowledging that she was right. I had judged her. I continued to judge her.

She said, "I'm young, and the way I look gives me a lot of power. I'm not giving any of it up; I'm not letting it pass by unused because it will pass by. And I won't be judged for that, even by you. There will be years and years to be reasonable and temperate and totally invisible but those years are not here."

"What about Hank? What about what he wants?"

"We've had this discussion before. I'm not holding him with chains or court orders. He's free to go. They're all free to go, just like I am. Hank is aware of how I live and he's not pleased, but there's nothing he can do about it."

She tapped out another cigarette, rolled it between her fingers, crushed it without lighting it. "What?" she said, looking at me more closely.

"Why don't you just cut him off, Angie? Why not tell him you aren't interested in him?"

"Because I am interested in him. I like him, I like sleeping with him, and I like offending Charlie's sensibilities. Continuing my sexual relationship with Hank serves many purposes."

"Where is Hank now?" I asked.

"Out."

The telephone rang and Angie picked it up as if it were her own home, her own line. "Vito! Hi. Yes, she's here." She looked at me but made no move to give me the receiver. "Oh, yeah? Well, I tried making that fish stock but I didn't have the patience to finish it. Sure. Well, the shortcuts didn't look to me to be anything that would make a difference. All right, all right. Here she is." She turned to me, her hand over the receiver. "He wants to talk to you," she said, as if this fact surprised her.

I took the telephone from her and turned away so she couldn't see my face. The cord kept me tethered to the room and she wouldn't leave, though everything about my posture and tone asked her to go. Vito said he had just wanted to say good-bye again before I left. He said he'd see me soon. I felt exposed, unable to get away from Angie's cool, assessing look. I hung up as quickly as I could.

"Are you and Vito friends?" I asked as I set the receiver back in its cradle. I didn't want her to be trying out Vito's fish stock recipe. I didn't want her to be trying out anything at all connected to Vito.

"He's an interesting guy." She sat back. "Don't you think so?"

I didn't answer. I felt suddenly cold.

"I haven't slept with him if that's what you're asking," she sighed. She lit another cigarette. "Sometimes we bump into each other. Taking walks. I've gotten a little insomniac. You could bang pans and dance naked around Hank all night and he'd sleep on and on and when I get restless sometimes I drift out the door. When Hank was on the Lawn, I'd bump into Vito in the middle of the night sitting on the grass. That's how we got to know each other."

"What did you talk about?"

"I don't remember." She studied me carefully again. "You know, as a little girl, you would march into whatever situation we pointed you at—fearless character, that was you. Now you gauge every step. Now you're even afraid of me."

"You want people to be afraid of you," I said.

"That might be true. But I don't want you to be afraid of me. Not you, Bear."

"Then you shouldn't be scary," I countered. "You shouldn't sleep with Hank just to hurt Uncle Charlie."

"I didn't sleep with Hank just to hurt anybody. Really, Iris. Listen to me." She leaned forward, seemed to consider taking my hand before thinking better of it. She looked fierce and unhappy. "That first time with Hank was the day I got the picture in my head of Eddie getting killed. I wasn't in my right mind. Right up until that day I'd kept Hank at a distance. I knew how much he wanted from me and I was being fair and restrained because he wasn't going to get it and I knew that and who wants to hurt Hank, anyhow? Right up until then I was being what I was supposed to be."

Her voice pitched up an octave and down, dropping audial quote marks around the words "fair" and "restrained."

She said, "I could do that. But that day . . . and there was Hank, and the chance of some relief from myself!" Her fists were clenched and the cigarette popped open between her fingers so the furry edges of its filter poked through the paper wrapper. She shook it loose onto the table.

I wasn't terribly moved. It seemed to me that all she could describe was her own position, her own desires; his didn't engage her imaginatively. Stupid Hank, to follow her with so much hope.

She continued. "You're different from me. You would have had Hank's feelings on your mind," she said. "I know that. But until recently you wouldn't have found so much fault in me. That's a new thing."

"Pisses you off, doesn't it?" I said.

"Yes." She thought a minute. "What's changed?"

I thought of the grassy smell of Vito's skin. I thought of my mother on an Animal Mother day, stuffing laundry into the washing machine in a rage. The image was both fresh and long-standing, since it had faded once but here it was back as plain as a yellow triangle trail marker. Quite clear.

"Nothing," I said.

She snorted. "Oh, come on."

"I don't like seeing somebody being used by somebody else who doesn't particularly care about his feelings."

"That idea that sex is one person using another is so small and mean— so parochial," she said icily. It was clear to me that it wasn't any idea she was describing. It was me. Any sorrow was gone from her.

I said, "Maybe it's outdated but it's still what's happening. Angie, Hank wants you to marry him."

She made a dismissive snorting noise. "Listen to me. If Hank survives long enough to be an old guy, or even a middle-aged guy, he is going to be glad I took him as a lover, with or without love. He won't have to look back and regret that it never happened."

"Maybe he'll look back and regret that it did."

She smiled. She flicked the cigarette remains off the table and onto the floor. "It doesn't matter that much, Iris. Not in the end."

Angie's expression had a weary experienced sharpness. Hank walked in the door before I could gather myself to respond. He was surprised to see me, not pleasantly surprised, though he put as much warmth as he could muster into his greeting. He bent automatically and plucked the cigarette remains from the linoleum, placed them in the ashtray before Angie. She smiled up at him as I excused myself, saying I had only dropped by to pack some things that were in my room before leaving for the lake.

Hank's and Angie's clothes lay scattered on the bed and chair and the room smelled vaguely of cocoa. Incense sticks and candles lined the dresser, the windowsills, every flat surface. A picture frame stood crammed onto the limited free space of the table on Angie's side of the bed and I lifted it up to get a better look at its contents. It was us: Perry, Eddie, Angie and me, tumbled in a pile like puppies at the end of the Lake House dock. It must have been taken the year we first went to Uncle Charlie and Aunt Eleanor. I didn't look more than four years old in the photograph, though, and they had become our guardians when I was six. In the picture I clung to Angie and laughed. The boys were clowning, pretending to grab me and upend me into the water. Only Angie was solemn, black eyes fixed on the camera, hair tangled and looped and shining, skinny little legs tucked under her to one side while one of her hands remained locked on my upper arm so the boys couldn't roll me off the dock.

I set the photograph down and went to the closet, yanking the jacket I wanted free in one pull. I pushed aside some sneakers at the far back corner. There were two of the manila envelopes holding Perry's drawings. There was the third folder, the one with Hank's draft records. I plucked all three up, folded them into smaller shapes and jammed them in my bag with some shirts and jeans. When I reentered the living room Angie and Hank fell into the kind of silence that indicated they'd been talking about me.

"Give me a ride to the train station?" I directed this question to Hank.

"Sure," Hank answered. "Let me get the car keys."

"So are you coming home this weekend or not?" I asked him as soon as we were on the stairs down to the driveway and out of Angie's hearing.

"I'll come when I can. I know it has to happen sooner or later." Then, "Iris, you don't have to mention the fact that Angie is here to my folks."

"If they ask directly I'll say the minimum. If they don't, I'll say nothing."

"We can't try to smooth things over with everyone's feelings still so burned. The way my daddy talks about Angie . . . it didn't seem to take Angie by surprise, but I was just astounded."

"You mean it was creepy? Like Angie said?"

"Basically. It's so painful. Here's this man who, on the one hand, is so responsible and experienced and generous. And then there's this other part of my daddy that's only just come to light, the part that calls Angie things I'd have to call obscene. I can see that we both look shallow and self-indulgent to him but I also know that he's wrong—he doesn't understand. If it was just politics maybe we could talk. But it's tipped over into something . . . personal. Sexual. He'd say moral."

"He's always taken the hard way, the way he thought was the right way," I said.

"That only makes it worse," Hank replied. "If you'd described what he looked like and what he said to me and I hadn't witnessed it firsthand, I wouldn't have believed you. Which is just to say that, for now, I'm not sure I want us at the Lake House."

"I'm sorry," I said.

"I am, too."

"If you come you know that Aunt Eleanor will keep things in check. She'll keep him civil."

"Yeah," Hank said, but he didn't say it with much conviction. "I never thought I'd think this but now's maybe a time I wish my own momma had some of your mother's style. She might have fallen apart quite a bit, but when she wasn't fallen apart, the woman could take on tigers."

"So I've been told."

I scrambled out of my side of the car before he could open the door for me—a habit that Uncle Charlie had insisted all boys should honor and one that Hank persisted in despite the changed times. I stood on the curb in front of the train station doors and leaned forward to kiss him on the cheek.

"This will all come out all right, won't it?" I asked.

He nodded. On the train ride into the mountains I could not reconcile the two faces: Hank's open, hopeful one, and Angie's, framed in the window when I looked up and waved from the drive—full of rage.

Who She Always Was

THERE WAS THE DISH OF THE LAKE WITH ITS EVERGREEN, OAK and birch border. For the first time in my life I stepped onto the property at the beginning of summer without a sibling or guardian at my side. I'd taken a taxi from the train station, and now I floated for a while at the end of the winding clay drive with my bag anchored to my left hand. When I first went to Charlottesville, I had imagined my arriving here at the beginning of summer with Hank, both of us feeling exactly the same happy lift at first sight of the property. I should smell bottlebrush, which I did, because bottlebrush would go on and blossom at this time of the month regardless of what happened in the human world. Angie was supposed to be trotting toward us waving, and Aunt Eleanor was supposed to be parting the curtains on the second floor to look out and confirm that the sound she'd heard had indeed been a car door slamming: us, returning to them. The windows were blank; the house stared balefully out toward the end of the drive, where I surveyed the scene and readjusted my expectations.

In previous summers there had been a clunky four-hand piano duet audible at this point or the sound of my brothers splashing perhaps thirty yards offshore. I stood, wondering why the very sounds in the air felt wrong. It took me a minute to realize that the mourning doves, mock-ingbirds and titmice were absent, and in their place was the metallic cawing of ravens who had driven them away and taken up residence in the oaks to the north of the house. They sat there now like iridescent black flowers in the trees.

I trudged down the orange dirt lane, dropping my bag on the porch before proceeding around the house and down the lawn to the dock. Wilma, daughter of the now-deceased Otto, wriggled through the kitchen dog door and came bounding out to greet me. Wilma had always liked me. She wasn't a barker so I had no warning of her approach. She flung herself at my back and knocked me over, then licked my neck and head, whining happily as I pushed her off and got to my feet again. Her entire body wagged as she positioned her head firmly at my left knee, pressing.

I scanned the side of the raft for the telltale rope and S-hook, which used to mark where the boys tied submerged nets of beer for retrieval after Uncle Charlie and Aunt Eleanor were asleep. They had allowed me to come with them on one or two nights so I knew what it all looked like: inky lake surface with a necklace of lit camp windows hung around the shore. We would stop at the raft just long enough to retrieve the Bud-weiser, kissing up against its wooden side as we wrestled the beer into the center of the rowboat. Then we would pull slowly around the lake, drinking and watching the electrically lit interior scenes. We had once actually managed to witness the first half of a middle-aged seduction through the windows of the Oosman cottage before the couple fell to the floor and out of sight. We hadn't known the participants. They must have been renters. I remember the man kissing her eyebrows before he pulled her down. Her hair had been so askew, so stiffly caplike that I'd wondered if she wore a wig. His lips had run along the length of her eye-brows as if he were combing them with his lips, smoothing them.

Impossible for any rope or S-hook to be there on the raft's side but still I looked.

I felt like an orphan. I hadn't felt like this when I understood that my mother was dead, or when my father remarried and made it clear that he would not be back. I hadn't felt like this when my brothers got on the plane to Vietnam, or even when we were told that Eddie was killed and Perry missing. But now, Angie and Hank banished from this childhood landscape and my brothers gone, I imagined myself sitting at a dinner table with only my aunt and uncle, just three people at a table the size of a prone Shetland pony with empty chairs all around us, pressing down. We were so terribly alone. How solemn and dark it was all of a sudden.

I called out to Aunt Eleanor as I entered the kitchen but there was no answer. Wilma pattered along at my side as I hauled the suitcase I'd left on the porch into the hallway. She glanced up every couple of seconds at my face. The dog's continued attention to my mood meant that Eleanor was not home. Had she been here, Wilma would have run to her now to announce my arrival. A torn notebook page lay on the kitchen table. *Charlie—gone berrying. Nothing with blood dripping off it is allowed one inch further than the porch steps. Take off your shoes. I adore you. —Elli.* A crooked little heart had been drawn around the "Elli." The note wasn't in the exact middle of the table. I pushed it dead center.

Elli? I had never heard my uncle call his wife anything but Eleanor. And why was my uncle here at the Lake House on a weekday? This early in the season he spent his weekdays at the winter house to be closer to Washington. He had, to the best of my knowledge, never in his life taken an actual vacation before August. Uncle Charlie allowed himself summer weekends at the Lake House, two full weeks every August and fall hunting season. Period. Nothing else had ever intruded upon his work schedule.

I had picked my way across the porch without seeing a single dead animal, so I assumed Uncle Charlie was still out. I walked to the fishing rod cabinet in the library, found it unlocked with an empty space where his favorite one typically hung.

Something else was odd about the room: piles of papers, a file cabinet—it looked as though someone was working out of this room; an unheard-of development. Uncle Charlie regarded the Lake House as a kind of sacred space. No briefcase, no business meetings or telephone calls had ever been tolerated under this roof. I moved toward the desk but stopped.

I ventured into the bedrooms with Wilma still ticking along at my side. Only my aunt and uncle's room had open windows. The others, Hank's and mine, which would normally smell of boxwood and Japanese clump dogwood at this time of year, were dusty and close. I threw windows open and turned down the bed. The sheets were dampish, unaired. Had I not been expected? What had made them think I wouldn't come to them?

I made my way up to the attic, the domain of the boys when we were growing up: a No Girls Allowed zone. It was hot in the summers but with windows open at either end of the loftlike space a breeze moved through the room, and its wonderful height provided the longest view of the lake. If Uncle Charlie were fishing I might be able to see his little skiff with the electric engine from the attic window.

Angie and I had come here to snoop around and feel pleased to be playing in forbidden territory. Hank had been offered the option of sleeping here with my brothers but he generally preferred his bedroom on the second floor. He visited but didn't reside. Angie and I scooted up the stairs whenever the boys were out with Uncle Charlie and Aunt Eleanor was obliviously busy. We would lean out the window, staring downward from this terrible height and scaring ourselves just the slightest bit with threats to jump or throw up. Then we would play with the toys we were denied in our brothers' presence: their electric train set chief among these delights, their cars and trucks right behind. They must have known we did this because we never got the trains and trucks back exactly where we'd found them, but they didn't say anything. It must have been enough for them that we wanted to come up here so badly and that we were denied access whenever they were present.

There were no cars or trucks here now; no electric trains. Otto had peed on the original base of the very first train set, warping the plywood and leaving an indelible and hard-to-ignore stain on the green felt that represented grass. Aunt Eleanor had laughed. My brothers were brokenhearted for a full four days: the scenery at that end of the platform had been perfection itself. Otto had been led upstairs to have his nose pressed to the still aromatic green felt before he was whacked on the nose with a magazine and banished forever from the attic. The boys let him back up the next week—Perry liked to sleep with him. Now the train platform was gone. Uncle Charlie must have broken it up and burned it.

When I opened the window I could hear waves sipping against the exposed tree roots at the water's edge. I could smell dirt and sun and felt thoughtlessly cheered before I remembered how things were. Wilma threw herself down beside me, panting, waiting, panting.

Lakes, Vito had said to me, were blockages, places where natural drainage and flow had failed. Basaltic magma rises and fills gaps. Gravel and boulders shed from this basalt block another egress. Glacial advances grind the surface down to impenetrable sandstone, and the water flowing downward is trapped. It didn't make the sight any less beautiful to imagine its technical history. It still had the same abstract effect on me.

Was that Uncle Charlie, just drifting behind the island and out of sight? It was shallow over there, and the bass liked that side of the island. Could be him. I pulled a chair away from the wall to set it squarely before the window so I could sit and keep looking. As I dragged it across the floor one leg caught on an uneven spot in the planking, and I craned my head back to take a look. Normally a rug covered that spot, so I'd never noticed this single unaligned seam. The plank didn't fit the floor. Its finish was blonder, less grimy and scuffed. I walked over to it and knelt down, wriggled at its edges. It popped up in my hand.

I lifted the plank up and set it to one side. I couldn't see anything clearly at first, my eyes adjusting to the sudden shift from the intensity of light blinking off the lake to the darkness of the room's interior. I dropped one finger gingerly down into the depression and touched what felt at first contact like a dead animal. Certainly it was fur. My finger flew back up into the light as if it had been bitten.

But it hadn't been bitten, and the fur hadn't taken on any of the grimy stiffness I knew from handling dead game. I sniffed, almost certainly eliminating the possibility of a small corpse: I smelled only dust. So I peered in again; dropped one hand down again, plucked at a fringe of fur and pulled the object up.

It was my stuffed Dalmatian dog. One of the boys had hidden him away from me in a game of hide-and-seek and then forgot him, leaving me to tramp around the house in desperation for four days' running before I decided he was irretrievably gone. Eddie had probably been the hider that day—he was the most aggressive and heartless hider among us. I examined the spotted creature now, dust puffing and drifting away from his little polyester body where my fingers squeezed him. Wilma rose and offered to chew him but I whipped him out of range and shooed her away.

I beat him against my leg and more dust rose up, drifted across a beam from the window and dispersed. The ear that Perry had sewn back on for me hung by a dozen threads. I had thought it was a miraculously perfect repair when he'd handed it over that day. Now I could see its clumsy earnestness, the big spaces between stitches and the not-quite-matching thread. I stroked the dusty little toy and set him down beside the opening I'd made before reaching my hand in to see what lay beneath him. My fingers brushed against plastic, followed the flat surface to its edge and got a hold. Out came a bag of Batman comics. For the next hour I sat by the window and read what had been denied me in my childhood by brothers who would never let my greasy baby fingers actually hold the comics and turn the pages.

I held Eddie's favorite, the Batman *Knightfall* series, which told the story of how Bane, son of a man who was killed in a military coup, was imprisoned to serve his dead father's sentence. Eddie had acted out Bane coming to consciousness after a month-long coma that followed a terrible fall, waking to a new character: a changed and violent Bane. Eddie had broken one of Aunt Eleanor's favorite dishes once doing this scene. He wanted Perry to play Batman in the story where Bane finally kills his nemesis, who was, of course, Batman. Perry never wanted to do that story. He liked the one where Azrael goes to the side of Batman and Robin in their fight against Bane. Eddie was Bane. Hank and Perry were

Robin and Azrael. They took turns with the role of Batman. Wilma got bored with me at last and retreated back down the stairs.

Reading the comic books was like falling through a hole into another, stranger place with a set of problems so clearly not your own that you could skate along on the glittering surface of the graphics, all bulging abdominal muscles and flaring capes. Thrilling; simple. I slipped them into their plastic sleeves and, not knowing what else to do with them, laid them back into their hiding place. My hand brushed against a plastic cylinder. I got it between my thumb and forefinger and lifted it to the light.

It was a pill container, its stickered label so faded and stained with age that I had difficulty reading it. I felt around in the depression under the plank and set off a rolling bustle of them, twelve in all, and the ones whose labels weren't faded had been rubbed to make them equally indecipherable. My mouth was suddenly very dry. I lined up the little platoon of smudged orange cylinders before plucking one from the line and rolling it in my palm. It cracked, so brittle that it imploded into shards before I knew how hard I was pressing. I switched on an overhead light and peered more carefully at the label. The typed text was faded and rubbed but on two of the bottles it was visible. *Jacqueline Sunnaret,* they read. And the date, as I'd expected, was the year of her death.

Two floors below me a door opened and a voice called out my name.

"I'm here," I called back. I swept the bottles back into their dark compartment, squared the plastic sleeve that lay above them and then laid my Dalmatian to rest on the cover of *Sword of Azrael.* I replaced the plank.

"I'm here!" I repeated, moving toward the narrow steps as quickly as I could while consciously thinking about how I was walking. I was sure that if I stopped thinking I would simply stop moving and be found here by my aunt. So I thought hard: left foot, right foot, left foot, right. Step down. Hold the banister. Step faster.

She met me halfway down the stairs to the first floor, Wilma swirling excitedly around her knees as she tried to keep climbing. Wilma had always been Aunt Eleanor's dog. "You didn't call to tell us when you were getting here!" she greeted me, happy and accusing at once. "Oh, Iris, when you said you were staying in Charlottesville beyond finals week, your uncle was afraid that maybe you were going to not come home at all this summer! I told him he was being ridiculous! I've wanted to call four times a day but he convinced me I was a fool. Wilma, get out from there! Why didn't you have us meet you at the station?"

I didn't know. I put my arms around my aunt and when I released her I was shocked to see tears in her eyes. "Has something else happened, Aunt Eleanor? Is there something else wrong?"

She shook her head vigorously. "No, no, no. I'm just so happy you're here."

"Uncle Charlie's here now, too? Right smack in the middle of the week?"

"Yes, and it's a disaster. I have no privacy anymore. He puts his fingers in things as I cook them and though he's here for three meals a day all week he still pretends that the dishwasher is a technological advance beyond his comprehension."

"Why is he taking so much vacation?"

"It isn't vacation, dear." Aunt Eleanor turned and motioned me to follow her out of the room. "Come pick through the berries for me while I start a crust so I can get a pie on the table tonight. Got a butterflied leg of lamb I'd like to see on the grill for dinner. What do you say?"

"I love grilled lamb."

"I know." She smiled and kept moving.

"So, Aunt Eleanor, what is it if it isn't vacation?"

But she was gone, twenty steps ahead of me and already calling back from the kitchen. "I knew you'd be along soon if not today. Bill Allen across the lake helped us get the dock in just last week."

"I thought Hank helped with that."

"Well, Hank started to help with that but then he wasn't able to finish the job."

"You mean he and Uncle Charlie got into a fight about Angie?"

"They did."

"Oh, Aunt Eleanor!" The keening edge to my voice snagged something in her and her eyes teared up again. She tossed her head like a mule testing a short lead line and pulled open the refrigerator. She slapped a pound of butter onto her granite bread-kneading board.

"If men could see themselves sometimes," she said. "See what helpless babies they turn into over not getting their way, not being the biggest dog. Charlie is just used to Hank doing as he's told. And Hank has reared up on his hind legs and decided all of a sudden that nobody is the boss of him. It started out friendly but in the end it was all yelling."

"Why is Uncle Charlie home in the middle of the week?"

She had transferred the butter into a bowl and was chopping it into a cup of flour with a serving fork. She set it down now to turn and give me her full attention. "Your uncle's security clearance was compromised. He was asked to cut off all contact with his two largest projects. He's home, basically, because they took away every bit of important work he had and set him down in a desk to push a little bit of paper around. So he just walked away. They'd've found something for him—given him other contracts because he's respected. But he said that if he stayed and didn't have the important work, it wouldn't take long for the respect to evaporate. And that would be the end of him; the end of him as he wants to be."

"I don't understand."

"Yes you do, my dear." I listened for bitterness in my aunt's voice but heard none. "When it was clear that he was never going to get another interesting piece of work, clear that nobody could talk to him freely, he didn't really have a choice, did he? Imagine working with people who stop talking whenever you enter a room, who never have a cup of coffee or lunch with you because they can't talk freely in your presence anymore."

"That's ridiculous. It can't all be because of Angie, can it?"

"Your sister's cash donations were made with money that came from your uncle's bank account. You know that."

"But Uncle Charlie didn't have anything to do with the people that Angie gave it to."

Aunt Eleanor didn't even bother to respond to this wobbly little protest. She knew that I knew that it didn't make any difference at all if the money were channeled through one of his dependents before it arrived in a dissident group's hands. It didn't make any difference that the men who had worked with my uncle for decades knew that he himself had nothing to do with radical fringe groups. He was connected, compromised, linked. He was out.

"Can't he fight this?" I asked.

She shook her head and resumed her deft slicing. "Keep going through those berries," she ordered. "Pie can be made whether or not your uncle has high security clearance or not. Pie is still pie, and I like pie."

"You're angry with Angie, I know," I began.

"I am indeed," she said sharply.

"And I know you feel upset about Hank's position."

"We already know all that. Say what's on your mind, Iris."

"We have to make Uncle Charlie see what it could turn into. He doesn't want to lose his son. And Angie—she's the last of my family, Aunt Eleanor. I mean, my biological family."

"Iris, the things that were said! The words that were used." Aunt Eleanor suddenly looked damp and uncertain: hopeless. She was shaking her head. "She's a beautiful and passionate girl," my aunt went on. "But she's also a little fool who doesn't understand a thing she's done, who's hurt my family and betrayed the very country her brothers died for and her father and Charlie served."

"It's who she always was, Aunt Eleanor! You can't stop loving her just because she's done some things that are entirely in character."

"You grew up in different times than Charlie and me, you girls. You never saw what other countries, evil countries, can become; you never saw everything you loved being threatened."

"I think Angie does see what she loves being threatened, Aunt Eleanor. I think that's why she gave money to those people."

"Those people, as you call them, are thugs and criminals—self-indulgent children who do not understand and therefore do not value their own country. I despair of them." My aunt put down her bowl. "And

I don't believe, really, that your sister is a political animal. I think she's simply angry and drawn to anger in others. That doesn't exonerate her. In fact it makes her actions worse. She has no goal, no ideal. She's just indulging a feeling that she'll grow out of, and along the way she's leaving wreckage behind her that she refuses to acknowledge. Perhaps that last is what I mind the most."

"Aunt Eleanor, the terrible turn things took—they weren't in her control. They weren't her responsibility. The way Uncle Charlie's employer is treating him, that's not in her control, either."

"You don't entirely believe that," she said to me, straightening herself, looking carefully at me while she said it. "Hank was so angry when he left. I didn't think he had it in him. It's like that girl is some kind of incubus, changing him." Aunt Eleanor smoothed her apron against her thighs and looked up. "Maybe it's just a matter of time. Maybe it's just a case of everyone needing a chance to cool off."

The room brightened and for a moment I thought it was simply the effect of her softening tone; but no, the sun had actually come out from behind a cloud and now the room was full of high contrasts where a moment before it had been gray.

Uncle Charlie came home with bass, which I helped him clean and dress as a first course. He had always insisted that fish needed to be eaten within an hour of being pulled out of the lake, so Eleanor was used to making room on a menu for them on short notice. But laid out on a big platter it was clear that there was too much of them. And there was too much lamb, too many potatoes, too many green beans. We sat amid piles of uneaten food, not talking about the missing people whose presence would have normalized this formerly normal-sized meal.

We took a walk with Wilma after dinner, still not speaking Angie's and Hank's names. We went to bed without having uttered them, and the next morning I rose early to go out fishing with Uncle Charlie with the world in the same state. The air was crisp, no fog or cloud cover, and we squinted whenever we had to face the rising sun snapping off the waves.

"Sunrise; sunset. Best times," was all he said to me as we pulled toward the little inlet he liked to fish in the earlier parts of the day.

"This is Hank's rod, isn't it?" I replied.

He looked up. "Looks it," he said.

"Aunt Eleanor told me about your losing the higher security projects, Uncle Charlie."

"I didn't 'lose' projects. They were formally taken from me."

"Angie didn't mean to hurt you, Uncle Charlie. I'm sure what she did wasn't connected, in her own mind, to what happened to you."

"Then she is an idiot."

"No she isn't."

"Then she's something worse. If she isn't an idiot, that means that she did it knowing what the consequences would be. Exactly where does she think all her little individual rights came from if not from the larger society that she lives in, and that she now claims is corrupt and unworthy of her support!"

I had nothing to say to this, so I said nothing. An hour later we pulled back to the dock without having caught a thing.

"Just as well," Eleanor greeted us as we pulled in with the morning's pinks gone to clear light. "I've had enough bass already to last me through the summer."

I went to the telephone in the study, feeling furtive, and dialed Vito's number. I would wake him, but that would be all right. But there was no answer. I knew his room: the telephone sat on a nightstand almost directly in his ear and would wake him, a lighter sleeper, within a half of a ring. I tried three times just to be sure I was dialing the right number.

Had he not been in his room, or had he not answered? No one would be calling him at this unlikely hour but me, so if he was there and had not answered, he had done so knowing I was probably the person trying to reach him. When the rings still summoned no one, I set the receiver in its cradle as if it were glass and crept back to the kitchen, flushing the toilet on my way to make it look more as if I'd simply left to use the bathroom and not a telephone in some odd private corner of the house.

I needn't have bothered. Aunt Eleanor and Uncle Charlie were entirely distracted by a pair of young men dressed in black suits who had just knocked on the front door to inform them that the FBI was now interested in Angie Sunnaret's whereabouts. She was being charged in connection with the shooting death of the twenty-nine-year-old policeman during the vandalizing of a draft board in Roanoke, Virginia.

No Answer

T HE NEXT MORNING I WOKE BEFORE AUNT ELEANOR AND UNCLE
Charlie, before dawn in fact. I slipped down through the gray light
to the kitchen, where I made a pot of coffee and considered dialing Vito's
number again before rejecting the idea. Then I changed my mind and
dialed.

He didn't answer. I craned my head around to get a look at the clock.
5:14 a.m. Could he sleep through this ringing? Where was he if he wasn't
home in his own bed?

Then I walked across the lawn to the dock, holding my mug in both
hands. A new sailboat bobbed on one side of the dock but I rejected it. I
managed to get into the old rowboat without losing more than an inch
of my coffee and I pulled myself out a few hundred yards with the cup
balanced on the plank by my side. There I sat and looked back at the
house, a light in the kitchen window throwing a little white patch onto
the lawn. I let one oar trail in the water, sipping my coffee while the boat
swung slowly around, leaving me facing a shapeless expanse of predawn
lake. I sat as the light came up and the masses of gray slowly became individual trees and rocks.

I had dreamed of Vito. I knew this because since I'd woken some strand of him had crossed my mind every few minutes. I had a dream aftertaste of him. My lips felt unnaturally warm and when I put my fingers to them the pressure recalled dream kisses, whole-body wraparound encounters that changed my heart rate and the temperature of my skin. I had also dreamed of the river of pills in Perry's drawing, the current carrying my mother away.

Aunt Eleanor had called Hank the night before and ordered him to come home. He received the news about the FBI and their charges in silence. He swore he had no idea where Angie was.

For the first time I felt myself wanting an outsider to stand with me as I considered my own family. If Vito were here I could talk about the bottles with him, and perhaps find my way through the foggy impression that the little orange canisters were linked somehow to the reason my brothers were lost and my sister was drifting toward a precipice.

The attic floor cache was clearly known to my brothers since it held their Batman comics, but why would young boys hide something like pill bottles? Had an adult hidden them there? I tried to imagine the woman who had stood before her mirror dabbing Shalimar between her breasts before walking up the stairs, loosening the plank, arranging the Dalmatian dog over the Batman comics.

No. That was wrong. My mother had not put them there. I sat in the gently rocking boat and made up other possible scenarios, these new ones all involving Eddie and Perry, whose domain was the attic. They had put the bottles there. Or one of them had put the bottles there. Or had it been Hank, not as averse to the attic as I'd thought?

I dropped an oar and pushed, changing direction again. I floated a bit more. I tried to imagine where my sister was at that very moment and what she might be doing, whom she might be with. I failed.

As I tied the boat back to its mooring and approached the house I felt disoriented in a way I couldn't describe with words. Aunt Eleanor greeted me at the door and told me that she'd found a law firm that she thought would be ideal for Angie's case, and a senior partner had agreed to come to the Lake House for our initial meeting. I could see that she had forgotten what she herself had said: that when people change things, things are changed and can never go back. You only had to watch her moving with brisk, purposeful energy to her coffeepot for a fresh cup to know that she harbored the hope that we could once again all be the way we were. I was a little frightened to see myself watching her from a distance and seeing her as a deluded though well-intentioned woman.

I was sure that it wasn't going to go back to the way it was. Now I saw that all the trusting, cheerful assumptions among us could be carried away as if they weighed nothing, which of course they did.

I wanted the young policeman to come back to life. I wanted the old Hank back, and I wanted my sister to release him. I wanted him to see that he would never be happy loving her so much when she loved him so little. I wanted the way I was with Vito to last forever.

Late that afternoon I carried a telephone up to the attic, where an unused jack was wired beside one of the boys' beds. I called Vito's number again, and again there was no answer. I called my own apartment and Hank picked up on the first ring. I asked him if Angie was still there and he said that when he woke the morning after they'd gotten the news about the subpoena she had been gone. He truly didn't know where she was.

I thought of the afternoon Vito had stopped me when I tried to pick up the ringing telephone. *No intruders,* Vito had said, shoving the telephone into a drawer and closing it ceremonially. I had been pleased, flattered that he made it clear that he would not be summoned away from me. My heart sank. Where had Angie's early morning hejiras taken her?

"I'm sure she'll be back or she'll call soon."

"Where would she go? Who does she know in town?"

"She's always done this," he said. "Always," he repeated.

I spent the rest of the day not calling anyone at all.

Playing with Poison

YOU CAN, I FOUND, DECIDE TO REMEMBER IN MUCH THE SAME way you decide to forget. It isn't like deciding to be a doctor or to eat a cheeseburger—it's more like the way you decide to let someone show you that the painting of an apple, turned just a bit at another angle, is also a painting of a child. I've known this—I just didn't use the knowledge. Think of the popular drawing that at first glance looks either like a well-dressed Victorian young woman, or an old crone, depending upon which details the viewer initially fixes upon. The challenge, of course, is that our minds resist simultaneously seeing one image in two ways. Few people see the two possibilities until someone says, *There's the nose, and the hat, and the eyes.* Then the different vision of the same image pops into view as plain as day and it's hard not to see it.

Some people refuse to see the feather, the eyelash, the tiny nose. They cling to their familiar first version and it keeps looking like a shawl, a squint, an enormous beak. Others accept the news that their first view was only that. The views don't contradict one another so much as coexist, and the mind resists this because it wants only one truth. A person has to decide to argue with her mind, and her nature, and keep looking. A person has to be very open to the idea of having been wrong.

That's what it was like to decide to remember. *Going looking,* Crooked River had told me, *that's the best way to find out what you want . . . who you really are.* So Eddie's humiliation before my father, Skinny's demise, my Animal Mother—now that I had decided to see them, their outlines were suddenly clear. Now I couldn't remember what the view had been like without them there in plain sight.

My brothers' fates had made this change, perhaps—shaken apart whatever part of my mind that had been in charge before. Or perhaps it was Vito. Wasn't that the way it happened in all the fairy tales? Sleeping Beauty finally woken by a kiss; Rapunzel trapped in her tower until the young prince freed her from her tiny, jewel-like prison? They were awakened by love, and what happened to them after they were changed is never known.

I waited for the meeting with the lawyer by being quiet, and retreating to the room that had once been my mother's. Angie had described lying here on her bed and watching her dress so often and so clearly that I could not be sure what was Angie's memory and what was mine. Had it always been raining as our mother decided which dress to wear? We lay on her bed and listened to the thrum of a thick downpour on the cocoa bean walks in the garden outside her window. The pillow always smelled faintly of Shalimar.

It's a deeply feminine scent, a not-mommy smell, and I loved it but it made the bottom of my throat feel heavy and closed. I associated it with the parts of my mother that snarled or grunted when we angered her, that drank scotch, that wore dresses without backs and little strappy shoes with heels like five-inch nails: my Animal Mother. This mother cried frequently, sometimes in ugly bubbled-up waves that ride in on shocking amounts of mucus—not the tissue-to-the-eye, dewy tears of television mothers.

But I also loved the smell because it summoned up the peaceful Queen Mother, the woman who had had only one drink and smiled on her children as they gamboled in the late-afternoon sunlight on the lawn. This is the woman who must have bantered with admiring three-star generals and put the officers' wives auxiliary jumping through whatever hoops she cared to set up. She got her way with other mothers and fathers, with generals, with school principals and all the other large people in the world I knew.

This mother sat on tiny chairs with Angie and me and sipped sugary tea from plastic cups. She rolled little cars down packed roads with my brothers in their dirt patch at the back of the yard, making *vroomvroom* noises with them and suggesting changes in the bridge designs. Their bridges and parking garages were made from dry-cleaner box parts and needed to be replaced every time the weather turned damp. She was particularly good at bridges. She laughed lightly. She didn't forget about dinner or getting dressed in the morning.

I couldn't tell if my father made my mother the Animal Mother or the Queen. When the telephone rang and he was coming home she was the second woman until his arrival. Then, a little way into his visit, she started showing signs of the first. She started as a Queen but always ended as the Animal Mother. I guess he made her both.

Angie loved only the Queen. She left the house the moment the Animal Mother made a hint of an appearance. Perry also felt happier with the Queen than the Animal, that was fairly clear. He went to bed singing on the nights she built cardboard bridges. He went to her jewelry box to bring her her pearls to wear in the dirt pile and she put them on and kissed his nose.

But Eddie seemed more satisfied on days when the Animal Mother was in ascendance. He was cheerier, more energetic. If she fell into weeping or snarling he squared off with her while the rest of us backed out of the room, out of the yard, off to a neighbor or up a tree. I was too little to be much good at seeking shelter on my own so I went with Angie to the creek if we were in the winter house or out on the lake in a rowboat if we were at the Lake House. We sought water, always. I was not upset: seeking shelter was what other people did for me. It wasn't my concern. I was safe.

Eddie sought conflict. He argued and taunted, produced all the objects and behaviors that he knew made our mother feel most powerless: nose-picking, swear words, dirt-bombs and bugs in the house, flaunted cigarette stubs. He could make her cry almost as consistently as our father could.

During these animal times I was often in Aunt Eleanor's company, driving somewhere, cooking, dancing in her kitchen. I regularly forgot my brothers and my sister. I was with Aunt Eleanor.

One day I was drawn away by the sound of my brothers arguing in the attic. I heard Angie's voice in the mix. I left my mother's room and drifted up just enough stairs so I could rest my chin on the floorboards at the top of the flight that led to the attic. From here I could see my siblings, all wholly absorbed with the contents of a pot that Eddie was stirring. Even from the top of the stairs I caught a stiff ammonia-like smell. If they were aware of my presence they did not acknowledge me. I saw bottles jammed under Eddie's bed and it was clear, given my siblings' physical positions and tones of voice, that the mixture in the pot was Eddie's doing and the source of the conflict. He crouched over the aromatic liquid, Perry squared off directly to the other side and Angie behind Perry and a bit to his left.

"It's just play," Eddie protested, and I sank my head down a bit to make myself more unobtrusive. "It's pretend poison."

"Get your face away from it, Eddie, or you'll pass out," Angie warned.

Perry had on his blackest face. He said, "It isn't play poison. You can read bottle labels and you know what it can do. You've got to just cut it out, Eddie. Pour this crap into the toilet."

This was the wrong thing to say and even I knew it. Eddie smiled. "Make me," he said, only he said it very softly, which was much scarier than saying it loud. Perry rose up to his full four feet and eleven-odd inches, pulled back a foot and brought it quickly forward smack into the side of the pot, which spun into the air. Ammonia-ish fluid sprayed along its path, wetting bedclothes and soaking cotton throw rugs. The room was suffused in tear-producing fumes.

"You clean this up!" Eddie cried.

"I don't think so," Perry said back, and now it was Perry's voice that was softer. "I think *you* need to clean this up."

Now Angie stepped forward. "There's too much for any one person to clean up and you two don't know how to run the washing machine! So we're all cleaning up."

They had frightened themselves. They had frightened me. I ducked before the crown of my head drew any attention and slid back down the stairs, keeping close to the wall to minimize squeaking. I tiptoed back to my mother's room and pressed my nose into her pillow to drive the ammonia smell out and the Shalimar smell in but the ammonia smell was too strong. Everywhere I went in the next week, there it was. "Do you smell anything?" I remember asking Angie the next afternoon as we walked by the stairway entrance to the attic.

"Nope," she said, staring blandly into the distance while she said it.

And when I insisted I smelled something, giddy with fear that she would say that yes she did smell something, she insisted I smelled Perry's shoes and that was all I smelled.

All that week we lived with the Queen Mother, calm and elegant and attentive. But Eddie had been transformed into Animal Eddie. Now it was he who snarled at the slightest thing and wept like his heart was cut to ribbons. When it was Eddie and not my mother who wept I could hear something that was in her voice all along but invisible to me until Eddie revealed it: rage.

What did my mother have to be angry about? She had us, which is all that a child believes her mother should need or want.

More confusing was Eddie. What did Eddie have to be angry about? We were all together, except for my peripatetic father. He had sisters and a brother who generally adored him—we even usually obeyed him. A beautiful mother; a glamorous father; manipulable and endearing siblings. This was what Eddie's life looked like to me.

Justice

BY THE AFTERNOON WE WERE MEETING WITH THE NEW LAWYER
Eleanor had found, I had still not succeeded in reaching Vito. I had
not stopped wondering where Angie was. Aunt Eleanor told us to prepare for the meeting with the attorney with open minds, and be ready
to do whatever he advised. No arguing, she said. He was the expert, of
course, and we depended upon experts, but our chances for getting
through this situation intact rested on all our shoulders as well. I wasn't
feeling hopeful.

The mood walking into the living room was reminiscent of the mood
on the day we heard Thompson the possibly drunken vet say that Perry
had killed Eddie. That day had been cold and yellow. The living room had
been peach, a shade just barely cooler than the light that bounced from
the leaves through the windows. The day after Thompson left, Aunt
Eleanor began painting the room a deep maroon. She painted a lot of the
rooms in the house new colors after his visit, and pitched away a good
deal of the furniture that had been in there when he introduced himself.

Now the room was the green of just-cut grass and the temperature of deep June Virginia shade. We could smell the lake, and a busky
waft of Wilma passing by the window: she'd antagonized a skunk the

week before and was consequently banished to the yard. She tended to prop herself up on her hind legs and press her nose against the screens when she was banished from the living room. Cries of "Down, Wilma!" or "Get off the damn screen, Wilma!" had punctuated our first day all together here as Wilma circled the building like the hound she was, trying to rejoin her pack.

It was clear that Aunt Eleanor and Uncle Charlie had spent the first days after receiving the FBI's news locked in a dispute that grew more bitter as they spoke less about it. Uncle Charlie made it clear that now Angie was in the law's purview and it would treat her as it would and should. He washed his hands of her and turned her over to the larger powers of the state.

Aunt Eleanor would have nothing to do with this position, which she regarded as wrong-headed or, if pressed, asinine. When Uncle Charlie said that the state would provide legal counsel if Angie so desired, she had countered with a description of the Washington lawyer she'd found. He had experience in cases like Angie's, she'd reported matter-of-factly. Uncle Charlie had protested. He had asked her if she didn't believe in the legal system's ability to try cases fairly. That's the foundation of our society's ability to trust, he argued, to proceed with good faith in our culture's legal processes. Aunt Eleanor said that she had more good faith in a process that provided a lawyer with a caseload of five clients (billing hundreds of dollars an hour) than she had in a process providing a lawyer with fifty cases (earning twenty dollars an hour). Nothing personal, she said. No slur on the American way. She'd already made the first appointment with him and given him a deposit.

My aunt Eleanor was at war, though she didn't have a clear bead on her enemy. Various things that flew out of her mouth made it clear that we all of us drove her crazy with our political posturing, our ill-conceived sexual attachments, our romantic ideas about the social contract, our idiotic naiveté about social protest. Only I seemed outside her first line of fire. As far as she knew, I had made no awkward intra-familial sexual conquests. I hadn't handed any cash over to so-called protesters who were only thugs with a fringe of political ideology. I wasn't getting in her way as she tried to keep Angie out of jail. I was still, still, the good daughter, the easiest child to love.

For the first time in my life I saw that this hurt Hank. He was bound by very deep ties to his mother and father. He accepted that his loyalty to Angie was received as an insult by them but he couldn't realign those stars. He was also miserable because Angie hadn't taken him into her confidence and he still didn't have the faintest idea where she was. Uncle Charlie didn't believe him when he said he had no idea where Angie was, but I did.

So now we were going to meet Aunt Eleanor's legal paragon, the young Turk who had defended at least a dozen high-profile cases in which protesters had faced charges ranging from trespass to assault and destruction of federal property. He had won each of these contests. He had also, though we spoke of this less, defended three Black Panthers against murder charges and gotten prison time for them instead of the electric chair. This would not have been so remarkable except that the murders had taken place in Texas, famous for its willingness to execute. He was so well known that when Aunt Eleanor had used his name, Hank and I immediately recognized it.

"You know it's not the money that makes me not like this idea," Uncle Charlie had said to her at breakfast.

"I know. That makes it worse," she said. "If we were poor I could actually understand your resistance to getting better legal advice. But we're not. So what does that mean, Charlie?"

The lawyer, Darren Winter, was much younger than Aunt Eleanor and Uncle Charlie would have liked. Still, he wore wingtips and suspenders, as did the junior partner who accompanied him on his trip to the Lake House; he drove a BMW and managed to balance civility with the clear expectation that everyone around him would do what he said.

He accepted an offer of tea, asked for lemon and settled himself in the room's best chair. To successfully implicate Angie in a murder charge, he explained, the opposition would have to prove that Angie was tangibly connected to the Roanoke draft board incident where the young police officer was shot and killed. As far as he knew, this wasn't going to be possible. One of the purposes of today's meeting, he explained, was to assure him that in fact there was no such evidence. If we knew of anything that could specifically link Angie to that time and place, we had to put it on the table right now. Because if this evidence exists, he said calmly, there is a possibility that the opposition will find it—so we have to have it in our hands to prepare our defense. Or, I thought, to destroy it.

We all shook our heads like owls. No, no—no evidence at all, we said. Hank, my uncle Charlie and my aunt Eleanor, all were able to assure him without a trace of doubt. Why, Angie was asleep in her bed in California on the day of the Roanoke draft board vandalizing, certainly. Too bad she lived alone and had no witnesses. Something about the way I spoke caught the lawyer's attention.

"Miss Sunnaret? You seem uncertain?"

The junior partner had a tape recorder as well as a pile of documents and a notebook, which he was using right now.

"No."

"No?" His tone was entirely neutral: a lawyerly just-repeating-your-language-for-clarity's-sake tone.

"No," I said, "I am not uncertain. I don't have any reason to think that anybody has evidence linking Angie to that particular draft board, or those particular people."

He smiled and nodded.

What was on my mind, of course, was the folder she had pressed on me with Hank's draft records. When Angie gave it to me for safekeeping I had only seen them as an annoyance. I knew they could be replaced within a few weeks. Now they weren't so inconsequential because they might be concrete evidence linking her to the Virginia draft board, and thus, the dead young policeman. The folder was sitting in a backpack upstairs right now, exactly where I'd dropped it when I arrived.

"You should look at records and papers you have carefully," Mr. Winter was saying. "Search for anything that could help pinpoint Angie's location that day. Perhaps one of you spoke to her and have the telephone bill records that can provide proof that she wasn't in Virginia at the time of the shooting. Perhaps you have a letter postmarked from California on that specific day. Just for the record, I need to inform you that destruction of evidence, even if it's inadvertent, is a serious offense."

This comment was for my benefit, I was sure.

"Are records from particular draft boards traceable?" I asked, crossing my legs and making shooing gestures toward Wilma, who had braced herself on the outside window ledge with her nose pressed against the screen. "Back to a specific draft board, I mean?"

"Most of them, yes. They're stamped when processed in ways that identify them with a particular place of origin. In other words, any papers from the Virginia draft board where the policeman was shot would be easy to identify as such."

My heart sank.

The lawyer watched for my reaction, registered whatever he saw and continued. "You have to realize as well," he added, "that the FBI routinely gets requests approved for wiretaps and searches. Expect your own lines to be tapped. If the FBI requests written transcripts of your telephone bills, of course, the phone company is legally required to tell you that they have been subpoenaed. But by then the damage is done. Expect a possible visit or two from the authorities. I'm sure you understand that cooperation with them is essential. We want to look confident, though responsibly concerned. We need to present a united front, uniformly describing Angie as a young girl with ideals who simply made a contribution to a group she did not entirely understand."

It occurred to me that as we stood in the driveway and watched the two wing-tipped attorneys pull away in their BMW that we were positioned in roughly the same configuration we'd been in the day we watched Thompson pull away in his crooked little chuffing Chevy. And just like on the preceding visit, no hands were raised in farewell. We stood like rocks in the dirt for a while, and then we turned away and limped back into the house.

Aunt Eleanor dispatched us in different directions: Uncle Charlie to his study to examine household telephone and utility records during the month of the draft board vandalization, Hank and I to check our own telephone records. We both simply threw away bills after we'd paid them, so this would require calls to Virginia Bell to get copies. We were to review the month with one another and describe any contact with Angie in writing. She sent us to the front parlor.

"This is ridiculous," Hank said to me as we closed the door behind us and sat down by the telephone, still holding the legal pads and pens she had thrust into our hands. "What does she think we can accomplish doing this?"

"She's just keeping busy," I said. "Convincing herself that she's working toward something."

"I know. But of course it isn't going to do any good. Any telephone records that we have access to, the FBI has already subpoenaed."

"It's just getting prepared, like the guy said," I cajoled. "So we won't be taken by surprise. And we might find something that helps Angie's case."

"But you know as well as I do that she *was* calling people engaged in 'anti-government activity' and she *was* giving them cash and she *was* meeting with them," Hank said. "And records from any residential telephone she might have used will prove it." He shook his head. "The only thing I can think of that we might need to find are the draft records she claimed she had—my draft records. I'm a Virginia resident and those draft records came from the Virginia office that got vandalized. She told me not to worry about them. Do you know if she destroyed them? Did she tell you about them?"

"Nope," I said. He wasn't really paying any attention or he would have seen my color change. So now two things were perfectly clear: Angie actually had been at the draft board in question, and she hadn't kept the information about his own records from Hank, as she'd told me she would.

"Hank? Doesn't it bother you that she was there?" I ventured.

"She didn't pull any trigger. She didn't hurt anybody herself."

"Hank! She was——"

"She was nothing! I just hope she burned the damn records so they can't be pulled out of some dumpster behind an apartment she was living in and used against her later. You know?"

I said nothing.

"This is just such a waste of time," he sighed, tossing his legal pad onto the carpet.

"Maybe," I agreed, "but we should stay in here for a while anyway and come out talking like we did something productive." I paused. Hank had known all along that Angie was part of the attack on the draft board and the young policeman's death. I felt myself hardening, looking at him with pity as well as some fear. He had let himself fall so entirely into her hands.

"Hank? Do you remember my mother taking a lot of pills?"

"Why?" He had become instantly reserved, wary.

"Do you remember a hiding place in the floor of the attic?" He shook his head vaguely from side to side. "Come with me," I said, reaching down and taking his hand. I led him up the narrower stairwell to the third floor and to the crooked plank. I knelt, popped it open and reached in, drawing out the cellophaned package of Batman comics. I handed them to him.

"My, my!" He laughed. "I finally get to touch the sacred Batman comics. I never thought this day would come."

I pulled out my Dalmatian dog, which was not so familiar to him. Hank had never paid any attention to stuffed dogs, or for that matter to me during those years when a stuffed dog was an important thing in my universe. I set the dusty little polyester creature down and plunged my hand in again, coming up with a clutch of orange cylinders. I lined those up next to the dog.

"What about these?" I asked.

"What about them?" he countered.

"The labels say they're my mother's. Why are they here?"

"Why are you asking me?"

"Because you were old enough to know and you were there."

"Eddie liked little pill bottles. Your mother must have known that and let him have them when they were empty. Or maybe he picked them out of the trash. I don't know."

I had known Hank all my remembered life, and I knew now that he was telling me so little that it amounted to lying.

"Let's go back downstairs," he said uneasily.

I didn't want to leave the attic with its sharply angled light, its low ceilings, its connection to my child brothers and the bottles. I actually curled my fingers around the window ledge behind me and hung on. "Tell me about the day she died. I don't remember the day she died."

He had reached the first of the flight of steps to the second floor but he stopped and sat down. "You were with my momma somewhere. That's why you don't remember."

"Where were you? Were you with Eddie and Perry?"

"Yes. And Angie. I'd spent the night with them, mostly here in the attic."

"Tell me about the day."

"It was so long ago, Iris."

"I know." He was saying that I shouldn't be interested now because I hadn't been interested before. But it was too late now to be what I was. I smiled reassuringly at him, encouraging him.

"Just tell me," I said. And he did.

THE DAY MY MOTHER DIED began quite happily for everyone, it seemed, but my mother herself. It was the day before Eddie's birthday, a connection that never became lodged in family history because we did not acknowledge the day of her death in any way in the years following it.

Because of that impending birthday, there were flour, eggs, sugar, vanilla, chocolate chunks and tiny decorative footballs made of sugar on the kitchen counter. My mother had roused herself and begun the procedure because the first birthday cake was due at the crack of dawn. But she'd lost steam. Her good intentions had seeped right out of her and she ended up sitting on the floor, where Perry found her in a soggy stupor sometime in the middle of the morning. *Perry,* Hank now told me that she had said, *I want you to go to my pills and only give me one pill. And I want you to keep the bottle with all the other pills hidden from me. Can you do that?*

Hank was positive that Perry knew that the contents of these bottles were something that our mother depended upon. Everyone but me, it seemed, understood her relationship with the pills. Hank had overheard enough in his own house to know that our mother struggled to take only three or four of them in a day, and that she often failed and he assumed, because of the deep silences that fell around the subject and because of the ways my mother sometimes seemed to drift far away from us even as she sat in the kitchen staring out at the lake, that my siblings knew this as well. Everybody knew that I didn't know.

On this day our mother gave Perry the bottle to hold and the order to give her only one of the pills. Just one. If she asked him to give her more, he had to hold out and not hand them over. Could he do that for her? Perhaps Perry was flattered by this request. Or maybe he was scared, but according to Hank he had accepted the job and solemnly carried the bottle up into the attic and reported on his duties to Hank and Eddie, who were building a cardboard city while Angie stood by, criticizing their work and making suggestions. I was gone. Hank didn't know where. I seemed to be gone often. Perry had lifted up the oak boards and set the full bottle down among the Batman comics. My mother, meanwhile, tried to scrape herself off the floor and plug in the eggbeaters. She failed. She wandered into the backyard, where Hank, Eddie, Angie and Perry could see her walk vaguely in larger and larger circles. Finally she sat down again, staring away from the house.

They had all—Hank and Angie and the boys—clustered at the attic window where they could see the lawn sloping down to the lake and our mother planted there in the grass, staring. They drew chairs up and waited for her to move. An hour went by. Finally she rose and drifted back into the house. They heard her moving around in the kitchen, rattling open the drawers. They heard her slow steps coming up the stairs and they sat very still and waited. The footsteps stopped, there was a pause, and then she called Perry's name from the second floor. He went to her.

Hank claimed now to have stood at the top of the stairwell with Angie and Eddie, the better to hear their conversation. He said they had all heard it: *Perry, I need you to get the pills now. I know I said not to give them to me but everything's fine and you can do it. You can trust me. I only need to hold the bottle. I'm fine. But you need to please do this.*

Perry had refused, just as he'd promised her he would. Then Hank, Eddie and Angie had heard more frightening noises—my mother shifting into the Animal Mother in the face of resistance, growling and then shouting. Then they heard the bright smack of an open hand on a face, and the bump of a small body falling back on the stairs.

"Eddie bolted down those stairs like there was a fire he was running into to save somebody's life," Hank said to me. "And he was actually frothing at the mouth—more mad than I'd ever seen him. Angie and I followed. We didn't know what else to do. And there was your mother on the stairs, shaking Perry from the nape of his neck like a dog, really shaking him, telling him to do what she said. Iris, she just looked crazy. I thought she was going to topple over and go right down the stairwell, still hanging onto Perry. Eddie was as crazed as she was. He charged up to her and Perry and started yelling at her to stop but she acted like she didn't hear him. Maybe she didn't hear him. He broke your mother's hold on poor Perry and then he pushed her. She slapped Eddie, hard, right across the face. They started yelling at each other like there was nobody else there and it was just between the two of them. Then she ignored Eddie, turned to Perry and told him to get the pills, kept saying *You can trust me.* When he didn't move to get the pills she just started hitting them—both of them. Finally Perry gets to his feet and he's crying and telling Eddie to go away—to stop yelling at her and stop fighting. Perry's trying to push Eddie back up the stairs and Eddie by now is more crazed than even your mother.

"Then Eddie turns his back on them all of a sudden, and he's stopped yelling now. He comes tearing into the attic past me and Angie and he pops up the little door to the secret cache. He pulls the pills out and goes back down the stairs and we can hear more yelling, Perry telling him to go away, to take the pills away; your mother yelling to give her the pills."

"Eddie gave her the pills," I said.

"Yes. Eddie walked back up the stairs to us, just turned his back on your mother and Perry and walked away, disgusted. But Perry followed her like a dog, begging her to give the bottle back to him. She acted like he wasn't there now.

"Perry finally gave up and left her. He came back upstairs where we all were just standing there waiting for him, and then he and Eddie had this fistfight—just the two of them knocking each other down over and over. Angie and I didn't do a thing to stop it. It must have gone on for forty minutes. Then they just sat there on the floor, and Eddie said, *She says you can trust her.* He said it like a taunt. A joke.

"While Eddie and Perry were knocking each other down, Angie and I were at the attic window, watching the lawn, waiting for your mother to come out or for I don't know what. I thought it was going to be okay. I mean, your mother had had the eggbeater on the counter. When I came through the kitchen that morning I'd seen the sugar and butter and flour in the pink canisters and that had been a kind of promise that she was going to finish the cakes and be there to hand them over at the birthday tomorrow. So today was safe because tomorrow had to happen. I wasn't afraid about the pills.

"Eddie and Perry finally stopped hitting each other. They got up and came over to the window with us when we heard someone light, someone who had to be your mother, step out the back door and onto the porch. She was humming. When she drifted ten yards more toward the water and turned to look straight back and up to the attic window, we saw that half her hair was missing. She held scissors in one hand and a hank of her hair in the other and she snipped as she turned away from the window and kept walking. From way up on the third floor looking down you could see how the clumps of hair made a path behind her. She was wearing one of your dad's military belts on the outside of a sweater. I remember thinking it was a perfect touch. Isn't that odd?

"It was Perry who ran to her. Angie and Eddie and I were just kind of frozen in place. He ran so fast he fell down twice and he called out to her the whole way. When he reached her she turned to him, surprised. She hadn't heard him even though he'd been screaming out 'Momma, Momma!' But then she reached down to put her arms around him and kiss the top of his head. We were too far away to hear what she said. Perry told the police later that she'd told him she was just going for a little cool-down in the lake and then she had to get the first cake in the oven. So he let her go. We saw him step back away from her and wave. She waved back."

I blinked. "She drowned accidentally," I said at last. "Just like Aunt Eleanor and Uncle Charlie have always told us."

"She had a will, Iris, and it had been updated a month before she died. She left the Lake House to you and Perry and Eddie and cut your father out. Why would she update a will?"

"Because that's what responsible parents do. They periodically update wills."

"But she wasn't a responsible parent," Hank said. "She changed her will just before she died and cut your father out. My folks asked him if he wanted to get a lawyer—contest it. But he didn't. When you and Angie are both twenty-five, it passes entirely into your control. See, this is the reason that Angie is so sure that Perry shot Eddie."

"I don't understand," I said. "The boys didn't care about money, or the house."

"No, not the money! Not the house! It's that Eddie gave her the pills— he pushed Perry aside and he gave her the pills."

"You just said that she told the boys they could trust her," I murmured.

"Right. Trust her. Look, Iris, Angie was always sure that Perry blamed Eddie for your mom's death. She's always thought that it's this thing between them."

"They loved each other."

"I know. I don't think I've ever known two brothers who loved each other more than Perry and Eddie did."

"They were just little boys."

"Remember the hunting trip where they fell into the gorge?" Hank went on. "Angie's convinced that Perry pushed Eddie in."

"If Perry pushed him, then why would Perry risk his own life to jump in right after him?"

"Maybe because Perry pushed him," Hank replied. "You can love somebody and wish they'd just die, both at the same time." He turned to look directly at me and spoke as if his next sentence flowed logically from the last. "Eddie knew what she'd do with the pills. And he handed them to her anyhow."

"But you said she'd started making the cake for the next day."

"Well," Hank said, standing and grasping the banister. "She sure fooled us. Liar, liar pants on fire."

"You have to trust somebody," I said. "It wasn't a bad thing to trust her." Hank didn't respond. "I always trusted Angie," I added after a moment. "Loved and trusted her."

"I know. So does she. She says that's why it hurts so much to see you don't trust her anymore."

So they had talked about me.

"Do you trust her, Hank?" I asked.

"Depends. Trust her with what?"

"Your happiness."

"Of course not."

"Then I don't understand," I said.

"She's not responsible for my happiness," he answered. I had turned away from him, but he took my arm. He said, "You know what she did the night your mother died? She baked Eddie's goddamned cake. And when my momma drove up with you that afternoon, Angie took you aside and told you that she was the Queen now, and you were the princess, and everything would be all right."

I remembered this the moment he said it—Angie's white face and my terror calmed as if by magic. Angie was the new Queen. I was the princess. It was terrible, but it was all going to be all right.

———————

ANGIE CALLED THE HOUSE that night and asked Uncle Charlie to arrange for her to have one last Fourth of July at the Lake House, unmolested by the authorities. She promised to turn herself in the very next morning.

Aunt Eleanor conferred with the lawyer, who was not happy with the plan. He pointed out that this case involved a police shooting, and the officers assigned were not going to want to risk losing her when they knew she'd be standing on the Lake House lawn on the Fourth of July. The lawyer told Uncle Charlie that he doubted anyone could dictate behavior to the FBI.

"I didn't work with those people for twenty years without knowing who to go to for a favor when I need it," Uncle Charlie replied stiffly. "If she wants to have one day at the Lake House without interference I think I can arrange that for her—and I think she should have it."

Aunt Eleanor slipped her hand in his and faced the lawyer squarely. "We'll come to your office on the fifth," she said. "Make whatever arrangements you have to make."

The Fourth

THE NEXT DAY WAS JULY SECOND—TWO DAYS TO THE BIG party. I had restrained myself from calling Vito Signori's number for three days now, but this had to be done if I was going to know for sure if he was coming to the picnic. He answered on the second ring.

"You've been out of town?" A bad start, I thought, but I couldn't control myself.

"I was out with two guys who are going to be in a graduate seminar I'm taking next semester. They claimed to know some phenomenal highway cut-throughs so I decided to follow them around for a week."

I knew by now that highway blasting was something that all geologists loved dearly, and his tone was cheerily unself-conscious.

"Angie asked me to give her a ride to the Lake House on the Fourth," he said, and my chest constricted again. "You'd already mentioned it, so I figured I was invited, right?"

"Right."

"So we'll show up around ten. Eleven."

I nodded into the telephone and then, remembering he couldn't hear this, said, "Great. That's great."

"Look, I'll swing by your apartment on my way out of town and scoop up any incoming mail." He hung up.

I'd waited for the intensity of my feelings for Vito Signori to plateau or diminish. Instead they'd sharpened, an experience that should have been a source of delight, but wasn't. I went out onto the lawn where Uncle Charlie and Aunt Eleanor piled logs and crates onto the bonfire pile. Uncle Charlie had made the traditional preparations: rockets, bonfire, torches. He'd set up the drum barbecue and filled it with coal. He'd ordered three cases of champagne, fifteen cases of soda, a keg of beer. Aunt Eleanor was already baking and butchering her way toward the big event.

"What song are you doing this year?" he asked me as I reached them.

"I haven't thought about it, Uncle Charlie."

"Well, we're not lighting the bonfire until you all do your songs," he said grimly.

"Uncle Charlie, maybe this year should be kind of edited." I could see Angie arriving with all the chords to "Eve of Destruction" or "The Great Mandala" worked out. The unspoken rules had all been broken and now anything might happen. Uncle Charlie didn't answer me, which meant that as far as he was concerned this year would follow exactly in the pattern of its predecessors.

"A friend of mine just called, Aunt Eleanor, and said that Angie would be getting a ride with him."

Uncle Charlie turned away from the bonfire preparations then. "Really?"

Aunt Eleanor snorted impatiently. "Oh, Charlie! Veedo is Iris's young man, not anyone Angie has an eye on!"

They began a heated discussion about paper napkin supplies. I drifted back up to the house.

One more day. We smiled when we ran into folks at the grocery store and kept inviting everybody we ran into, just as we always had done. Friends were called and told yes, yes, everything was going ahead just as always—please do come! Jell-O molds and little paper flags on toothpicks littered the kitchen counters. Eleanor had decided to slow-roast a

pig as well as do the full chicken-hamburger-hot-dog-marshmallow barbecue. As soon as she found a butcher two towns over who could handle the order she set Uncle Charlie to digging the pit. This was not
normally the kind of challenge he enjoyed, but he took his shovel meekly
and kissed her on his way out to pick a site.

I baked cupcakes and impaled them with little toothpick flags, arranging them on their platters into perfect rows of paper squares waving over red, white and blue icing. I carved a watermelon into a
saw-toothed basket and went on runs with Uncle Charlie to buy new softball bases and balls, prizes for games, paper bunting to hang around the
porch. I did these things and all I could think while I did them was that
Angie had always had her way, had always trampled over the feelings of
anyone obstructing her path, had always cast herself as the superior moral
being at exactly the time she was indulging in the most questionable
moral behaviors. She had told me she loved me, but that was a patroniz-
ing self-serving lie, offered up only to give the impression that she was
capable of loyalty, which she was not.

Hank had stayed at the Lake House after the meeting with the lawyers,
working on the party, being terribly civil and pleasant with his parents.
Now Uncle Charlie called him off to work on the barbecue pit with him.
They were still there, poking at coals, when Vito and Angie pulled up two
hours later. Angie wore a black leotard and bell-bottom jeans, silver at
her throat and hoops on her ears. She looked jangled and ill-tempered.
Vito wore what I knew was his best shirt and a pair of khaki pants and
he, too, looked as if he'd been interrupted mid-argument. They pulled
up, so involved in the end of some difficult conversation that they were
oblivious for the moment to the house and yard and to me, walking toward them. As Vito pulled up the parking brake he reached toward her
lightly with one hand, tracing her chin in one quick, delicate line. The
gesture was so intimate it stopped me dead at the top of the drive. I controlled an impulse to retreat into a bush so as not to intrude—and not
to see—and forced one foot out before the other again. Angie saw me
and waved. They unfolded themselves from the front seat and Vito smiled
in my direction, started walking happily toward me. Angie was humming

blandly, swinging her hair over her shoulder and reaching into the trunk for a backpack. Vito called to me and I responded by breaking into a trot. I couldn't have responded any other way if I'd tried. Angie raised an eyebrow at this open display of eagerness but I proceeded directly into his embrace. Then I turned to her.

"I'm so glad to see you, Angie." The touch to the cheek could have been essentially meaningless. The sight of her was, actually, welcome. She grinned at me and I felt the old, unthinking pleasure.

She looked around her. "It really is beautiful," she said, as if this fact made her sad. She had spoken with such resignation—almost something I would call despair—and I felt a pang.

"Thanks for coming back," I said.

"It had to happen sometime, didn't it? And this is the ideal day—lots of distraction, lots of history. Remember the Fourth that Jerry Ploughrite almost drowned when he dove in after Otto because he thought the stupid dog couldn't swim? He didn't drown in the end but he scared the shit out of Otto." She laughed.

"I don't remember."

"I guess you were too little. So. Where's Uncle Charlie?"

I nodded toward the back of the house, where he would be nestling the butchered pig into the coals. She sighed. "Okay. Here I go." She trotted off, whistling vaguely.

"Is this your Veedo?" Aunt Eleanor had found her way to our side. "Come along, young man. I have a job for you."

"Vito, this is my aunt Eleanor. Eleanor, Vito Signori. Let me show him around first, Aunt Eleanor. I'll turn him over to you as soon as I'm done, I promise."

"Fine. Are all the flags in the cupcakes?" She actually sounded a bit anxious.

I nodded, and she released us temporarily, swarming off to get the early arrival ten-year-olds some softball equipment.

"She looks like a sparrow on Dexedrine," Vito observed.

"She can normally handle a hundred guests without breaking a sweat. But Angie's situation, Hank being back . . . she's not herself."

I led him into the house and through all the rooms, showing him where I had hidden things in childhood, where we had scrawled messages on the walls of closet interiors, where various dramas had taken place that I'd described to him during our long afternoons. When we reached the attic he pulled another manila envelope from the Iroquois Nation out of a pocket. It had been folded into eighths to fit.

"Take this before I forget it again. It came to the Jefferson Avenue apartment."

I flattened the thing as well as could be expected and opened its top flap before inverting and shaking. A breeze flowed steadily between the two attic windows, lifting the drawings as soon as they were free and carrying them across the floor. Vito retrieved them. They were portraits, both of Eddie. He looked squarely at the artist with an open, affectionate expression, a cigarette between his lips and his arms spread like wings to either side of him as he lay sprawled on sandbags. In the second portrait he was picking something out of a bowl with his free hand, grinning. The grin was exact to him, electric and pure. Beyond the sandbags bush and elephant weed rose up. A cloud of mosquitoes had been painstakingly included above and just to the left of the subject's ear. "What's in that bowl in the second drawing?" I asked Vito.

"Looks like cut-up jackfruit," Vito said.

"He looks happy," I said. "What do you think?"

"I think," he said, "that this picture was done by somebody who loved his subject, and I think the subject loved him back."

"It does look like that." I shook the envelope again, hard, and out popped a small spiny vegetative chunk of something. It was flattened, of course, brown with green and yellow tints at its base, spiked with a thorn as long as my thumbnail.

"What is it?" I asked Vito again.

He plucked it up from where it had fallen and rolled it in his palm. "Looks like a jackfruit spike. This is the outside of the fruit. It's sweet in the center. They start about the size of an avocado and can get as big as a healthy five-year-old." His brow accordioned.

"What's the matter?" I asked.

"When I push at it, there's some resilience. Some give."

"Well, you said it's a tropical, almost cactus-y plant. They'd hold their moisture longer than other kinds of plants, right?"

"Yes," he said, looking up. He smiled uncertainly at me. "I'm sure they would."

"So what did you and Angie talk about on the ride over?" I asked, taking the spiky bit of husk from him and rolling it between my thumb and forefinger.

"You, of course." He smiled. "You."

"Me and what else?"

"She's a fascinating person, your sister," he offered. "But she's not like you."

"Who's she like?" I asked.

"Me," he answered. "Before Vietnam. Before detox."

Just then my aunt looked up at the house from where she was stationed on the lawn by the hot dogs. "Iris! Iris and Vito, come on out here!" she called. "Your time's up!"

"Tell me what that means," I asked, "that she's like you."

"Your aunt is calling. Come on. I have to make a good impression. This is my first visit, after all."

"No arguments," I ordered. "No fights."

He snorted. "You think I don't know how to behave myself at a party?"

"Well then, come on. Now you'll know what the Fourth of July is like at my house." I led him back out to the lawn, and my aunt.

"When everyone goes home tonight," Eleanor said as we joined her, "we'll all sit down and try to get right with this. We'll figure it out."

Then Eleanor handed me tongs and a flipper, positioned me in front of a platter of parboiled chicken and raw hamburger and let herself be swept away by a group of incoming guests. She glanced back over one shoulder as she walked away. I saw her eyes find something and track it anxiously from across the lawn: Angie, walking toward Vito and I.

"Well," Angie said the moment she joined us. "I see some buckets back there with what look like champagne corks sticking out of the top."

"Angie, it's not even noon." I could hear how it sounded to Angie the moment it was out of my mouth but it was too late by then.

"Yep," she said, and walked toward the buckets of champagne. Vito and I remained standing side by side. We watched as she made her way down the lawn toward the water, reached her destination and popped a bottle of champagne. She plucked one of the plastic flutes from the pile beside the drinks, turned to raise it in a toast in our direction and stepped into the growing crowd with the bottle in one hand and the glass in the other.

"What does she think she's doing?" I muttered.

"Leave her alone," Vito replied. "Maybe she just needs to blow off some steam."

"You don't have to protect Angie from me."

"I know that."

"Angie!" Aunt Eleanor called in my sister's direction. "There's a sack race out here that has to happen. Come help me get it off the ground!"

Angie pretended not to hear her. I handed Vito the flipper and headed toward my sister. When I got close enough to speak to her in an un-eavesdroppable hiss I said, "Angie! For Christ's sake, just do what she asks you, okay?" Angie turned her back on me and drifted deeper into a group gathered around a croquet set, apparently deaf and dumb. I followed. "Don't be an asshole, all right?" I went on. "You said you wanted to be here. So now you're here—get the sacks."

"Fuck you," she said mildly. Then she sighed. "All right, Bear. Fine. Anything to blend. Anything to oblige." She carried the bottle with her when she went to get them. Its presence in her hand and the overheard "Fuck you" kept the older children out of her path as she moved along, but the little ones weren't sensitive to these cues. They clamored for sacks.

Perhaps it was the khakis and pressed shirt that drew Uncle Charlie to Vito. Among the dotted and op-arted mini-skirts and cut-off dunga-rees, these clothes had a vaguely military effect that I knew my uncle found reassuring. By the time I turned to see where he'd gone, Uncle Charlie had positioned himself by the hamburgers and was offering advice. Vito had cocked his head at an attentive angle and started to nod steadily toward my uncle. When I reached them they were discussing pigs, fire pits and melted fat. Vito was describing pigs he himself had roasted in the past. He handed me back the flipper and walked off with Uncle Charlie. I heard the words *steeper edges and some more heat-holding rocks at the bottom,* and then they were behind a group of people holding hot dogs and cans of Fresca. My aunt saw them walking together and smiled at me, nodding in their direction. I could see how worried she'd been, and how relieved to find that the Veedo I'd invited was an apparently friendly competent undemanding man. I turned my attention to the meat. Once cooked and bunned, hamburgers had to be arranged in the positions of the American flag's stars; hot dogs had to be laid out as stripes. Aunt Eleanor and I had punched actual star shapes out of the top buns with a cookie cutter. The flag they formed covered an entire folding table. It was my job now to replace parts of the flag as soon as they were eaten by passersby.

By the middle of the afternoon, Uncle Charlie and his helpers had carved the pig into a skeleton. Its flesh had been offered to children as well as adults, but younger picnickers preferred their pig in the disguised form of a hot dog. Most could not be convinced that the animal whose form could still be clearly made out on the spit was not like them—did not have feelings and did not mind being roasted and sliced, served with barbecue sauce and pickles. The adults were not generally bothered by this spectacle, and had sawed into the body with real enthusiasm.

Vito used the first break in his assigned duties to find me. "I just came from an interesting conversation with Hank," he said. "He says there are some missing draft papers." Vito kept smiling as he spoke and nodding at people passing by whom he had met during the afternoon. "He says if they're around, Angie could get quite a few years; if they're not, she's a shoo-in to walk away."

"Really?"

"I don't understand," he said. "When all this started you told me that draft papers weren't important."

We had swiveled to face each other. He held a cupcake in one hand and its little toothpick flag in the other. I held a package of hot dogs.

"Well now it seems they are," I explained. I could feel hot dog juice dripping on my foot and moved the leaking package farther away from my clothes. "They're from the Virginia draft board that got vandalized— the one where the policeman was shot. They're Hank's papers but they were in Angie's hands, so they could be used to argue that Angie was there that day. That she took them. Or at least that she was involved with those people. . . ."

"The ones she's already given money to," Vito finished. I nodded. "I see," he said. He didn't look surprised.

"Angie looks very beautiful today, doesn't she?" I said.

"Yes. She's always beautiful."

The plastic seam at the bottom of my bag of hot dogs burst. I bent to retrieve the scattered wieners and when I stood again Vito had been summoned into the kitchen by my aunt Eleanor and ordered to carry ice out to various buckets full of soft drinks and champagne.

I turned my attention to the clamoring voices asking for food, then helped Eleanor restock cups and plastic forks at various tables on the lawn. I strode by three neighbor children, all under nine, winding themselves in the bunting along the porch and popping the few nails holding it to the rail off into the viburnum beneath the overhang. Beyond them was the lawn, and my sister Angie drifting toward the dock, champagne in hand. Was that the same bottle she'd started out with this afternoon? Hardly likely. It was around six o'clock now. She could easily have moved on to a second bottle. Perhaps a third.

"It's getting overcast," Aunt Eleanor said as she strode by with a basket of prizes for games. "We might have to set the fire earlier than usual."

She sounded worried again. I looked around at the people on the lawn—the largest crowd of neighbors and friends that I had ever seen at a family Fourth of July. Aunt Eleanor had been afraid that they would stay away out of pity or awkwardness, this first one since we lost the boys. She had worked very hard to make it known that no, it was quite the opposite, and the friendly thing to do was to come, insist on being served her triple-berry frozen pops, play all the games, bring your pre-bonfire lighting song, drink just a little too much beer, yell at the softball umpire as if you really cared. Our property was sprinkled with people who were here because they cared for her, and for Charlie. They were playing games as if their very lives depended upon it; ripping at the remains of the skewered pig as if it were some prize taken on the fields of war and they the conquering army.

I walked purposefully away from Vito and down to the dock.

"So how was your drive?" I asked her.

"Very interesting. Vito is always interesting company. I have a favor to ask."

"What?"

"I want you to give the draft records that I left with you to the people who are charging me," she said.

"That would hurt you," I answered evenly. "That would be a bad thing for you." She held a plastic cup in one hand and the bottle of champagne in the other. She poured. "Don't do that," I said. "You're already slurring."

Angie sighed, a disappointed-in-my-limited-view kind of sigh. She poured again so the liquid reached the very top of her plastic cup. She drank. "I looked for them so I could give them to the police myself but you'd moved them."

"I did."

"I want them back now," she said softly.

"No." I was speaking softly back.

She shook the bottle at me. "I don't want to walk away from this," she said grimly. "I don't want to keep it small and quiet. I want it to be in the papers! Most of the people here"—she gestured broadly with the champagne to encompass the guests—"would think I was right to do what I did. It was the right thing to do, and they'd all come out and say so if they had the nerve! I want us all to go through with this—you and Charlie and Eleanor and Hank and me!" She raised her plastic cup for emphasis and some champagne slopped over the rim.

I stopped my hand a few inches into its rush to slap the cup out of her loose grasp.

"Why are you acting like this?" I said.

"I owe you nothing," she answered. "You owe me everything."

"You are full of shit." I was right in her face now, our feet perhaps four inches apart at the toes. "And you aren't making any sense at all. Stop drinking that stuff." I reached for the bottle but she swept it behind her back.

"I kept you safe," she said in an almost dreamy tone. She had stopped looking at me and leveled her gaze out over the darkening water. A pre-rain breeze had kicked up, tearing little whitecaps off the tops of the waves. "I loved you. But you've turned out to be one of those small people who only want to protect their little territories. Your Hank. Your Aunt Eleanor and your Uncle Charlie. Your Vito."

I tensed. She saw it. She didn't contradict what she knew was in my mind. Instead she sighed again. "So limited," she breathed. "So small."

"You're drunk," I said.

"That may be but I want you to give the folder to the police anyway. And when I'm sober I'll still want you to give it to them. If I knew where you'd put it I'd go get it myself right now and hand it off to the prosecution." Here she swung the bottle as a kind of punctuation to her statement.

"Angie, come up to the house and lie down for a while. I'll make you some coffee."

"No. I think I'll take a sail."

"You're too drunk to take a boat out."

"Fuck you." She spoke matter-or-factly, cheerfully even. She bent and began to unwind the ropes holding the little sailboat. Its gunwale bumped reassuringly against the tires I'd nailed to the sides of the dock the summer before and she leaned far, far over to place the champagne bottle carefully on a seat. I grabbed an elbow and pulled her back from the boat. Angie swiveled and struck me forcefully in the ribs with one fist, breaking my hold and leaving me doubled over, breathless. When I could speak again I said, "Uncle Charlie and Aunt Eleanor deserve better than this from you—they love you, too, Angie."

When she spoke she sounded almost close to tears. "You look at them, at Eleanor and Charlie, and you see picnics and rides, pretty domestic scenes with you and Eleanor in matching aprons. I look at them and I see the birds, pecking at the soft places: the inside of the mouth, the eyes. They killed Eddie and Perry. They sent them off. I don't know why, but they did it."

She dropped one foot over the side, tipping the hull but managing not only to get in but to snatch the bottle from its perch on the seat before careening into the boat herself. Her movements had carried the little ship away from the dock.

I still could have stopped her. I could have caught the rope trailing from the stern divot. I could have jumped in and pulled her back while she was still wobbling and thumping around only a few feet from the dock.

"Come back," I said without conviction.

"Fuck you," she called back gaily. She was hoisting the boat's single sail. She was moving away in the quickening breeze, even heeling already a bit.

"Angie!" This time I could hear more anxiety in my tone. "Where are you going?!"

This time there wasn't any answer from her. She waved her free hand, then the one holding the champagne bottle. The boom swung toward her head and I saw her duck awkwardly, pop up again on the other side of its trajectory, laugh and wave again. "Bye!" she called out. "Good-bye!"

I stamped away back up the lawn. The breeze had quickened and the sky had darkened. Eleanor was right—we would have to light the fire earlier than usual. Eight small bodies jammed into sacks bounced by on my left. Vito had been corralled into organizing them in my absence. He had spun them off from the starting line in the time it took Angie to become a little thumbnail-high figure in the distance.

I stood and watched. This difficult drunken woman floating away from me with a bottle of champagne in her hand was the same creature who had protected my place as favored child in our adoptive family, taken my side against ill luck and occasionally bossy brothers, shown me what a lake looked like from its center in the middle of a starlessly rain-black night. I knew that. I knew that.

"Iris! Dorcas Ruffel won, and I've told her you'd award the prize. She wants you to do it," Vito called.

Certainly. Dorcas should get her prize. I was a member of the hosting family for this day just as I had been for all of my remembered life and I would go get Dorcas's prize. Dorcas had a little crush on me—I had taught her how to mock and joke her way into a boys' softball game last year when she'd faced resistance and she considered me a font of kindness and wisdom. She was standing by Vito now, tugging his shirt and looking shyly in my direction. She wanted me, only me, to bring her prize.

I went to the kitchen to retrieve one of the plastic Statues of Liberty that had been assigned to sack-race winners, smiled beneficently as I crossed the lawn again to reach the little competitors and bowed as I presented it to the seven-year-old winner. She beamed back at me, completely happy, happy in the way you can be when the moment immediately before you is all. Lucky Dorcas, I thought, watching her skip back across the lawn to show the prize to her mother, who was helping Aunt Eleanor clear the remains from the hamburger table and move on to ice cream.

Aunt Eleanor's voice floated across the lawn to me. She was waving as well as yelling. Poor Aunt Eleanor. "Iris, we need some more ice and milk for coffee!" she called. "And some Fresca or Tab! Set it up in the dining room! I can smell the rain coming!"

I strode off to the kitchen and the waiting coffee percolator. Angie could go to the other side of the lake and get stuck behind the island's calm where the winds vanished the instant you cleared the large hunk of granite on its southern tip. She could sit there all night. Sit there for eternity.

I yanked the filters off the top cabinet shelf, shoveled coffee out in uneven spoonfuls. Angie had been the one who told me that I could manage the high dive on the raft when I was eight and nobody else thought I had the nerve. She'd bet Eddie five dollars that I could do it and won. She bought us ice cream from her winnings. When Uncle Charlie said nobody could swim across the lake alone, she'd volunteered to come with me and we splashed out triumphant on the other shore two hours later. She had checked my eighth-grade algebra homework and taught me how to get a seat at a decent cafeteria table. She'd guarded my ignorant happiness while all along she herself had been living among strangers who didn't, as far as she could tell, know her or love her.

"Iris!" I hadn't heard Vito come up behind me but here he was within an inch of my shoulder and hip and I could smell him, a roasted chestnut and dirt smell with an acrid finish—he was sweating. I felt myself lean in toward him so far I brushed the hairs of his neck with my nose as I breathed in. Then I pulled away.

Angie's balance had been both literally and figuratively compromised when she teetered away from the dock. A turn in the wind could take the tiny boat right over. A person could get tangled in the sail or the rigging, no matter how well she swam. Angie was an exceptional swimmer.

"I need to get a case of Tab. Excuse me." I pushed myself out of Vito's loose grasp. He had slipped his arm around my waist.

"The world won't end if another case of Tab doesn't appear." He skipped backward and directly into my path. "I never touched Angie. That's it, isn't it? That's what's going on now with you?"

But I was in some state that made what he said irrelevant. Perhaps it was too late to get this news from him, assuming that it was the truth. I didn't know. If Uncle Charlie had seen the way she looked when she left, he would have asked someone to drop an engine on the back of the rowboat and go look for her right this instant.

The pig was reduced to bones, my neighbors' fluent knives having worked on it all afternoon, and now they were on to the songs, precursors to the bonfire. The weather looked unsteady and I could feel Uncle Charlie moving us toward the fire at a steady uncompromising rate, the clouding sky on his mind. "This Land Is Your Land," "When Johnny Comes Marching Home Again," "Off We Go into the Wild Blue Yonder," "Liberty Bell March," "The Battle of New Orleans," "The Caissons Go Rolling

Along," "Dixie," "Stars and Stripes Forever," "My Country, 'Tis of Thee," "Anchors Aweigh," "America the Beautiful." The national anthem.

We stood in a ring around the pile of logs and packing materials and old crates. Uncle Charlie raised a torch, lit it, flipped it into the center of the pile. It answered with a roar.

I stepped out of the circle and walked into the bedroom I was supposed to share with Angie that night. The draft papers were a bit dirty and raggedy where I'd creased them before jamming them into the backpack. I slid them into the front of my shirt, wanting no questions about what I was carrying, and returned to the fire. I made my way to the opposite side of the circle from my aunt and uncle, fumbled at my shirt buttons until I freed Hank's draft papers. I stepped forward and held them into the fire, held them until they caught and had been half consumed in my hand before I let them drop into the larger mass of twisting flames.

The draft records with the Roanoke, Virginia, draft board markings were gone, reduced to ash. I'd kept them in the direct flames until my own fingers were blistered. Now there was no evidence against my sister. She would make her way through some legal posturing and then she would go free.

I felt something brush my hair, then my arm. Raindrops. They spattered around us, emissaries from the larger stormfront that moved slowly along behind them. The bonfire had gained its full momentum by then and was not threatened by this light rain. It burned on, snapping and fizzing in the thickening downpour while our guests ran for cover into the house. The women among them stopped to help take food and plates and bowls to the shelter of the kitchen. I walked through them, moving in the opposite direction toward the dock.

I stood at its end as the rain came weeping across the water. I could smell and hear the weather more clearly than I could see it since the incoming rain had drawn a curtain over the evening sky, leaving us in a thickening darkness. The water lapped against the tires where the sailboat had been moored. I stared into the darkness but could make out no sail's outline, could hear no water slapping against a polyurethane hull or rigging clanking against pulleys. Behind me the house lights flowed out of the windows and I could see the lines of rain coming down in the narrow illuminated columns. When I turned to face the lake there was only darkness and sound.

Then my name called from the shore, footsteps on the planking, and Vito beside me. He listened, too. "Looking for something?" he said at last.

"No."

"Iris, what did you do with the papers? The draft records?" he asked.

"What draft records?" I continued to stare out at the water.

"All right. I'll go with that," he said. He pulled his shirt over his head and unzipped his pants, stripping them off in two brisk yanks. "You could scuba dive in this lake," he said, lining his toes to the last plank on the dock. "You're certified. You didn't ask me how my attempt to retake the scuba class went."

"How did it go?" I asked.

"I flunked again."

He lifted himself on the balls of his feet and swept his arms over his head and I was astounded at my physical reaction to the sight. My pulse altered, the walls of my chest contracted, all the blood in my body rearranged itself, spiraling down from the belly and up from my thighs.

"I love you," I said to him.

He swiveled and dropped his heels to the decking, walked up to me. "Good," he said. He came to a stop only when we stood so close our breastbones might have been bolted together. He kissed me. He tipped me off balance, picked me up and walked again to the dock's edge. "I love you, too," he said. Then he jumped.

I'm not somebody who panics in the water and he'd certainly given me enough lead time to be ready but for some reason I hit the surface utterly unprepared and went under still breathing through my nose. I crashed back up to the surface choking, fighting off feelings that were connected to my difficulties breathing but not entirely explained by them—I was just in a full-blown panic.

We were in darkness with a hiss of rain all around us, and a first flash of lightning on top of that. Vito did not see my mood. I started counting automatically when we saw the flash and reached five by the time the thunderclap followed. It was a rolling explosive thing, so close that when the sound hit the water it left my head vibrating. The wind thickened.

"Only five seconds between. With a wind. Vito, get out of the water." I heaved myself back up onto the dock with all my clothes streaming.

"You're sitting at a higher elevation than me now," he answered, floating on his back a few yards from me. "I'm entirely safe as long as you're there to attract the lightning."

"I'm serious."

"Come back in. Don't waste this." He raised one arm from the water, reaching toward me.

"It's not safe." Vito had heard my childhood biography in enough detail to know that we had swum regularly in electric storms, playing games and ducking when we saw flashes even though it was clearly too late by then to avoid a descending lightning bolt. Even Uncle Charlie and Aunt Eleanor had been casual in our childhood about calling us in during storms.

He started swimming out into deep water. Another flash. Another clap of thunder. "There's no incoming here," he called back to me. "Nobody's booby-trapped the water. Everything's perfectly, absolutely safe."

I had a sudden sharp image in my mind of birds perched on the remains of a forehead, pecking at eyes and the insides of mouths, hopping farther down to work at the genitals. I stood up, peeled off my saturated shirt and jeans and launched myself into the black water.

Vito met me when I surfaced. He embraced me with both legs and both arms, pulling us immediately beneath the choppy little waves and holding me until my lungs burned. I broke free and kicked upward. Vito popped up a second after me.

"Come to the island," he said, tugging at one of my hands. "Swim out with me."

I looked out into the lake. The island was a deeper darkness in a dark night, its outline barely visible. The thought of swimming toward it was immeasurably attractive—consoling and thrilling at once. Rain would hiss around me, I would proceed stroke by stroke toward this large dark shape and no one but Vito would know where I was. I thought of Uncle

Charlie yanking at the starter rope on the old twenty-horsepower row-boat engine, preparing to putter out onto the lake to look for me in the middle of a dark thunderstorm when he discovered my absence. I thought of Aunt Eleanor looking anxiously out into the lake, seeing nothing.

I shook my head. "No."

Angie was out there right now—perhaps stuck somewhere, too drunk to unscramble her cables and catch the wind. That's what Angie did.

"I'm going in," I said. Three kicks brought me back to the slimy ladder; two heaves brought me up and onto the planks. I stood there for a moment looking out at the round dark ball of Vito's head bobbing in the chop. Another flash of lightning. Another deafening boom. "Please come in, Vito. Please."

He sidestroked reluctantly to the ladder and pulled himself up. Aunt Eleanor came striding down the lawn with a tablecloth over her head, one end tossed elegantly over a shoulder to keep it from tearing away in the increasing wind. She came right up onto the dock before she said a word. "Someone said the sailboat was gone and I couldn't believe it." She tapped a foot angrily. "The only person I can't account for is your sister." This to me. "Darkness, thunder and lightning, and off she goes! I'm going to ask the neighbors for their motorboat." Aunt Eleanor didn't say anything at all about the fact that I was standing in my underwear and Vito's clothes lay in a heap at our feet.

"How drunk do you think she was?" I asked Vito.

He pulled on his shirt, bent to pluck up his pants. "Your aunt or your sister?"

"This isn't funny."

"I have no idea. I don't think I saw her more than once early on in the day."

Uncle Charlie trotted across the lawn and joined us. He stood by Aunt Eleanor on the dock and looked out into the succeeding curtains of rain. "She's likely just fine, Eleanor. Angie's been swimming across this lake since she was ten. And how much sense does it make to put another boat out into that? The thunder and lightning seem to have passed by, but still, you can't see more than ten feet, and it's a big lake."

"The MacDermotts have a floodlight on their boat, and a horn, too," she answered him. She turned to glare at my uncle and we all saw the accusation in her icy manner. Everything about the way she stood there demanded to know what sort of wimpy response was that, to say that she'll come home when she feels like it, when any fool knows that tonight is not like any night that has ever preceded it and what Angie could or could not do as a ten-year-old swimmer has no bearing whatsoever here. None at all.

"I'll ask Mr. MacDermott about his boat," Vito offered.

"No, no. I'll go speak to Oscar. I'm sure he won't mind at all. He might even insist on coming with us," Uncle Charlie sighed.

"I'm coming with you as well," Vito said. "I have night vision you wouldn't believe."

Uncle Charlie considered, looking Vito up and down.

"And I'm already wet so the weather makes no difference to me," Vito added. This fragile little joke decided my uncle. He smiled. Nodded.

"Come back to the house and get some dry clothes on," Aunt Eleanor sniffed at me, taking my hand. We walked side by side, slowly, back up the lawn to the lights of the house. Vito and Uncle Charlie had set a much faster pace and we saw them enter the house and then leave, headed toward Oscar MacDermott's dock a few hundred yards down the shore. The keys to his boats were always left in the ignition.

We stood in the rain just outside the reach of the house lights and listened until we heard the engine crank and fire. Its floodlight snapped on and threw a long pencil-thin tube of light ahead of the boat. We could see the rain driving through the beam of light when the boat passed close to shore, and then it was only a yellow line that got smaller and furrier at its perimeter as the boat moved out into the lake itself. The boat's path took it behind the island, and it vanished.

"Look at us standing in the rain," Aunt Eleanor said. Then, "How I hate being the one who stays behind and waits." She sighed.

"Should we send somebody else out? It's a big lake, Aunt Eleanor."

"Not that big. Charlie knows every ripple and inlet of it. He'll find her." Aunt Eleanor turned away from me then and trudged toward the porch's screen door. We could see our neighbor Lamont Philbrook through the French doors that separated the porch from the living room. His sleeping two-year-old was draped over one shoulder and he was calling to his wife. "Look," Aunt Eleanor said. "People are leaving. We have to towel off and get back in there. Be at the door to say good-bye." The last syllable on the word "good-bye" wobbled unsteadily. "Come on, dear. Remember to ask after Mr. Philbrook's mother, who's sick in a hospital in Tallahassee."

I nodded, though she had turned herself toward the French doors by this time and launched herself over the porch threshold. She didn't see me.

An hour later the last guest was gone. Vito and Uncle Charlie had not returned. Right until the third trip to the trash can with a bag full of empty bottles and paper plates I was confident that Angie had merely indulged herself in a snit, and that we would all find our ways back to one another when Uncle Charlie towed her back home. I had destroyed the only evidence that could hurt her legally. I had saved her. She would endure a brief court appearance, be freed, and we would all be normal again.

The storm abated, though the sky remained dark, and when I stood behind the house on my way back in and looked out over the lake I might as well have been standing at the end of the world, staring out at a great disk of sea.

But I was not at the end of the world. I was in my childhood's summer backyard and I had stood by—with some satisfaction—and watched my drunken sister take a boat out when she had no business doing so. And when the alarm went up and people took to the water to find her, I'd said nothing.

And why was this?

The answer came to me in much the same way my birthday wish for Eddie's death had come to me—I had imagined her tangled in rigging and trapped under a boom while the wind tore off the tops of little shattered waves, which it then threw in her face—and I'd let her go. This was true at the same time that I had wanted to destroy anything that could hurt her. I'd listened to the expensive lawyer explain that destroying evidence was a federal offense, and then I had dropped the papers into the flames. I remembered who we were and that I loved her.

"I see their light," Aunt Eleanor said to me from her sentry post at the window. She walked briskly out of the house and toward the shore, me struggling to keep up. The moment we were beyond the house lights and into the darkness of the night lawn we could see that they were alone: no sailboat was in tow. Aunt Eleanor accelerated into a trot and then a run. I kept pace, suddenly afraid. Uncle Charlie did know every inch of this lake, and they had been gone for hours. How had she eluded them? Where was she?

"We need to call in some help and do a sweep," Uncle Charlie said as he pulled up to the dock. "I can only think that she was drifting steadily along just behind or ahead of us. I can't think of any other explanation for our missing her. That hull was unsinkable. Even if she'd capsized, it would never have just sunk."

I had not spent my childhood summers on a lake for nothing. I knew that all boats could, given the right circumstances, sink.

"I'll call the police," Aunt Eleanor said grimly. "And some neighbors."

An hour later I sat in one of a half dozen boats that slapped across the water in a choppy sweep looking for Angie. By early morning the darkness was again shot through with rain, now driving, now merely spattering. The unnatural silence that settled over the searchers contributed to a dreamscape feel. Logic and chronology were not the guiding principles of this night.

We searched on and did not find her. The rain stopped and the stars became visible just before dawn. They turned the lake surface a pure silver. The air softened and dried and the water became platelike. It was going to be a beautiful day. Then, just as there was enough light in the sky to make out individual trees and rocks, a cry went up on the side of the line nearer the island. Four boats rushed toward the call, pulling up finally around an irregular and deep inlet on the side of the island directly opposite our house. There, behind two white birch whose exposed roots still had all the raw clumped-dirt signs of being pulled from the earth only hours before, was the boat.

"It looks like it drifted in here and got stuck when the trees came down," someone said.

My uncle had already jumped off the bow of his boat into waist-deep water. He scrambled through it frantically, outpacing the younger men who had lowered themselves over the sides as their own boats arrived. I stayed firmly rooted to my place on the seat of Oscar MacDermott's Chris-Craft, unwilling to approach the tangle of branches and rigging. The sailboat was keeled over, half submerged. Uncle Charlie dove down into the cabin and stayed there so long I could see the men gathered around the stern nervously counting, their lips moving and their faces darkening as the lips said *a hundred and one, a hundred and two* . . . Vito didn't wait. He followed Uncle Charlie in at around *fifty-two, fifty-three*. They emerged together, both whipping their heads from side to side to sheer off water and then shaking them more soberly to communicate that no, they had not found Angie. Eight men pushing on the port side righted the sailboat and pushed her back out into deeper water to get her upright. Now I, too, slid over the side and joined the slow walk all around the hull, looking for holes, scrapes, any news about what had brought the little vessel to shore. It offered up no news. An inspection of the deck and cabin yielded nothing as well.

The two policemen who had joined us during the night assured us that they could call in divers. They would get dogs to walk the farther shore and search the island to look for signs of her reaching land. How strange, I thought, to be on the other end of the kind of call that our scuba instructor got fairly regularly. I straightened and said, "I'll go with them if they can lend me a wet suit and a tank. Some weights."

"You're not going anywhere," Uncle Charlie said brusquely. He chopped one hand to the side to emphasize his authority on the question of my going anywhere.

"The lake's got a spring on its southern end," I said to the policeman. "They'll need people who are comfortable working at fifty feet or so."

"I said you're not doing that," Uncle Charlie repeated.

I ignored him.

"I'll go, too," Vito said.

"You aren't certified to work outside of a bathtub." I hissed so as not to be overheard and it made the words sound more harsh.

"Nobody knows that but you."

"You'd be an unsafe partner and I'll out you if you try to lie about it." I pushed past him, both of us in fairly deep water. He grabbed my arm and I lost my balance, slipping under the surface. He hauled me back up.

"You aren't going to tell anyone, and I'm going, too," he said to me when I was breathing normally again. "I'll be your partner. You'll protect me and I'll protect you."

I jerked my arm out of his grasp. "Why are you so insistent?"

He was taken aback at my vehemence. "She's your sister!"

"I know that!"

"Iris, I'm not insistent because of any feelings for Angie. I'm insistent because you love her."

I did love her. I loved her and I had imagined her white body held beneath the surface by a twist in some rigging, all her hair floating around her like a dark plant—I had imagined this and felt satisfaction.

"You want me in the water with you," Vito was saying, "just like I wanted you with me on the first test dive."

I just barely made out his meaning. He seemed to be so far away, just lips moving in a face that floated up at me from a distance. When I decoded his words at last I said, "You flunked your first test dive."

"Yes. But without you there, I might have finished it in an emergency room."

"If you can convince them that you're certified and you can get them to lend you gear, I won't stop you."

So in the end, Vito swam ten yards down the line from me. The police hadn't questioned him when he volunteered—they'd wanted as many points on their sweep as they could get and he'd listed his credentials quickly and not very clearly. We flippered in long lines up and down our assigned areas. We dropped down another ten feet and moved out, farther away from the shallow island perimeter. We repeated the pattern. Repeated it again.

I had not imagined that my lake, this blinking blue eye in the face of our mountain valley, could be so full of Coca-Cola cans and old bent fishing rods, debris from a thousand casual crossings. I came upon a black plastic garbage bag, here so long its sides were furry with weed. Something heavy and solid bulged at its sides. Only a week before, I would have approached the bag, poked it, lifted, thought of its contents as an engaging puzzle. Now the sight horrified me and I would not touch it. Vito broke it open in the end. Old cans and broken glass poured onto the lake floor beneath it as he lifted it up and shook.

Perhaps it was our thirtieth sweep, perhaps our fiftieth, when we surfaced to excited shouting from the farthest end of the line. Someone had found something, and I could hear the pronoun "her" called out over the water.

It was a person. A woman.

I didn't realize I wasn't breathing until I had trouble making my legs kick, and traced the problem back to respiratory distress. I stopped, let the troubled legs drop directly under me in the water, treaded until I was taking regular breaths and started again toward the end of the line with my ears kept above water to catch any other scrap of news. Vito remained at my side. It made for slow going, and I could see the scene coalesce and unfold as I approached. The three divers who'd reached the position first sank down, leaving a little boil of bubbles marking the site.

I dog-paddled up, fully expecting to see them surface before my eyes with my dead sister hanging between them. But they rose up again without her—without anything. The three boats that had rushed up bobbed now with all their noses pointed toward one another. People started yelling.

They had found a body, its clothing disintegrated and its remaining flesh pulpily spongelike, a long rope of graduated pearls around its neck and a silver Marine Corps buckle still hanging from what was left of its leather belt. I had reached them by now, and treaded water within a few feet of the diver who reported this.

"Look for a plastic bottle," I whispered.

"What?" This from the diver.

"Go back, and look around the body for an orange plastic prescription medicine bottle," I said, louder this time.

They found it. They found the bottle, my father's old belt, which she had cinched over her sweater that day, the pearls that she had let Angie play with when she dressed for evenings out, twenty-seven cents in change from her pockets, the remains of the body itself and a little wax candle—no doubt plucked at the last moment from the birthday party preparations she had been struggling to organize when she decided, instead, to kill herself.

Suspect Terrain

I LOVE THE VOCABULARY OF GEOLOGY. THINK OF "POLAR WANDER." When I first heard the term I thought of the way people's particular north stars move, how the emotional world is one way on Monday and another by Christmas.

In geology, "polar wander" was the term used by scientists who looked at electromagnetic data from different rocks and found that they sometimes all pointed north, as they should—and sometimes arranged themselves less predictably. Compass needles lie flat at the equator and stand up straight on end at the poles, with all gradations of those angles in the latitudes between. That's why you can look at the paleomagnetic compasses in rock and tell not only when the rock was born but also where it lay in relation to the poles when it was created. A rock that formed in Vermont should have essentially the same electromagnetic gradations as a rock that was formed right next to it in New Hampshire because they lay in the same position relative to the North Pole—which they all point at. When that didn't always prove true and neighboring rocks didn't match, geologists had to figure out if the rocks had moved, or if the North Pole had moved. It seemed logical that one thing or the other had happened.

Only fifty years ago the accepted answer was that the poles had moved; thus, polar wander. Then tectonic plate theory swept the wandering poles idea off the table, convincing people that it was the rock after all that had moved, and not the North Pole.

I learned this when Vito explained to me that one reason we know that the Virginia Tidewater once lay cheek-by-jowl next to what is now Africa is because the paleomagnetic compasses in rock from these places point at exactly the same angle. If only we could zip up the ocean between them, he said, we would see that these different continents fit together quite well. This places both of them clearly at the same moment in geological history, smack next to one another and sitting in exactly the same relationship to the North Pole.

But those poles are not steadfast, and the tectonic plate explanation doesn't explain everything after all. When geologists drilled into rock to compare different depths and thus different time periods, they found that even in the same bored tube of rock, the electromagnetic alignment of the samples from progressively distant time periods faltered, and then—every hundred thousand years or so—completely reversed. In other words, the North Pole and the South Pole have switched places. We have no reason to believe they will not do so again. The last switch took place about ninety thousand years ago, so another reversal is near. I use "near" in its geologic sense—meaning any minute now or maybe in ten thousand years. Compasses in some parts of Asia and Australia are already refusing to do their duty, an early warning sign of an incoming shift. It's going to happen: tape recordings will be twisted into unusable patterns; our magnetic-stripped cards will get wacky.

Before Vito, I wouldn't have given this phenomenon a second's thought. Now I think about it for hours: little faltering losses and shifts building into a convulsive and global reversal, ending in upside down but ultimately restored order. I think of how rock from the same bored tube looks one way at one depth, entirely different at another, though both samples are from exactly the same spot. This doesn't disturb me because it makes too much sense.

My favorite geologic term is "suspect terrain"—something that the

Virginia Piedmont, and to a lesser extent the Blue Ridge, have in great quantities. Suspect terrain is just rock that formed someplace else and then slid along a fault line to a new home. It is squeezed out of its native place and settles in entirely foreign terrain, where it is adopted and assimilated. They are orphan rock formations. In the end, both polar wander and suspect terrain are terms that geologists use to explain things that otherwise make no sense.

So our Lake House, so deceptively solid and square on its handkerchief of lawn, is merely floating along above the mantle like everything else, vulnerable to collisions with other floating masses or to eruptions that push new materials to the surface with the force of several hydrogen bombs.

It's easy to forget all that. The curtains are blowing in a lovely breeze. I see them from where I sit, and the mountains in the distance are so pretty, their silhouette a furry rolling expanse of green. I know that if I walked into those mountains I'd find dazzling bodies of water, and the slopes leading into the valleys would be roped with glittering creeks. It's all a matter of perspective.

The plates pull apart, create oceans; collide, create mountains. A person has to accept that wherever she stands, she is moving. Old seafloor is plowed ahead of these advancing sheets, down into deep ocean trenches where it melts, lightens, rises up again as volcanoes to become Laos, Cambodia, Vietnam.

This is how I think now. This is what's on my mind as I look out at the lake and sit beneath the same tree where Angie and I tried to build a treehouse twenty years ago. My two daughters have strung a tightrope between this and another tree about sixty feet away. I forbade tightrope walking without a net, sure that they would never find one. But they dug up a yellow pages listing for used gymnastic and circus equipment, called a number and were told that tightrope act nets could, indeed, along with many other delightful objects, be purchased if only we traveled to an obscure warehouse with a hundred and thirty dollars in cash and asked for Jimmy McPhee. I agreed to do this. Vito then laid out the perimeter for the netting, drove support hardware into appropriate trees that could serve as part of the web and poured cement to reinforce edge poles. The girls were falling off their tightrope on a regular basis within minutes of the cement drying. They tell me that by the end of the week they will have stopped falling altogether. They are confident, and beautiful in the way only the untouched smooth surface of adolescence can be beautiful.

I cannot look at them without seeing the young Angie, who has become the largest absence in my life, larger than my brothers, larger than Hank, who has married a senior-level executive at Raytheon and moved with her to Saudi. Before Saudi she took him to Turkey. After Saudi she thinks a transfer to an Australian project is likely. Hank does not make his way back to the Lake House more than once every two years or so, and we are very polite with each other. He tells me that his wife does not want children and so they will never have them. He has made some attempts to renew his bonds to Uncle Charlie and Aunt Eleanor but for reasons I do not entirely understand, nothing holds. There is no purchase to Hank; no spot to get a toe in. Perhaps the way he felt about Angie ground them all away. At any rate, Aunt Eleanor and Uncle Charlie have lost him. I don't believe I have ever seen a lonelier man in my life. Once I asked if he regretted Angie, and he said he was grateful to her and to everything he'd been with her—just as she had told me he would be.

After graduation I took deep-dive courses, then an ocean-dive course, then instructor certification. Within a year I was learning how to work with different oxygen mixes and investing in my first dry suit. In the end, I did the deep-wreck dives that had interested Vito, who proved to be a repeat dive-school flunky. He got nosebleeds at twenty feet and popped eardrums at thirty. Poor visibility and darkness could set his heart off like a wind-up toy. Submerged, he was hopeless. But I graduated from quarries to lakes to Pacific reefs and then on to the breakers and tidal currents of the Atlantic coast. I developed a reputation in diving circles as a calm, clear guide. I had a killer nose for wrecks, and the locations of three long-lost wooden sailing ships are attributed to search teams that I led.

Uncle Charlie's professional life never regained its energy and direction—no one in his old world trusted him again after he lost his security clearance. Most people came to think of Angie as being dead, though her body was not found, and that death worked on him in ways that even the boys' loss did not. For months he sat in a chair in front of a television. Nothing could lure him away, not calls from the office or the beginning of hunting season or the smell of an apple pie on a cool evening. Aunt Eleanor waited, unafraid and protective.

It was my daughters who brought Uncle Charlie back from that dark place. Aunt Eleanor watched, mystified, as he offered to babysit and change diapers. When they were babies I would find him sitting in their bedroom, rocking by their snoring little lumplike forms. For a long time that rocking chair looked to me to be the only place he seemed happily settled rather than shipwrecked. He and Aunt Eleanor would come to visit and he would drift away from us and take up this favorite post of his, keeping watch over nap time. When they could crawl, they crawled to him. He hadn't been like this with his own baby boy, Aunt Eleanor told me, equally amused and irritated with her husband's transformation.

My girls took their first steps in Uncle Charlie's direction, waged some of their biggest and earliest battles while in his care: who had cheated, who got to go first, what was fair—he discovered childhood's moral fervor refereeing their fistfights with the world and with each other. He knew them and loved them, and they paid him back with something approaching worship. Their devotion returned him to the living.

Aunt Eleanor plays both handmaiden and idol to my girls, alternating roles about once every three months depending upon their mood. Even now, weighing in at ninety and a hundred and eleven pounds respectively, they leap into her lap whenever she seems open to the idea. When they were toddlers she took them to get rides on the same mechanical horse in town that I rode. On their birthdays they receive two cakes, the first offered before they get out of bed and accompanied by joke gifts, the second following dinner and offered with an invitation to make a serious wish. Eleanor bakes the first and I bake the second.

I watch Aunt Eleanor carefully now, looking for clues about how to be an adult. I know that a good deal of my early, happy ideas about how easy it is to walk around in the world was a gift I got from her and Uncle Charlie. They gave me the most elusive and celebrated forms of happiness—the ones that rest on the invisible idea that you are free to enjoy your Popsicle and the sun on your face because any threats to you are not your business: the grown-ups must deal with those. At my daughters' ages I never knew or cared what providing that freedom cost them. This ignorant narcissism was mine because they let me have it. I think I always knew that, even as I sat in the sun as a little girl and licked my Popsicles, trailing my feet in the water off the dock at the Lake House and waiting for my breasts to grow, wondering how my toenails would look if I painted them like Angie's. Now I do what they taught me to do, watching my own young charges hoot and push each other off balance above me on a tightrope.

The Lake House belongs to me now. Aunt Eleanor and Uncle Charlie talked about moving out for years before they actually did because I resisted the idea. I was perfectly happy with us all under the same roof, but Aunt Eleanor made noises about my having a family of my own and needing the space and privacy. In the end she packed herself and Uncle Charlie up and called the moving truck.

It didn't take. They ended up buying a large mossy place a half mile down the lake from where I sit now. They still have the winter house outside Washington, but between May and October they are so close that I can hear Wilma's two doggy sons hit the water when they hurl themselves off Uncle Charlie's dock to swim out and greet him if he's rowing in. I can still climb to the attic and look out for Uncle Charlie's little boat at sunrise bobbing on what he has always argued was the island's bass hideout.

The girls have never known any other arrangement. They regard Aunt Eleanor and Uncle Charlie as their grandparents, though they know that their biological grandfather lives on in Paris with a beautiful Frenchwoman in an apartment that Aunt Eleanor told me looks as if it were ripped directly out of French Indochine. Because their family history is entirely available to the girls, they have no real interest in it. They are still new enough to live essentially in the present. They are young and beloved and I assume that there is nothing in their lives they'd decide to forget. Still, no one's life is entirely transparent. It's possible that my sunny daughters have already decided to bury something that they will later have to either choose to retrieve and live with, or not. I will tell them, if they ask, to retrieve and live. I will tell them that memory is the ground under your feet, and though it might feel like suspect terrain, you still stand on it.

The only history that visibly amuses them at the moment is geological, which is lucky because Vito is their father and he is, as he planned to be, a geologist. He takes them into the mountains and shows them how the terrain shifted and washed, how to decode the colors and shapes around them, how to judge juxtapositions and angles. Even when he is not home, which is often, my older girl goes off on Saturday mornings with little vials of chemicals, miniature hammers and bags for samples. At home she drowses by fires and reads. She is dreamy, bookish, squinting, inquiring. She is also affectionate—the one who is easier to love. I take pains to hide this from her and her sister.

My younger child is not even vaguely bookish or dreamy. She loves the mountains not as a geologic curiosity but as a hunting ground. She wanted to go into them with Uncle Charlie when she was about the same age as Hank, Perry and Eddie when they first went with him. Charlie has modified his views on girls and hunting, and he takes her. They pursue various animals, kill them and return with bloody carcasses that he has taught her to disembowel out in the woods before she lugs them home. I don't allow them past the porch steps until they're butchered and hosed. This second child is a very good shot. Aunt Eleanor tries to teach her how to cook what she's killed but she resists. Her sister is teachable, however, and she and I often find ourselves in Aunt Eleanor's kitchen bent over a stubborn thigh bone with a hacksaw.

Vito and I married the year he asked me to come with him on his first visit to Proover Davies's family. One year after Angie vanished he told me he had decided to go and asked if I would just ride along. I agreed, and proposed to him halfway through the Cumberland Gap on the return trip.

Now every year we unfailingly travel to Proover Davies's hometown at the mouth of this valley. Our girls know Proover's nieces and nephews, his aunts and his parents, his godfather, Lenny, and his little sister, Prudence. We take a picnic into the mountains with this group, jamming the whole of it into two cars and one truck. Vito hands out little hammers to anyone younger than fifteen and leads them in a mission to hang off cliffs and chip at rock. They squeal when they find anything interesting and can be heard at quite a distance.

Proover's family does not know, and never will know, that Vito believes he killed their son. The other people he killed, the ones he used to see so regularly, have receded. When they do surface now they are generally civil.

The only person I could be said to have killed, on the other hand, surfaces often. She is not always civil. In her presence I am more aware of the pleasures of being physically daring in a dangerous world. When she makes appearances I am more likely to wear five-inch heels, to float our raft into the middle of the lake and lure Vito there in order to seduce him in the middle of the night, to take on a dive assignment that could go very wrong if luck didn't accompany my skills. I am bolder, occasionally even beautiful instead of innocuously pretty. I am so grateful.

The sister who lured me gaily into lakes during rainstorms and sat hip-to-hip with me in my bed and called me Bear is plainly visible in my daughters. I show them her picture and wait for them to recognize her face in their own mirrors, but they haven't yet. I describe the life I lived with my brothers and Hank and Angie to them—the part of my life that in my simplicity I had thought was simple: cakes and roasted meat, fireworks and the smell of pine, trips to a mechanical horse and the confidence that birthday wishes meant something. They nod because this sounds familiar—it is, in fact, a good deal like the life I've shaped for them. They believe in it and don't have any thoughts of change.

No one, not even Vito, knows that I stood on the dock and let my sister indulge a self-destructive drunk and go drown herself. This scene is mine alone. Some days it feels like a cool polished stone in my chest—not unpleasant, but very dense. Other days the memory of her silhouette against the black water is shattering. I see one hand holding the bottle of champagne and the other flying toward a grip on the seat—a mysteriously graceful figure that summons up the idea of flight. In a matter of a few years my daughters will look just like she did the year she sailed off with a bottle of champagne in one hand.

Crooked River tells me that I need an animal familiar, and that Mary Beaver Dam has already suggested that I may find my match in the goat nation. They point out the goat's cheerful self-sufficiency and pragmatic attitude, its daring when challenged. I tell them that they only want to pass off some of the surplus generated by Mary's new 4-H goat group, but I may be at the end of my resistance. Crooked River and Mary Beaver Dam are often right and I keep forgetting that it saves time to agree with them earlier in the discussion rather than later.

Crooked River has learned many healing incantations and medicines from Mary Beaver Dam, and was the first to correctly diagnose and treat my younger daughter's recurring headaches. My daughter claims he altered her dreams as well as stopping her headaches but I don't believe her. She says she has much more realistic nightmares now. I tell her that's just getting older—it isn't some old Indian's medicine.

Every August we go with Crooked River and Mary Beaver Dam to the state fair in Syracuse, where he shows Tadodaho's great-great-great-grandchildren to admiring judges who often give them blue ribbons. Besides her new goat club, Mary Beaver Dam is cultivating a small group of ferret breeders, but ferrets present a host of erratic behaviors and aren't an ideal hobby unless you're comfortable with the prospect of being greeted one day with an affectionate animal and the next with a creature who won't speak to you after it has finished shredding the furniture and boring into all the cereal boxes. I don't hold out much hope for this new club.

Crooked River continued sending me pictures through the first year of my marriage. They became more domestic in nature—little boys standing by jackfruit that reach their shoulders, ceramic pots holding cooking fires, men sitting in meditation on salt-and-dirt-packed floors in huts. Then the little box arrived directly from Vietnam—no intervening upstate New York postmark. I kept it for three days before I opened it. I'd fallen into the pattern of waiting until I was entirely alone before I sliced open any mail from the Iroquois Nation and it had taken a few days of waiting for Vito to take off for a job in Alaska and the girls to be at school. I happened to be in between classes and dives—no calls from the police department, no calls from fellow dive instructors needing help: I was free to walk around the package for quite a while before I finally bent down and sliced through the tape holding one side shut. Out popped the box, sealed with some waxy substance that yielded to a prying knife. The contents made a little *thunk* when they hit the table.

Batman.

No note. I shook the envelope and box vigorously but found nothing. No drawing, no letter, no return address—only the Vietnamese postmark and stamp. It had been mailed ten days before from Saigon. A string was wrapped around one of Batman's arms so many times that it was thicker than his torso. I left the thing right there where it fell and went to the telephone.

Aunt Jenny didn't answer. She had always said she didn't believe in answering machines. Had I bought her one she would have left it in the box. She is a confirmed Luddite. Crooked River himself chased telephone linemen off his little handkerchief of dirt-packed property if they tried to hook up telephones anywhere near him. When Jenny finally answered in the late afternoon I bullied her into promising she would ask Crooked River to call me collect. Of course, she reminded me, nobody could get Crooked River to do a damn thing he wasn't about to do anyway. But he called within the hour.

"You were supposed to know already," he said. I could feel his shrug even if I couldn't see it. "There were so many signs. The jackfruit needle, still fresh. I let that stay in the envelope. The way the paper smelled. Once there were threads from a gingerroot. White girls can't tell new root from old. You should have known."

"Do you have an address for him, Crooked River? Does he write you? What do you know?"

"That he's still there. That's all I can say I guess," Crooked River replied.

"The pictures—are they from the war, or were they all done after the war?"

"Makes no difference," he said. "I don't guess there'll be any more of them now."

"Why?"

"Because you say he sent Batman," Crooked River explained. "Your brother is doing a pass-off. You hand Batman off when you don't need him as much as the next guy. Maybe Batman comes back your way but you can't count on it after a pass-off. That's the way we worked it."

"Maybe he's coming home," I said.

"No. He's not coming home. He's happy where he is. That's why he could send you Batman."

I held the little black plastic hero between my thumb and forefinger, rolling him back and forth. I said, "You know, Crooked River, I should send Batman to you. You took the string off, but he could still be keeping your family stories, right?"

"Eyeah. But he's holding other family stories now. You say he came with string? Who's to say whose string that is. I'd say he's more yours than mine."

"I never gave this Batman a story before in my whole life."

"Well. Now's your chance, little sister."

"He killed Eddie, didn't he?"

"That's not my story," Crooked River replied. I could tell from his tone that he was shrugging.

I kept the Batman. I can see him sitting on the kitchen windowsill even from where I am under this tree in the yard. He is proof that I have a brother, alive and thinking of me as I think of him. But the ground beneath both of us has shifted.

This morning my day opened under a soft sky, a deep green lawn rolling to the lake's reflective bowl. There are my daughters wobbling over my head and the sound of Otto's granddaughter barking at the door for Aunt Eleanor to let her in. Vito will be home by sunset and we will swim out to the raft together after the girls are in bed. I have already sunk some beer over the side. Perhaps we'll pull the rowboat around this end of the lake after dark and see what there is to see.

This Fourth of July there will be fire, but no fireworks, which remind me now of military explosions. There will be no songs to nationhood and glory. All comers who wish to sing are encouraged to choose music from *West Side Story, Saturday Night Fever* or *My Fair Lady*. Entries from *The Sound of Music* will be discouraged. Dancing is good as long as it isn't disco.

For this year's Fourth of July party I intend to fill the lake itself as well as the lawn, and have already hired a pontoon party boat and a dozen little paddlers. I tell every person I invite to bring a bathing suit and expect to get wet. I invite what must be hundreds of people—anyone I see. Roast pig will continue as a tradition. Crooked River and Mary Beaver Dam are bringing some of their 4-H'ers, and this year they want to roast a goat. They have offered to bring it themselves, and Aunt Eleanor is going to show them how to butcher it. I suspect they will bring several goats, attempting to leave one as my friend. I will resist, and roast him.

When Uncle Charlie heard that there would be no flags or Jell-O molds in the shape of the capital building he said he was going to continue the holiday as it should be done on his own property farther down the lake. I nodded and reminded him that people tended to come to where there's the biggest fire and I promised him that I would be building the bigger fire. When he protested that the whole thing was getting too circusy, I went out and rented a trapeze for the girls, and found a company that rigged nets under them and gave people their first lessons at flying through the air with whatever ease they can muster.

Now the only decision left is whether to resign Batman to the flames.

I will be surrounded, this Fourth of July, with all the people I love. If they can't come or have changed forms, that's all right. I can remember. There is Uncle Charlie on one bent knee asking me to accompany him to the fanciest restaurant in Virginia; there is Perry lovingly sewing my dog's ear back onto his head; there is my mother bent over our play tea table, smiling and offering sugar lumps; there is Aunt Eleanor rowing the roast out to the dock where I have insisted my birthday dinner will take place; there is Vito standing on Proover Davies's porch on the afternoon he reached their door for the first time; there are my lump-like sleeping babies on a sweaty summer afternoon; there are Mary Beaver Dam and Crooked River urging Tadodaho's children to victory in the rabbit competitions.

And there is Eddie lying on the kitchen floor, facedown before my father, with one pant leg pushed up over a patch of white skin and the other in place. There is Hank's drowned expression as he tracks Angie's path across the lawn in her denim bikini. There is her silhouette, one hand clutching a champagne bottle while the other seeks a hold on the boat's side.

There are my brothers moving through the elephant grass side by side, moving slowly and looking for a sign—a leaf at a different angle than its fellows perhaps. They walk point together, so far ahead of the other members of the platoon that they are effectively alone, cut off from anyone but each other and whatever is ahead. A thin green sawing insect sound hangs in the air like scent, and they walk on, holding M-13s at chest level and pushing the elephant grass to either side as they move.

They reach a clearing and Eddie steps directly into it, turns to Perry with a quick swivel of his head and his face lights—an electric, pure grin.

ACKNOWLEDGMENTS

Many people with direct experience of the Vietnamese conflict wrote about serving there, or waiting for those who served, and I turned to their work for guidance. Tim O'Brien's *If I Die in a Combat Zone* and Michael Herr's *Dispatches* both responded to and shaped that time in American history. I also owe debts to Peter Goldman and Tony Fuller's *Charlie Company,* to Al Santoli's *Everything We Had,* to Nathaniel Tripp's *Father, Soldier, Son,* and to Marian Faye Novak's *Lonely Girls with Burning Eyes.* Alfred W. McCoy's *The Politics of Heroin in Southeast Asia* offered an intriguing and controversial discussion of the complex relations among U.S. government agencies, military branches, and Asian operatives and allies.

For a better understanding of Vietnamese myth, folklore, medicine and daily life, I thank Lynette Dyer Vuong and Vo-Dinh Mai for *Sky Legends of Vietnam;* Vuong and Manabu Saito for *The Golden Carp and Other Tales from Vietnam;* Norma J. Livo and Dia Cha, for *Folk Stories of the Hmong;* and Quang Van Nguyen and Marjorie Pivar for *Fourth Uncle in the Mountain: A Memoir of a Barefoot Doctor in Vietnam.*

Thanks to John McPhee for *Basin and Range,* a book on geology that would accurately be categorized as a thriller.

Without Liv Blumer, peerless guide, interpreter, medium and agent, this novel would not have happened. Thanks to my editor, Aimee Taub, whose clear vision and capacity to amuse and be amused make her the invaluable colleague that she is. I am indebted to people who read the manuscript as it developed, including Susan Saranno, Terry Grobe, Susan Schotz and Ellen Ruppel Shell. David Silverman saved me from myself and from my fifteen-year-old computer on many occasions when technology defeated me.

And to Mark and Claire, who gracefully tolerate all intrusions from my imaginary friends, my gratitude.